COMING HOME TO OTTERCOMBE BAY

Bella Osborne has been jotting down stories as far back as she can remember but decided that 2013 would be the year that she finished a full-length novel.

In 2016, her debut novel, *It Started at Sunset Cottage*, was shortlisted for the Contemporary Romantic Novel of the Year and RNA Joan Hessayon New Writers Award.

Bella's stories are about friendship, love and coping with what life throws at you. She likes to find the humour in the darker moments of life and weaves these into her stories. Bella believes that writing your own story really is the best fun ever, closely followed by talking, eating chocolate, drinking fizz and planning holidays.

She lives in the Midlands, UK with her lovely husband and wonderful daughter, who, thankfully, both accept her as she is (with mad morning hair and a penchant for skipping).

Also by Bella Osborne:

It Started at Sunset Cottage
A Family Holiday
Escape to Willow Cottage

Coming Home to Ottercombe Bay

BELLA OSBORNE

AVON

A division of HarperCollins*Publishers*
1 London Bridge Street,
London SE1 9GF

www.harpercollins.co.uk

A Paperback Original 2018

2

First published in Great Britain by
HarperCollins*Publishers* 2018

A catalogue record for this book is
available from the British Library

ISBN-13: 978-0-00-825815-3

Typeset in Minion by Palimpsest Book Production Ltd, Falkirk, Stirlingshire
Printed and bound by CPI Group (UK) Ltd, Croydon CR0 4YY

Acknowledgements

Firstly, thanks goes to my editor, Rachel Faulkner-Willcocks for a fabulous job editing this book and to Sabah Khan, Elon Woodman-Worrell and the amazing team at Avon for all their support. Thanks to my agent, Kate Nash, who is my constant safety net, and special thanks to Kim Leo for yet another stunning cover.

Special thanks to Henry Yates at Burleigh's Gin and Graham Pound and staff at the Seven Stars Public House in Rugby for sharing their vast gin knowledge. Thanks also to everyone who has so enthusiastically supported me in my gin research – I feel we did a thorough job.

Thanks to the lovely people at the RNLI, Sarah at Devon Bat Group (she bears no resemblance to Tabitha in case you were wondering) and Christie from the National Bat Helpline – yes, there really is such a thing!

Thanks to Morton Gray for her knowledge of tarot cards and to my niece, Emma, for checking my terminology wasn't getting old and past it.

As always, my heartfelt thanks to all my writerly friends – I hope you know who you are because there are far too many of you to fit in the acknowledgements!

Thank you to all the fabulous bloggers – you are amazing,

as are all the lovely readers who continue to buy my books and write reviews. It really does mean the world.

Finally, the biggest thank you to my wonderful family for their unwavering support and acceptance of the voices in my head. I love you beyond reason.

For my mum – thank you.

Chapter One

Daisy's bum didn't feel like her own thanks to four hours on an old motorbike. A pretty village sign welcomed her, but Daisy felt a long-buried sadness creep over her like frost across a windowpane. Coming back to Ottercombe Bay was a big mistake. If only I had a choice, she thought.

A good-looking man in an unattractive high-vis jacket interrupted her thoughts as he stepped out in front of Daisy's motorbike. She hastily swerved and braked, and the ancient vehicle spluttered to a halt.

'You can't come this way,' the young man said, his muscled arms clamped across his luminous chest.

'Please,' she said, followed by her best cheesy grin; something familiar about the man's mop of dark hair had her memory working overtime.

'No way,' he said, pulling back his shoulders.

Daisy flicked up her helmet visor with an air of defiance; she wasn't easily intimidated. 'Don't be daft. I need to get to Trow Lane.' She looked longingly down the main road. She was only three streets away.

'You'll have to go around.' The man was peering at Daisy. 'Do I know you?' he asked, a frown appearing briefly on his tanned face.

'I doubt it. Look, it's daft to go miles out of my way. I'm only going down there,' she said, pointing. Daisy was tired after her long journey and didn't need this jumped-up workman telling her what to do, especially when she could see no reason why the road was cordoned off on a sunny Saturday evening in late June.

She revved the motorbike back to life but high-vis man stepped up to her front tyre, blocking her path. They glared at each other. Daisy revved the engine again and made the motorbike hop an inch forward. He didn't even flinch. She was vaguely aware of a crowd gathering nearby. Then she heard it – a distant clanging sound. She frowned and the man glared back. The clanging sound drew closer and Daisy recognised it as drums accompanied by what sounded like someone trying to get a tune out of an elephant. She spotted the bunting crisscrossing the road. The penny finally dropped – it was carnival parade night. He was right, there was no way she would be able to ride her bike through town tonight. She slammed down her visor and grumbled an apology before she skidded the motorbike away leaving the smug-looking high-vis man swathed in a fug of black smoke.

Daisy was still cross when she pulled up at Sea Mist Cottage. She stopped the bike, tugged off her helmet and tore the heavy backpack off her aching shoulders. This was not a good start and it was further confirmation that she shouldn't have come back. She turned and looked at the cottage. It was like being transported back in time – it hadn't changed a bit. The ancient building still looked like the sad face Daisy had imagined she saw when she was a child, with its heavy overhanging thatch eyebrows and symmetrical windows with half pulled down blinds giving the impression of drooping eyelids. The simple porch jutted out like an afterthought of a nose and its small front door like a forlorn open mouth was just a stride away from the pavement. She remembered that the door used to stick a bit but that was years ago, it had most likely been fixed by now. Daisy watched the silhouette of someone through the frosted glass as they gave the door a shove and stumbled outside.

'Daisy, love. You made it,' said Aunt Coral, enveloping Daisy in a tight hug. It had been a long time since anyone had embraced her like that. Daisy had forgotten there was no escape from Aunt Coral's hugs.

'Let me look at you.' Aunt Coral held Daisy at arm's length. Daisy shook out her mop of caramel-blonde hair, which had been cocooned in the helmet for the last four hours.

Tears welled in Aunt Coral's eyes. 'Oh, Daisy, you have grown into a beautiful young woman.' She bit her lip. 'And you look so like your mother.'

At the mention of her mother Daisy felt the sorrow settle on her afresh. Even after all these years it still hurt like it had happened yesterday. The sense of loss was exactly the same, as was the empty sensation clutching at her gut. Ottercombe Bay held only sadness and bad memories for Daisy.

Despite this, Daisy forced a smile because she knew this was the required response and Aunt Coral beamed back at her. 'It's good to see you. Come in and I'll get the kettle on,' she said, ushering Daisy inside. As Daisy reached for the door handle a strangled screech of a bark made her flinch. Further frantic barking accompanied the arrival of a small black dog now pogoing up and down on the other side.

'Oh, Bugsy Malone shush now,' said Aunt Coral, bustling

past Daisy. She tugged open the door and the small black dog shot out and started to nip at Daisy's boots, making her jump back. 'Now, now,' said her aunt, scooping up the protesting canine who continued to bark at Daisy.

'What is it?' said Daisy, recoiling from the snarling bundle that was trying to escape from her aunt's clutches. Daisy didn't know much about animals; she didn't have anything against them and some seemed quite cute, but her nomadic lifestyle meant there had never been an opportunity for pets.

Aunt Coral chuckled. 'He's a pug,' she said, leading the way into the cottage. Bugsy continued his vocal assault. Daisy followed at what she hoped was a safe distance.

'He doesn't seem very happy,' said Daisy over the high-pitched yaps.

'He's a bit out of sorts since your Great Uncle Reg died. Devoted to each other they were. I don't think little Bugsy can work out why he's not here any more.' Aunt Coral's voice went a bit wobbly. She cleared her throat and popped Bugsy out of the back door where he was temporarily distracted by the smells of the garden. 'Right. Tea?'

'Yes, please. Milk, one sugar,' said Daisy with one eye on the paws now trying to carve their way back into the cottage. The kitchen was filled with the smell of freshly baked sponge. Daisy breathed it in greedily and her mood lifted. She dropped her rucksack and sat down at the small kitchen table with its pristine white tablecloth. She looked about her whilst Aunt Coral busied herself with the tea. It was as though time had stood still. The kitchen was just as it had been when she was a child; the only changes she could spot were that the walls had been painted yellow, when they used to be blue, and there appeared to be the addition of a corkboard with a variety of pieces of paper and notes pinned to it. She spotted the last postcard she had sent from France and her good mood quickly faded when she remembered the disaster of her French boyfriend Guillaume.

Daisy looked down at her rucksack. Everything she owned was in it, apart from the motorbike. That was it. All her worldly goods in one package. She pulled back her shoulders and gave herself a mental shake. This was the way she liked it. No ties, nothing to keep her in one place or hold her back. She was as free as a bird and that suited her just fine. Aunt Coral ferried a large tray with a teapot and a pair of fragile-looking cups and saucers to the table and sat down opposite Daisy. She pointed at the rucksack. 'You're not planning on staying long, then?' There was a sadness in her eyes as she poured their tea.

'No, sorry. I need to leave straight after the funeral.' Daisy broke eye contact and picked up the delicate teacup. She didn't know where she was heading next. She had been staying in a hostel in Canterbury, hopping from one job to the next, when Aunt Coral had telephoned. It had seemed like an ideal opportunity to make it a permanent departure from Kent. As to where she was going next, she had no idea, but she wouldn't be staying in the small Devon town any longer than was absolutely necessary.

'Well, you can't leave directly after the funeral, I'm afraid, because there's the will and—'

A knock at the door was simultaneously accompanied by frantic barking from the garden making Daisy feel she was under attack from two different directions. Aunt Coral calmly got up and headed for the front door. As soon as Daisy heard the high-pitched voice a bell started to ring in the deepest recesses of her mind.

The visitor's Devonshire accent was strong and her voice

got louder and faster as she approached. 'OhMyGod. I can't believe it's actually you. I mean I hoped it was when I saw the bike because I don't know anyone with a bike like that. Not round here. And it is you, you're here!' A young woman with long straight dark hair flung herself at Daisy and hugged her tightly. 'I've missed you so much,' she said, sitting down without taking her eyes off Daisy, which was quite disconcerting.

'Tamsyn,' said Daisy, recognising her. 'It's lovely to see you. Do you still live next door?'

'Yeah, with Mum and Dad. They'll be thrilled to see you too.'

'Tamsyn has been a wonderful help keeping an eye on Reg while I've been at work. Reg has kept every card or letter you have ever sent from all your travels and I think he's read them all to Tamsyn a few times over. And you know how he always liked to tell stories and you featured in quite a few of those too.'

'Not the fantasy ones with dwarves. You weren't in those,' said Tamsyn, her face deadpan.

Daisy wasn't sure how to respond, but thankfully Aunt Coral started speaking again. 'I don't know what I'd have done without Tamsyn these last few months. She's virtually one of the family now. Aren't you, Tamsyn?'

'OhMyGod. Does that make us sisters?' said Tamsyn, jigging about excitedly in her chair – the same action being mirrored at the back door by the dog.

'I don't think so,' said Daisy with a chuckle. Tamsyn was joking, wasn't she? Here was a prime example why people should leave home and explore the world, thought Daisy. Staying here had turned Tamsyn into Ottercombe Bay's answer to Phoebe Buffay from *Friends*, blurring the line between adorable and certifiable.

'Where are you going next?' asked Tamsyn, wide-eyed, cupping her tea with both hands. Daisy wished Tamsyn would blink more often – it couldn't be good for her eyes. Daisy spotted Aunt Coral also looking at her intently; she felt under pressure to say something and oddly the need to impress.

'Um, I'm not sure. Abroad again probably . . .' She didn't have the money right now but her long-term plan was definitely to travel more extensively. 'South America,' she blurted out. It was somewhere she had always wanted to go but living hand to mouth meant it was only ever going to be a pipedream.

Tamsyn's mouth dropped open. 'Wow, you are my absolute hero.' She turned to Aunt Coral who gave a proud nod.

Daisy felt awkward and it showed on her face. She dropped her gaze to her teacup. She began to recall more about Tamsyn as her brain rearranged her archived memories. She remembered the little girl who followed her everywhere, who went beachcombing with her and liked to collect shells but screamed if she found a crab. She remembered sitting on the edge of the pavement watching the carnival procession together. She remembered them as gawky teenagers swigging cider behind the beach huts. She remembered a friend.

'You not going to the carnival tonight?' asked Daisy.

Tamsyn grinned. 'I was on my way out when I spotted the motorbike.'

'Sorry,' said Daisy. 'You shouldn't miss it for me.'

'Uh, no way. You're far better than any crumby old carnival. I was only going to get a look at the men in uniform.'

Daisy recalled the officious bloke in the high-vis top. 'Really?'

'Oh, yeah. Police, firefighters, lifeboat crew, they all have floats in the carnival now.' At the mention of lifeboat crew Aunt Coral and Daisy exchanged looks.

'It's a shame my brother couldn't make it for the funeral,' said Aunt Coral, her nose twitching slightly. Daisy noted the offhand reference to her father.

'Dad's really sorry. He sends his love though,' said Daisy, who had hoped her father would have made the effort to attend but given he lived in Goa it was never really on the cards. Aunt Coral nodded her understanding.

'Oh, I remember your dad. He rescued me once when I built this amazing sandcastle with a moat and I was so busy trying to keep the water out I hadn't noticed the tide creep in and it was all around me and he waded out to save me,' said Tamsyn, as she machine-gunned the story out.

Daisy smirked. 'I remember that day. It was only ankle deep; you didn't need rescuing at all.' Daisy laughed.

Tamsyn pouted playfully. 'Huh, I could have been swept away – the current here is very strong.'

Before she realised it, Daisy was deep in conversation as the memories flooded back. And for a change they were pleasant ones she was happy to recall. Time seemed to whizz by and Daisy was vaguely aware Aunt Coral was now walking around wearing pyjamas. She checked her watch, causing Tamsyn to look at the kitchen clock.

'Crikey it's late,' said Tamsyn, making Daisy grin at the old-fashioned turn of phrase. 'Mum and Dad will be wondering where I am.' Getting to her feet Tamsyn gave Daisy another huge hug. 'I am pleased you're home,' she added, then turned to Aunt Coral and kissed her cheek. 'Bye. See you tomorrow.'

'Yes, thanks Tamsyn.'

'Tomorrow?' asked Daisy as the sound of the porch door being vigorously shoved announced Tamsyn's departure.

'She comes around most days.'

'Doesn't she work?'

'Oh yes, good little worker is Tamsyn, but it's all a bit erratic at the beach café. They have school kids working there in the summer, pay them next to nothing and only have poor Tamsyn for the lunchtime rush.'

Daisy pondered this. She'd always thought her lack of being able to land a decent job was because of her frequent moves but it seemed even if she'd stayed locally she'd have been no better off. Her thoughts were invaded by a disgruntled-looking Bugsy rushing into the kitchen. He marched up to Daisy and shook himself. Daisy offered him a finger to sniff and he promptly wiped his nose on it.

'Ew!' Daisy recoiled, pulled a tissue out of her pocket and wiped her hand. Bugsy looked quite pleased with himself, he even gave a brief wag of his curly tail before he turned around and presented Daisy with his bum.

'Right, I'm off to bed,' said Aunt Coral, picking up the dog. 'It is lovely to have you back even if it's only for a few days.'

'Oh yeah, that reminds me. What were you saying about me not being able to leave after the funeral?'

Aunt Coral's eyebrows danced. 'Oh yes. You need to stay for the reading of the will. Great Uncle Reg has left you something substantial – that was what the solicitor said. Night, love, see you in the morning.' And with a fleeting kiss on the top of Daisy's head she disappeared upstairs.

Chapter Two

Daisy was woken by something scratching at her door. She was coming round, whilst wondering where she was, when the bedroom door sprung open and something burst in. Daisy leapt in fright but quickly realised it was only Bugsy. At virtually the same time the dog seemed to spot who was in the bed. He snorted his disgust and strutted out of the room. It seemed Bugsy's wake-up calls would be a disadvantage of having a bedroom on the ground floor.

It was Monday morning, the day of the funeral. She had tried to talk to Aunt Coral about the will yesterday but she didn't know anything more than she'd already shared except to say Daisy's father, Ray, hadn't been left anything because Reg had helped him out financially in the past and Ray had agreed he'd already had his fair share of any inheritance. This in itself had been a revelation to Daisy, but looking back her father had rarely had a stable job while she'd been growing up so the money they had lived on must have come from somewhere. Reg had always been generous to a fault, one of the many things she'd loved and admired about him.

She wondered what Great Uncle Reg had left her in his will. She thought back to the last time she'd seen him, it had been almost three years ago, shortly after she dropped out of university for the second time and she felt a twinge of guilt. He had seemed full of life despite his advancing years. She recalled his mane of grey hair and wayward beard that always seemed at odds with his otherwise smart appearance, which invariably included a cravat. He'd said something to her then about securing her future but she hadn't paid much attention – she now wished she had, the suspense was killing her.

A light tap on the door pulled her from her thoughts. 'Good morning. I'm glad you're awake. Tamsyn will be here shortly and we've got a truckful of sandwiches to make for the wake,' said Aunt Coral. 'Or "pallbearers party" as Reg liked to call it,' she added with a chuckle before she disappeared into the kitchen.

The truckful of sandwiches was no joke, because shortly after Daisy was up to her elbows in a buttery production line whilst Tamsyn did her best to update her on who she may know at the funeral.

'You remember Max, don't you?' she asked.

Daisy jutted out her lip and slapped a piece of ham on the buttered bread Aunt Coral had just handed her. 'Not sure.' But even as she said it a picture of a cider-fuelled teenage snogging fest loomed ugly in her mind. Whilst she had left Ottercombe Bay at seven years old she had returned each year for a two-week holiday, giving her a snapshot of the life she'd been pulled away from.

'You doooo,' said Tamsyn. 'Max Davey, he never tucked his shirt in.'

'Sounds like every boy at primary school to me.'

'Jason Fenton, remember him?'

Daisy paused with a slice of ham held aloft. 'Skinny kid, played with trains at break time?'

'Yes. That's him. He's a policeman now,' said Tamsyn, with a firm bob of her head.

'Wow, well done Jason. Why would Jason and this Max be coming to my great uncle's funeral?'

Tamsyn opened her mouth but Aunt Coral was already on the case. 'They're both lifeboat crew and your great uncle supported the lifeboat his whole life. He was Lifeboat Operations Manager for many years,' said Aunt Coral proudly. 'Max and Jason both used to meet him for a coffee once in a while to hear his stories.' She paused briefly mid-spread with her buttered knife aloft. 'There's lots of people in this town who are going to miss him.'

Daisy patted her arm, Aunt Coral gave her a wan smile and returned to spreading.

Daisy shed a few tears during the service but overall the funeral was surprisingly cheerful, which reflected Reg's personality. A few people told their favourite stories of Reg – one of them involving a donkey and a top hat, which had them all belly laughing – so as everyone filed out of church most of them were smiling, which was exactly what Reg would have wanted.

Daisy studied the floral tributes and wondered who all these people were who knew her great uncle but who she'd never heard of, especially some calling themselves Bunny and Toots.

'Hi . . . again,' said a deep voice behind her. Daisy turned to see a ruggedly handsome young man. 'I'm sorry Reg died, he was a sound bloke. You okay, Daisy?'

'Hi . . .' She paused where his name should go as a cavalcade of memories bombarded her.

He twitched his head. 'Don't remember me? For one thing, I stopped you riding your bike through the carnival procession on Saturday. Prevented a potential massacre, I reckon,' he said, his local accent soft and barely noticeable.

'Ah, yes,' said Daisy feeling more than a little embarrassed at her behaviour that night. 'Sorry about that.' He didn't look half as aggressive now, with his hair groomed and wearing a smart shirt and tie although he kept running his finger around his collar giving the impression he wasn't very comfortable in the outfit. 'You're Max. You were the boy who always had his shirt untucked at school.' She was keen to avoid reminding him about their teenage antics.

The corners of his eyes crinkled. 'Yep, that'd be me, all right.'

'And you were friends with my great uncle?' It still seemed an odd pairing to Daisy.

'Yeah, me and Reg used to catch up from time to time. I'll remember him fondly.'

The look in Max's eye intrigued her. 'What will you remember most about him?'

'He taught me I'm as good as anyone else . . .' Max blew out a long slow breath and looked for a second like he was going to get emotional, '. . . and how to judge the tides.'

'That's nice,' said Daisy feeling awkward; her memories weren't quite as profound. 'I'll remember being curled up next to him watching films with a steaming mug of hot chocolate.' In a flash a memory of the film *Bugsy Malone* popped up and she had a 'doh' moment when she realised where the dog's name had come from. They'd watched that film many times when she was little.

'Ah, here you are,' said Aunt Coral joining them. 'Daisy, you can come back to the house in car one with the oldies; I'm in car two with the Exeter crowd.' She turned her attention to Max. 'Lovely of you to come today, Max. Are you coming back for the wake?'

'No, sorry, Coral, I'm working. I swapped my shifts so I could see old Reg off. Raise a glass for me at the party.'

'Okay. If you're sure.' Aunt Coral gave him a fleeting pat on the shoulder and went to organise some others.

'I 'spect I'll see you around, if you're staying here for a bit,' said Max.

'Unfortunately, I won't be staying,' said Daisy. 'But it was nice to see you again. Bye.'

Max paused. 'That's a shame,' he said, his eyes warm and intense making her almost rethink her decision.

The next morning Daisy found herself in a warm and stuffy solicitor's office sipping a strong filter coffee.

'Do you think he would have liked the party?' asked Aunt Coral.

It was an odd question, but she knew Aunt Coral had been worrying about giving Reg a deserving send off. 'He would have loved it. He definitely would have approved of all the port.' Aunt Coral visibly relaxed and Daisy felt a swell of affection for her. The wake had been well attended and diverse, with some serious talk about coastal erosion and an impromptu singalong. It had been exactly what Reg would have wanted.

Daisy didn't really want to hear his will read. She didn't need anything to remember Great Uncle Reg; she had her memories. Although she had to admit she was curious about what he had left her that could be described as 'substantial'. Cash, perhaps, but she wasn't sure Reg had a lot of money. She needed some cash; she hated living hand to mouth. Possibly a share in the cottage, which would be very tricky because it was Aunt Coral's home and she definitely wouldn't want to sell it. Daisy decided she wouldn't think about that option as it made her uncomfortable.

14

Maybe it was a family heirloom, although the only items she could think of were pieces of furniture. That's probably it, she thought. The large clock in the hallway and the dresser in the kitchen could both be described as substantial. Her mind wandered off and imagined her on the *Antiques Roadshow* trying hard to master her 'I'm not at all disappointed it's only worth tuppence' face.

'I am terribly sorry to keep you waiting,' said the solicitor, hurrying into the office with a folder in his hand. 'Now, I shouldn't keep you long.' Daisy was warming to the old gent already; she was keen to get packed up and head off up the M5. She hoped to get as far as Gloucester tonight but she wasn't sure where she was heading afterwards.

'This is the last will and testament of Reginald Montgomery Fabien Wickens . . .' There then followed a paragraph of formal jargon before Daisy tuned in again. '. . . To my niece, Coral Anne Wickens, I leave the property of Sea Mist Cottage, Trow Lane, Ottercombe Bay, in its entirety . . .' Aunt Coral let out a small sob and Daisy took her hand to comfort her. Daisy's heart was starting to increase its speed. 'To my great niece Daisy May Wickens, I leave the property and grounds of the former Ottercombe Bay Railway Station and adjoining car park, subject to her being resident in Ottercombe Bay for a full twelve months from the date of the reading of this will. My residuary estate is to be divided equally between Coral Wickens, Daisy Wickens and the Royal National Lifeboat Institution Ottercombe Bay Station. Should any beneficiary fail to meet the conditions of bequest their share will be divided equally between the other beneficiaries. Signed Reginald Wickens.' The solicitor laid his hands flat on the document and patted it gently. Nobody spoke.

Daisy's mouth had gone dry, she was baffled and a quick glance at Aunt Coral showed she mirrored how she felt. Daisy put her hand to her necklace and closed her fingers around her locket for comfort. 'I'm sorry, but he's left me what exactly?' she asked.

'Ottercombe Bay Railway Station and car park.'

'But there's not been trains here for years,' said Aunt Coral.

The solicitor shuffled through a pile of papers and leaned across the desk to hand something over. It was a dog-eared auction notice. 'The railway station at Ottercombe was decommissioned in 1975 and bought by . . .' he checked his notes, '. . . a Mr Arthur Wickens who bequeathed it to your great uncle on his death. There are also some historic planning applications for demolition and site development that were refused in 1989, 1992, 2001 and 2010.' He removed his glasses and smiled at them warmly from across the desk.

Daisy stared at the piece of paper in her hand. She was looking at a faded photograph of a Victorian railway station building. 'He's left me an old railway station?'

Aunt Coral was peering over her arm. 'Do all those refused planning applications mean there's not a lot she can do with it?'

'Not at all. It simply means the council weren't in favour of it being demolished, although there is a letter here saying they would be open to an application for change of use but it's dated 2010.'

'Can I sell it?' asked Daisy, her voice coming out a little croaky.

'Once it has passed to you formally following the adherence to the conditional clause.'

Daisy stared at him. Why didn't these people just use

normal words? 'And when does it pass to me formally exactly?'

The solicitor twitched. 'One year from today, assuming you have been resident in Ottercombe Bay for the full twelve months. This is also for you,' he said, handing Daisy a thick cream envelope with her name beautifully written on the front in fountain pen; she recognised it instantly as Great Uncle Reg's handwriting. 'I believe this letter will explain things a little further.'

For once Daisy opened her mouth but could not think what to say so she shut it again. What was going on?

'This may be a stupid question,' started Aunt Coral, 'but I'm guessing this is all legal and watertight and there's no way to get around the conditions he's set?'

'I'm afraid not,' said the solicitor, who started to discuss paying for the funeral and the process of probate. Daisy thumbed the envelope in her hands and studied the writing. There was a slight wobble in the letters but it was unmistakably Reg's; she could imagine him sitting in his favourite chair writing it.

'I wasn't expecting that,' said Aunt Coral, as they left the solicitor's office a few minutes later. 'How do you feel?'

'Flabbergasted, but I'm fine,' Daisy said, when she really felt like running away.

Daisy hardly spoke a word on the way home. She could feel an uncomfortable sensation take hold, a feeling akin to claustrophobia; a sense of being suffocated and chained down that she needed to fight against and escape from. Back at the cottage she changed out of her smart clothes quickly and shoved her things into her backpack.

'Cup of tea?' came the call from the kitchen.

Daisy started to panic. She couldn't stay for tea, she couldn't stay another minute. This place was simply not good for her; she was uneasy most of the time she was here but knowing it was only for a couple of days it had been bearable. A whole year was unthinkable. She stood for a moment and gripped her locket. As long as she had it she could be anywhere and her mother would be with her. She took a deep steadying breath before replying to Aunt Coral, 'No thanks. I'm just going out.' She grabbed a pencil and searched for a piece of paper. She scribbled a note on the back of an old envelope.

I'm so sorry but I have to go. I'll be in touch. Take care of yourself. Love D x

She left the note on her pillow, picked up her bag and left the bedroom as quietly as she could. Panic rose as she wrestled with the porch door. It was one thing to run away but to be foiled in her attempt would be excruciating. 'Bloody thing,' she grumbled but a whimpering at her feet drew her attention. Bugsy was sitting watching her, his head on one side. He studied her with his abnormally big eyes. She stopped for a moment, for some odd reason she felt she needed to explain to him why she was leaving, although she suspected he wouldn't be sad to see her go.

'I have to go,' she whispered. 'This place has too many bad memories for me. Too many ghosts.'

Bugsy stood up, turned around and she heard a sort of phht sound, which was followed by a foul smell. Daisy shook her head, gave the door one more shove and slunk out.

She pulled on her helmet, got on the bike and was thankful it started first time. She surveyed Sea Mist Cottage one last time, opened the throttle and drove away. Hopefully this would be the last she'd see of it for a very long time.

Chapter Three

In a few short minutes her breathing had steadied and despite a small niggle she knew she was doing the right thing. She didn't like not saying goodbye to Aunt Coral but she would only have tried to make her stay. She turned into the high street and pulled up at the traffic lights. Tamsyn jumped in front of her waving her arms.

Oh cock, thought Daisy.

'Hello. I knew it was you; your bike sounds ropey. Wasn't it a lovely service? Proper good send off, lots of people, which is really lovely, especially for an old person because sometimes there's not many people there because all their friends have died, but everyone loved Reg. Why have you got your rucksack with you?'

'Umm,' mumbled Daisy.

Tamsyn came to the side of the bike. 'Are you leaving?' Tamsyn's face fell, she looked instantly despondent.

Daisy wished she was a better liar as she lifted her visor. 'Sorry, Tamsyn, I need to go. You take care now.'

'No. You've only just come back, you can't leave now . . .' Her eyes filled with tears and Daisy felt like she was torturing a toddler.

The traffic lights changed. 'I'm sorry,' said Daisy, she

meant it. She flipped down her visor. Someone behind hooted and Daisy revved the engine and started to pull away.

'Sandy wants you to stay!' shouted Tamsyn with desperation in her voice.

Of all the things she could have shouted after her this was the one thing that would have the desired effect. The words were still ringing in Daisy's ears as she pulled her bike into the kerb and switched off the engine. Tamsyn walked over looking anxious.

Daisy felt numb. She pulled off her helmet and stared at Tamsyn.

'What do you mean "Sandy wants me to stay"?' snapped Daisy. Daisy's mother was called Sandy, was this who she meant?

Tamsyn nibbled her bottom lip. 'You remember my mum, Min?' she said, sounding like she was saying a tongue twister.

If this was going to be another long drawn out story Daisy was likely to scream. 'Yes, why?'

'She kind of gets these feelings. It's a bit like a spiritual medium but not really the same. They're like a sixth sense message from those who've left us. And she said to tell you but I wasn't sure if you'd think she was mad or not and I didn't want to upset you and—'

'Tamsyn, please spit it out.'

Tamsyn took a deep breath. 'She felt your mum's presence. She said she could tell Sandy was pleased you were home and she wanted you to stay.'

Daisy didn't know what to think. She had seen no evidence herself of life after death so she had no reason to believe in it. But the thought of some sort of contact from her mum had such a powerful draw it wrestled hard with

20

her logical mind. Daisy swallowed. Another car honked at her and overtook, nearly clipping her bike.

'We can't stay here. Get on,' instructed Daisy.

Tamsyn shook her head. 'It's too dangerous without a helmet.'

'I'll go at like five miles an hour – it'll be fine. Or better still, you can have mine.'

Tamsyn shook her head. 'It's illegal. Hang on, I have an idea.' She ran off towards the barbers. Moments later she came out wearing a black crash helmet featuring a bloodied skull design, which looked interesting when teamed with her long flowing summer dress.

'Barber has a motorbike,' she said and she climbed on the back. Daisy didn't question her, she restarted the bike and pulled out safely into the traffic. She could have ridden anywhere but one particular place sprang to mind. She headed out of the town centre and turned onto the coast road. A short way along she turned off onto the gravel area that was both a small car park and viewing spot.

Daisy left the bike and walked off along the coastal path with Tamsyn following dutifully, a lot like it had been when they were children. Up ahead Daisy caught a glimpse of the sea – the dark blue smudge expanding as she neared the headland. The perfect crescent of Ottercombe Bay came into view on Daisy's left side. From her high vantage point she had a good view of the divide that had existed in the bay for almost a hundred years; on one side of the beach were rows and rows of fishing boats of varying shapes and sizes and on the other a multitude of deckchairs, picnic rugs and tourists. The occasional shout of a child drifted up to her before ebbing away but otherwise it was peaceful high up on the cliff top.

As the sea breeze caressed Daisy's senses she started to

feel calmer and some of the frustration at having her escape plans interrupted diminished. She could smell the sea, the fresh scent quite like no other which reminded her of the summers she had returned to the bay with her father, year after year until he could bear it no more. For Daisy returning to the bay meant being reunited with her sadness but when they left there had also been the ache of being ripped away from everything familiar.

They walked to the far end of the headland; the tip of the crescent on one side of the bay. Daisy took off her leather jacket, laid it on the ground and she and Tamsyn flopped down on it.

'I love this view,' said Tamsyn at last. Daisy was amazed she'd managed to keep quiet this long.

'Me too.' She had forgotten how much she loved it. Pictures of the picnics she had had there as a child swam in her mind's eye. Her mother and father dancing while she giggled and snuck an extra biscuit. The sun shining down on them whilst the sea beat a steady rhythm below – they were happy times. Her parents had loved this spot too it seemed, as it was somewhere they had come regularly. Daisy ran her fingers through the grass and wondered if her mother had sat on that spot and done the same thing; it felt likely. A familiar sense of loss pulled at her gut. Daisy was reminded of why she was here. 'Is your mum some sort of psychic?' she asked.

Tamsyn dragged her eyes away from the sea. 'Not officially, but she's always had these sensations and thoughts that weren't her own. My dad calls it a load of witpot but I think there's something in it.'

'What makes you think there is?' Daisy turned to gauge her reaction.

Tamsyn tipped back her head and stared into the

cloudless sky. 'Because she never lies. I mean like *never* – she can't even tell a white lie. If I ask her "Do you like my hair up?" she'll just go "No, it looks better down." She never lies. So when she says things about people who have passed then I have to believe that too, don't I?'

Daisy wasn't convinced. 'Who else has she had messages from?'

'They're not strictly messages,' said Tamsyn, bringing her gaze back to earth. 'She was in the paper shop a couple of months ago and Mrs Robinson was blathering on about gardening, like she does, and my mum had this thought about Mrs Robinson's dad being unwell. Now she doesn't know him but she says "How's your dad?" and Mrs Robinson says "He's fine".'

Daisy pulled a strained face. 'If he was fine then—'

'Ah, that's the thing. Mrs Robinson called round on the way home and her Dad was dead in the armchair.' Tamsyn lay back on the jacket.

Daisy gave a pout and let out a slow breath. This wasn't exactly the cold hard proof she was hoping for. 'What exactly was the message or whatever it was she had about my mum again?'

'She was in our garden and she rushed inside saying she felt cold and to be honest of late she's only been overheating. Dad says she's about the right age for the change. She told me she had a sense of Sandy being with her. She couldn't see her or anything. Do you think she's bonkers too?' Tamsyn sat up abruptly and eyeballed Daisy.

'No, she was always lovely your mum, she used to make me laugh. I don't think she's bonkers.' Daisy remembered a kind woman with a wicked sense of humour. But whilst she had seemed nice that didn't add any weight to her credibility as a conduit to the afterlife.

23

'Why are mad people called bonkers and not people who bonk?' Tamsyn, asked, looking at Daisy as if she was expecting her to provide a sensible answer.

'Erm, I don't know, Tams. Our language is weird.'

'It is. Phrases confuse me too. Why do people say, "You can't have your cake and eat it"? What else are you going to do with cake?'

Daisy laughed. 'Very good point.' Tamsyn had a way of putting you at ease and taking your brain off on an unexpected tangent so you forgot about all the serious stuff.

'Why were you leaving?' asked Tamsyn, plucking a daisy and tucking it behind her ear.

Daisy thought for a moment. 'Because Great Uncle Reg is trying to make me stay.'

Tamsyn looked excited. 'Did you get a message from beyond the grave?'

Daisy sighed. 'Sort of. He left me some old railway station in his will and said I had to stay here for a whole year to get it.'

Tamsyn sat up poker straight. 'He left you a railway station? What like Exeter or Marylebone?'

Daisy laughed. 'No, the derelict one for Ottercombe Bay.'

Tamsyn startled Daisy by starting to clap her hands together in front of her as if she was doing a sea lion impression. 'Wow, this is amazing. That is the cutest building ever.' Daisy raised a doubtful eyebrow. 'Seriously, it's beautiful. I mean it's all boarded up and has been for years but . . . this is so exciting!' She let out a tiny squeal and Daisy couldn't help but laugh at her enthusiasm. 'And he wants you to stay here for one whole year?' Daisy nodded forlornly. 'I love that man.' She threw her arms around Daisy and hugged her tight. She pulled away and her grin faded. 'Please say you're staying.'

Daisy gave a tiny shake of the head. 'I don't think so, Tams. I've not stayed in the same place for a whole year since . . .' She had to think about the answer. 'University I guess and then I was only there in term time.'

'One year will go quickly and at the end of it you'll own your own railway station. Which is totally amazing.' Tamsyn made a noise like a train and Daisy chuckled. 'You have to stay. You really do.' Tamsyn clutched Daisy's hand tightly and looked hopefully into her eyes. 'It's like you've been set a quest and you can't say no to a quest.'

'A quest?' Daisy blinked hard. 'This isn't medieval times.'

Tamsyn bent forward. 'No, but I love reading fantasy novels and usually there's a quest for the main character and it's dangerous but they always succeed in the end and live happily ever after. This is your quest and your happily ever after could be at the end of it.'

Daisy laughed until she noticed Tamsyn was deadly serious. She didn't believe in happy-ever-afters but she wasn't one to shy away from a challenge.

Daisy hugged her knees, stared out across Ottercombe Bay and thought. 'We'd best take a look at the place before I make any rash decisions,' she said, but before she'd finished the sentence Tamsyn was dragging her unceremoniously to her feet.

In front of her was an odd sight. It was a single-storey ornate building sat on its own with a railway platform and portion of train track in front of it. Daisy stood with her hands on her hips and took it all in as Tamsyn ran backwards and forwards along the platform like a toddler in a toyshop. Daisy was standing in what apparently had once been the station car park and was now a waist-high weed jungle with a series of increasingly bigger potholes where there had once been concrete. The railway track was also overgrown and in its entirety only measured about a hundred metres; on it was a dilapidated old railway carriage. The station building itself was in better condition, it looked grubby but its golden Victorian brickwork was easily visible. Daisy felt like she was in a Poirot movie and despite the lack of more track a steam train was going to puff into view any minute.

Tamsyn stopped running up and down the platform and held her arms out wide. 'What do you think?'

'Probably make a nice museum.' Daisy squinted in the sunlight.

'But it's soooo pretty. Isn't it?' said Tamsyn, jumping down from the platform and landing on the railway line. Daisy could see why her grandfather, Arthur, had wanted to build on the land, it was in a prime location about a mile inland where the ground got flatter, close to the town but convenient for the main roads and just a stroll to the beach. It was prime holiday rental territory but if the council weren't going to let them build on it she couldn't see much use for it – even if it was a pretty little building. Tamsyn came to stand next to her.

'I love the three chimney pots,' said Tamsyn, studying the tall stacks spread across the roof.

'Hmm,' said Daisy. 'I'm guessing inside it's split into three rooms.'

'Dunno. Shall we open it up?'

Daisy looked at the boarded-up windows and door and the missing roof tile. 'We'd need tools. I don't think there's a lot of point to be honest, Tams.' She glanced at Tamsyn who was gazing at the building the same way children look at Cinderella's castle at Disney World – it was a look of complete awe. Daisy had another look herself, perhaps she was just more of a realist than Tamsyn.

'Come on, I thought you were the adventurer – you're not telling me you don't want to explore inside?' said Tamsyn, giving Daisy a small dig in the ribs.

Daisy had to admit she was curious. She liked old buildings. Daisy shrugged. 'I wouldn't mind a snoop about but—'

'Right come on then. My dad has tools,' said Tamsyn, striding back to the bike. Daisy took a deep breath, she knew it would be easier to simply go along with her. She checked her watch. She wasn't going to get far tonight, she may as well stay, have a good home-cooked meal with Aunt Coral and head off tomorrow. She didn't feel good about sneaking out earlier: Aunt Coral deserved an explanation before she moved on, it was the least she could do. She hoped she hadn't already found the note she'd left.

Back at the cottage Tamsyn went to hers to get the tools and Daisy slunk inside quietly in the hope Bugsy wouldn't go off like a house alarm. A quick peek through the kitchen and she could see Aunt Coral was in the garden. Daisy let out the breath she was holding in and scurried through to her bedroom. She dropped the rucksack and went to retrieve the note from the pillow but it wasn't there. She hunted about the bed and floor but there was no sign of it. Her heart sank. What must Aunt Coral think of her? For a moment she considered making a run for it anyway but something twanged at her heartstrings and she decided she'd simply have to face up to things. She went through to the kitchen and was about to go out the back door when a flash of black and white caught her eye as it scooted under the table. She crouched down. There was Bugsy with the envelope she had written the note on.

'Good boy, Bugsy, give me the envelope,' she asked politely stretching out a hand but he reversed away emitting a low growl, his teeth clamped tightly to his treasure.

'Drop it,' she hissed. 'Leave, give. Hand it over.' But nothing was working. Bugsy backed away. He looked from his treats cupboard to Daisy. 'Are you blackmailing me?' This creature was smarter than he looked – but she supposed that wasn't hard.

As Aunt Coral turned the handle of the back door Daisy lurched underneath the table and made a grab for the envelope. She had a grip on it but so did Bugsy. They both pulled and the envelope ripped in half making Daisy topple backwards and bang her head on the underside of the table. 'Cock!' said Daisy loudly as Aunt Coral came in.

'Oh dear,' said Coral. 'Are you all right?'

'Yeah, sorry about the language.' Daisy shuffled from under the table rubbing her head where she'd bumped it. 'I was just leaving you a note to say I'm going to take a look at the railway station and Bugsy stole it. But now I don't need to leave a note,' she said quickly screwing up her half of the envelope and shoving it into her pocket. She eyed the dog who was now defiantly tearing his half to shreds, which was perfect and she felt a sense of superiority at outwitting the canine blackmailer.

Tamsyn's dad gave them and the toolbox a lift to the old railway station and Daisy hauled the large box of tools out of the boot. 'Right, where shall we start?' Daisy asked Tamsyn who still had one foot in her father's car and was checking her phone.

'Oh, SOS. The café want me to come in to work. Tell me tonight if you find any treasure. Good luck,' she called before getting fully back in the car and being driven away.

'Great,' said Daisy. She tucked her locket inside her t-shirt and walked onto the platform, where she stopped by the boarded-up door and opened the toolbox. She found a useful-looking small crowbar and set to work trying to prise off the boards. It was hard work and she tired quickly. Her arms started to throb, but she continued all the same. It took her some time but eventually she felt the lower board give a little and it spurred her on. Another heave and the nails gave way and pulled free.

Daisy felt a sense of accomplishment as she dropped the crowbar and stuck her head through the gap. Her nostrils twitched. 'It whiffs in here,' she said, which was something coming from someone who had experienced the toilets in the remote corners of Goa. This was an altogether different, more musty smell. She peered inside but with everything boarded up and only an odd tile missing from the roof it was dark. There was little point going in.

Daisy went to put the crowbar back in the toolbox but found herself having a quick rummage instead. She soon came upon exactly what she needed – a head torch. She pulled it on, adjusted the strap and crawled inside the old building. She stood up, dusted herself down and looked about her. She was in a perfectly square room. There were two boarded-up windows – one next to the door and one on the far wall – and a cursory swipe over with the torch showed them to be intact. On her right was a find that made her face light up almost as much as the torchlight: it was an old-fashioned ticket window. She was in the ticket office.

She went through a doorway to the right to find another square room with a large cupboard. She peered inside. Its many shelves were well worn and she suspected this may have been some sort of luggage storage. She crouched down to find a dusty sign on the bottom shelf. When she went to pick it up she was struck by how heavy it was for something half the size of an A4 sheet of paper. Most likely cast iron, she thought. It had a red background and gold letters that read 'Beware of the trains', which she thought was a bit obvious at a train station but you never could account for the stupidity of some folk.

A further grope around uncovered a brush with GWR painted on it but not many bristles and a box of papers that generally looked quite dull apart from the beautiful script of the writing; sadly she doubted they were worth anything. She popped the heavy plaque and old brush into the box and carried them out through the ticket office and into the last room, the door to which still had a sign on it saying 'Waiting rooms'. The door was heavy and ornate and the hinges groaned when she opened it. Inside it was like stepping back in time. This had two more rooms off it labelled 'Women's waiting room' and 'Men's waiting room' but it turned out they were simply single toilets.

The ceiling was lower here and had a loft hatch. She'd need a ladder to get a look inside there. The room itself had a large fireplace that had long since lost its surround but a long wooden bench remained as well as a large wooden station sign saying 'Ottercombe Bay'. Daisy was grinning as she plonked the box on the bench and created a cloud of dust that caught in her throat. She started to cough violently.

'Who's in there?' A fierce male voice came from outside. 'Come out now.' Daisy couldn't answer but she continued to cough. 'Don't make me drag you out!' the voice shouted. Daisy didn't like the tone and as she managed to get the coughing under control she grabbed up the small cast iron 'Beware of the trains' sign. It would be dark outside by now and she didn't know if she may need it to defend herself.

As Daisy pushed on the door into the main ticket office someone pulled on it and she lurched forward brandishing the sign.

'Argh!' the other person shouted and brought up their forearm quickly making Daisy react by giving them a swift whack with the sign.

'You're trespassing,' she shouted lifting the sign ready to strike again if necessary.

'Bloody hell. Daisy?'

Daisy took a step back and tried to assess who she was blinding with the head torch. 'Max? What the hell are you doing?'

'Investigating who's breaking into the railway building. And all I get for my trouble is a broken arm,' he said, nursing his injury whilst muttering swear words.

'I was defending myself because you lifted your arm to hit me.'

'I lifted it to shield my eyes from your bloody light.' He pointed with his good arm.

'Oh, right,' said Daisy, a little more conciliatory. She pulled off the head torch and it shone at a more comfortable level. 'Let's look at your arm.' She didn't wait for him to offer it she just took hold making him wince. She ran her fingers over his taut forearm carefully, noting the muscle definition. 'It's not broken.'

'Are you sure?' Max gave his arm a thorough inspection.

'Fairly sure.'

'You a doctor or nurse?'

'Nope, but I worked in a specialist hospital once . . .'

'Specialist?'

'Actually, I cleaned out the cages at a vets near Nice.'

'Bloody hell,' said Max again but this time there was laughter in his voice and Daisy started to lighten up too. 'If the police see you in here you'll be the crime of the century. You'd best make a run for it.'

Daisy gave him a quizzical look. 'You think I'm stealing?'

'Er, yeah. Why else would you break in here with a crow-bar?'

'Good point,' said Daisy, she would most likely have come to the same conclusion. 'I was just having a look at my inheritance. Turns out there wasn't much.'

'Inheritance?'

'Yep. This is all mine,' she said her voice dripping with sarcasm. She retrieved the box and Max looked inside.

'Did Reg own this place then?'

'Apparently my grandfather bought it and then left it to his brother, Reg, and now he's left it to me. Proper family white elephant. They've tried four times to get planning permission to build on the land and every time it's been refused.'

They heard the distant sound of a police siren and Max became uncomfortable. 'Come on, we'd better get out of here. I don't want to have to explain all this to the local constabulary,' he said already heading for the door.

Once outside Daisy put down the box and picked up the board that had covered part of the door.

'Here, let me,' said Max taking it from her. She passed him the biggest hammer from the toolbox and with a few swift knocks the board was back in place whilst she tried to ignore the sight of his muscular forearm.

'Arm's all right now then?' asked Daisy with a smirk, noting how easily he hammered it back in place.

'It was the other arm,' said Max, returning the sneer.

'Thanks for helping . . .' Daisy paused. Max seemed to have grown up to be an okay sort of person despite her previous impression. 'Let me buy you a pint.'

'So I don't put in a claim via a personal injury lawyer?' said Max, looking serious.

Daisy's eyebrows knitted together. 'You'd better be joking.'

'I am. Come on, I'm dying for a pint.' Max bent down, put the box with the railway items under his arm, picked up the toolbox and headed off across the platform. Daisy wasn't keen on being dictated to but she was intrigued by Max and right now he was walking off with her stuff so she pulled herself together and followed.

Chapter Four

The Mariner's Arms was very much a local pub and virtually everyone greeted Max by name as he walked through the bar.

'You don't come in here much then,' remarked Daisy.

'Nah, almost never,' he said putting down the boxes when the barman approached.

'Usual Max? You're early tonight,' said the barman, with a cursory nod in Daisy's direction.

'Please Monty, and I'll have a whisky chaser seeing as the lady's paying.'

Daisy thrust her hands into her jeans pocket and was thankful to find her last two notes there and some change – it was all she had.

'Everyone calls me Monty on account of my surname being Python,' said Monty, offering his hand across the bar, which Daisy dutifully shook. 'What can I get you?' he asked.

She would have liked a large gin and tonic but she needed to ration her cash and it looked like they only served the standard green bottled offering anyway. 'Small Diet Coke, please.'

Daisy paid for the drinks and they moved to the end of

the bar with Max nudging the boxes along with his foot because both his hands were full.

'I knew old Reg liked trains, not as much as Jason mind, but I knew they were an interest of his. He never mentioned owning the railway though, the dark horse.'

'It's not exactly something to shout about though, is it? You've seen inside it now. It's a tip.'

Max tilted his head. 'Yeah, it's been neglected but it's not a wreck. It mainly needs repairing, cleaning and fitting out if you're planning on living in it.'

'Living in it?' Daisy nearly spat her drink out. 'I don't think so.'

'Why not?' Max appeared genuinely puzzled, which made Daisy consider her answer.

'It's basically three rooms and two toilets in a rubble-strewn car park. The only plus sides are it's in a good location.'

'Bedroom, kitchen cum living room and bathroom. What else do you need?'

Annoyingly he had a point. 'I guess,' said Daisy. 'I'm not sure the council would be keen.'

'Then ask. It's only a phone call to the planning office, they'll soon tell you what they will and won't be happy with. Is it listed?'

Daisy shrugged. The thought hadn't crossed her mind. 'Don't know.'

'You'd need to investigate first to know what restrictions are on it. If you didn't fancy living there yourself holiday lets do well around here. Or there's commercial use.'

'Not many trains now though,' said Daisy, before taking a swig of her drink.

'Huh, you're funny. I mean turning it into a business. People love olde worlde venues for parties, and cafés always thrive in seaside resorts. It'd make a really quirky bar. You could have loads of railway memorabilia up on the walls.' He brushed his wayward dark hair off his forehead.

Daisy reached down to the box at her feet. 'Like this?' she said pulling out the almost bald brush.

'Yeah, exactly, people go crazy for that sort of thing.'

Max made her smile. She wasn't entirely sure why, maybe it was because he was uncomplicated and easy to read. She liked that.

'Look I'd better make a move,' said Daisy. 'Aunt Coral will be expecting me back.'

'But you're a big girl now.'

She paused, there was nothing to rush back for. 'Okay, I'll text her while you get another round in.'

Max checked his pockets. 'Diet Cokes all round then.'

Daisy went to the loo. She noted the lack of graffiti as she entered the cubicle, but when she pulled down her jeans she felt something scratch her bum. The surprise made her leap forward and bump herself on the cubicle door. 'Ow,' she cried.

'You all right in there?' came a thick accented voice from the cubicle next door.

'Yeah, sorry. I just . . . actually, never mind. I'm fine thanks.' Daisy tugged her trousers back up and pulled the offending thing from her back pocket – it was the letter the solicitor had given her.

Daisy roughly opened the envelope and pulled out the thick folded sheet inside, Great Uncle Reg's words dancing in front of her eyes.

My Dearest Daisy,
*   I am sorry to think that I will not see you again.*
One of my greatest regrets in life was not being blessed

with a child of my own. However, as my great niece, you have more than filled that gap in my life. From the moment your dear mother handed you to me at a week old I knew my heart was lost. As humans we are capable of love on many different levels and I am happy to say I have loved you your whole life as if you were my own. I have seen life strike its blows and watched you stand up and fight back and I am immensely proud of the rounded adult you have become.

I would have loved you to make your life here in Ottercombe Bay, but I understand your reasons for not doing so. I have enjoyed following your travels but it was always bittersweet to see you start to settle some-where only to uproot yourself and move on again. I believe you are a restless soul, Daisy, and it troubles me. I am the first to encourage young people to explore this amazing world but that needs to be done from a solid base – a firm and secure home. The nest to return to in times of storm if you like.

This is why I want you to spend one year in Ottercombe Bay. I do not wish to restrain you but to help you mend your wings in order to fly higher next time. A stay here will help you to finally lay to rest the ghosts of your past, something your father never managed to do.

The railway station was left to me by your grand-father but I always felt I was only minding it until a time it should pass to you. You have great flair Daisy and the cheek of the devil so I'm sure you will make good use of this to fund what I hope will be a very happy and healthy future. Until we meet again, I remain your ever-loving

Great Uncle Reg

She folded the paper and blinked back the tears before opening it again and rereading it. She knew Reg had loved her and had to admit he had been a worthy stand-in for her grandparents who had seemed to die in quick succession when she'd been in her teens. Sadly people dying had not shocked Daisy at the time – she expected people to die, her mother had and if the most important of all people could be wrenched from you then nobody was safe. She had spent her life cocooning herself, keeping a safe barrier from other people to save herself from future heartache as best she could.

When she rejoined Max at the bar he was playing with a beer mat.

'I thought you'd gone out the window,' he joked.

'Not my style,' she said, although as she uttered the words she realised exiting tricky situations via the quickest route possible was exactly her style but Max didn't need to know that.

'What is your style?' asked Max looking interested. 'I've no idea what you do for a living.'

Daisy hated questions like this because they made her think about her career path to date, which was uncoordinated, some might say haphazard. 'I've got quite a few strings to my bow,' she said. But Max appeared to be expecting a more detailed answer. She thought back. 'I studied Film Production and Design for a while at uni where I did some part-time bar work but quit early to be an extra on a film set in Ireland. I got on a ferry and basically worked my way around half of Europe. I did some work in a call centre before travelling through the Netherlands, Germany and Italy waitressing mainly.

'Then I went to stay with Dad in Goa for a few months and worked in a hotel for a while but it wasn't for me. I decided to go back to uni to study Environmental Management but it was the wrong decision. A few months later I set off to do the other half of Europe, starting with Spain where there was more waitressing and bar work then went to France and met this guy . . .' As soon as she'd said it she wished she hadn't, she could see the look in Max's eyes. She focused on the table and continued. 'He had big ideas, mainly get rich quick schemes, all of which failed but we set up a mobile food van. It wasn't glamorous but it was a steady business we could grow. Then he bought into another stupid scheme and we lost everything.' She took a deep breath. 'So I came back to good old Blighty and I've been working around the South East for the past few months.'

Max blew out his cheeks. 'Quite varied then.' Daisy agreed and they both fell silent. Perhaps she had over shared.

Daisy took a sip of her drink. She held her locket between her thumb and forefinger and gave it a little rub. 'Reg left me a letter. There's a condition attached to me having the railway station. I have to stay here for a whole year.'

She thought for a moment and then tugged the letter from her back pocket and pushed it across the table. She studied Max as his eyes slowly made their way down the paper. He had dark intense eyes, ridiculously long eyelashes and a warm even tan. She didn't really remember him at primary school but she did remember the gangly youth who used to hang around the beach when she visited. She recalled a row with her father about him too and she racked her brains to try to remember the reason. It was rare for her to fight with her dad.

'What happens when the year's up?' said Max at long last, folding the letter back up and returning it.

'I'd sell it and go travelling.'

Max sniffed. 'But he wants you to settle down.'

'It's blackmail from beyond the grave, though, isn't it?'

Max chuckled. 'Not at all. We talked about you sometimes, me and Reg,' he said. He sipped his drink. 'He cared a lot about you.'

'I felt the same about him,' said Daisy, sounding defensive. She carried the guilt of not visiting often enough but she'd tried to keep in touch through regular phone calls and postcards.

'He worried about you.'

'He had no need to,' said Daisy, her voice flat. She felt uncomfortable that Max knew things about her, it put her at a distinct disadvantage.

Max lifted his shoulders languidly. 'Maybe not, but he worried all the same. Sounds to me like he thinks you need to stop globetrotting and make a life for yourself here.'

'But I don't want to.'

'But maybe it's what you need.'

Daisy was taken aback and it showed on her face. 'What gives him the right to make me?' She was starting to feel irritated and Great Uncle Reg wasn't here to debate this with, but unfortunately for Max he was.

'He was a close relative and he cared. It's not a crime.'

'But you can't just decide things for other people and then try to make them do it. That's like slavery.'

Max laughed and Daisy's irritation hitched up a notch.

'Do you think maybe you're overreacting to someone trying to help you?' Max leaned forward and watched her closely.

'No. It's not helping if it's manipulation.'

Max pulled a face. 'Reg's intention was good. By my reckoning that makes it okay to offer you some help.'

40

'I don't need help. I need people to mind their own business!' Daisy got up and almost tripped over the toolbox and box of railway items. Cock, she thought. She was never going to manage to carry them both all the way back to Aunt Coral's on her own. Max turned and followed her gaze and a wry smile formed on his lips.

'Do you, er, need me to *help* you with those?'

Daisy plonked the railway box on top of the toolbox and lifted them into her arms in one awkward movement as her muscles tried to cope with the weight. She turned and glared at Max who was looking annoyingly smug. 'No, thanks,' she said, walking unsteadily out of the pub.

Her anger propelled her quite some distance before the heaviness of the boxes weighed her down and her arms longed for her to stop, but she knew if she did it would be even harder to set off again. She tried not to think about the letter or the railway or Reg for that matter, but it was impossible because they were all swirling around in her head and overwhelming her.

Chapter Five

Back in the pub, Max was just finishing his Diet Coke and still chuckling about Daisy when Jason came in wearing tailored shorts and a neatly ironed polo shirt.

'Perfect timing, it's your round,' said Max meeting his friend at the bar.

Jason glanced skywards. 'I doubt it but what are you having?'

'A pint please.' Monty was already on the case without the order having to be relayed. 'You won't believe who just bought me a drink,' said Max raising one of his eyebrows.

'I like quizzes,' said Jason. 'How many questions can I ask?'

Max rolled his eyes. 'Bloody hell, Jason, just give me some names.'

'Okay, okay. Is it someone famous?'

'No, and it's not twenty questions, just guess already.'

'Someone who looks like the photofit of the bloke who stole the gnome from the garden centre?' Jason was a police officer who was keen to work his way up the ranks.

Max was shaking his head in despair. 'No, and that was just someone who left it on the bottom of the trolley and forgot to pay.'

'This is what happens. Common crimes start to become acceptable and before you know it you have a crime wave on your hands. It's like insurance fraud. Years ago nobody would have dreamed of putting in a false claim but nowadays practically everyone falsely claims for a new camera and sunglasses on their holiday insurance.'

'You included.' Max gave him a knowing glance.

Jason looked outraged. 'Good God, how many times have we had this conversation? I left my Ray Bans on the bus in Tenby and nobody handed them in.'

'Yeah, that's what they all say. But you, an officer of the law. Tut, tut, tut,' said Max loving every minute of winding up his friend. 'One last guess, I'm getting bored now.'

Jason's expression changed to one of serious concentration. 'Right. I'm going to say . . . my mother?'

'No. Daisy Wickens.' Max leaned back on the wooden chair and put his pint to his lips all the while watching Jason's reaction. Jason's face lit up and he searched the pub, his eyes darting about before they came back to Max.

'Really, where is she now?'

'Dunno, she got the hump and left.'

Jason frowned. 'Did you upset her?'

Max took a long slow sip from his pint and then placed it back on the table.

'Not intentionally,' said Max, but the corner of his mouth twitched.

'Bloody hell, Max, do you get some sort of kick out of upsetting people?'

'No, she's always been a stroppy mare. She used to swan about for a couple of weeks each year like she owned the place. One minute she'd be hanging around with us, the next she'd ignore us. I can't cope with that.' He knew too well what sort of person she was. She was fickle and never

43

lasted anywhere more than five minutes and those sorts of people were always going to hurt you eventually. He'd had it happen too many times – first his mother, then his father and more recently a now ex-girlfriend. If someone wasn't likely to be a permanent feature in his life then he'd learnt, for his own self-preservation, to keep them at a distance.

'I always liked her,' said Jason his gaze drifting to his shandy. 'She went through a lot with her mum and everything. She was only a kid.'

'We all have stuff in our past that could mess us up, Jay. It's no excuse.'

'Agreed. But she was nice to me, you know, she'd show an interest. Didn't mock like some.' He regarded Max.

'What? I've never mocked you,' said Max. Jason tilted his head to one side. 'Okay, maybe once or twice but it's only banter.'

Jason sipped his pint. 'Shame I missed her though. I expect she's off on her travels again soon.'

'Yeah, I guess but Reg has left her the old railway station if she stays.' He sat back in his seat and watched Jason's reaction. Jason sat up straight. 'I thought that might interest you.'

'Like I said I always liked her. It would be lovely if she moved back here permanently.'

Max grinned. 'I meant I thought the old railway station might interest you.'

Jason went a bit pink round the edges. 'Oh, well, yes. You know I'm an enthusiast, that goes without saying.'

'She's got a box of old train stuff, heavy old metal signs, that sort of thing. If you run you'll catch her up. I doubt she's got far lugging that lot and a full toolbox.'

Jason looked concerned. 'You left her to carry it all?'

'Like I said she's a stroppy mare.'

Jason took a couple of large glugs of his half pint of shandy and stood up. 'You amaze me sometimes, Max.' He shook his head as he left.

'Two stroppy mares in one night,' he muttered to himself. He finished the last of Jason's drink and pulled a face. 'How does he drink this crap?'

Daisy was grateful for having the lamppost to rest the boxes against but she knew she had to press on. She'd calmed down now; the boxes were unbelievably heavy and she was regretting getting cross with Max. She could have done with a hand lugging them back to Aunt Coral's. She wished she'd arranged for Tamsyn's dad to come back and collect his toolbox – hindsight was a wonderfully annoying thing.

She took a deep breath and lifted up the load again and set off with a purposeful stride; the sooner she got back the sooner her arms would stop aching. She heard a car coming and expected it to zoom past, but she could tell it was slowing alongside her. All I need now is some pervy kerb crawler or the police, she thought. Daisy had to admit she probably looked an odd sight, and more than a little suspicious. She wasn't sure whether to keep going or stand her ground. She heard the car stop, a door slam and then footsteps behind her.

She turned around to see a tall man approaching her, with the streetlamp behind him it was difficult to see. She got ready to lob the toolbox at him if necessary.

'Excuse me, can I help you with those?' he asked, which wasn't at all what she was expecting.

'Er, no, thanks,' she said, wondering what his game was.

'It's no problem. Come on, I'll give you a lift.' Daisy

hesitated. 'It's okay. I might not be in uniform but I'm a police officer.'

'My dad told me not to get in cars with strange men,' she said and he laughed.

His laughter evaporated. 'But you know me, we went to school together. Played together in the holidays when you came home, Daisy.'

Something about the way he said her name rang a bell. She tried to get a good look at his face but it was dark. An embarrassing silence followed.

Daisy quickly scanned her memory for boys from primary school. It was all a haze of oversized uniforms, bad haircuts and playing tig. Something Tamsyn had said glued the puzzle pieces together in her mind.

'Jason,' she almost shouted it as recognition struck. 'Of course. I'm sorry. You've got a lot taller since I last saw you.' Jason had been one of those boys who was picked on by the others. If she remembered correctly, Max had looked out for him when they were younger.

Jason looked happy with her response as he took the heavy boxes from her with annoyingly little effort but then he hadn't been carrying them for half a mile. 'It's lovely to see you again, Daisy. I hear you're staying for a while.'

'Bloody hell, the grapevine here spreads faster than a Kim Kardashian selfie.' This was one of the major down-sides of a close-knit community. 'And no, I'm afraid I'm not staying.' She followed him to the car and waited whilst he put the boxes in the boot.

'Oh,' Jason looked downhearted. The short trip was conducted in relative silence, just the odd clink coming from the toolbox in the boot. Jason pulled up outside the cottage and got out. Daisy got the feeling she was upsetting a lot of people tonight.

She met him at the boot of the car. 'I'll take the toolbox back to Tamsyn's dad.'

'I'll take this one inside then,' he said, picking up the railway box and having a sneaky peek inside.

'Feel free to have a look through if you're interested. And thanks for the lift, I do appreciate it, Jason.' She hauled out the toolbox and headed next door.

After saying her thank-yous and politely refusing their offer to come inside three times Daisy finally escaped Tamsyn's parents. She could see Jason and Aunt Coral were standing just inside the porch chatting. Daisy tugged on the door, it swung open and Bugsy made a break for freedom. She tried to make a grab for his collar but what he lacked in aerodynamics he made up for in speed as he dodged her like a professional rugby player and disappeared into the darkness.

'Bugsy!' shouted Aunt Coral as she lurched past Jason. Daisy wasn't sure which way Aunt Coral was going to go and in the split second she had to make a decision. She made the right one so they didn't collide but Daisy managed to leave her foot jutting out slightly. Aunt Coral was moving at speed, she caught her toe on Daisy's foot and fell spectacularly through the open doorway, landing with a thud.

'Are you all right?' asked Daisy, crouching down at her side. Jason joined her and together they helped her up.

'Yes, I'm fine,' she said brushing herself down. 'Where did he go?' she asked, looking about frantically. Aunt Coral stepped forward and seemed to stumble. 'Ow, my ankle!'

Jason put an arm around her and guided her back inside. 'Let's get you sat down and we can have a look at your ankle. I'm trained in first aid.'

'But we need to catch Bugsy,' said Aunt Coral hobbling inside.

Jason looked at Daisy and there was a slight pause before she realised she needed to do something. 'Yes, of course. I'll go look for him.'

'Thanks, love,' called back Aunt Coral.

It was late and it was dark. Not just average town or city dark, no this was middle of nowhere, no light pollution, Ottercombe Bay dark. Only the main streets had lighting, so in Trow Lane it was blacker than the inside of the old railway building.

Daisy wasn't exactly sure what she was meant to do. Standing there in the dark on her own she felt a complete idiot. 'Bugsy,' she called half-heartedly. It was unlikely he was going to come back because she'd called him, they hadn't exactly warmed to each other. She stopped and listened. She could hear something. It could've been the sound of small paws on gravel or perhaps a bird in the hedge. Daisy wandered off into the night but it was pretty pointless looking for a small black dog in almost total darkness.

She decided to walk to the end of the lane and back again to at least show willing. Every few steps she called his name feeling like a total idiot. He hardly knew her so he wasn't likely to come running. When she reached the end of the lane she took a moment to look out over the few rows of houses to the sea beyond. The moon was casting its jewels on the surface of the water and painting a halo over the cottages. Daisy had to admit it was a sight to catch you unawares. She watched the jewels sparkle for a while until a faint bark drew her attention away. When she got back to the cottage there was still no sign of the dog.

Inside Jason had a first-aid box out, presumably from the car, and had done a good job of bandaging up Aunt Coral's ankle, which was now resting on a cushion on the coffee table.

'Did you find him?' asked Aunt Coral, looking hopefully at Daisy.

'Sorry, it's hard to see out there.' Daisy was just about to flop onto the sofa when Aunt Coral replied.

'Take the torch from the kitchen then. He likes to go up onto the headland so take care.'

'The headland? That's gotta be over a mile away.'

Aunt Coral frowned. 'It's his usual walk. He's probably just gone off on the route he's used to.'

'In which case he should come back then,' said Daisy, hoping this was her get-out clause, but Aunt Coral's pleading look said different as did Jason's slight headshake of disapproval.

'Right, I'll walk up to the headland and look for him. I'll stop for chips on the way back, do you want anything?' She hadn't eaten so at least it wouldn't be a completely wasted trip.

'No thanks, I'll be getting off,' said Jason. 'Doctors tomorrow if that's still swollen, Coral, okay?'

'Yes, thank you, Jason.'

'Bye then,' said Jason to Daisy, somewhat frostily.

'Thanks again for the lift,' she said and she went to find the torch.

An hour and a half later she was walking back eating her chips having not seen any sign of the dog. She had had a proper look for him and even called his name numerous times up on the headland but it had been met with silence. As she munched her way back along the lane she thought she heard something. She stopped and for a second the sound continued and then stopped. She ate another chip, walked two steps forward and then stopped and the sound repeated and then halted moments after she did. There was someone behind her. She spun round quickly with the torch but there was no one there – until she shone the torch on the ground. A couple of feet behind her was Bugsy. He blinked when the torchlight shone in his eyes.

'Great, how long have you been following me?'

Bugsy ignored her, stuck his squat nose in the air and strutted up to her, sat down and looked hopefully at the last chip. Using the chip as bait Daisy coaxed him back to the cottage, threw it in the porch and he thankfully followed it, devouring it quickly while Daisy pulled the door closed and heaved a huge sigh of relief.

'I found him,' she called feeling quite pleased with herself. That was one point she could chalk up to herself in the Bugsy versus Daisy battle and it felt good.

Chapter Six

The next morning Aunt Coral was still thrilled to have Bugsy back and was fussing over him, the fact that his escape had caused her ankle strain seemed not to have registered with her. Daisy, on the other hand, was well aware and was watching the dog closely. He wasn't as daft as he looked, and to her mind he did look daft. The pug was just about as far removed from the origins of the wolf as any dog breed could possibly be. He reminded her of a cork piglet she'd made at school, which still sat on the kitchen windowsill. The squashed face and the curly tail made it a good likeness. The only difference was the piglet was painted pink and had tiny eyes whereas Bugsy was completely black with disproportionally huge eyes like two eight balls stuck in his face. He gave her a smug look when Aunt Coral gave him another small piece of bacon.

Yeah, I've got the measure of you, thought Daisy, she wasn't going to be outsmarted by a tiny bug-eyed dog.

'Jason says you can get some money for the railway memorabilia you brought home. He knows some specialist who can get you the best price, if that's what you want.'

Daisy munched on her toast. 'Sounds good. The place

is just a shell. I don't know what Reg expected me to do with it.'

'You've got a whole year to work that out; you don't need to trouble yourself right now. And of course you're welcome to stay with me. I'd be glad of the company but if you wanted to get your own place I'd understand.' Coral patted her hand.

'Thanks.' Daisy knew now probably wasn't a good juncture to explain her imminent departure. She couldn't walk out now Aunt Coral was laid up with her ankle. Daisy was lots of things but she wasn't unkind or callous. She was still set on leaving but she couldn't dispel the mixed feelings she seemed to be experiencing. Daisy blamed it on Great Uncle Reg's letter and what Tamsyn had said about her mother – both were playing on her mind. She'd stay for just a couple more days, which would give Aunt Coral's ankle a chance to recover and her an opportunity to speak to Tamsyn's mum, Min, and lay that particular ghost to rest, then she could leave.

Seeing as she was here a bit longer than planned she decided she'd call it a holiday. Holidays were what people came to Ottercombe Bay for. She would write it off as a vacation and then at the end she would depart just like all the other tourists. She took a deep breath; she knew leaving also meant walking away from a share of Reg's money, and money was something she was lacking. But, no, her mind was made up. No amount of cash was worth being trapped for, especially not for a whole year. Daisy finished her toast, ignoring the dog's whiny pleas for her to share.

Daisy's bedroom was currently doing a good impression of a bombsite. She amazed herself at how quickly she could turn an ordered space into a chaotic jumble – perhaps it was a skill. She didn't know anyone else as talented at being untidy as she was. She only had the one rucksack but it was enormous and when she'd left Canterbury she'd had to ram everything in to get it all to fit. She had since had to pull everything out to get to the things at the bottom and now the contents were strewn about the room. Luckily Aunt Coral wasn't the nosey sort, so Daisy could shut the door and know it would be fine. Well, nobody was perfect after all.

It was mid-afternoon when Daisy found herself lying on the pebble part of the beach on a rather thin towel while she waited for Tamsyn to finish her shift at the beach café. Every summer the council tipped a few tons of sand onto the top half of the bay making it perfect for the holiday crowd, but unless you were there super early you got relegated to the pebbles further down. Despite her bumpy bed she was enjoying herself. The sun was warming her body gently whilst she listened to the sound of the sea washing the shore and parents arguing with small children over sun cream and ice-lollies.

On a summer's day Ottercombe Bay was a hive of activity, all the rental properties would be full and all the second homers would be maximising their investment, and days like this were ideal for making you feel good about yourself and your decisions. A couple of days of sun and relaxation was going to do Daisy good. She hadn't had a proper break for months, let alone the chance of a holiday so an opportunity to do nothing was one not to be missed because soon she would be back on the road hunting down her next job.

'You'll get a well weird tan line if you leave your necklace on,' said a voice above her, throwing her into shadow.

'If you stand there, Tams, I'll get no tan at all.' Daisy instinctively put her hand to her locket.

Daisy shuffled over to make room on the towel and Tamsyn bunched up her long flowery skirt and sat down. Daisy gave her the abridged version of the previous evening's events.

'How's Coral now?' asked Tamsyn.

'Cheesed off mainly, I think. The painkillers are working but it's a bad sprain. She'll be hobbling about for a while.'

'I'm sorry about her ankle but if it means you're staying, yay.' Tamsyn clapped her hands together.

Daisy hauled herself up onto an elbow. 'It's only temporary while Aunt Coral recovers.'

'Okay,' said Tamsyn despondently. She looked about her. 'You could've brought Bugsy to the beach. He loves it down here.'

Daisy pulled an unimpressed face. She had forgotten about walking the dog, although he'd probably had enough exercise last night to last him for a while. 'He doesn't like me much,' she said.

'Oh, don't be silly. Bugsy is totally adorable isn't he?'

Daisy's expression didn't change. 'He's totally untrainable.'

'But he's the cutest thing imaginable,' said Tamsyn.

'He's ugly.' Daisy's face was full of scorn.

'What?'

'Oh come on. He looks like he spends every day smacking himself in the face with a frying pan. And those bulbous eyes – they're way too big for his head.'

Tamsyn was shaking her head. 'I can't believe you're saying that. He has gorgeous eyes and I think he's beautiful. Maybe it's your attitude he doesn't like.'

Daisy took a sharp intake of breath. 'My attitude? That dog is 99 per cent attitude.' And one per cent pig she thought to herself as she flopped back onto the towel and was reminded it was lying on a bed of stones; but she wasn't going to let on to her discomfort.

'Well, Reg loved him and Reg loved you. It kind of makes you related,' said Tamsyn, settling herself down.

Daisy shot bolt upright. 'No, it doesn't.' She shook her head at the ridiculous suggestion. 'I am not related to a bloody pug.'

'I think you're in denial,' said Tamsyn shutting her eyes.

Daisy opened her mouth to argue further but realising it was pointless she shook her head and lay back down, a little more gently this time.

'I hear you met Jason last night,' said Tamsyn.

'Is there some sort of live feed or webcam I don't know about? Or am I actually part of a TV programme like *The Truman Show* – The Daisy Wickens Show?' She was amazed how everyone seemed to know what was going on almost before it had happened. This was the problem with small towns. To the untrained eye, Ottercombe Bay probably seemed an average-sized town but take out all the holiday lets, all the camp sites, the second homers and day trippers and the core of locals was actually a lot smaller. It was most definitely a village and a peculiar one at that.

'No, silly,' giggled Tamsyn. 'There's a hole in the wall between our cottages.'

'What?' Daisy was outraged and found she was covering her precious areas with her hands.

'Only kidding, but you should have seen your face. No, Jason told me he'd seen you.'

Daisy heaved a sigh of relief. It wouldn't have surprised her if there were a hole in the wall. She gave up on lying down and sat up. 'Are you and Jason together?'

Tamsyn gave a tinny laugh. 'Noooo, he's not my type. Too geeky.'

Daisy scrunched her face up. Given Tamsyn's interesting dress sense and love of fantasy novels she thought perhaps she shouldn't be throwing stones at someone else's glass house. 'Okay, who would be your type?'

Tamsyn's gaze drifted off to sea. Daisy was moments away from waving a hand in front of her face when she eventually spoke. 'I like my men beefy and broad shouldered. Intelligent but not geeky. Romantic, kind and caring, like Flynn Rider.'

'The cartoon character?' queried Daisy, although she wasn't sure why this should be a surprise to her.

'Yes, he's perfect and Tangled is my favourite film ever.'

'Okay, anything else?'

'Someone who likes the same things I do, like fantasy novels, vintage, dragons, crafting, pineapples and buttons. And they have to be an animal lover.' She shot Daisy a withering look.

'That's some list. You found anyone who fits your criteria?'

'Not yet. How about you?'

Daisy felt uncomfortable, she wasn't big on sharing at the best of times. 'Nope, no one.'

'Oh, come on, there must have been someone in the last zillion years. Don't fob me off. All those trips abroad to exotic destinations full of hotties, there must have been a few.'

Daisy admired Tamsyn's tenacity. 'There was one guy.'

'Only one?' Tamsyn tilted her head. 'You guard your heart like a dragon guards its hoard.'

Daisy was momentarily stunned by Tamsyn's profound insight. 'Anyway . . . I meant only one serious one. His name was Guillaume.'

'Gee-om?' mimicked Tamsyn with a titter. 'How do you spell it?'

'Trust me that won't help you. He was very French, olive skinned and utterly gorgeous.'

Tamsyn bore the expression of the perpetually bewildered. 'Was his skin like black or green olives?'

'Neither,' said Daisy with a chuckle. 'It's a warm tone, like having a good tan.'

'Okay.' Tamsyn still looked perplexed but she settled down for the story anyway. 'What went wrong?'

'We rowed a lot. Mainly about money. He was a huge risk taker. We had a good thing going in France and we lost the lot because of his stupid get-rich-quick schemes.' Daisy's voice was tinged with temper.

'But now Reg has left you some money, could you try again with Gee-womb?'

Daisy was already shaking her head. 'No. I couldn't trust him not to blow every penny. I'm better off on my own.' She knew this was true, but she also knew it wasn't that simple. Guillaume had hurt her greatly. It was rare that Daisy let down the barriers she had erected around her heart but she'd let him march in and he'd torn it to shreds. 'Anyway, I like being on my own.'

'I don't believe you,' said Tamsyn bluntly. Daisy looked taken aback. 'I mean, you must miss your parents.'

Daisy felt uneasy and pulled in a steadying breath. 'Dad and I keep in touch. He seems happier in Goa. A little more at peace than he ever was in the UK. And of course, I miss Mum every day.' Daisy thumbed her locket. She couldn't begin to explain the emotions just thinking about her mother trawled up.

Tamsyn patted her leg. 'Your mum was lovely. It was sad she died. Such an awful accident.'

Daisy swallowed. This was a subject she was uncomfortable discussing but she couldn't let Tamsyn's comment go unchallenged. 'But we don't know it was an accident.'

Tamsyn became animated. 'You don't believe the rumours that your dad killed her, do you?'

'No,' said Daisy. She was shocked by the statement, even though she was familiar with the rumours. Despite his best efforts, the suspicions had still reached her and she knew it was one of the main reasons they had left the area a few months after her mother's death, just before her eighth birthday. 'But someone else could have caused her death. We know she drowned but not how exactly. The inquest was an open verdict.' This still haunted Daisy.

Tamsyn bit her lip as if considering her next sentence. 'Or it could have been suicide.'

Daisy shook her head. This was an idea too awful to entertain. 'But why? Why would she kill herself? She had people who loved her. Dad said she was the happiest person he knew.' And she had me, she thought, how could she have left me? Daisy concentrated hard to keep control of the emotions starting to bubble inside.

Sadness clouded Tamsyn's face. 'I guess we'll never know,' she said, giving Daisy's leg another pat.

Daisy paused for a moment while she considered something. She liked Tamsyn and she was beginning to feel she could trust her. She undid the clasp on the chain of her locket and handed it to Tamsyn. 'I think this holds the key.'

'There's an actual key inside?' Tamsyn's eyes were wide like Bugsy's.

'No, I think it holds the clue to what happened to my mother.'

'Is there a message engraved on it or a note inside?' Tamsyn studied the locket closely.

'No, there's no message.' Sometimes Tamsyn was hard work. 'It was with my mother's effects when the police handed them over. Dad has always maintained he'd never seen it before and even tried to give it back to the police but they insisted it was hers.'

'So who's right?' asked Tamsyn.

'I don't know, but if my mother had it with her the night she died then I believe it holds the answer to what happened.'

Chapter Seven

When Saturday morning dawned Daisy wasn't entirely sure how she had been roped into going to the local fête. She knew it meant a few locals selling plants and a bunch of screaming kids high on candy floss, but Tamsyn was excited and desperately wanted Daisy to go too. Perhaps she just wanted to share the ordeal.

The little town was humming with activity as yet more cars squeezed into the already overfilled place. Daisy had wrestled her wayward hair into a flowery bandana and put on the only summer dress she owned. They joined the throng of people heading towards the recreation ground.

Daisy was stopped at the gates by an overly smiley woman. 'Fifty pence entry, please.'

'What?' said Daisy astonished. 'You're charging people actual money to come in?' Daisy chuckled but she handed over her entrance fee and took the proffered leaflet.

'It's a shame Coral couldn't come,' said Tamsyn, appearing at her side. Today she was wearing a bustier top, floaty skirt and flip-flops that didn't match.

'She's saved herself fifty pence – that's very wise.' Daisy scanned the leaflet. It was a timetable of events. 'Events' seemed a bit grand for the local fête.

'I'm going to look at the buggy racing first and later the falconry display,' said Tamsyn. 'You coming?'

'Buggy racing?' It was like being in a parallel universe where Ottercombe Bay had woken up to the wonders of the twentieth century – still a century behind but, hey, it was progress, thought Daisy. Clearly the fête had advanced somewhat since she'd last been. She followed Tamsyn with a spring in her step and her expectations raised.

Although Daisy couldn't argue that there was buggy racing it was on a smaller scale than she'd been expecting. 'They're model cars.' Daisy pointed at one speeding past and watched it hit a bump, momentarily leaving the grass.

'No, they're remote control,' said Tamsyn, waving at someone she knew who was grappling with a controller. They both watched as a buggy on the other side of the course crashed into a tyre wall. 'Whoops, let's check out the other racing,' said Tamsyn striding off.

The other racing had Daisy standing there literally open-mouthed. 'Goat racing? Since when did you get racing goats?' she asked.

'Oh, they've been doing this for a few years. It's great. They used to have teddies for jockeys but they kept getting eaten. You can bet on them,' said Tamsyn pulling out her purse and heading over to a large blackboard where their old head teacher was frantically updating odds on an interesting list of names.

'Hiya, Mr Templeton,' said Tamsyn.

'Oh, hello Tamsyn. Who are you betting on?'

'Any top tips?' she asked with an exaggerated wink.

'Couldn't say but Hairy Potter has failed to finish twice so you might want to steer clear of him,' he said, with a tap of his nose. He looked past Tamsyn and watched Daisy for a minute while she giggled at the names on the board.

'I know you as well don't I?' He narrowed his eyes. Daisy stopped giggling and swallowed hard.

'Daisy Wickens. Hello Sir,' she said feeling seven years old again.

'Lovely to see you again, Daisy. And where did life after Ottercombe Primary take you?' He was looking genuinely interested, which made the very unimpressive answer all the harder to muster.

Thankfully Tamsyn stepped in. 'She's been travelling round the whole of Europe.' She emphasised this by waving her arms in a giant circle and almost knocking off Mr Templeton's glasses.

'Careful there, Tamsyn. That is wonderful, Daisy, well done you for continuing your education by taking in some of this wonderful planet. Will you be having a bet with us today?'

Daisy opened her mouth and closed it again. Everyone always assumed that travelling meant she'd been on one long holiday when in reality she'd been an itinerant worker living on a sporadic and pitiful income, which wasn't the sort of education he meant but she loved his optimism. 'Thanks. I'll have a pound on Billy the Kid, please.'

'Good choice,' he said, taking her money and giving her a ticket.

'One pound on Barb. E. Cue and a pound on Hot to Trot. Thanks, Mr T,' said Tamsyn, taking her tickets and leading Daisy over to a roped-off area. In the ring were some miserable-looking teenagers hanging on to a number of recalcitrant goats of varying sizes. Daisy was about to put her ticket away when a large goat snatched it from her hand and promptly ate it.

'Hey Gollum!' said the youth on the other end of the goat's rope.

'He's eaten my betting slip!' said Daisy, throwing up her arms.

'Sorry,' said the youth, dragging the goat away.

'Great. I hope I don't win now,' said Daisy, as they watched the goats being taken round to the starting line.

'Mr Templeton will honour your bet anyway. He always liked you at school,' said Tamsyn. The truth was, like all the teachers, he pitied Daisy. She was always the poor little girl whose mother died. She could tell what they were thinking by the way they looked at her.

They squeezed through the crowd to get a spot where they could see down the track to the finish line.

'Runners and riders ready?' asked the compère to nobody in particular. 'On your marks, get set, go!' A length of board was dropped and the goats were free to run the course. It appeared they all knew the drill as they set off at a good pace with only one stopping to try and steal a child's ice-cream.

'And I'm a Llama takes an early lead with Billy the Kid and Vincent Van Goat close behind . . .'

'Oh great, I'm second,' said Daisy, unsure if she was pleased or already worrying about the conversation she would have to have with Mr Templeton: *Sorry Sir, the goat ate my homework . . . I mean betting slip.*

'I think mine's at the back,' said Tamsyn, trying to lean over for a better view.

The commentator continued '. . . and Hot to Trot and Norfolk Enchants are the back-markers as we start the second and final lap. The carrots are now on the course so watch those runners gallop home.'

He wasn't wrong. The goats seemed to sense the arrival of the treats now in a tub at the end of the course and they went even faster.

'. . . and as they come to the line the winner is Billy the Kid, with Goaty McGoatface in second and I'm a Llama in third.'

'Ooh, you've won a fiver,' said Tamsyn happily.

Perhaps it was worth an embarrassing conversation with Mr Templeton after all. As it turned out he was completely lovely about it and she hadn't been the first that day to have their ticket eaten, which made her feel a little better, especially when he reassured her the goat would be fine. Daisy put her five pounds away quickly to avoid a similar incident.

They saw a crowd gathering nearby for another event and made their way to the front. They got there just in time to see a man raise his arm and say 'Take the strain.' Followed almost immediately by 'Pull!'

'Now this is something I am happy to pay fifty pence to see,' said Daisy, whilst she and Tamsyn admired the sixteen men in straining shorts and tight t-shirts battling in the Tug of War competition.

'There's Jason,' hollered Tamsyn, wildly pointing to the middle of the team on the right. Daisy was distracted by the person behind him. She was working her way up from his muscular thighs and perfectly rounded backside when she realised it was Max. His biceps were literally bulging as his team started to inch backwards. It was a most appealing sight to witness. Their anchor stumbled and in the confusion to get everyone back on their feet the other team took the advantage and pulled them over the line. Max looked like he was swearing under his breath until he glanced up and saw Daisy. She felt caught out and threw up a hand to shield her eyes from the sun, which was behind her, but hopefully he wouldn't think she was ogling him.

The second round was over all too quickly but thankfully Jason and Max's team won so it all hung on the final pull.

'This is really exciting,' said Tamsyn, her face total proof of her statement.

'Take the strain,' said the judge and both Daisy and Tamsyn tilted their heads to one side in unison as they watched the men's muscles swell in anticipation. 'Pull!' The other team must have had a lucky first round because within seconds Jason and Max were inching backwards and the contest was over. Daisy was quite disappointed, she had been comparing muscles along the row and now they were all dispersing.

'Best of five?' shouted Daisy and everyone turned around including Max. He strode over, a frown etched on his forehead.

'You're still here then,' he said.

'Obviously,' said Daisy, sensing the hostility emanating from him.

'Thought you'd have run off by now.' He indicated running with his fingers and chuckled. What had she done to him? It was him who had let her walk half the way home with two heavy boxes, *she* should be mad at *him*. And now she thought of it, she was.

'I'm not stopping long though. I've far better things to do than hang around this provincial backwater.'

Max's eye twitched. 'Don't let us simple folk keep you from your big ambitions.'

'Oh, don't worry, you won't,' said Daisy firmly. Why did Max irritate her so much and how did it escalate so quickly?

'We should go and get seats for the falconry display.' Tamsyn tugged at Daisy's arm pulling her away.

Despite the altercation with Max, Daisy was enjoying the fête. It wasn't what she had initially thought, or what the events schedule had led her to believe, it was far more entertaining. She chuckled as she passed a wheelbarrow full of cans of beer surrounded by disappointed men checking raffle tickets.

A little girl skipped past with a bright pink teddy bear, hugging it so tightly Daisy feared it might pop its stuffing. Her mind filled with a memory of being seven years old and at the fête with her mother, the last summer before she died. Her dad had been working and it had taken her mum many goes to knock over the cans and win her a teddy. Her teddy had been white with a large yellow bow and she'd loved it dearly. Daisy was cheered by the memory but a lump caught in her throat and she realised she was crying. Even her happy memories made her sad, that was why she couldn't stay. Daisy hastily wiped her eyes.

The seats at the falconry display were a place on a hay bale, but Daisy wasn't complaining. The cloudless sky was paint pot blue and the sun was gloriously warm. The falconry display was in a large arena and a series of T-shaped wooden posts had been knocked into the ground at various intervals. Daisy looked around, the 'seats' were filling up fast. An elderly man walked slowly into the arena dwarfed by a huge bird of prey on his gloved arm.

Daisy looked closer. 'That's never Old Man Burgess. Is it?'

'It is,' said Tamsyn.

'Bloody hell, have they embalmed him already? He must be at least a hundred.' Daisy remembered the man being seriously old when she was a child and he appeared to have shrivelled up further and become even more prune-like.

'Ninety-five,' said Tamsyn. 'He had a party just after Easter.'

He had always reminded the children of a character from *Scooby Doo* and, true to their beliefs, he would regularly shout at the kids to get out of his garden, which only perpetuated the myth that he was up to no good. He looked frailer now, wobbling precariously when the large bird disembarked his arm and took to the first post.

'Testing,' came the Devonian voice with an added loud screech from the sound system. 'Ahh that's better. Good afternoon ladies . . . and gentleman, and welcome to the Ottercombe Bay . . . falconry display.' He spoke as slowly as he walked. This could be a very long afternoon, thought Daisy.

'Now, this is Nesbit . . . he is a sea eagle or a white-tailed eagle as they are sometimes called. The Latin name is . . . *Haliaeetus albicilla*. He's six years old and . . . was bred in captivity. I have Nesbit's favourite food here . . . I'm going to leave a little bit on each of these perches . . .' Old Man Burgess continued to provide information about sea eagles as he walked the length of the arena placing what looked like bits of mince on each post. Nesbit was watching him closely and the audience was watching Nesbit, the children were enthralled. Old Man Burgess explained carefully what would happen next.

'When I give the command Nesbit will fly to each perch in turn and then return to me here and that's when you give him a . . . big round of applause.'

Old Man Burgess gave a whistle and right on cue Nesbit took to the sky. He was impressive in full flight and a few oohs went up from the crowd as his vast wingspan propelled him across the arena, narrowly missing a few spectators near the edge. They all watched Nesbit get higher and higher with each rhythmic thrust of his wings and also further and further away as he flew out of the arena.

Daisy leaned into Tamsyn and whispered. 'Was he meant to do that?'

'I don't think so,' came her hushed response.

Muttering spread throughout the crowd as Nesbit became smaller and smaller.

Old Man Burgess cleared his throat. 'Well, I'm afraid ladies and gentlemen . . . that's the end of the falconry display but don't forget Percy Winkle's . . . racing ferrets will be in this arena in about half an hour's time. Thank you.' There was a final screech from the speakers and a smattering of weak applause. Daisy clutched her sides finally giving in to the laughter.

'That's the funniest thing I've ever seen.'

She had to pull herself together because Old Man Burgess was making a bee-line for them but she had a few minutes to compose herself given the speed he was walking. ''Allo Tamsyn, 'ow are you?'

'Very well, thanks, Mr Burgess. I'm sorry about Nesbit. Will he come back?' asked Tamsyn, anxiously biting her lip.

'Don't worry about Nesbit. He's a little bugger, for sure, but he'll be back when he's . . . hungry. We're still training him, my son and I. Still hopeful of releasing him one day.'

'Around here?' said Daisy rather loudly as she visualised what it might be like for a fish eagle to steal your chips or, worse still, poo on you from a great height.

'No, no, no,' chuckled Mr Burgess. 'Isle of Mull, Scotland.'

'Good. We have enough trouble here with the seagulls.' She gave a grin but no one else was smiling. 'Does he do this often?' asked Daisy, trying hard to look serious.

'Yes. He does bugger off quite a bit actually. But it could have been . . . worse.' Mr Burgess nodded wisely.

Daisy looked about her, there were a lot of disappointed

faces and no eagle. 'How could it be worse?' she asked and Tamsyn shot her a look.

'I once took him to a fête near Lyme Regis and they had a local owl . . . sanctuary there with the wee little owls all tethered to perches. Nesbit took to the air but . . . this time he went for one of the little owls. Tore it to shreds he did in front of the kiddies.' Old Man Burgess was shaking his head and Daisy and Tamsyn were both looking wide-eyed and terrified. It was an image Daisy would struggle to erase.

Chapter Eight

In the few days since the village fête Daisy had become restless. The wanderlust was kicking in, as it always did, and she felt the need to get away. So much so she even offered to take the dog for a walk before she went to bed.

'Thanks,' said Aunt Coral, grimacing as she lowered her sprained ankle onto a floral cushion. It wasn't improving at the speed Daisy would have liked. She wanted to leave Ottercombe Bay as soon as possible, but she couldn't leave Aunt Coral when she was still hobbling about.

'No problem,' called Daisy, clipping the dog's lead onto Bugsy's collar. 'Have a rest while I'm gone. Bye,' added Daisy and she made steps to leave. Bugsy had other intentions. Daisy realised he wasn't planning on going with her when she found she was dragging the reluctant dog up the hall.

'Come on, Bugsy, let's go walkies,' she trilled. Bugsy stared unblinking at her, his giant dark eyes fixed on hers. Daisy gave a gentle pull on the lead but Bugsy stayed put. Daisy bent down to the small dog and put out her fingers so he could take in her scent. She guessed he was still missing Reg and having this stranger in the house was probably confusing for him. He sniffed Daisy's

70

proffered hand of goodwill and sneezed his response all over it.

'Oh, come on,' hissed Daisy, losing her patience and wiping her hand down her jeans. She was met by the same stare of defiance. Daisy stared back. She tugged on the lead and the stocky little dog slid along the polished floor on his bum but as he met the rough surface of the doormat he found his feet and trotted outside.

'Huh,' said Daisy with great satisfaction mentally marking up a point each on the imaginary scoreboard. She hoped that would be the end of it, that Bugsy would now see who was boss. It was the least he could do, if it wasn't for her he wouldn't be going for a walk at all – he could show a little gratitude.

It was a warm July evening, with a clear starry sky. The first few minutes of their stroll were uneventful until Bugsy bobbed down on a small patch of grass, gave Daisy a superior look before turning his back and straining hard.

'No!' yelled Daisy frantically checking her pockets for the poo bags she knew weren't there. Daisy searched about her. It was getting dark; perhaps she could just walk away and leave Bugsy's little deposit? But at that moment someone came around the corner a few feet away. Bugsy spotted them too and made a big show of scuffing up the grass and inadvertently his own deposit. There was little Daisy could do but watch as the piece of poo flew through the darkness and disappeared.

'Hello, Daisy,' said the over-friendly policeman.

'Hi Jason.'

She had never felt quite so guilty as she did right now. The orange sign on the lamppost, stating the maximum penalty for dog fouling was £1000, was at head height with Jason and was not helping one little bit.

'You okay?' he asked.

'Yes, of course,' said Daisy, feeling increasingly uncomfortable. She tried to keep one eye on him whilst attempting to locate the errant piece of poo. An excruciating silence followed where Jason bobbed his head encouragingly as if expecting Daisy to say something – or was he expecting a full confession? He couldn't prove the poo was Bugsy's, she'd deny everything. 'You, um, on the late shift tonight?' she said, sounding a lot like Aunt Coral and wondering how long it would be before she was shopping at Marks and Spencer.

'I should have finished half an hour ago but someone thought they saw Nesbit on the church spire. It was just a very large seagull. Would you like me to walk with you?' He pointed towards the beach.

'No, it's okay. We're on our way home now, thanks. We've been out ages,' she lied, shooting a look at Bugsy just in case he had a canine way of contradicting her.

'Oh, okay,' said Jason, looking thoroughly disappointed.

'Another time,' said Daisy and instantly regretted it.

Jason's glum face lit up. 'I'd love to. That would be . . . well . . . lovely,' he said, his grin so broad she was surprised he could form words. 'Thursday perhaps?'

'No, sorry I'm busy.' She crossed her fingers behind her back. She didn't like lying but Jason wasn't her type, in fact, nobody was right now – she didn't need the complications that came with dating.

'How about tomorrow? I need to drop the railway memorabilia back to you.'

'Okay, great. Thanks,' she said. She couldn't wriggle out if he was helping her.

Daisy saw her chance to escape. She kept to the roadside edge of the pavement as she skirted around Jason, keen to avoid the missing lump of poo. 'Bye,' she said, giving a tug on Bugsy's lead and he begrudgingly followed her. She heard Jason let out a yelp and turning back she could see him standing on one leg trying to inspect his other shoe. It appeared Jason may have found Bugsy's lost deposit. Daisy put her head down and hurried back to Aunt Coral.

They reached the porch and Daisy decided she needed to have a word with the dog about calling a truce. Daisy crouched down and Bugsy stood his ground.

'Now listen, Bug.' She felt the shortened name suited him better. 'You and me need to get along for Aunt Coral's sake.' Bug tilted his head to one side so he at least looked like he was listening. 'It's what Reg would have wanted.' At the mention of Reg's name Bug barked. It was a short sharp yap that in this close proximity made Daisy jump and she promptly toppled backwards and landed on her bum. She was not happy. Bug on the other hand looked very pleased with himself. He sniffed the air, turned around and scuffed up the ground just as he had done to cover up his own poo. It felt to Daisy like a clear statement of how he felt.

Daisy got up and brushed the bits off her backside. 'Right, fine. Have it your way. But I'm warning you . . .' she said as she took him inside. Bug marched through the door without a backward glance and the battle lines were drawn.

'Hi, love, everything okay?' called Aunt Coral.

'Yeah, we're good,' said Daisy unclipping the lead and wagging a finger at Bug, which he studiously ignored.

'You weren't gone long.'

Daisy openly sighed. 'No, Bug . . . Bugsy wanted to head back.' At the mention of his name Bug turned and glowered at Daisy like he knew what she was doing. She mimed that she was watching him. He turned away and trotted in to see Aunt Coral who greeted him warmly. Daisy went to put the kettle on and a few minutes later came in carrying two cups of tea. Bug yapped his disapproval at Daisy and she nearly spilled the drinks.

'Oh, now Bugsy,' said Aunt Coral with a chuckle. 'He's asking where his tea is.'

'What, now?' said Daisy, as pleasantly as she could manage.

'Bugsy sometimes likes a cup of tea. Well, a bowl of tea. Would you mind?'

Yes, she minded very much. She didn't want to be Bug's slave. This dog was playing mind games and he was super effective at it. 'I don't think tea's good for dogs,' said Daisy, giving Bug a smug stare.

'It's decaff and he only has a little bit with milk.' Aunt Coral's eyes were almost pleading.

'Okay,' said Daisy, her lips pinched. It was absurd.

Daisy returned and put the tea on the floor near Bug. He sniffed it, sneezed in it and trotted out of the room. Another point pinged up against his name on the imaginary scoreboard.

'Daisy, I've been having a look at Reg's accounts.'

'Hmm,' said Daisy distractedly – she was contemplating how to restore the balance of power between her and the dog.

'He had rather more money than I realised,' said Aunt Coral, passing Daisy a bank statement.

Daisy scanned it and came to the high five-figure balance. 'Bloody hell.' Aunt Coral looked amused. 'Sorry,' added Daisy automatically.

'I know. The solicitor has been in touch about distribution. They are transferring mine in the next couple of days. Yours will be held by them for the year but if you needed me to lend you some money in the meantime I'd be happy to.'

'Thank you, that's really kind.' Daisy handed back the statement. She did desperately need some cash.

'The Lifeboat will be thrilled when they get their share.'

'Yeah, I bet they will,' agreed Daisy. Her mind whirred with possibilities. She could do a lot with her share of the money. Flights to South America would no longer be out of the question. It would be a chance to properly explore far-flung countries without working all hours. The world was once again her oyster but to get that money she had to stay in Ottercombe Bay for a whole year and she wasn't sure if she could. Being in one place went against all she was used to, moving on was her norm. Ottercombe Bay filled her with sadness as there was no escaping her mother's death. Everywhere she went, all the people she saw were a constant reminder.

The next morning Daisy was woken by piercing yaps outside her door and she had to quell the desire to shout at the dog to shut up. She checked the clock, it was six thirty. Bug's demands to be let out in the garden were getting earlier and earlier. He definitely had the upper hand, or paw, because the thought of clearing up his wee was worse than dragging herself out of bed. She eased herself from under the covers and stepped over yesterday's clothes.

She quickly gathered herself up, flung open her bedroom door and marched into the hallway where she met Aunt Coral.

'Good morning, love. Did you sleep well?' Aunt Coral's kindly question caught Daisy unawares.

'No, Bug keeps barking.' She was tired and grumpy – not a good combination.

'Oh, he doesn't usually. I hope he's all right,' said Aunt Coral, inching her way towards the kitchen.

Why can nobody else see his villainous plan? thought Daisy. He is an evil dictator. Perhaps he's the reincarnation of Mussolini, she thought, or an even better fit might be Vlad the Impaler. Perhaps Min could get a message from him she wondered.

'You go back to bed. I'll put the kettle on,' said Aunt Coral, her expression jolly. Daisy's shoulders sloped forward, she'd never get back to sleep now. Thanks to Bug her brain was well and truly awake.

'No, it's okay. You rest your ankle I'll get us some breakfast.'

'Perhaps before that you could give Bugsy a walk? I think he didn't go far enough last night. That's probably the problem.'

Daisy gritted her teeth and headed for the kitchen muttering about Vlad the Impaler.

A couple of hours later Daisy was chewing her toast in silence while she and Bug had a staring competition, which annoyingly he won paws down. A rap of knuckles on the front door had both Daisy and Bug heading in that direction.

When she entered the porch she could see it was Jason and Max. What did they want?

'Is this a bad time?' asked Jason. He held the old railway box aloft. 'I have some good news about the memorabilia.' He gave a toothy smile.

Daisy tried to look welcoming. 'Thanks, Jason, you'd better come in.' Max averted his gaze and followed Jason in. You buy one, you get one free, she thought.

Aunt Coral met them in the hallway. 'Good morning, boys.'

'Good morning, Coral. Lovely to see you up and about. How's the ankle?' asked Jason. Everyone followed him into the living room. Max stepped back to let Daisy go in front and she acknowledged his gesture. She was still mad at him for their altercation in the pub and the snide comments at the fête.

Jason put the box on the table and unpacked the items. 'The documentation isn't worth anything but a serious GWR collector might give you a few pounds for it.'

'GWR?' asked Daisy.

'Great Western Railways. They ran the branch line that ran from Exeter to here. Some people specialise in certain railway companies,' said Jason. He continued unpacking. 'The brush isn't in great condition but should still fetch a few pounds. These pamphlets are quite interesting.' He held up three yellowing booklets. 'These are probably worth about ten pounds each.'

'Ooh, that's fabulous, Jason.' Aunt Coral was leaning forward with interest, whereas Daisy was already quite bored. The effort of selling them was outweighing the return. Max looked similarly uninterested.

'These photographs were in an envelope and they're well preserved. Probably local interest only but worth five to ten pounds each. The real star of the show, however, is this.' He held up the cast iron 'Beware of the trains' sign and everyone waited. He was building up his part and even Daisy was a little intrigued. 'We could be looking at as much as eighty to a hundred pounds for this.'

'Great,' said Daisy with a yawn and she went to get the rest of her toast. She paused in the hallway as she heard the conversation start up in the living room after she'd left.

'Is Daisy okay? Only Tamsyn said she saw her crying at the fête,' said Jason.

'Oh, poor love. She tries to put a brave face on it but it must be hard,' said Aunt Coral.

'Are we talking about her mother topping herself?' asked Max.

'Cause of death was drowning,' said Jason.

'She could have drowned herself,' said Max.

'It was unclear if abrasions on Sandy's forehead were caused before or after she died.' Jason had a look of Hercule Poirot about him.

'Nobody knows exactly what happened. They just found her washed up on the beach one morning,' said Aunt Coral with a shudder.

'Sorry, that was just what I heard,' said Max, his tone conciliatory.

'Poor Daisy,' said Jason. 'It must be hard being back here with all the memories. It is a proper mystery, perhaps . . .' Daisy strolled into the room and Jason stopped speaking. He cleared his throat. 'Sorry, Daisy.'

'Is this what it's going to be like? A year of everyone whispering behind my back. All the speculation dredged up again. Because there are no answers, you know?' She clutched her locket as she spoke.

'We just care about you, that's all,' said Aunt Coral.

Daisy shook her head. 'I don't need you to—'

Max stood up. 'People around here try and look after each other, you'll have to get used to it *if* you're sticking around.'

'I don't know if I'm staying but either way I can look after myself.' Daisy was trying hard not to shout.

'You are so selfish and if you don't appreciate that people will want to help, maybe you should leave.' Max's voice rose to match hers.

'If staying means everyone meddling in my life, then perhaps I should.'

'If you consider it meddling then, yeah, go!' shouted Max.

'Fine!' Daisy stormed out of the room.

'Now, Max. That was uncalled for,' said Aunt Coral, swinging her legs off the cushion and standing up.

Max pushed his hair off his face. 'I'm sorry, Coral. I didn't mean to upset you—'

'But evidently you did mean to upset Daisy,' she scolded, hobbling out of the room.

Jason carefully put the plaque back in the box and looked at Max. 'I guess none of us handled that well.'

Max patted him on the back. 'It's okay mate. Come on, let's get going if you're still giving me a lift to work.'

'Daisy, please don't overreact,' came Coral's voice. Max and Jason were in the hall when the thundering footsteps on the stairs announced Daisy's arrival. She was clutching an orange wash bag and wrestling with an overstuffed backpack.

'I'm sorry Aunt Coral, but Max is right. I don't belong in Ottercombe Bay and no amount of money is worth staying for.' She shot a glare at Max whilst she continued to struggle with the rucksack.

Daisy finally got the bag done up and pushed past the men, gaining some satisfaction from shunting Max to one side. She gave the front door a shove and strode outside.

'You know I really think we should intervene,' said Jason, watching Daisy over his shoulder as she put on her motorcycle helmet. Jason and Max walked to the police car.

'She was never going to stay,' said Max. He shook his head and got in the passenger seat. Aunt Coral was standing in the doorway with a yapping Bugsy under her arm. Both vehicles started at the same time but Daisy got away first. She blew a kiss to Aunt Coral and rode off in front of Jason.

Daisy's heart was thumping. She was cross and quickly overheating thanks to the combination of leathers, backpack and temper. Max had pressed all her buttons. She had to put herself first, that was how it had always been. If she didn't look out for herself, who would? It was a self-preservation thing and it had served her well. She indicated and followed the coast road, she may as well have one last look at the sea. She saw the headland and felt a twinge of sadness at seeing her mother's favourite place. But she felt the locket against her skin and was reassured. Turning her head briefly to catch a glimpse of the coastline something caught her eye. A figure in long flowing clothes was standing on the cliffs. Mum? For a moment Daisy lost concentration and the bike wobbled. She gripped the handlebars and maintained control but a loud noise behind startled her. It was the sound of a police siren. She checked her mirror – it was Jason.

Jason or not, it was still the police so she pulled over and the patrol car stopped behind her, its blue lights flashing wildly. She removed her helmet and took a deep breath. Max glared at her from the passenger seat and Daisy sneered back; she was tempted to stick her tongue out but decided against it.

Jason strode over. 'Daisy, please don't go like this.'

'Jason, you are lovely, but it's honestly best for everyone if I go.' She looked over to the headland. The figure in flowing clothes was now walking towards them and she was reassured to see it was Tamsyn. For a moment she'd wondered if she was hallucinating, although that hadn't happened since the mushroom soup in Goa.

'You know I could arrest you? If that's what it takes to make you stay,' said Jason, the corner of his mouth lifting. 'There were a couple of traffic violations back there.'

Daisy gave a half laugh. She was touched by Jason's attempts to keep her there.

'Hiya, what's going on?' asked Tamsyn, and both Jason and Daisy turned to look at her in her bohemian outfit.

'Daisy's leaving,' said Jason.

'No. You can't go. You promised,' said Tamsyn, clutching at Daisy's arm.

'No, I didn't,' said Daisy, to both of them. She did put herself first, that was true, but she didn't break promises and she'd never intentionally upset Tamsyn.

'Well, no but it's the same,' pleaded Tamsyn. 'Please stay.' Tamsyn gazed at her doe eyed. Daisy looked from her to Jason who had an equally sorrowful look on his face. For the first time in a long while she felt people wanted her around and it was an unusual sensation and sadly something she wasn't used to. She could usually announce her departure and people would send her off with nothing more than the occasional card and a wave. This was an altogether new experience. She took a deep breath and the scent of the sea struck her. Not in a bad way – it seemed to conjure up memories of happier times and she tried to blink them away.

'If not for us, stay for Coral,' said Jason. 'She misses Reg terribly and I know she's loving having you here.'

Tamsyn gesticulated enthusiastically. 'Her ankle's not getting any better. What if she had another fall? You'd never forgive yourself,' said Tamsyn dramatically. Daisy started to think. She hated being put on the spot, but it felt like she needed to stop threatening to leave and make a commitment either way. Stay or go, but which would it be?

'Everyone is actually on your side, Daisy. We were insensitive back there and I for one promise not to discuss it again.' Jason sounded sincere.

81

'Let her go. I'm going to be late for work!' shouted Max out of the car window.

'Who's being selfish now?' called back Daisy already starting to feel better. Jason was right, Aunt Coral had only ever been supportive and with her ankle still causing her problems it wasn't fair to jump ship. And however much she didn't want to think about it the money was also a big pull. Right now she had the grand sum of one pound, sixty-eight pence on her. She was impulsive but she wasn't completely stupid and she knew if she left now, by the end of tomorrow she would be regretting throwing away her inheritance. It was decision time. But could she stay put – in Ottercombe Bay of all places – for a whole year? There was only one way to find out. There was also the added advantage of annoying the hell out of Max if she were to stick around and that seemed to tip the scales.

She took a deep breath. 'Okay, I'll stay,' said Daisy. Tamsyn cheered and clapped. 'Just for the year.' Even saying it had her breaking out in a cold sweat but she knew in her heart, despite all her efforts to avoid it, this was what she must do. 'Now, go and get grumpy arse to work,' she said smiling and waving sarcastically at Max who was turning an interesting shade of red, like a cross beetroot.

Jason gave her an impromptu peck on the cheek. 'You won't regret it,' he called as he jogged back to the car. Max was waving his arms about wildly as he was driven away. Daisy waved back and flashed him a cheesy grin, knowing it would make him all the more irate.

Tamsyn linked her arm in hers. 'Jason's right. You won't regret it. I'll make sure you don't.'

Chapter Nine

Now Daisy had it firmly in her mind that she was staying in Ottercombe Bay, it no longer felt like a prison sentence; it was more like a challenge with a pot of gold at the end and she was already mapping out how she was going to spend her prize. If she could focus on the money and the fact that she was following Great Uncle Reg's wishes she might just make it through but she needed to have a plan otherwise the next fifty weeks were really going to drag.

She was sitting one evening with a highlighter pen and the local paper. Having read the headline story about the crime wave of shed fires and vandalism to a tree, she was feeling Ottercombe Bay may be the safe haven she needed for a while. She needed to ignore Max Davey, he was an unfortunate irritation she would have to put up with, a bit like thrush – though less colourful and possibly more irritating.

She sat back and studied what she had highlighted. There were three jobs she had experience for – they weren't mind blowing but they would be something to fill the hours and enable her to contribute to the housekeeping. Despite Aunt Coral's kind offer, she wasn't a charity case – she always paid her way.

'I think I'm going to venture back to work tomorrow. The pharmacy is struggling without me,' said Aunt Coral, lifting up her ankle and placing it carefully back down.

'Hmm?' said Daisy idly. 'If you're sure.'

'What have you got there?' asked Aunt Coral, putting on her reading glasses. Daisy handed her the paper and guided her through the highlighted adverts.

'I'm looking at jobs. There's one at the charity shop; not a volunteer role but minimum wage.' She pulled a face. 'Or a server at the Fish and Chip van on the seafront and this one . . .' she tapped the page for emphasis, '. . . receptionist at Stabb and Lakey.'

'Ooh the law firm?'

'Yep, I really want that one and it's good money.'

Aunt Coral read the advert carefully. 'I'm pleased you're staying.' She reached out and squeezed Daisy's hand.

'I'll apply for the charity shop one too, as a backup,' she said.

The charity shop job had already gone by the time Daisy enquired and she didn't fancy working in a chip van because she would always have a faint aroma of grease about her. Everything was riding on the receptionist's job. Daisy liked a challenge and she knew she could do the job – she just had to convince them of it and, with the aid of her well-crafted CV, she had already cleared the first hurdle and secured an interview. Thanks to a small loan from Aunt Coral she looked the part with a new cream skirt, navy top and smart navy shoes. Her hair was neatly plaited against her head and her make-up was subtle.

She shooed Bug off the sofa and sat down to watch the clock. Bug gave her a disapproving look, farted and left the room. She waved a hand to clear the air. That creature is rotten inside and out, she thought. She fidgeted about on the sofa for a bit but she couldn't settle. She decided instead of squirming for the next hour she might as well walk into town and get a coffee.

The walk was pleasant, the sea breeze calming her senses as the July sun gently caressed her skin with its warmth. She was definitely a warm weather person; she liked the heat far better than the cold, which was another reason why South America appealed to her. The thought of being able to travel but not have to constantly work was what would keep her going this year. She walked along daydreaming about the solitude of the Atacama Desert in Bolivia and the wonder of the Inca legacy at Machu Picchu and soon found herself in the centre of town not far from the Stabb and Lakey office.

It was quite busy in the cramped coffee shop as it was coming up to lunchtime. She ordered herself a double espresso, something she'd got a liking for in Italy. She took the overfilled cup, watching it closely because it was balanced precariously on a mismatched saucer. She turned just as a man barged past her to be served next.

'Oi!' barked Daisy. The coffee slopped over the sides of the cup and down the front of her cream skirt. 'No!'

'Sorry,' came the curt reply making Daisy's head shoot up to inspect her aggressor.

'Oh, typical. I might have guessed it'd be you.' Daisy scowled at Max, who looked nonplussed and carried on giving the lady at the counter his order.

Daisy flushed crimson. She was furious. Her interview was in less than thirty minutes. She didn't have time to walk back and change and get back in time and if she did she was severely lacking in anything appropriate to wear. Most of her clothes were screwed up on her bedroom floor. She made a mental note to sort them out when she got in.

'Would you like a cloth?' asked the kindly woman behind the counter.

'Yes, please. Thank you,' said Daisy, leaning over and taking the cloth. She dabbed at her skirt but the strong dark liquid had already seeped into the soft material. She went to the ladies to see if she could improve things where she discovered it was actually possible to make things worse. She now had a very large wet patch in the middle of her skirt and the coffee stain was only slightly faded. She downed what was left of her espresso and headed out of the coffee shop.

'Have a nice day,' called out Max but she ignored him. The short stroll to the Stabb and Lakey offices had her sodden skirt sticking to her legs. As she approached she decided it may look better if she turned the skirt around. At least their first impression would be of someone smartly dressed, she may even be able to get away without them noticing.

She gave her details to the current receptionist who seemed a little bored. Daisy took a seat in the waiting area and as she sat on the coffee side of her skirt she felt the now cold wet patch adhere to her thighs and start to seep through her pants. It was more than a little distracting but she wouldn't be put off, she really wanted this job. It was about time she had a decent job; she'd been bouncing from one rubbish zero hours contract to the next and a proper role in a good small firm would be ideal. It would be good for her CV too, which would hopefully mean better jobs when she did move on.

A tall, thin man meandered into the waiting room and appraised her. He proffered a hand. 'Miss Wilkins?'

'Wickens,' corrected Daisy, standing up.

'I'm Mr Lakey.'

'How do you do, Mr Lakey?' asked Daisy in her most professional receptionist voice.

'Very well, er . . .' His eyes had wandered to the front of her skirt and now hers did the same. The stain was on the back so what was he looking at? On the front of her skirt, which had once been the back, was a large patch of black fur making it look like she had some sort of pubic wig. Bloody Bug, she thought as she remembered sitting on the sofa in his favourite spot. She quickly twisted the skirt around her middle in an attempt to make the black hairy patch disappear but as soon as the wet patch came into sight she regretted it.

'You see someone spilled some coffee just before I got here – not me I'm not clumsy or anything it was some idiot in the coffee shop. And the black hair is my aunt's dog, he sits on the sofa and he sheds fur everywhere.' Mr Lakey's eyebrows were doing a tango as the two offending patches whizzed past numerous times whilst Daisy continued to twist the skirt around her waist. Daisy stopped the skirt at the halfway point so she now had the coffee stain to her left side and the black furry patch to her right. She looked up and smiled at Mr Lakey and eventually his eyes met hers. He blinked.

'I like to make a good first impression,' she quipped.

'Shall . . . we continue?' he asked with a definite hesitation.

Daisy agreed and, gathering up what was left of her dignity, followed him into the office.

A few hours later Daisy was sitting on the floor at Sea Mist Cottage feeling sorry for herself. Bug walked in and stopped abruptly at the sight of a forlorn-looking Daisy.

They observed each other warily. Daisy decided she couldn't be bothered to match wits with the dog today so she let him win the staring contest and he strutted off to make his spot on the sofa even more furry.

The interview hadn't started well and had gone downhill from there. It turned out they were looking for a career receptionist – someone who was going to stay and grow with the company. Something Daisy wasn't prepared to commit to. She hadn't known how much there was to being a receptionist; her experience extended to welcoming people and serving tea and coffee. She hadn't expected to have to take all the phone calls, manage the diary and appointment system, type letters and look after the petty cash. And with each question it had become evident she wasn't experienced enough, which was a depressing realisation. She had emphasised her ability to absorb things quickly and her willingness to learn, but after a string of temps Stabb and Lakey wanted someone who already knew what they were doing and that wasn't Daisy.

She had been to university – for a while, at least. Surely, she thought, two thirds of a degree across two subjects still counted for something? But she was starting to think this was an incorrect assumption. The lack of a finished degree along with her many short-lived roles only seemed to highlight her lack of dependability. It was a depressing truth that she had got to this point in her life with no credible career.

Daisy tried to console herself with the memories she had of the places she had visited and all the people she had met, but it was difficult to recall them without feeling how transitory it had all been. Nobody had ever pleaded with her to stay like Jason and Tamsyn had. It affected her in a way she hadn't expected; it had chipped away at her hardened heart.

She dragged over the box of railway stuff. If she didn't have a job she could at least sell some of the railway things. She rifled through for the photographs she'd missed when she'd found the box in the gloom of the old building. She pulled out the large envelope, which was a similar size and shape to the bottom of the box explaining how she had missed it the first time. She scattered the photographs onto the carpet in front of her and was drawn to one of the larger pictures. It was a great scene, with the railway building to the left of the picture and a large steam engine billowing out white vapour as a throng of people waved from the platform.

Daisy picked it up and studied it closely. Everyone seemed happy and relaxed and she suspected from the clothing it had been taken in the 1930s. She continued to sort through the pictures and wondered about the people in them, what had they each achieved in their lives? She suspected most had lived their whole lives in Ottercombe Bay but perhaps the arrival of the railway had opened them up to new opportunities.

Daisy was surprised when she checked the clock; time had evaporated, and she decided to start cooking dinner because Aunt Coral would be back from work soon and getting some food ready was the least she could do. By the time Aunt Coral came gingerly through the front door to the rapturous barks of an excited Bug there was a lasagne in the oven and vegetables boiling merrily on the stove.

'How was your day?' asked Daisy, keen to avoid reliving her own.

'Not too bad. Ankle is still sore if I move about on it too much but otherwise okay. How did the interview go?' Aunt Coral had made it to the living room doorway and had a look of hopeful expectation about her that Daisy was afraid she was about to crush. Daisy shook her head and Aunt Coral mimicked her headshake. 'Not well then, love?'

'Nope, it didn't get off to a great start.' She shot daggers at Bug who was hopping around Aunt Coral's feet. 'And I wasn't what they were looking for anyway. It turns out all my years of various jobs add up to not very much at all.' Daisy absentmindedly put her hand over her locket.

'Something'll turn up, it always does,' said Aunt Coral with an uneasy smile. 'Something smells nice.'

'You rest your ankle and I'll serve up.'

When she finally found herself nodding off on the sofa in an empty living room Daisy decided it was time she went to bed. She padded into her bedroom, liking the fact she didn't have to drag herself upstairs, and looked around; she didn't have much stuff but what she did have was strewn everywhere. She had meant to sort this out but she hadn't got around to it yet. Being untidy wasn't the worst sin in the world but it had annoyed a few people in the past. She'd tidy it all up tomorrow because depressingly she had nothing else to do.

It was warm in the bedroom so she threw the window wide open, kicked off her shoes and took off her locket. She gazed at it, turning it over in her hands. She was sure the police couldn't have made such a howling error as to put someone else's effects with her mother's; she must have been wearing the locket when she died. In which case, where did she get it from and why had her father never seen it? Of course, she had had these discussions with him before but they had often ended in an argument or, more often than not, with her father simply refusing to talk. In his mind it was not Sandy's locket and he couldn't seem to think beyond that. Perhaps the possibility there was

90

someone else with her the night she died was too much for him to deal with?

What had happened that night ate away at Daisy. Knowing what had transpired would never bring her mother back but somehow she felt it would help her to move on. The fact she had spent all these years not knowing if her mother had killed herself, or worse still been murdered, was always with her – it was a shadow that never went away.

Sometimes she thought of what might have happened to Sandy; it played out in her mind like a film and occasionally brought her to the brink of tears because there was never a happy ending for her mother. She felt she had cried a lifetime of tears the day her father said her mother had gone to heaven to be with the angels because she was too beautiful to stay on earth. She vowed nothing would ever break her heart the way her mother's death had done.

Daisy ran her finger over the intricate scrolled pattern on the locket; it was quite distinctive, she'd never seen another one like it and she'd been looking for a few years now. A jeweller had once told her it was sterling silver and made in France in the mid-1700s, which only added further fuel to the mystery. Daisy placed it carefully on the bedside cabinet, turned out the pockets of her jeans and dropped them on the floor – there was no point in folding them up, they were going in the wash tomorrow. Perhaps tomorrow would be a better day, she thought, as the light breeze from the open window ruffled the curtains gently and she drifted off to sleep.

It was morning when something made her stir and for a change it wasn't Bug. She reached for her locket. Something she did every morning, wherever she found herself, it was the first thing she put on. She couldn't lay her hands on it. She sat up and stared at the bedside cabinet. Apart from two empty glasses and a long-forgotten mug of tea there was nothing else there. Daisy swung her legs out of bed and started to scrabble about on the floor, the breeze from the open window must have knocked everything off, she thought, although the window wasn't wide open now. But there was nothing on the floor. A crumpled five-pound note and her precious locket were gone.

Chapter Ten

Daisy whipped open the bedroom curtains, almost expecting to see someone standing there, but all she saw was the strip of front garden and her old motorbike. What had happened? She scanned the bedside cabinet again, still in disbelief that her precious locket could have been taken. Daisy ran upstairs.

'Um, Aunt Coral, are you awake?' she asked hesitantly at her aunt's bedroom door.

'Yes, love,' came the answer from the bathroom behind her making her jump.

'Have you seen my locket?' Daisy asked the bathroom door.

'The book-shaped one you always wear?'

'Yes,' Daisy said, rolling her hands over and over in front of her as if trying to hurry Aunt Coral along.

'Then yes I've seen it.'

Daisy felt elated as the relief washed over her. Aunt Coral opened the bathroom door and Daisy was tempted to hug her but she was brushing her teeth.

'Where is it?'

Aunt Coral looked blank. 'Last time I saw it you were wearing it. Have you mislaid it?'

'No,' said Daisy shaking her head and looking desolate. The awful sense of loss reappeared immediately gripping her insides. 'I put it on the bedside cabinet last night but this morning it's not there. I think it's been stolen.'

Jason arrived quickly with a colleague carrying what looked like a large briefcase. 'Scene of crime officer,' he explained. 'We'll check the whole house for any fingerprints, residue or material fragments.'

The SOCO coughed behind him. 'Actually I'm just going to dust around the window frame for prints. It's not a murder enquiry. Can you show me where to go?'

'Of course, officer,' said Aunt Coral, leading the way. 'I'm afraid they've made quite a mess of the room,' she said, opening the door and revealing the room in a total state of disarray. Daisy opened her mouth to speak, but paused. Was there any benefit in owning up to the fact she'd created the mess? It wasn't going to make any difference to what had been stolen. Perhaps she'd tell Jason on the quiet later.

Jason strode in putting on latex gloves, making them ping at the cuffs. 'My word, they have roughed the place up. What could they have been looking for?' he said, picking up a discarded bra on his pencil and placing it on the unmade bed. Daisy cringed. Tidying up before they arrived would have been a good move, but she'd barely had time to get washed and dressed before they were banging on the front door. She guessed there wasn't a lot of criminal activity in Ottercombe Bay. Jason whipped out his notebook and started scribbling. 'And you were in here at the time? I guess they woke you up?' He waved his pencil at the mess. Daisy bit her lip and gave a brief shake of her head. 'Interesting,' said Jason, continuing to scribble. 'Did you see anyone? Hear anything?' Daisy shook her head again. Perhaps honesty would have been the best policy, she thought. 'Where were the items taken from exactly?'

'On here,' said Daisy, pointing at the bedside cabinet.

Jason stuck his head out of the window. 'They must have taken them as a consolation prize when they didn't find what they came for. If it was purely opportunist they could have just reached through the window and taken them off the cabinet as it's right under the window.'

He was very good, thought Daisy, and she opened her mouth to explain but Aunt Coral was already speaking. 'Would you like a coffee, boys?' she asked.

'Please, and a slice of your Vicky sponge if you have any?' asked Jason. Daisy thought how unlike *CSI* it was as she left the embarrassing scene and went to join Aunt Coral in the kitchen.

An hour later the SOCO was long gone and Jason had moved on to sketching the locket as the only photos Daisy could find of herself wearing it wouldn't zoom in with enough focus for the detail to be seen properly.

Daisy couldn't believe it had gone. All these years it was the first thing she put on each morning and the last thing she took off at night. It had always been with her since her mother died. It was her comfort blanket and she felt bare and vulnerable without it. She kept putting her hand to her chest and every time she was shocked not to feel it under her fingers. She knew she would never get used to not wearing it.

'I'm quite observant,' said Jason. 'Your locket was rectangular, wasn't it?' Daisy nodded. 'Was it solid silver?'

'Yes, there's a funny symbol inside it.'

'Did it have any other distinguishing features?' asked Jason, his whole face alert. Daisy didn't like him referring to her beloved possession in the past tense. She thought how odd it was that in her time of distress here he was in his element, doing the job he loved.

'Is it likely I'll get it back?' she asked, the sorrow evident in her voice.

Jason paused, his pencil hovering. 'We'll do our best to recover your locket but I suspect whoever took it will be looking to sell quickly.'

'Basically no chance then.'

Jason gave a weak smile and carried on sketching. 'Does this look right?' He turned the page around for Daisy to see the drawing better.

Daisy took the pencil from him. 'The shape is right,' she said. 'But the pattern was different.' She made an oval in the centre and started to sketch the scroll pattern within it. She knew the locket so well – she knew its smooth edges, its intricate patterned front and simple swirls on the reverse. She always knew it was immensely important to her, but was not prepared for the sense of loss she felt. The locket, like her mother, was irreplaceable.

After a few minutes Daisy noticed droplets splosh onto the picture and she stopped drawing. She was crying. Jason passed her a tissue. 'I promise I'll do absolutely everything I can to get it back.'

She nodded. Daisy feared if she tried to speak she'd end up sobbing and she and tears had an unhappy relationship. She always went blotchy and got a headache when she cried and she had done far too much of it in her lifetime.

After Jason eventually left she had barely shut the door when Tamsyn appeared on the other side. Daisy let her in and was immediately swamped by a bear hug.

'This is sooo awful. To think hard end criminals have been in this house . . .' Tamsyn paused. 'I wonder why they call them that?'

96

'It's not hard end, it's hardened, as in toughened by their experiences. Do you want a cuppa?' Daisy sloped off to the kitchen and whilst she got cups out Tamsyn hovered in the doorway.

'Actually . . .' started Tamsyn and Daisy paused with the kettle under the tap. 'Can I look at the crime scene?'

Daisy sighed. 'Yeah, be my guest.' Once again she was a point of local interest – a stop on the sightseeing tour of life, something to ogle and wonder at. Well, her bedroom was anyway. Daisy waited at the table and sipped her tea while Tamsyn's slowly lost its heat.

Tamsyn came scuttling back and slid into her seat opposite Daisy. 'They've made a right mess in there. What did they take?'

Daisy suspected she would get asked this quite a lot. 'A few quid and my locket.' She looked into her teacup.

'The swines,' said Tamsyn with feeling, then realisation seemed to permeate and her hands flew to her face. 'Your mum's locket?' she asked, with a gasp.

Daisy flicked her eyebrows in response; she didn't want to unlock the emotions bubbling uncomfortably below the surface. It was best if she tried not to think too much about it, although that was hard not to do. They sipped their tea in silence for a bit.

'Right,' said Tamsyn forcefully. 'What you need is cheering up.' Daisy wasn't sure this was even worth attempting. 'I know what we'll do. We'll go to the donkey sanctuary.'

Daisy felt herself physically slump. Wandering about looking at animals who were permanently miserable would do little to lift her mood. 'I don't think—'

'I'm not taking no for an answer,' said Tamsyn, standing up. 'First of all, we'll sort out your bedroom. Come on.'

'It's fine,' said Daisy, but the words were said to an empty room. By the time she'd washed up the teacups and wandered through to her room Tamsyn was plumping the pillow and doing the final adjustments to her bed. The room looked perfect.

'There. You'd never know they'd been in here.' Daisy didn't like to point out it was highly unlikely they had been in the room because everything on the bedside cabinet was reachable from the open window.

'Thanks, Tams. This is kind of you.' Daisy vowed to keep her room tidy from now on. She wasn't sure how long it would last, but at least she'd try.

'Right, let's go,' said Tamsyn with gusto. She linked arms with Daisy and marched her out of the house, giving her barely time to grab the house keys. 'We can look out for Nesbit the eagle on the way. He's been spotted in a back garden over that way. He frightened the life out of an old lady hanging out her washing.'

Thankfully it was a short drive in Tamsyn's battered Nissan Micra. The car either had an issue with its steering or Tamsyn's driving was a little on the erratic side. She seemed to stray over the white line on more than one occasion making their arrival in the car park a welcome relief.

On the walk to the entrance the sound of braying donkeys welcomed them. Tamsyn was looking excited even before she'd seen a donkey. Daisy was surprised to see it was free to enter and became intrigued by the map promising all manner of donkeys, a gift shop, a café and a variety of walks around the many donkey enclosures. Daisy decided that if she was to get through the next couple of hours she had better upgrade her attitude. She took a deep breath, slapped a smile on her face and followed Tamsyn through the gate. Her friend was trying to take her mind off things, the least she could do was try to look as if it was helping.

'I love it here,' said Tamsyn, her face one large grin. 'It's my happy place.'

The first couple of enclosures had some bored-looking donkeys on the other side of their paddock who had no intention of making the long walk across to say hello. Tamsyn read out the information on the small board and Daisy listened to the sad story of Bernard and Biscuit, two of many rescue donkeys now leading a happy life at the sanctuary. By the third enclosure Daisy was starting to feel a bit better about things, some of the poor animals had suffered terrible neglect and had bounced back and here she was making a fuss about a possession. Learning about the suffering of another was good at giving you perspective, even if it was a donkey.

They walked through some pretty gardens, past a children's play area where the volume rose above a comfortable level and then it changed to near silence as they reached a tree-lined area where many benches were dotted about. Each bench had a neat shiny plaque and they stopped to read them, noting the increasingly tear-jerking dedications. She was glad to come to the end. A sign announced the Poitou donkey enclosure and Daisy found her mouth tweaking at the edges at the sight of the giant hairy donkeys. They were friendly and came to the fence to be fussed. She discovered scratching a donkey's ears was quite calming. A large gingery donkey cantered over, announced his arrival with a loud bray and barged the others out of the way.

'Steady on,' said Daisy, checking the name on his collar. 'Hiya Guinness.' Guinness wobbled his large head and tried to eat Daisy's shirtsleeve, which made her laugh.

'You feeling better?' asked Tamsyn tentatively.

Daisy gave her friend a half hug. 'Yeah, I am. Thanks for getting me out of the cottage.'

'It's what friends do.'

'Let's get a coffee. It's my treat,' said Daisy, and they followed the signs to the café. They took their tray outside and settled themselves down with a view of some white donkeys being fed their lunch.

'Are you working today?' asked Daisy in between mouthfuls of heavily buttered teacake.

Tamsyn gave a heavy sigh. 'Yeah, they want me in at one o'clock, but they may not need me past four when everyone starts leaving the beach. I can never be sure what I'm going to get paid. Dad hinted again last night that I should be thinking about leaving home but even with saving all I can I don't stand a chance of being able to afford my own place. Especially not around here.' She sighed again and sipped her latte. 'Sorry, I shouldn't moan. Especially not after the day you've had.'

'My day has got a whole lot better,' said Daisy. 'Thanks to you.' Tamsyn gave a weak smile, which quickly changed into a huge grin.

'I'm going to hand in my notice. I'm going to quit the beach café.'

'Whoa there. Let's not get hasty,' said Daisy. She wasn't the best source of advice but at least Tamsyn had a job, however crap it might be.

'No, I should have done it years ago. If I quit then I have to get something better.' She picked up her coffee to clink mugs with Daisy.

'Or you could keep the beach café job whilst you look for something else,' she suggested. 'That way you still have some income.' How did you tell someone you cared about that this was the worst idea ever?

'Hmm,' said Tamsyn, appearing to consider this.

Daisy stared on wide-eyed and fearful. 'What'll you do?'

Tamsyn slowly ran a finger across her eyebrow. 'I might do reading . . .'

'I don't think anyone will pay you for that. Unless you mean like a book editor – I think that's all they do all day.'

'No, palm reading, silly.'

'I didn't know you were like your mum.'

'I'm not sure I am but if I don't try I won't know.' Tamsyn was still grinning, the obvious flaws in her plan clearly not obvious to her.

'You should probably test out your skills first. Punters will be hacked off if it turns out you can't tell them their future.'

Tamsyn appeared to ponder this. 'Let me try on you,' she said, taking Daisy's hand.

Daisy looked about her quickly, what would other people think? It looked like Tamsyn was about to propose. 'I think you're meant to read it not hold it,' pointed out Daisy, embarrassment stealing over her.

'I'm seeing if I can sense a connection.'

A loose connection in Tamsyn's head was all Daisy could think of. Tamsyn shut her eyes and gripped Daisy's hand. Daisy acknowledged an elderly couple who went past shaking their heads. Daisy waited. 'Anything?'

'I'm not sure what I'm meant to be sensing.'

'Usually people with a gift tell you something about yourself you don't already know.'

'How can I not know something I'm telling you? Makes no sense.' Tamsyn looked confused.

'If you have the gift. You tell me something I know but you don't.' Tamsyn opened her mouth looking as if a light bulb had just pinged on above her head. 'And not something

Reg told you,' added Daisy quickly. Tamsyn's face dropped. 'Just relax and see if you can sense anything.' Daisy offered Tamsyn her hand once more.

'Okay, let's try again.'

Tamsyn held Daisy's right hand for a while. Daisy noticed her coffee was going cold so picked it up with her left hand, which felt odd and she clumsily put it to her lips.

'A-ha!' shouted Tamsyn her eyes snapping open.

Daisy slopped her drink down herself. 'Cock,' said Daisy and Tamsyn gave her an old-fashioned look making her feel she needed to amend her swearing. 'Cock . . . a-doodle-doo?' Tamsyn seemed happy with the alteration. 'Did you sense something?'

'Yes,' said Tamsyn emphatically.

Daisy was preoccupied with wiping the spilled coffee off her top. 'Okay, what was it?'

'Teaspoons!' said Tamsyn her voice triumphant.

Daisy stopped what she was doing and blinked. 'What about teaspoons?'

Tamsyn straightened. 'My mind was a complete blank . . .' This did not surprise Daisy. 'And then teaspoons popped into my head. Do you collect teaspoons?' Daisy shook her head. 'Hmm. Have a fear of teaspoons perhaps?' Daisy shook her head again. 'Do you even like teaspoons?'

'Not especially,' said Daisy, as the serviette she was using to mop up the coffee began disintegrating.

'Ahh, but you don't dislike them.'

'No.' This was possibly the oddest conversation she'd ever had.

'There you go then.' Tamsyn seemed pleased. 'I think I might have something.'

'It's a bit of a cliché but seriously Tamsyn I don't think you should give up the day job.'

'O-kay.' Tamsyn's tone was sulky.

'You need to plan what job you really want to do. What are all the things you love? Think of those and they may uncover a wonderful opportunity.'

'I love buttons,' said Tamsyn and Daisy bobbed her head enthusiastically whilst she tried desperately to think of an associated job.

In that moment Daisy realised she also wanted something more – to do something she loved and not just for the money. She was here until the end of June and she couldn't spend her time doing nothing because then it would seem like a life sentence. In the back of her mind something Max had said started to germinate. Perhaps it was worth having a chat to the planning office about the railway building; it couldn't do any harm.

Jason was sitting in the pub engrossed in a newspaper headline about a drugs raid in Exeter, not taking his eyes off the page as he sipped his half of shandy.

'All right?' Max pulled out the stool opposite noting Jason's intense expression. This was the stuff of his dreams – a big police case.

Max was wearing his lifeguard's uniform and his orange shorts strained when his muscled thighs flexed as he sat down. He put his pint down and looked across the table. It made Max smile that as well as the drugs raid, Nesbit the eagle's safe return home had also made the local front page.

'Have the shed arsons made it to the nationals yet?' he joked.

'Don't ridicule it, it's a serious crime, Max. Mr Patel's shed was torched on Monday and his tortoise was burned alive.' Jason's face was sombre unlike Max who was already cracking up.

'Toasted tortoise. It might become a delicacy,' said Max, bringing his laughter under control.

'He was very upset,' said Jason, folding up his paper precisely and laying it on the table.

Max snatched up the paper and turned to the sports pages. 'I hear you've got another big case to crack.'

'Yes, a second burglary took place this morning.' His eyes widened as he spoke.

'Proper crime wave,' said Max, with a smirk.

'It could be the start of something. Perhaps organised crime.' There was no mistaking the excitement in Jason's voice.

'Steady on,' said Max, before taking a long slow drink. 'Not likely in Ottercombe Bay though is it?'

Jason raised a finger. 'Now, you say that but a place where you wouldn't expect to find an underworld cell has to be the perfect place to hide one.'

Max couldn't disagree with the logic, however unlikely it was in reality. It was hard to keep a straight face. He started to hum a melody.

Jason gave him a longsuffering look. 'And you can stop with the *Midsomer Murders* theme tune as well.'

Max and Jason had always been mates – an odd combination of the once local troublemaker and the ultimate goody two shoes. They had diverse upbringings and therefore differing outlooks on life but their differences were what made them a good team. Max encouraged Jason to be brave, to step outside the rules occasionally and Jason tempered Max's wayward streak.

Jason and Max were both from local families who could trace back their ancestry to multiple generations of Devon residents – but there the similarity ended. Jason had doting parents; a mother who worked part time and a father who was a coach driver and shared Jason's love of trains. They were still very much in love after umpteen years of marriage and were immensely proud of their son, the policeman.

Max on the other hand had mainly been brought up by his mother who to all intents and purposes had been a single parent through his formative years because her husband had been in and out of prison as his petty crimes got bolder. She had finally moved to Scotland with a new boyfriend when Max was eighteen leaving him with his dad. His father had tried to stay on the right side of the law but it simply wasn't profitable enough to support them both. Max turned a blind eye to his father's antics until he tried to persuade him to join him on a criminal venture – that was the last time Max had spoken to his father.

Jason adjusted his jacket and leant forward a fraction. 'Your dad must be due for release soon. Isn't he?' he asked, looking slightly embarrassed.

Max's expression changed. 'Not for another couple of months. Let's not go pinning anything on him just yet.'

Chapter Eleven

Jason was turning out to be a useful person to know. As the local bobby, everyone knew him and therefore he had a wide network he could tap into, particularly as he had a colleague with an uncle working in the local planning department. After a warm-up phone call from Jason he was happy to meet Daisy for a chat. She had made an effort, steered clear of both espresso and Bug's furry patch on the sofa, and she felt ready for her meeting.

An older-looking gent with thinning hair and thick glasses collected her from the waiting area at the council offices and they did introductions.

'Thanks for meeting me,' said Daisy, starting to feel a little less prepared as she followed him into an office and saw a mountain of paper on his desk.

'No problem but you will need to submit a formal application through the proper process. Anything discussed here today does not in any way constitute agreement of any changes to the property or land we are discussing. I hope you appreciate this?'

Daisy swallowed hard. With formal wording like that he would get on well with Great Uncle Reg's solicitor. She hadn't even suggested anything yet and she was being told off. 'Yes, of course. I'm just looking for guidance. Some ballpark areas that may be worth exploring.'

'This is the last application we received for the property,' said the planning officer, passing Daisy a pile of papers. She had a quick flick through and spotted some blueprints – it looked like her grandfather had taken the whole thing seriously and spent some money in the process.

'And I think the solicitor said this was turned down, as were the other ones before it. I'm guessing the same would happen again if I were to suggest building a new property in what was the car park.'

'I think that is a fair assumption. There are properties nearby that would be affected and the apartment building previously proposed would have looked out of place in the surrounding area and had a visually overbearing impact.'

'How about smaller buildings? Single-storey properties perhaps?' Holiday cottages could be a profitable option, thought Daisy.

'Very unlikely,' he said, a crease deepening on his forehead. 'You see the car park has a designated public right of way through it.' He drew a line with his finger across the blueprints virtually cutting the car park in half.

'And knocking down the platform and railway building?' She had to ask.

His frown intensified. 'The railway station is considered a historic building. It is grade two listed and is therefore subject to a number of conditions. Demolition is not an option.'

'Can I open the car park and charge people to park there?' This felt like an easy way to make money although, now it was August, the summer season was already well underway.

'Subject to obtaining a parking permit, public liability

insurance and undertaking a risk assessment to ensure there would be no environmental damage caused by vehicles or inconvenience to pedestrians.'

Daisy had to control the urge to huff out her frustrations. 'Could I not just take down the fencing and charge £5 a day?' she said, failing to hide a brief pout.

'I'm afraid not.'

'Right, so what can I do?' Daisy was starting to feel this was a pointless meeting.

He nudged his glasses down his nose and viewed the file over the top. 'Subject to application you could apply for a change of use.'

'What else can you use a car park for?' It was hard not to sound cheesed off at this point.

'I meant the building itself.'

Daisy perked up. 'Could I convert it into somewhere to live?' One holiday rental would be better than nothing, she thought.

'It's possible,' he said, although his face said different. 'But I believe something commercial that retains the original features of the property and complies with the grade two listing would be the most likely to be looked upon favourably.'

Daisy wasn't sure what else you could do with a railway platform and dilapidated ticket office. 'Like what?'

'A railway museum perhaps?' He looked the most animated he had since she'd met him. What was it with men and trains?

She felt her shoulders slump forward in surrender. 'I don't think that would bring in much money.'

'You'd be surprised. There are a lot of railway enthusiasts who would be interested and it would likely cover the increase in rates that would accompany a change of use.'

'Increase?' said Daisy sitting up, meerkat-like.

'Yes, there is an annual cost associated with the property, which will fall to you as the owner. Any change of use will incur a review and a likely increase.'

Bloody brilliant, thought Daisy, not only could she do nothing with it, which would mean it would be virtually impossible to sell, it was also going to cost her money. Great Uncle Reg hadn't thought this through.

The planning officer went on about what she could do to keep the site secure as they had had some complaints over the years of kids messing about and playing ball games in the car park area but Daisy let it wash over her, agreeing at what she hoped were appropriate moments. There was no way she was throwing good money at it. She thanked him for his time and advice, took his business card and vowed to think carefully about all he had said. But it was unlikely she would be submitting a planning request any time soon.

She decided she needed something stronger than an espresso and headed for the pub. Monty gave her a warm welcome and she sat at the corner table where she had sat with Max and sipped a large glass of Rioja. She had taken a liking to red wine whilst living in Spain and Rioja was one of her favourites, but it didn't taste the same today; there was a certain bitter aftertaste.

Just when she thought she was at today's low point, Max walked in, looking tanned and relaxed like he didn't have a care in the world. He scanned the bar and when his eyes alighted on Daisy his face fell and Daisy involuntarily huffed. She didn't like him because ever since she'd come back he'd seemed to annoy her; what with leaving her to lug home the heavy boxes, suggesting her mother had killed herself, knocking coffee down her before her interview and generally being hostile. It appeared to be a mutual loathing; although she wasn't sure what she'd done, she got the feeling he was on Great Uncle Reg's side when it came to what was best for her. She began studying the contents of her glass. Monty materialised and started to pull Max a pint – it appeared a bob of the head between them was communication enough. Daisy wondered how Max could afford to drink out virtually every night and then realised she had no idea what he did for a living.

Max took his drink, turned around and scowled briefly at Daisy.

'You can sit here too, if you like.' Daisy indicated the empty seats. She guessed it was most likely Max's usual spot. She wasn't going to move but she would attempt to be civil, however hard that might be.

Max gave a quick look around. There weren't any other tables available. 'Okay,' he said looking rather reluctant as he sat down opposite Daisy sending across a whiff of freshly showered man. 'Sorry to hear about the burglary.'

'Thanks.' She noted his clean t-shirt and casual jeans. Even his clothes mirrored his customary relaxed demeanour.

They sat in silence for a few minutes, sipping their respective drinks and avoiding eye contact until Daisy could bear it no more. 'My day was shite. How was yours?'

Max sniggered. 'Not great, but possibly not as bad as yours. What's up?'

'Met a planning officer about the old railway. Turns out it's grade two listed so I can't demolish it and I can't build near it. All I could do is apply for change of use and make it into a boring museum for railway nerds.'

Max was frowning. 'If you can apply for change of use I'd have thought there were more options than just a museum?'

'He said commercial use, but there's not a lot else you can do with a moth-balled ticket office,' she said glumly.

'Er, yeah there is,' said Max, taking a long drink of his pint.

'Like what?' There was more than a hint of a challenge in her voice.

Max sat back in his seat and let his knees part. 'If you think about the other ones locally there's one that holds craft workshops, they seem to do okay. There's one they converted into a pottery shop, another one is an antique shop – they specialise in railway memorabilia so they might be interested in your stuff.'

'Hmm.' She didn't look convinced.

'What about all the other old buildings that get converted, like banks and post offices? I've seen them turned into bars, coffee shops, restaurants, offices and one of them is even a car showroom.'

'I can't see the planning officer going for any of those; he seemed quite set on the railway museum idea. And all your suggestions sound like they'd cost a lot to fit the building out.'

'You're just on a downer – nothing I say is going to be a good idea because you've already decided you don't want it to be a success.' Max took another easy slug of his beer.

'What? Of course I want it to be a success.' Daisy was starting to get riled. She tried hard to control it with a mouthful of Rioja.

'No, you don't. You don't want old Reg to be proved right. You'll sabotage your time here just to prove a point.' He shook his head.

'You are talking nonsense. I'm here aren't I? And I have every intention of staying the full year.'

'But then what?'

'I'll go travelling. There is a whole world outside of Ottercombe Bay, but you probably hadn't noticed because you have your head so far up your own arse!'

'And you running away again was precisely what Reg was trying to avoid. He's given you an opportunity most people would jump at. But you're just too stubborn to see it or even try.' Max stretched out his arms, folded them behind his head and raised an eyebrow as if in challenge.

'Travelling opens you up to a world of possibilities and experiences and—'

'It's still running away.'

Daisy was fuming. 'I have neither the patience nor the crayons to explain this to you.' She downed the rest of her wine, slammed down her glass and stormed out.

Daisy sat on the headland, her face pointed out to sea but she wasn't really looking at the view and she certainly wasn't seeing anything. Her hand was resting near her throat where her mother's locket used to sit. Her aunt had offered her one of her necklaces to wear but it wasn't just the feel of the jewellery against her skin she was missing. She missed the connection she felt to her mother, the reassurance she had when she touched it. She knew people wouldn't understand. It wasn't a lucky talisman: to Daisy it was her connection with the past.

Losing the locket had given her a renewed desire to know more about her mother's death, but she didn't know where to start on a case the police closed eighteen years ago. She wished she'd done more investigating when she still had the locket – she was convinced it held the key.

She lay back on the grass, the sun warming her skin, and stared up at the wispy clouds drifting aimlessly above her. She watched the shapes slowly change. She remembered lying in the exact same place trying to see pictures in the clouds as a child – at moments like this it didn't feel that long ago. She wondered how different her life would be if her mother hadn't died. It was likely they would all still be living in Ottercombe Bay and she would never have travelled further than Exeter . . . or maybe she was doing her parents a disservice; perhaps as a strong unit of three they would have seen the world together – she couldn't be sure.

She knew if she wanted to search deeper into her mother's death she probably needed to call her father but that was always a difficult subject to broach with him. It would need careful planning, rather than rushing in – something she was famous for. She puffed out a breath. She had come up here to calm down and it had worked.

The row with Max in the pub had escalated quickly. Now she was thinking more rationally she knew some of what he had said was right, even if she hadn't wanted to hear it. Great Uncle Reg had always looked out for Daisy, so she knew he only had good intentions when he had left her the old railway building and his forcing her to stay in Ottercombe Bay in order to inherit it was his attempt to get her to put down some roots. But when you had been nomadic for such a long time, it wasn't that simple.

When her mother had died, her father had been devastated and the local rumours of how she might have died tortured him until he had packed up their things, flung them in the back of their old car and left the bay, taking Daisy with him. They rarely made it to a year in one place so she spent her formative years travelling around the UK. It didn't take long for it to feel completely normal. They only ever came back to the bay for two weeks' holiday each summer. That was all her father could cope with.

Daisy sat up and looked around. She watched the painted sky lighting up the horizon as the last drop of sunlight dissolved silently into the sea. The vibrant colours were reflected on the cliffs, giving the bay an ethereal glow – nature's light show was beautiful. There wasn't a lot to dislike about Ottercombe Bay. It was busy in the summer – the tourist trade was both a blessing and a curse. The tourists overran the place in high season but the locals needed that income to get them through the stark winter months.

She would have to apologise to Max at some point, he was infuriating. She thought back to Max's suggestions for the railway building. There was no way she was going to turn it into a railway museum, she couldn't think of anything duller and an antique shop wasn't a lot better – she'd always disliked the smell of them. The bar was an interesting idea and the one that really stuck out. She had come across a few great bars on her travels. In particular, a few amazing gin bars. Gin was very popular in the Netherlands, where it originated, and certain areas of Spain and whilst there she had sampled more than her fair share of locally made gins. Gin bars also seemed to be on trend in the UK and the ones she had been in were heaving with people, which was always a good sign.

Daisy closed her eyes and an image of the inside of the railway building popped up. The ticket hall was the main space which would be the bar and seating area. Perhaps the office and luggage cupboard could be where she kept a glasswasher, sink and storage? The other end of the building wouldn't need much alteration – it was already toilets. In a blink she could picture the railway building as a bar. Lots of noise and happy people crammed into the small space, with her manning the optics. Max popped up into the picture and she opened her eyes quickly. Max had no place in her gin bar fantasy – even if it was sort of his idea. But getting it from an idea to reality was far easier said than done.

Chapter Twelve

Daisy pushed her salad around her plate aware Aunt Coral was talking about what had happened at the pharmacy that day, but she wasn't really tuning in.

'. . . and then the gorilla stuffed a packet of paracetamol up his nose, jumped onto the counter and demanded I do the tango with him. Daisy are you listening?'

Daisy lifted her head and tried to recall what Aunt Coral was going on about. 'Not really, sorry.'

'I thought not. What's the matter, love?' She reached a hand across the table and patted Daisy's wrist.

'I want to do something useful with the year I'm here. Either get a decent job to have something substantial on my CV or . . . I don't know.' Daisy tailed off and speared a cherry tomato that ceremoniously squirted juice over her pristine white t-shirt. Daisy groaned.

'A job is definitely a good idea but what was going to come after the "or" in your sentence?'

Daisy was busy sponging off the tomato juice with a cloth. 'I don't know,' she said with a half-hearted shrug.

'Come on now, yes you do. What was it?' insisted Aunt Coral who had now put down her cutlery and was looking intently at Daisy.

'The planning officer basically said I couldn't do anything to the building apart from change of use and all the suggestions he gave sounded dull, but I was speaking to . . . someone and they've given me an idea.' Aunt Coral became alert as Daisy seemed to lose interest in her own suggestion. 'Ahh you know it's probably a dumb idea anyway and it would take loads of money to make the changes. I should probably just go for the job in the fish and chip van.' Her shoulders slumped forward and she resumed pushing her lettuce about.

'Stop being defeatist,' said Aunt Coral, in an uncharacteristic snap. 'You've always been impulsive so what does your impulse tell you this time?' She softened a little and fixed her gaze on Daisy.

'Go for it,' said Daisy, almost without thinking. In her gut she had a rumble of excitement caused by the thought of a new venture.

'Great,' said Aunt Coral enthusiastically. 'What is the idea exactly?' She bent forward in anticipation.

A small smile played on Daisy's lips. 'A gin bar.'

Aunt Coral's eyes widened. 'Oh my, now that is something new. Would it only sell gin?'

'Not exactly. Different types of gin would be the main theme. Gin is quite big right now.'

'I've always liked a gin and tonic and your Great Aunt Ruby was a big fan. Do you think it would make money?'

'Yeah, I do. They're very popular. I think it would pull people in and if we stock good quality craft gins they should keep coming back.'

Daisy could see Aunt Coral was thinking. 'I do like the idea and I can see the tourists lapping it up but what about in the winter months when it's just the locals?'

They both sat back in their chairs a little and looked to

the ceiling for inspiration. Aunt Coral had a good point. Daisy knew the seasonal change in seaside resorts was dramatic.

Aunt Coral jumped in her seat as if someone had stuck a pin in her. 'Lantern parade!' she shouted.

Daisy blinked. 'What?'

'Oh, sorry you've not been here for the lantern parade yet. Each December the children make paper lanterns, pop a battery light inside and walk from the church to the prom and they give out prizes and hot chocolate. If you were shut for the winter it would be a good thing to open up for. I bet the adults would like a shot of gin before they set off. It's usually a bit chilly.'

'I can't shut for the winter – I'd need to be able to make it work all year round. The parade sounds great, but even if I start sorting the place out now and go through the planning consent process I'll be lucky if I'm open for December.' Daisy's face fell. She'd be bankrupt by Christmas. She certainly couldn't wait until next year's holiday season to open up. Something Aunt Coral had said was swirling around Daisy's brain. 'How about hot chocolate?' Daisy asked.

Aunt Coral looked thoughtful. 'I think they get a job lot of the cheap stuff from the cash and carry . . .'

'No, I mean when it's not a gin bar it could be a hot chocolate cabin.' Daisy's enthusiasm was flooding back but Aunt Coral looked sceptical. 'Think about it. Proper hot chocolate, like Great Uncle Reg used to make, not the powder stuff and in all sorts of flavours – mint, orange, toffee all covered in cream, marshmallows and sprinkles. Do you think that would bring in the locals in the winter?' Daisy held her breath and waited, Aunt Coral appeared to be on pause.

'Yes,' she said at last. 'I think it would. It's an excellent idea. I've never heard of a hot chocolate cabin before.'

'I just made it up,' said Daisy.

'Reg loved a hot chocolate.'

'I know, I remember,' said Daisy in a soft voice.

Her excitement was short lived as she realised this was all going to cost a lot. 'I hope the bank is feeling generous because I'll need to borrow to get this off the ground. Do you think if they speak to the solicitor they'd loan me the money knowing I have my inheritance to come next year?'

Aunt Coral was frowning, which was not looking positive but her frown melted and a smile slowly replaced it. 'I'll lend you the money out of my share.'

Daisy put her hands up. 'No, I couldn't let you.'

'Why not? It's the same as the bank, but I won't charge you interest. You just pay me back instead of getting charged by the bank. I was only going to put it in a savings account anyway. It might as well make itself useful.'

She had a point. 'You'd have to have something in return though. How about free gin and hot chocolate?'

Aunt Coral let out a hearty laugh. 'Free gin. I think you'll definitely be bankrupt. How about if at the end of your first year I take back my investment plus a few per cent? That's all the bank was offering me in a savings account. But only if you're in profit, mind.'

'Deal,' said Daisy standing up and offering an outstretched hand. She had a good feeling about this, and now all she had to do was convince the planning officer a gin bar was a better idea than a railway museum. It was a good thing she liked a challenge.

Aunt Coral stood up, shook Daisy's hand, then pulled her into a spontaneous hug, which set Bug off on a yapping marathon. 'I'm excited for you, Daisy,' said her aunt giving her another hug. 'And Uncle Reg would be too.' Clearly Bug disagreed, because he was still barking at maximum volume as he circled the two of them.

When Jason called round on the pretext of providing an update on the burglary, Daisy was saddened she hadn't thought about her beloved locket for a few hours. Aunt Coral busied herself with making tea while Jason and Daisy chatted in the living room under Bug's watchful glare.

'We are making progress. We have run the fingerprints we found and they were all either yours or Coral's. We have asked all antique dealers in the area to be alert to anyone bringing in a locket like yours and we've circulated the sketch.' Jason appeared pleased with his summary.

Daisy let the pause linger before she spoke. 'But basically you're no closer to catching them or finding my locket then?'

Jason's enthusiasm waned slightly. 'We're doing all we can at this stage.'

Daisy took a deep breath. She needed to stay positive and concentrate on the good things. 'I've got some ideas for the railway building and I'm going to submit a request for change of use to the planning office.' It felt good to voice it out loud.

'Excellent. What are you going to do?'

'Hot chocolate cabin by day and gin bar by night.' Daisy found she was grinning as she said it.

'Wow. It sounds perfect. Will it have a railway theme?'

Daisy hadn't thought about themes beyond gin and hot chocolate. 'I guess the building itself sets the theme, because I won't have the money to change it much.'

'I think keeping it original will appeal to lots of people. If I were you I'd use those old photographs and railway signs you found: they're part of the building's history and add interest for both locals and tourists. I've also got some bits and pieces you might be interested in. I don't want anything for them; it would just be nice for them to be on display.'

Daisy didn't want to think too much about Jason's bits and pieces on display but it brought a smile to her face anyway. 'Thanks, that's kind.'

Aunt Coral came in at that point in the conversation carrying a tray that wobbled precariously. Jason jumped up and took it from her. 'There's some boxes in the shed marked railway in Reg's handwriting. I don't know what's in them but you never know.'

Jason became animated. 'Shall we take a look now? I've got a few minutes.'

They were soon hauling garden tools out of the way and dragging out the two large boxes Aunt Coral had mentioned. They eagerly opened the first one. Daisy pulled out the yellowed newspaper on the surface and Jason gasped. 'Model railway.' He reached into the box like a child grabbing sweets, but when his hand closed around the engine he went into slow motion and brought it up to his face to study closely. Daisy's enthusiasm had evaporated as soon as the contents had been revealed. Toy trains were no good to her. She watched Jason, his eyes full of childlike glee as he started to carefully hand items to Daisy. 'Tea's getting cold,' she said feeling boredom take hold.

'You're right, I could be here for days,' he said and she believed him.

'Why don't you have them, Jason? I'm sure Reg would want them to go to a good home.' She was sure Aunt Coral wouldn't mind him having them; she seemed rather fond of Jason.

121

'Oh, I couldn't. These are worth quite a bit.'

'We can check with Aunt Coral but I don't think she'll want anything for them. Come on, I'll give you a hand putting them in the car,' said Daisy, putting back the ones she was holding. They lifted the box together and lugged it across the back garden. Jason looked at Daisy, the corners of his mouth twitching.

'Do you fancy going out with me . . . for a drink . . . tonight?' asked Jason, his face flushing up to his neat hairline.

Daisy hated moments like this, everything instantly became awkward. 'Mmm, that's kind of you, Jason, and I'd love to go for a drink as a *friend*.' She emphasised the last word and hoped that was enough.

Jason nodded. 'As friends would be lovely,' he said gallantly, making Daisy feel even more horrid than she already did. She liked Jason, she really did, but he was not her type and the last thing she needed now was the complication of a relationship with someone local who she would see every time she came back to visit Aunt Coral. She surprised herself at the thought she would be coming back to visit even after having done a whole year here. Already Ottercombe Bay must have been growing on her more than she cared to acknowledge.

That evening Daisy and Jason exchanged awkward smiles at regular intervals over their drinks. Whilst the pretext of their drinks was clear to them both it still felt uncomfortable. Daisy didn't want to ask how work was in case he thought she was asking about the break-in again so she searched her brain for a subject to end the crippling silence.

'Did you get a chance to look through the box of trains?' she asked, almost hopeful this would send Jason off on a monologue about model railways. Oh how her life had changed.

'Not properly, but there is a 1968 die-cast Flying Scotsman in there. It's quite rare but it has been well played with, making it a bit battered.'

Daisy was bored already. They had nothing in common and conversation was painful and stilted. When she thought it couldn't get any worse the pub door swung open and in walked Max. Daisy felt her face drop and her last shreds of optimism with it. Max strode over and slapped Jason on the back almost making Jason spill his shandy.

'All right matey?' he asked. He gave a cursory tip of the head in Daisy's direction. 'Daisy.'

'Good thanks,' said Jason.

Daisy wasn't sure why she decided to take the route she took next. 'Very well thank you. Having a quiet evening out with Jason.' She held Max's gaze as his eyebrows danced and he looked to Jason for an explanation.

'Drink out with a friend but always room for one more. Pull up a chair,' he said. Daisy felt her bravado plummet.

'As long as I'm not being a gooseberry.'

How fitting, thought Daisy. He had lots of hair, he was bitter and she didn't like him very much – he was exactly like a gooseberry.

'No, it's just a drink,' said Jason.

'Sure?' asked Max, looking at Daisy's empty glass. 'Or are you two about to go for a snog behind the beach huts?' Max teased, his face alight with mischief.

'Another gin and tonic please,' asked Daisy.

Max leaned over, picked up her glass and sniffed her current drink. 'One lemonade and a shandy,' he said, turning his back and waving to get Monty's attention.

Why was Max so annoying? He clearly had never grown up; he was still the seven-year-old who pulled her plaits and threw grass at her after the school playing field had been mown. There was something about him that annoyed her even when he wasn't trying very hard. She realised she was frowning and Jason was studying her closely. Poor Jason, he was such a sweetie. She changed her expression and tried to relax.

'I'd like to be involved in the transformation of the railway building. You know, if you need a hand with anything at all you only have to ask,' said Jason, giving a toothy smile.

Daisy opened her mouth to reply but Max was quicker. 'What's this?'

'Daisy is going to turn the railway building into a business venture,' said Jason moving his chair a fraction nearer to Daisy.

'I'm hoping to turn it into a gin bar and hot chocolate cabin,' she said haughtily.

Max sucked his lip in through his teeth and it sounded like air being squeezed from a lilo. 'Monty won't like that,' he said, his voice a fraction louder than was necessary.

'What won't I like?' asked Monty, passing over their drinks. Max pointed at Daisy. She felt like she'd been hit in the face with a frying pan. She knew her eyes were bulging so she guessed she probably looked a lot like Bug. She blinked as Monty waited for an explanation.

'It's still just in the planning stage,' Daisy started in a small voice. 'I'm thinking of turning the old railway into a hot chocolate cabin . . .' She left a long pause. Monty's expression was changing. 'And gin bar.' She said the last words super-fast and then bit her lip in anticipation. Monty frowned hard.

'It'll be themed around the railway,' said Jason and Daisy nodded along. 'It'll help keep the history of the Ottercombe Bay station alive. And gin has quite a growing target audience.'

Max was grinning mischievously as he put down his pint and sat at the table. Monty's eyes flicked around the three of them.

'You'll be selling more than just gin though, won't you?' Max asked Daisy.

Daisy glared at him, he was trying to cause trouble. 'Yes, but the main focus will be the gin. We won't be in direct competition,' she said with a squeak of a laugh. Monty didn't look amused.

'I think we will, but only if you get planning permission,' said Monty at last. 'Will you be seasonal only?' He raised an eyebrow and looked hopeful.

'It needs to be open all year round,' said Daisy.

'Not enough trade here in the winter as it is, we don't want it spread even thinner. Will you be doing food?' Monty was narrowing his left eye as he spoke, which was quite unnerving.

'We won't be doing main meals. Just cakes and snacks.'

Monty appeared to relax his shoulders a fraction. 'That's something I suppose.' Another customer caught his eye and he walked to the other end of the bar.

Daisy let out a huge sigh of relief and then remembered who had stirred it all up in the first place. 'Thanks, Max.'

'He was going to find out soon enough,' Max said, maintaining his air of calm aloofness. Daisy didn't like the fact he was right or that this was most likely just the start of the opposition she would face. All of a sudden, all the other local businesses that may be affected popped into her mind. Basically anyone who sold hot drinks, cake or alcohol was going to challenge this. Inwardly she groaned.

'It's pointless isn't it?' she said before picking up her drink. 'It's a small place, which already has lots of businesses all vying for a share of limited trade. They will all oppose me and the planning officer will have to decline my submission.' She looked to Jason and Max to contradict her.

'Not necessarily,' said Jason. 'Businesses change hands and premises change use fairly regularly and it wouldn't happen if everyone opposed everything. The way I see it, you aren't in direct competition with anyone. It's similar, yes, but we used to have three pubs, all very different in their own way, and now we have two. It's only like the third one opening up again.'

Max looked dreamy eyed. 'I loved the Smuggler's Rest. Great little pub.'

Daisy looked at Jason and he mouthed 'Complete dive.' She giggled. Jason was sweet and he had a way of making her feel better about things and right now she needed a few more Jasons on her side.

Chapter Thirteen

The next few weeks were a whirl of phone calls and filling in forms. The planning officer seemed especially receptive when Daisy pitched her ideas under the banner of maintaining the original features and making it a railway-theme bar and café. There were no guarantees with the planning process; it was now a waiting game where Daisy could do little more than start to tidy up the building.

When Daisy got back to the cottage it was approaching dusk, the September night cloaking the bay in an inky twilight like a cosy blanket. Coral gave a tired sigh as she sank into the old sofa and lifted her foot onto the cushion.

'You okay?' asked Daisy.

'Ankle's playing up a bit, that's all.' As if on cue Bug jumped off the chair where he'd been sleeping, stretched heartily, gave a loud whistling trump and went and sat in front of Coral expectantly. 'Oh blast. You want a walk don't you?'

Bug's curly tail waved about excitedly. Daisy didn't move her head but her eyes travelled towards the dog and her aunt. She knew what she had to do. 'I'll take him,' she said, trying to sound enthusiastic as she got to her feet.

'Ooh that would be a help. Thanks, love,' said Aunt Coral sinking even further into the sofa.

'Right. Come on, Bug,' said Daisy and the small dog quickly turned his head to look her in the eye. 'You and me, walkies,' she added in a sing-song voice, mainly for Aunt Coral's benefit. She and the dog both knew they would be doing this under duress.

Bug dashed out of the living room and Daisy then spent five minutes searching the house for him, trying her bedroom last, where she found him rolling on the bed.

'Hey,' said Daisy loudly, making Bug freeze, which was a good opportunity to clip on his lead. He looked annoyed at being caught off guard and lay down flat as if trying to sink into the duvet. 'Come on,' said Daisy, giving the lead a tug. Bug didn't budge, he looked up at her with his giant sad eyes and she felt something not dissimilar to empathy.

Daisy crouched down by the bed, level with Bug. He shuffled a little closer. 'I'm going to be sticking around for a bit so we should try and be friends if only for Aunt Coral.' Daisy knew talking to the creature was a complete waste of time but she continued anyway. 'You and me are going to make an effort, starting now with a nice walkies. Okay?'

Bug lurched towards her face. Daisy was convinced he was about to rip her nose off and she threw herself backwards. Bug leaped off the bed and landed on top of her. 'Argh!' shouted Daisy as Bug tried to lick her face. His breath was nearly as bad as the smells that came from his bum. Daisy managed to grab him and place him on the floor next to her.

'Yuck.' She rubbed her arm across her face to remove the worst of the doggy tongue assault. It hadn't been pleasant but it was better than being bitten. Maybe it was Bug's way of calling a truce.

Daisy took his lead and set off for what she hoped would be a short and uneventful walk. By the time she reached the headland Daisy was barely aware she was taking Bug for a walk. He was trotting along beside her nicely and her mind was busy trying to work out how long it would take her to clear up the railway building and if one big standard weed killer would be enough to clear the wilderness in the overgrown car park. What occurred next happened in a nanosecond. There was a flash of something small and greyish-brown to her right, which must have been a rabbit. Bug saw it too because without warning he went from snail pace to locomotive, wrenching the lead from her hand. Within a moment he was swallowed by the darkness and gone.

'Bug!' she shouted but there was no sound at all. Not even a distant bark or the sound of paw on path – nothing. 'Bugsy Malone come back here.'

The gloom devoured her words and she felt suddenly alone. A breeze she hadn't noticed until now swirled around her giving her goosebumps. Perhaps he'd come back when he realised the rabbit had gone down a hole, or would he try to follow it and get stuck? She called a few more times but there was no response so she followed the path down to the cliff edge. It was difficult to see where the cliff ended. She was careful not to get too close. What if Bug had gone over the cliff in his excitement to catch the rabbit? She knelt down and crawled to the edge and slowly looked over. A gust of wind came up to hit her in the face making her blink. The tide was in, so if he had fallen he'd have gone into the sea. All she could see was a dark swirly mass with foaming white edges below her. She convinced herself he wasn't quite that dumb but the thought of going over the cliff made her stomach flip and she quickly scuttled back from the edge.

She couldn't stop her thoughts jumping to her mother.

Her body had been found in the middle of the beach but there had been the possibility she may have jumped, been pushed or fallen from the cliff edge into the sea. Was this how it had been for her? Did she walk too close to the edge on a moonless night? It was unlikely because she had lived here her whole life and she knew the coast like she knew all the words to *Let's go to San Francisco*. It suddenly seemed far more likely someone else was involved. Daisy looked around quickly, her heart starting to pound. She saw a dark figure silently walking towards her, their footsteps hushed by walking on the grass rather than the path. Daisy glanced about her. Her pulse sped up. She had nowhere to run. This was ridiculous . . . was history about to repeat itself?

Daisy looked behind her, she was about two feet from the edge. If she ran off to her left she didn't know it well enough not to trip and go over the cliff anyway. If she went to her right she would be running straight at whoever was coming her way. She had no choice, attack was the best form of defence. She took a deep breath, started shouting wildly and ran towards the figure in the darkness. She went to dodge around the person but they put out an arm to grab her and she screamed.

'Bloody hell, Daisy,' said Max holding on to her firmly.

She wrestled herself free. 'Max? You idiot! I thought you . . . I thought it was . .' She couldn't finish the sentence without revealing far more than she wanted to.

'Hey, calm down. What spooked you?'

'You did,' she snapped, still breathless.

'Sorry, I saw someone acting strangely on the cliff top and thought I should check it out.'

Daisy felt her panic subside. He was only trying to help; it was her overactive imagination making her panic.

'Don't suppose you have a torch with you?' she asked. 'Bug has run off.'

'Nope, sorry. I've got the one on my phone but there's not much charge left. I'll help you look for him though.'

'That's easier said than done. It's like a real version of the phrase trying to find a needle in a haystack. Trying to find a black dog in the dark.'

She thought she saw him smile but in this light or lack of it, it was difficult to tell.

'Let's try this way,' said Max, leading the way along the coastal path. 'You shouldn't have let him off the lead.'

Daisy bristled. 'I didn't. Technically he's still on the lead. I'm just no longer attached to the other end of it.'

'Hmm, I hope he doesn't catch it on something, he could strangle himself.' Telling her that didn't make her feel any better.

'Let's hope he has more sense then.'

She followed Max in silence. She was aware how near the edge she was and was keen not to trip and fall to her death. She wondered if everyone else thought like her or if it was her graphic imagination. There was a noise to their right and Max stopped without warning, making Daisy bump into the back of him. Somehow she managed to catch her toe on the heel of his shoe and stumbled. She gasped as her foot slid towards the edge and she struggled to keep herself upright. A strong hand grasped her arm and yanked her back up straight.

'Have you been drinking?' asked Max, his face looming closer.

Daisy couldn't speak for a moment and the sound of her pulse was deafeningly loud. 'No,' she said breathlessly. 'It's that bloody dog. I swear he's an evil genius hell bent on bumping me off.'

Max started to laugh and Daisy dashed around to stand on his other side a safe distance from the edge even if it did mean walking on the uneven grass. As Max was still laughing she decided to comment further. 'You think I'm joking but I'm telling you, he hates me.'

Max paused to look at her. 'Seriously? He's just a little dog. I doubt his emotions stretch beyond fear and happiness.'

'Ooh, that's very deep.'

'If you're going to mock . . .' he said striding off making Daisy trot to catch him up.

'Sorry, you're probably right.' Perhaps it was best if she kept her theory on Bug's plans for world domination to herself.

A few strides further and they both heard it at the same time. A scratching noise accompanied by a low whimper. Max put his phone on to torch and waved it across the grass in front of them. It soon picked up a small black blob not too far away.

'Bug!' called Daisy and the dog gave a fleeting glance in her direction before continuing his attempt to dig out the rabbit. Max grabbed the lead and handed it to Daisy.

'Now hold it tight.'

Daisy pulled a face. She didn't like being told what to do almost as much as Bug didn't like being pulled away from his quest to unearth the rabbit who had evaded him. She gave the lead another tug. Bug didn't appear to want to leave. He walked backwards for a few paces before reluctantly falling in step.

Daisy was keen to get back to Aunt Coral but now Max was walking alongside her she didn't know if he just happened to be going the same way or if he was walking her home.

'Thanks for your help tonight. I'll be fine from here,' she said when they reached the end of the path and the welcome sight of streetlights.

'No, it's okay. I'll see you to the end of your road, I'm heading home myself.'

'Oh, okay.' She didn't mind so much if it was on his route home. 'Where do you live?'

'I've got a place in Tinkers Lane. They converted a couple of the old council houses into bedsits.'

Daisy quelled the urge to comment on the appropriateness of his address. At least he had a place of his own, that was more than Daisy could claim. 'Are your mum and dad still local?' Sometimes she amazed herself with her dullness.

'Nah, Mum moved away,' said Max. 'She lives in Thurso in Scotland. She literally got about as far away as you can get but still be in the same country. With the exception of the odd oil rig,' he added with a chuckle

'And your dad? I liked him,' said Daisy recalling the funny man who had always been up for a game of cricket on the beach.

Max looked uncomfortable. 'He's away too but at her majesty's pleasure. We don't keep in touch.'

Daisy felt awkward and tried to think of something to lift the mood. 'I remember when we were kids, you were a lifeguard at the local swimming baths and you loved it because all the girls used to swoon over you.' Daisy laughed at the memory. 'What do you do for a living now?'

There was a long pause. Max was frowning deeply and Daisy sensed there was something amiss but was unsure what it was exactly. Eventually Max spoke his voice clipped. 'I'm still a lifeguard.'

An awkward silence lay between them with only the sound of their in-time footsteps to break it. Daisy opened

133

and closed her mouth a few times but couldn't think of a single thing that wasn't going to make the awkward situation worse.

'Go on say it. I'm a loser,' said Max, at last.

'No, you're not. Because if you're a loser then I am too and I refuse to believe that.'

'You've got a bit further than me though,' said Max. 'I'm still doing the same crap job I was ten years ago. At least you've travelled.'

'Travelling isn't all fun. I was working all the time, I didn't have any money for sightseeing. Now I'm back in the same place I started. I can't get a job and I'm living at my aunt's. I wouldn't say that's the CV of someone who's made it.' They laughed amiably until it dwindled and they both took a moment to think through the life choices that had brought them to this point.

'You're part of the lifeboat crew,' said Daisy as it struck her. 'That's pretty incredible. I mean, how many lives have you saved?'

Max shrugged. 'A few. It's just what we do,' he said modestly.

'I think it's amazing,' said Daisy and she meant it.

'Here,' said Max thumbing through numbers on his phone. 'This is the coastguard's number. If you ever see anyone in trouble you just call it and they'll get a boat and crew in the water within minutes.'

Daisy noted it down in her phone and they carried on walking. A few silent minutes later they reached the corner of Trow Lane. 'Here we are,' said Daisy, sounding like someone from the Famous Five. She stopped but Bug carried on and got stopped sharply by his collar.

'Thanks for the chat. I'll go home and slash my wrists now,' said Max, with a faint smile.

Daisy looked at him in the orangey glow of the nearby streetlight. His hands were shoved in his pockets making his shoulders look oddly high up. His head was bowed low and his full lips almost pouting. He looked thoroughly fed up and she felt a tiny bit responsible. She took a breath. 'Look, this idea of changing the use of the railway building . . . that was your idea.' It took a lot for her to admit it, but it was true. The hot chocolate part was all her own work but the gin bar he could claim as his own.

Max wasn't looking convinced. 'How?'

'You went through the things other old buildings had been converted into and I couldn't get the bar idea out of my head. The only reason anything is happening at all is down to you. So you're officially not a total loser.' She gave him a playful nudge with her elbow.

He looked up at her through his tousled dark hair. 'Thanks,' he said with a bob of his head.

'You're welcome.' She mimicked his head bob.

'Jason said he was giving you a hand with a few things. If you need a thick loser who can lift stuff, you know where to find me.' He started to walk away.

'I might do that,' said Daisy with a smile and they went their separate ways. Daisy gave a tug on the lead, much to Bug's annoyance as he was now investigating a particularly interesting smell around the street sign. He grunted his displeasure and trotted after Daisy.

Chapter Fourteen

Daisy and Tamsyn were sitting in Tamsyn's garden drinking her mum's homemade elderflower cordial and going over the previous evening's events. 'Poor Bug must have been scared,' said Tamsyn, her eyes like Bambi and her accent strong.

'Give over, that dog is hard as nails. I could have been killed last night—'

'If it hadn't been for Max coming to your rescue,' Tamsyn cut in not breaking eye contact. 'If you'd been wearing a leather bikini and fur it would have been just like . . .'

'A fantasy novel?'

'Yes. How did you know?'

'Lucky guess.'

'We are so in tune,' said Tamsyn, clapping excitedly.

Daisy shook her head. 'I didn't need rescuing, he just happened to show up.' She was annoyed at the very thought of being rescued by anyone, let alone Max. She emphatically crossed her legs.

'It would be nice to be rescued by someone though wouldn't it?' Tamsyn went dreamy eyed.

'No,' said Daisy appalled at the prospect. She never had bought in to the fairytale princess stories. In her book women were completely equal to men so they should be rescuing themselves. You got yourself into it, you can get yourself out of it, was what Great Uncle Reg had always said.

'Don't you ever dream of someone coming on their white charger and taking you away from all this?' Tamsyn's gaze drifted off down the pretty garden.

'Never,' said Daisy truthfully. Life had dealt her a cold hard dose of reality at a young age giving her an unsentimental view of the world and a realistic perspective on the likelihood of anyone stepping in to help – it simply didn't happen. There was only one person you could rely on in life and that was yourself, and in her experience occasionally that was questionable.

'It's a shame you lost your locket,' said Tamsyn, appearing to come back from whatever fantasy she had drifted off to. A random switch in conversation was typical Tamsyn.

Daisy brushed imaginary crumbs off her hoodie. 'Yep, but these things happen.' She had to be blasé about it, it was the only way she could cope. If she thought about it for more than a moment a great lump would appear in her throat and she'd be moments away from blubbing, and she was such an ugly crier.

'My mum was going to do a reading with it. You know, try and find a connection to your mother.' Tamsyn spoke like this was as normal as taking out a library book.

'Right,' said Daisy, not knowing how to respond. 'Thank her for me.'

Tamsyn sipped her drink. 'Do you ever feel like your whole life is a film?' she said.

'No one would to pay to see this,' said Daisy, with a hollow laugh.

'I would,' said Tamsyn, changing position. 'It's like you

left the bay to go on a quest to avenge your dead mother. Sorry,' said Tamsyn as Daisy's eyes widened.

'That was no quest. I just moved away.' Daisy wasn't sure where this was going but it was likely if Tamsyn was in the driving seat it was an uncharted place far off the normal bus route. 'If this was a fantasy novel, then I guess Reg was the wise old wizard?' suggested Daisy.

'Yes, and I'm his remarkable but undervalued understudy,' said Tamsyn.

'What am I then, a hairy-toed hobbit?'

'If the ring fits? No, you are the one true heir who has to fulfil their destiny and slay the dragon . . . obvs.'

'Obvs,' concurred Daisy, feeling stupid using the abbreviation.

Tamsyn sat bolt upright. 'Maybe your locket was an enchanted amulet.'

'Please tell me you're joking.' There was only so far down the path of the merrily insane she would allow herself to wander.

'Of course I was,' said Tamsyn, with a weak chuckle but her eyes were darting about as if she was trying to solve a scientific equation.

They sipped their drinks in silence and Daisy zipped up her hoodie when the autumnal breeze made her shiver. Daisy's phone beeped and her eyes idly skimmed the screen. A friend request on Facebook wasn't anything unusual. However, this was a request from Guillaume. All sorts of questions flooded Daisy's mind but before she could order them she had pressed the decline button. The emotions swirling through her caught her off guard. She had cared greatly for Guillaume and he'd hurt her badly, he was the last person she wanted to be friends with. What was he doing trying to get in touch after all this time?

'You know when you get that burning sensation?' asked Tamsyn, interrupting Daisy's thoughts.

'Yeah, it's usually a urinary tract infection.'

Tamsyn tried to give her a playful swipe but she missed. 'Nooo, I mean when you're with someone you like.'

'And who might this someone be?'

Tamsyn bit her lip. 'I don't want to say. Mum did my cards and she sees a soul mate in my future.'

'We'd all like one of those. Who?'

'She doesn't know.'

Daisy mulled it over. 'What did you mean exactly by a burning sensation because now I've said it out loud, it's all kinds of wrong.'

Tamsyn went coy. 'Sort of like someone is drawing squiggles in your tummy. I'm wondering if it might be love. How do you know for sure?'

Daisy took a moment to think. She wasn't the most experienced in this field. A long string of wankers had failed to turn up a potential candidate for love and lifelong happiness. 'I don't think you ever really know,' she said and they both studied the autumnal colours of the garden, lost in their own thoughts.

Max was thinking about Daisy as he strolled down the hill towards his bedsit. He never considered it as home, maybe he wouldn't let himself because he only ever wanted it to be temporary. However, it was going to be difficult to get anywhere better on his wages. It was true his hours weren't exactly full time but it was hard to get another job to fit around them. He'd done a few bar jobs, even a brief stint as a cocktail waiter, but he was far better suited to being on the other side of the bar with a pint in his hand.

He liked the idea of working on the old railway building. Max had always been a little bit of a secret nerd. When they were kids he'd spent many a happy hour at Jason's house playing with his train set. It wasn't something he would admit to though. He remembered the excitement of days out by train with Jason's family and he could recall each trip vividly. He rarely went anywhere by train now – in fact he didn't go anywhere at all, on his income travel wasn't an option.

Max was Ottercombe Bay born and bred – it was in his blood. Despite wanting more from his life, what he knew he didn't want was to leave the bay. He had seen many friends move away but they had often ended up either coming back or finding somewhere else on a coastline. When you grew up with the sea on your doorstep it was hard to be away from it for any length of time. It always drew you back like the tide. Max found the rhythm of the sea soothing, apart from when he was out on the lifeboat in treacherous conditions; then it was a challenge to be met. But either way he needed it, it was his anchor.

The fact everyone around him seemed to move on had troubled him, but Reg had helped him to see it differently. He'd helped Max to view it as his choice to remain in the bay, rather than a lack of ambition or apathy. There had been few people in Max's life he truly valued but Reg had been one of them and sadly like many people in Max's life he too had left him. He missed Reg a great deal.

Max had that sixth-sense feeling that someone was watching him. He lifted his head and scanned the path ahead. The next streetlight was a distance away but there was someone near it casting a shadow. Max was interested because they were standing still, if they had been walking he wouldn't have taken any notice. As he approached he knew instinctively from their outline who it was and it unsettled him more than he liked to admit.

Max straightened his back and quickened his pace as he drew level with the shadowy figure.

'Max.' A man stepped out from the darkness and put a hand out to block his way. He reluctantly stopped. Max could feel his body go into fight or flight mode as adrenaline coursed through his system. The man lowered his hand. 'Hello, son.'

Max sucked in a breath and held it for a second trying to stay calm and measured. 'Dad.' He gave a brief dip of his head and tried to walk on.

'Ah, come on, matey. Haven't you got a hug for your old dad?' Pasco had a cheeky glint in his eye as he threw his arms open wide. 'It's been a while.'

Not long enough, thought Max bitterly. His father pulled him into a hug regardless of the fact Max still had his hands firmly rooted in his pockets and had no intention of reciprocating. Max's body tensed at the contact and he waited for the embrace to end.

Pasco held him at arm's length and looked him up and down. 'You look well,' he said, a tear forming at the edge of his eye.

'I'm fine. I see they let you out early,' said Max, when he was at last released.

'Good behaviour.' His father turned up his collar and flashed his mischievous smile that often had everyone doing what he wanted. Not this time, thought Max. The dark silence grew heavy between them. 'Do you fancy a pint?' Pasco tipped his head in the direction of town.

'You got any money?' asked Max, narrowing his eyes.

'Ah. That's the thing. I have some stuff in the pipeline but until they come through . . .'

'That's a no then.' Max's voice was flat.

'If you could sub me a little I'd be grateful and you'd get it back.'

'I doubt it,' said Max and he started to walk away. His head was spinning with the effort of keeping his emotions in check. Seeing his father again after all this time was a shock and it brought back all the unwelcome memories of the night Max had so badly betrayed him. Max shook his head as if physically trying to shake them out of his head.

'Max. Matey,' Pasco called but Max didn't turn around, he put his head down and kept on walking until the darkness swallowed him up.

It was a bright September morning and Daisy was up early with a spring in her step. She even gave Bug a quick scratch behind his ears before she tied her mass of curls up in a scarf out of the way. She had hard work planned for today and the last thing she needed was hair flopping in her face. Today was going to be productive, she had worked out all the things she would need initially and with her aunt still keen to invest she could now start to get things moving. She wrote a long list of cleaning products for Aunt Coral and left the house.

Daisy got off her bike and pushed it across the car park. She was amazed to see Max sat on the station platform with his legs dangling over the edge. 'You're a bit early for opening. At least two months early,' she called and his head shot up.

'Jason said you were starting work today but he was on shift so I thought I'd stop by.'

Daisy glanced at her watch. 'You're keen . . . or did you wet the bed?'

'You're funny,' said Max, with a look on his face that told

her she wasn't. 'Don't give up the day job . . . oh hang on, you don't have one.'

'Whilst I enjoy a bit of banter first thing in the morning, are you here to help or just depress me?'

'Bit of both.' Max scratched his head. His hair was lolling about with a will of its own.

'Okay,' she said with a shrug. She didn't entirely trust Max and she was now more than a little suspicious of his motives for turning up to help out of the blue. They'd done nothing but annoy each other for the past three months. 'You know I can't pay you?'

'Not expecting a penny. Just here to help. You know, the thing we locals do for each other.'

Daisy wasn't going to rise to the bait. 'Then thank you, you're very kind.'

'I know.'

Daisy raised an eyebrow. 'Aunt Coral will be dropping off a load of cleaning stuff and a couple of brooms on her way to work but for now . . .' She held up a crowbar and a shovel.

'Did you carry those on your bike?'

'Yep, you'd be amazed what I can do on it,' she said, but immediately felt her cheeks colour and turned away.

Max looked impressed. He took the crowbar and they set to work. Within minutes they had the boards away from the door and were inside. It smelt as fusty as Daisy remembered but with a good sea breeze and a scrub it would soon improve. Max carried on taking down the rest of the boards whilst Daisy set about shovelling debris out onto the platform. As each of the boards was taken down from the windows more and more light streamed inside, making Daisy blink. By the time the last board was down things looked quite different. It was still smelly, damp and empty, but the light had breathed new life into the neglected space. The walls were bare brick and despite being covered in cobwebs their look was original and charming. The vaulted ceiling in the main room was impressive and underfoot she had uncovered smooth slate flagstones that after a scrub and a polish would look striking.

A hoot of a car horn sounded the arrival of Aunt Coral and Daisy went out to open up one of the metal barriers for her to drive in. Right behind her was Tamsyn in her car and she waved excitedly.

'I had to come,' said Tamsyn through the now open window before the car had come to a complete standstill. 'Coral said you were opening it up and I had to have a nose around inside. This is a historic moment. It's like the opening of Tutankhamen's tomb.'

Daisy laughed. 'Not exactly, Tams, but thanks for your enthusiasm.'

Coral opened the car boot and they formed a chain to pass things from the car up onto the old platform. There were boxes and boxes of cleaning stuff thanks to Coral agreeing an initial loan to start getting the place tidied up and give Daisy a little money in her pocket. 'I think I've got everything,' said Coral, handing Daisy her list back.

'You're a star. Thank you.'

Tamsyn screeched as she entered the railway building and Daisy went to see what was wrong. Tamsyn was standing in the middle of the ticket office twirling around like a hyper five-year-old, her pineapple emblazoned skirt splaying out around her. 'This is a magical place,' she declared.

'Have you been drinking?' asked Max, who was standing casually nearby. The crowbar was resting against his shoulder making his bicep flex and with a strategically

144

placed smudge of dirt on his cheek he looked a lot like a photo from a calendar.

'No,' said Tamsyn although she staggered about when she finally stopped spinning. 'Doesn't it just feel like you could be transported to Narnia at any second?'

Daisy was about to agree but Max was already laughing. 'I think that was a wardrobe, not a railway.'

'No, she's right,' said Daisy. 'In the second book . . . was it *Prince Caspian*? The children are unexpectedly transported from a railway station back to Narnia.'

That wasn't the only thing Tamsyn was right about; there was something strangely magical about the place. Perhaps it was because it held stories of people setting foot in Ottercombe Bay for the first time, as well as those who waved their final goodbyes on the platform. It was alive with history and it gave Daisy a buzz to think it was her who was uncovering it.

Tamsyn was nodding vigorously and Daisy felt a connection to her. The friendship had always been there but it was only now Daisy was realising she cared greatly for Tamsyn and how much she'd missed her. Tamsyn brought a whole new level to quirky but she was uniquely Tamsyn and that was what Daisy loved about her. After a guided tour, which didn't take long, they were soon waving off Aunt Coral and Tamsyn. Max and Daisy looked at each other.

Max broke eye contact first. 'Back to work then,' he said going inside. Daisy took a moment to look around her at the weed-filled car park, the rickety railway track, the shabby platform and the neglected little railway building. It was a pleasing thought that in nine months' time this would be hers to sell. She felt for her locket and, realising it was no longer securely around her neck, she put her head down and went back to work.

Chapter Fifteen

After a few hours, Daisy was fed up with the dust and general grime and her arms ached from brushing the walls and beams. She wasn't entirely sure how somewhere that had been boarded up for years could be this dusty, but there was a thick layer on everything. Max had taken a break from inside and was blasting weeds with the industrial weed killer Aunt Coral had dropped off. Daisy took a deep lungful of fresh sea air and sat down on the platform edge.

'We should get lunch,' she called to Max. He checked his watch and came over.

'I'll finish off spraying first because I know how far I've got. Then I'd better go straight to work.'

'But you'll need to eat.'

'It's okay, it'll take me about twenty-five minutes to walk to the leisure centre. I'll grab a pasty on the way.'

Daisy hesitated. 'Or I could give you a lift.' She pointed at her motorbike. 'Then we'd have time to eat the pasties in the café. It's not good for your digestive system to eat and walk at the same time.' She had no idea what she was going on about.

'On that death trap?'

'It hasn't killed me yet,' said Daisy getting to her feet. 'There have been some close calls, mind.' She dusted herself down – what she would give for running water right now to wash her hands. She had rung the water company but apparently with a disused building it wasn't as straightforward as just turning the water supply back on, she would have to wait until they paid her a visit.

When Max had finished distributing the weed killer he strolled over to stand next to Daisy making her notice exactly how tall he was. He was towering over her and she wasn't short at five foot seven. She looked at Max and she looked at her little bike. What was the worst that could happen?

Daisy put her helmet on, got on the bike and waited for Max to join her. He swung his leg over the seat and she felt his body engulf hers as he bent his knees and his legs rested on either side of her thighs. She hadn't thought this through at all. It seemed extremely intimate to have Max's body pushed up against her. She could feel the heat radiating from him and her treacherous body was delighting in the closeness. She straightened her back and her resolve.

'You okay without a helmet?' she asked over her shoulder. At least she didn't have to make eye contact like this.

'Yeah, it's not far.'

'Just in case Jason is about I'll stick to the bridleway then technically we're not breaking the law.'

Daisy froze and she waited for Max to put his arms around her waist, but instead he put his hands behind him and gripped the sissy bar at the back of the bike. Daisy tried to let the large breath she'd been holding in escape subtly. 'Let's go.' She revved the old engine and it spluttered into life.

The first few metres across the car park were a bit bumpy,

as was the bridleway but otherwise it was okay until they reached an incline and the bike started to struggle. Daisy could feel things weren't right. Come on, at least make it to the top of the hill, she willed the machine, but it wasn't receiving the message. The power faded and the bike quickly slowed and stopped. Daisy put her feet down just in time to stop it toppling over and unseating both of them. She felt her heart sink.

'What's up?' asked Max, putting his feet down to steady himself.

'I think my bike just died.' Daisy tried to start it again but there was only a lonely clicking noise and no sign of life. 'Yep, it's dead.' Daisy was gutted. She loved her old bike. She'd had it since she came back to the UK, almost a year ago, and it had served her well. It was exactly the same as the first bike she'd owned and she'd had a connection with it straight away, which had been a bonus because it was all she could afford at the time. She patted the seat as if comforting an ageing pet.

'Let's push it to the café. We can lock it up there,' said Max. 'Don't worry,' he added catching sight of her face. 'It can probably be fixed.'

Daisy didn't reply, she just carried on pushing. She knew how old it was and the mechanic at the last MOT had warned her the carburettor was barely passable and wouldn't last much longer and she knew the engine was on its last legs as it frequently cut out. The hill climb with two passengers had obviously been too much for the poor old thing.

By the time they reached the café Daisy could feel the sweat trickling down her back. She locked the bike up and they went inside. She paid for the two pasties and went and sat near the window.

'Cheer up,' said Max, in between mouthfuls. 'We got quite a bit done this morning.'

Daisy looked up. He was right. The bike dying was inconvenient but she may be able to get it fixed and if not, it didn't exactly owe her a lot. The problem was more that she had a sentimental attachment to it. She didn't own much and the bike was her transportation – her mark of freedom; losing it sent a mild dose of anxiety through her at being marooned. She bit into her pasty to distract herself and the familiar peppery meat and potatoes took her back to a time when having her sandcastle washed away was the biggest of her worries.

Max finished his pasty at lightning speed. He brushed his hands together. 'Right, I'd better go if I'm walking.'

'Oh, sorry,' said Daisy, realising the impact of the dead motorbike on Max.

'Not a problem. Thanks for lunch. Same time tomorrow?'

'Max, you know you don't have to do this.'

'I know,' he said with a warm smile. 'But it's cheaper than going to the gym. See you tomorrow.'

She finished her pasty, savouring every last morsel. She'd had an unexpectedly enjoyable morning with Max. She was still wary of him and his motives but she couldn't deny he'd been helpful. A shadow at the window interrupted her thoughts and she turned to see Jason's grinning face. He was in uniform and he waved enthusiastically, before striding inside.

'Hiya Daisy. You okay?'

'I'm okay but my bike's died, which is a bit of a bummer.'

She could see Jason was thinking. 'Leave it with me. I'll get it brought home for you.'

'Really?' Daisy was stunned at how quickly people seemed to be able to solve her problems.

'It doesn't do to be the local police officer if you can't pull in a favour occasionally,' he said, with a jaunty raise of his eyebrows.

'If you're sure. Any update on the burglaries?'

Jason's expression changed to serious, he pulled out Max's vacated chair and sat down looking every inch the sombre detective.

'There's been a third theft.' He scanned over his shoulder in a shifty fashion making Daisy do the same.

'Where?'

'Fagins,' said Jason.

Daisy frowned. 'The gift shop?'

Jason nodded. 'They took a picnic blanket.'

'Did they break in?'

Jason leaned across the table and lowered his voice. 'No, it was almost closing time and the owners were bringing things in and noticed someone had taken the blanket from the hook outside.'

'Probably kids or maybe the shopkeeper miscounted,' suggested Daisy, already feeling this wasn't on a par with her loss.

Jason shook his head. 'I think there's a puzzle to be solved here. You mark my words.'

Daisy tried hard not to smile. Jason was funny. It was like he'd been born to the wrong generation – he would have been far better suited to her great uncle's era or possibly even further back, but he cheered her up. She had been lucky enough to live in a number of countries and some big cities and she was aware of the many crimes taking place all the time. Ottercombe Bay was in its own little bubble and here was Jason the bubble master.

The thefts all sounded like petty pilfering to Daisy. The only thing taken of any value was her locket and if she hadn't made it stupidly easy for them to steal they would never have taken it.

'It sounds like another opportunist theft to me. Most likely if I'd put my locket in the bedside drawer I'd still have it now.'

'I doubt it,' said Jason looking grim. 'They turned your room over good and proper. I've still no idea why.' That was when she realised Jason still believed the thief had come into her bedroom and caused the unholy mess she naturally achieved with very little effort.

Daisy took a deep breath. 'Jason, I'm really sorry but I may have misled you.' The sweaty feeling returned but this time not through strenuous effort but from embarrassment and guilt.

'How so?' He tilted his head.

'I don't think the burglar who took my locket actually came into the bedroom.'

Jason was waving her sentence away. 'But the excessive mess was a key indicator . . .' Daisy was shaking her head.

'The excessive mess was mainly . . . actually all of it was made by me.' She felt awful. It was excruciating to watch the look of bewilderment on Jason's face turn to disappointment. 'I'm truly sorry. I should have said before. I was embarrassed in front of everyone.'

A crease twitched across Jason's forehead but he recovered his easygoing nature quickly. 'That would have been helpful but it's a lesson learned for me too: I jumped to the wrong conclusion. Thank you for putting me straight.'

Daisy tilted her head. 'Sorry.'

'Let's forget it. It doesn't make a great difference; the same items were stolen.' Jason paused for a second and twitched. 'I take it they were . . .'

'Oh God, yes. I wouldn't lie about something like that.'

Daisy was mortified and clutched at her throat despite the locket no longer being there to comfort her. Jason saw the gesture.

'No, of course. Sorry, but you understand I have to ask.' Daisy nodded. 'Right, I'll make a few calls and get your bike picked up. Do you need a lift somewhere?'

'The railway building please, but only if you're going that way.' Daisy still felt sheepish after her confession.

'No problem. To be honest I'd love to have a nose around. You know how fond I am of trains.'

'I'll give you the gold standard guided tour,' she said, getting up from the table. It was the least she could do.

Jason was suitably impressed with the tour, which basically consisted of Daisy pointing him in the direction of the luggage store and toilets. Jason was soaking it all up. 'This is such a marvellous piece of history. You are doing a public service by restoring it.'

'I'm only giving it a wash and brush up at the moment. And to be honest,' she said – she felt she could be nothing else now having grubbied her reputation, 'even if I get planning permission, I'm only going to take out half of this wall.' She tapped the wall between the ticket hall and the ticket office. 'And put in a counter top for the bar. We need new hinges on the loo doors, general repairs, painting and some furniture but the rest will pretty much stay the same.'

Jason bobbed his head in approval. 'That's as it should be.'

Another morning spent trying to rid the railway building of grime and Daisy's hands were raw. She decided to take a break and investigate the abandoned railway carriage that sat beside the station. She leant forward until her body tilted enough for her to put her hands on the carriage window. She was a fraction overbalanced – it wasn't a comfortable position to hold for long. With the blind pulled down there was only a slit she could look through and it was dark inside. She cupped her hands to shield her eyes to help her see better. It appeared to be an empty shell. She wasn't expecting fitted seats and tables like in modern trains but she wondered if there may be some furniture. However, there was nothing but a few cardboard boxes scattered about. With no obvious treasure, the carriage would have to wait in line while she focused on the ticket office.

'What are we doing to this?' asked Max, when he saw her inspecting the old railway carriage.

Daisy noted his use of the word 'we' and raised her eyebrows. He seemed to be getting his feet under the table and it made her suspicious. 'I think that's part two of the project, assuming I can get part one off the ground.'

'It's worth having a look inside though. There might be more railway memorabilia in there.' The excitement was evident in his tone. 'You never know if you might find some original posters or . . .' Daisy was amused by how animated he was becoming at the thought of more train knick-knacks. Max pulled himself up and his expression changed to nonplussed, '. . . you know, in case there's something you can sell.' He coughed and tried the nearest door handle but found it locked. Daisy went to check the luggage cupboard and came back with the bunch of keys she'd seen there. Thankfully it was easy to identify the right one thanks to the large keyhole, and after squeezing some washing-up liquid into the old mechanism to provide some lubrication the key finally turned.

Daisy looked at Max and they shared the same gleeful

expression. They both reached for the door handle at the same time. Daisy stared at her hand covered by his. Neither of them moved or attempted to pull their hand away. Her pulse quickened. 'Okay, let's open it together. Three . . . two . . . one . . .' The handle turned with a reluctant creak as did the hinge when they pulled open the carriage door.

Daisy stepped over the gap into the carriage and straight away the smell hit her. She put her hand over her nose and turned to see Max's expression change as his nostrils were assaulted by the overwhelming stench of cat wee.

'Pissing hell,' said Max.

'Exactly.' Daisy reversed past him and almost fell out of the carriage in her haste to get away from the smell. Max grabbed her arm roughly. 'Ow.' Daisy tugged herself free and stepped onto the platform.

'Sorry,' said Max following her. 'I thought you were going to fall down the gap.' He pointed to the wide space between the carriage step and the platform.

'I'm fine. Thanks,' said Daisy her appreciation reluctant. She was perfectly fine, she knew the gap was there, he didn't need to keep trying to rescue her.

Daisy walked along the platform to one end of the carriage where a broken window was covered with board. 'I bet cats were getting in through this window until someone boarded it up. But they made a hell of a mess beforehand.'

'I hope they got the cats out before they boarded it up,' said Max, peering back in through the open door. 'I don't fancy zombie kitties.' He had a wide grin on his face.

'Zombies?'

'It could happen.'

'Okay, now we've found your level.'

'I'm going back in. If zombies attack, remember only a

head shot will kill them.' He leaped dramatically back inside the carriage making Daisy laugh.

Moments later he stuck his head out and waved at her. 'This place is full of cat poo but the good thing is it's so old it's fossilised and I can sweep it up.'

Daisy had to smile at his eagerness to clear up poo. 'Here you go,' she said, handing him a broom.

'It's the carpet that stinks, if we rip it out things will smell better a whole lot quicker.' He disappeared inside and Daisy stepped up onto the door plate but no further inside.

'No memorabilia then?' she called in to the carriage thinking of his earlier comment. 'Or little bits of history?'

'No, but the lamps are still in place and the walls are wallpapered – it's pretty amazing really—' Daisy's face registered her amusement and he quickly added '— if you like that sort of thing. You know, train nerds like Jason would love it.' Max swept harder and bits of rock-solid poo, like pebbles, shot into the cardboard box he was using to collect it all in.

'And you?' said Daisy. 'Come on, admit it, you're into this kind of thing too. Aren't you?'

Max didn't say anything – he continued to fire the ancient cat poo into the box like he was playing some weird game crossed between curling and target practice. Eventually he paused. 'Look, I'm not a full-on train geek like Jason. I just liked them a bit when I was a kid. I mean, what little boy doesn't want to be a train driver when he grows up? It's no big deal.' It was a plausible argument but Daisy wasn't convinced. She decided to leave him to it and get back to scrubbing the loos. Oh, the glamour, she thought.

Max didn't spot his father until he turned away from the bar with his pint in his hand and saw Pasco sat on the other side of the room staring at him. Max's heart sank; it was the same sensation he felt when he spotted a floater in the swimming pool. But in this case his instinct was to walk away. Avoiding a discussion with his father was always his preferred approach but having just bought a pint he wanted to savour, he was reluctant to down it, and he definitely wasn't going to leave it. His hesitation sealed his fate and his father made his apologies to the two men he was sitting with and came to join Max.

'Hello, son. I figured you'd turn up here eventually. I can't believe they shut down the Smuggler's Rest. Great little pub. Is this your regular now?' Pasco asked, pulling up a chair and gesturing for Max to sit. This was how he did it. He was a talker, a charmer and he drew you in every time. Max reluctantly sat down.

'Wouldn't say it was my regular but, yeah, I come in occasionally.' Max pushed his chair back to put some distance, as well as the table, between them.

'Oh, right. Monty said you were in most nights, but didn't run a tab.'

Max blinked slowly. Nice one Monty, he thought. 'Definitely no tab and I'm not starting one for you.' His voice was grim.

'Wouldn't expect you to,' said Pasco, knitting his fingers together in front of him, which emphasised the fact he didn't have a drink.

Max rolled his eyes, shoved his hand into his pocket and pulled out a five-pound note. 'Here, get yourself a drink. But that's all there is.'

'Thanks,' said Pasco patting him liberally on the back as he stood up.

Pasco soon returned with a drink and no change. 'I figured you were doing all right. What with the two jobs.' Pasco sipped his pint but watched Max intently for his reaction.

Max frowned. 'You've been spying on me?'

'Just taking an interest,' said Pasco. 'You're my son. I care about you.'

Max huffed. 'I'm just helping out a friend.'

'She's a very pretty friend.'

'It's Daisy Wickens.'

Pasco narrowed his eyes and then they sprang open as if he'd been poked with a pin. 'I remember her. Coral's niece. Right stroppy little mare.' He laughed at a memory. 'Her old uncle is a funny old sod too. What's his name?'

'Reg,' said Max, reluctant to fill in more information than was necessary.

'Yes. That's him, Reg.'

'He died,' said Max flatly.

'Not surprised – he must have been a hundred and fifty. Hang on, does this mean little Daisy has come into some cash? Is that why you're helping her out?' Pasco's tone was curious rather than accusatory but it hit a nerve; he had no idea how much Reg had meant to Max.

'No, it bloody well isn't,' snapped Max, deeply offended but not surprised. 'I'm not you, remember?'

'Yeah, I remember. If you'd been more like me, I might not have gone back inside.'

Max gritted his teeth and shook his head slowly. 'I wondered when you'd mention that. You still blaming me for getting caught?'

Pasco's tone softened considerably. 'No, Max.' He shook his head. 'And you shouldn't go blaming yourself either.'

'I bloody well don't. I count myself lucky I had the sense

not to turn up otherwise it would have been both of us banged up.' Max downed the rest of his pint. If he didn't leave now he'd say something he'd regret and whatever Pasco was he was still his dad. 'You might want to speak to Jason. There have been some break-ins so if you give him your alibis up front he may keep off your case.'

Pasco held up his hands. 'Not me guv. I'm on the straight and narra,' he said in a mock cockney accent. Max rolled his eyes, Pasco was still milking the lovable rogue routine.

'You planning on staying long?'

'I've just got back,' said Pasco, leaning back in his seat and putting his arms behind his head as if relaxing on the beach. 'I'm in no rush.'

'Bloody perfect,' said Max and he got up and left.

Chapter Sixteen

Max was dragging a huge piece of the rank carpet out of the carriage when Daisy arrived. He was putting in almost as many hours as she was, which was incredibly kind of him but she felt she should be paying him. The odd pint and pasty here and there didn't seem to match how much she appreciated his help. Being in almost daily contact had dampened the irritation between them as they focused on a shared goal and Daisy was thankful for it. It was tiring being annoyed with Max all the time, although she still had a niggling suspicion as to why he was being so helpful.

She looked around the car park: the weed killer had worked wonders and Max had cleared some of the dead plants. It was definitely looking more like a car park and less like a jungle.

'Morning. You're keen.'

'No, I wet the bed,' called back Max with a grin.

Daisy strode over. She had definitely warmed to Max. They had a similar sense of humour and despite his laddish exterior she was beginning to realise he was one of the decent ones. 'Here, let me give you a hand,' she said, grabbing hold of the carpet and giving the final tug it needed to pull it through the small doorway. They flung it onto the big pile of carpet Max had already removed.

They both eyed the large mound of old carpet with its interesting stains and heavy dose of eau de cat urine. 'What do we do with this now?' asked Daisy giving the pile a nudge with her shoe.

'Burn it,' said Max. 'I'll drag it to the middle of the car park and stick a match to it. Quite safe, there's nothing around to catch fire.'

'I don't think you can,' said Daisy, scratching her head. 'I read it in one of the many leaflets the man from the council gave me. I think we'll need a skip.' There wasn't much else to put in a skip making it seem like an expensive option.

Max puffed out his cheeks. 'Leave it to me. I'll sort it. At least in the meantime the pong will keep vandals away.'

'As long as I don't get more cats moving in.'

'Come and have a look inside,' said Max. He waved Daisy into the carriage and followed her. With all the blinds up it was filled with light. The carriage windows were big and although it was long and thin there was a surprising amount of space. 'I reckon you could get eight tables of four in here, and if you only turn half the tables that's forty-eight covers a night.'

Daisy laughed. 'Turning tables and covers? Where has all this jargon come from?'

'I looked some stuff up. That's all. It gave me some ideas.' Max looked embarrassed. Daisy hadn't meant to sound ungrateful; Max had just doubled her available space.

She gave him an affectionate nudge with her shoulder. 'What other ideas have you had?'

'Nothing else for in here but for the main building I think, if we're just serving drinks, some high-legged tables and stools would work well.'

'Sounds good.'

'I'll let the air circulate in here for a bit then we'll use it as a secure place to store stuff while the ticket office is being done up.'

'Thanks Max, you've done a great job.'

Max looked awkward. 'It's nothing. Come on, I need help fitting the new toilet seats.'

He really knew how to kill a moment.

While Daisy was holding the toilet seat in place and Max was concentrating hard on adjusting nuts and washers, she took the ideal opportunity to ask him a few questions and satisfy her curiosity. 'I've been thinking about what you said about your dad being in prison; he was always such a great bloke. Aunt Coral said he got mixed up with something.'

Max kept his eyes on the task. 'He's not a major criminal but he's also not as smart as he thinks he is. He knew what he was doing the night he got arrested and he paid the price.'

'What was he doing exactly?'

Max stopped tightening a nut and looked Daisy in the eye. 'He was smuggling.'

Daisy's brain went into overdrive of all the things he could have been smuggling. Drugs? Guns? Or perhaps even people? 'Smuggling what?' She tried hard to look nonchalant and not wide-eyed and eager.

'Wine and tobacco.'

Daisy was disappointed and it showed on her face. It wasn't exactly the crime of the century. 'Couldn't he just have gone on a booze cruise?'

'This was quite a bit bigger. He was meeting up with another boat offshore, from Belgium, full to the brim with cut-price high-end wine.'

Daisy was getting into the story now the danger level had perked up a little. 'What went wrong?'

Max pushed his hair out of his eyes. 'He was late . . . and the Belgian boat had been spotted by a trawler. He was on his own so by the time they had transferred everything to his boat the authorities had been alerted and he was picked up.' Max sat back on his haunches and sighed. 'And it was my fault.'

Daisy let go of the toilet seat and it make a clunk as it hit the porcelain bowl narrowly missing Max's fingers, but she wasn't thinking about that any more, she was focused on Max. 'How?'

Max rubbed his chin. 'I was meant to be helping him that night. If I'd been there he would have left on time, loaded up and got away much quicker.'

Daisy watched Max for a moment. He looked forlorn. 'Were you and your dad in on it together?'

Max shook his head. 'Not exactly. I got into a bit of bother when Mum left. Just petty stupid teenage stuff and one night this copper, he's retired now, he gave me such a bollocking, told me I was going to end up like my old man and he shut me in a cell for the night. He rang Dad but he was out. I was there all night and half the next morning until Dad bothered to start trying to find me. Being locked up freaked me out. The thought of being shut up for hours on end when you're used to total freedom and the sound of the sea. I knew then I couldn't cope with going to prison and vowed to sort myself out. Dad kept on badgering me to do this one job with him and he wouldn't let up. He told me everything depended on it and it would be his last job. He said maybe with some cash behind him he could get Mum back.' Max gave a cynical half laugh. 'In the end I caved in. I said I'd help him but when it came to it, I couldn't. I was terrified of being caught. Of being locked up. I chickened out.'

'And you blame yourself for him being arrested?'

'Of course, wouldn't you?'

'No. He knew what he was getting into. He's a grown man. You did the right thing by not getting involved.'

'Only I never bothered to tell him. I just didn't show up.'

Daisy stood up straight, her thighs were starting to burn from being stuck in a crouching position. 'It's still not your fault.'

'Maybe.' He didn't look convinced as he got back to work on the toilet seat. There was a knock on the window and Pasco's face loomed at the frosted pane. 'Talk of the Devil,' said Max.

Daisy went to let Pasco in. 'He's in the loo,' she said, inviting Pasco inside. She was about to shut the door when Aunt Coral's car hooted announcing she was outside the railings. Daisy jogged across the car park to let her in. 'Hi, everything okay?' asked Daisy, starting to pull open the makeshift gate.

'It's all right. I don't need to come in. I brought you this.' Aunt Coral handed her an innocuous-looking plain white envelope through the car window but as soon as Daisy saw it she realised why Aunt Coral had bothered to drive it over. The franking informed her it was from the council offices. Daisy thumbed the envelope and stared unblinking at her name and address.

'Are you going to open it?

At last Daisy tore her eyes away from the envelope. 'Actually, I think I might wait. I'm in the middle of some-thing right now.'

Aunt Coral watched her. 'It's up to you. I just hope it's good news. But if it isn't, remember it's not the end of the world.' Aunt Coral leaned out and patted Daisy's arm.

'Sure. Thanks,' was all Daisy could manage.

Aunt Coral restarted the engine, but something behind Daisy made her aunt stiffen and Daisy instinctively spun around to see what had had that effect on her. Pasco was standing on the station platform chatting to Max. Daisy looked from Pasco and back to Aunt Coral, she had gone quite pale.

'Are you okay?' asked Daisy.

Aunt Coral swallowed and seemed to pop out of her trance-like state. 'Is that, um . . .'

'Pasco, Max's dad.'

Aunt Coral looked flustered. 'Well, now. I need to . . . um . . . dash.' She crunched the gears of the car and laughed awkwardly at her mistake. As Pasco turned in the direction of the car Aunt Coral set off the windscreen wipers and with an unexpected blast of the horn she finally slammed the car into reverse.

'Bye, love,' she said with one last peek at Pasco. Daisy waved her off and wandered back across the car park onto the platform and sat down with a thud letting her legs dangle over the edge.

'Right, I have places to be. I'll leave you kids to it,' said Pasco and he strolled away turning up his collar against the autumn breeze. There was something about the way he walked that reminded her of Max – perhaps it was the confident swagger. She stopped watching Pasco and focused on the innocuous white envelope in her hands. Whatever was inside could change everything or nothing. Daisy took a deep breath, held it for a second and then folded up the envelope and hastily shoved it into her back pocket. She needed a bit of time to work through how she would feel either way. She needed to be prepared. She always liked to be prepared. She hated surprises, they were just a shock in disguise and the only way to handle them was to be well prepared. While she was mulling this over she went inside to find something to keep herself busy.

A couple of hours later Max stuck his head around the door to the luggage store where Daisy was busy washing down the walls. 'Come on,' he said. 'I'm buying you an ice-cream.' Except for the breeze it was oddly warm for late September and the thought of an ice-cream was always appealing.

They locked up and strolled down the hill to the beach café. Unsurprisingly it was quiet; a few local boys were kicking a football about and the fish stall was shutting up. Daisy went and sat at one of the many empty picnic benches while Max got the ice-creams. The picnic benches were a permanent feature in summer as the tide didn't reach that far up the beach in the warmer months with the occasional exception of a freak storm.

'Here you go,' said Max, handing her a giant swirly white mass balanced precariously on a wafer cone with two chocolate flakes sticking out at odd angles.

'Wow. It's huge,' said Daisy, taking it from him and starting to lick around the edges.

'You can thank Tamsyn for that,' he said, motioning towards the beach café where Tamsyn was waving furiously. 'I only paid for small ones.' Daisy gave her a thumbs up with her free hand and took a bite off the nearest flake.

They sat in silence for a while both demolishing their ice-creams. When Daisy popped the last bit of wafer into her mouth and savoured the remnants of the sweet creamy mixture, Max started to chat.

'I'm guessing that's the decision from the planning office.'

He pointed to the letter lying ominously on the picnic table between them.

'Yep. What do you think it says?' She raked her teeth across her lip and searched Max's face for reassurance.

'You'll only know if you open it.'

'That's what I'm afraid of.' She ran a finger across her name on the envelope. She couldn't think of anything before that had so determined her future. Perhaps if she'd stayed long enough to finish a degree this is how receiving the results would have felt.

She knew Max was right and she had to open the letter but as soon as she did everything would change: either it would be a yes and she would have to get serious about developing the old railway as a business or it would be a no and she would be facing the best part of nine months in Ottercombe Bay with nothing to do. Or would a no mean it was time to move on regardless?

'For Christ sake. The suspense is killing me.' Max shoved the envelope closer to Daisy. Without thinking she picked it up, ripped it open and pulled out the letter. Her eyes scanned the lines quickly but her expression gave nothing away.

'Well?' asked Max. 'Are we in business?' For the first time, he looked apprehensive, as if he too had a lot riding on this decision.

Daisy pursed her lips, folded up the letter and returned it to what was left of the envelope. Her eyes downcast she said nothing but looked totally dejected.

'Crap,' said Max reading the situation. 'They're total idiots at the bloody council. But this isn't the end. You can appeal, we'll fight it. I'll help you.' He reached a hand towards her but it only made it halfway across the picnic bench. 'Come on, Daisy. Don't give up. Turning that place into a gin bar is still a brilliant idea.'

'You would say that, it was your idea,' she said, flatly keeping her gaze down but a treacherous grin spread across Daisy's face. 'But it was a brilliant idea and that's why they've approved the planning permission!'

The whoops that followed had people stopping and staring at the two mad people jumping up and down on the top of a picnic table.

Chapter Seventeen

Tamsyn checked her watch as she entered the pub and nearly bumped straight into Jason. 'Ooh, sorry.'

'We were nearly bang on time,' said Jason, standing back to let her go first.

She giggled. 'Were you summoned too?'

'Yes, but I didn't expect Max to be here yet. He said if I got here first I was to get a round in.' Jason scanned the pub and headed for the bar. 'You grab a table and I'll get the drinks. What would you like, Tamsyn?'

Jason was such a gentleman, thought Tamsyn. 'Martini and lemonade please.'

Jason got their drinks and sat down next to Tamsyn.

'I'll get the next round. I'm not totally broke.'

'Sure,' said Jason.

'And I'm researching how to become a curator of buttons in a museum.'

'That would be a perfect job for you,' said Jason, his expression genuine.

'I know. I just need to find a museum with a large button collection.'

'I'm guessing Max and Daisy have some big news to share,' said Jason.

'Do you think they're an item?' Tamsyn excitedly bobbed up and down in her seat.

'I doubt it. They bicker all the time.' He took a sip of his shandy.

'I think that's all sexual tension.'

Jason flushed slightly. 'Or they just can't stand each other.'

Tamsyn looked disappointed. 'Could be, I guess. I was hoping they would hit it off and Daisy would stick around. I like having her back.'

'Me too,' said Jason.

'Have you got a bit of a crush on Daisy?' asked Tamsyn, looking at him through her eyelashes.

Jason started fiddling with the tray. 'Goodness, no. She's very lovely, of course, but way out of my league.' He gave a sad little laugh.

'You're right; I think she's out of both of our leagues.'

'How do you mean?' asked Jason, a little more colour coming to his cheeks.

'As a friend, I mean, she could do way better than me,' said Tamsyn and they both sighed and sat back in their seats.

'Will you hurry up. We are seriously late,' said Daisy, putting her hands on her hips. They had worked hard for the rest of the day buoyed by their good news. Max had ducked out for a couple of hours to give a few swimming lessons and then he'd insisted on removing the shelving from the cupboard, which was trickier than it looked.

Max glanced casually over his shoulder. 'Chill out. Tamsyn and Jason will be fine.'

'You don't know they'll both turn up. Either of them might be sitting there all alone thinking it's a joke.'

Max stopped fiddling with the lock and gave it a final

tug to check it was definitely secure. 'Really? Have you not met Jason the Timekeeper and Tamsyn the On Time fairy?'

He was probably right but she still didn't like being this late, although she had enjoyed herself today. Everything was now clean and prepared – all she had to do was hire a builder, have the wall taken out, and get the water and electric connected and she was almost in business.

A thought struck her. 'Cock-a-doodle-doo.'

'What?' said Max spinning around, his face contorted in glee at her choice of swear word.

'When they knock the cocking wall down everything will get covered in dust. What a total waste of time.'

Max patted her shoulder and her body jolted at the contact. 'They'll put plastic down and I bet they won't make as much mess as you think. Come on or we'll be late,' he teased and jogged off across the car park.

When Max and Daisy dashed into the pub like they were ending a race, they both clocked Jason and Tamsyn sitting very close to each other chatting animatedly.

'See they're fine,' said Max. 'And they've got the drinks in.' He strode over looking pleased with himself.

They seemed more than fine to Daisy. There was something about their body language, something about how they were looking at each other. There had been a change and it felt significant.

'Hiya, this mine? Thanks,' said Max, picking up the full pint and taking a long drink.

'I'm sorry we're late . . .' started Daisy pulling out a chair.

'You're not late,' said Tamsyn.

'Actually they are,' said Jason leaning into Tamsyn to show her the face of his wristwatch.

Daisy and Max both spotted the closeness and raised their eyebrows in unison as Jason and Tamsyn dissolved into childish giggles. When they realised Daisy and Max were watching them they slid apart.

Jason straightened. 'What's the reason for calling this auspicious gathering?'

Daisy put down her wine glass. 'I—' She started but then looked at Max, she could feel his eyes on her. 'Actually, *we* wanted to share some good news with you both.'

'See I told you,' whispered Tamsyn to Jason.

'I heard from the planning officer today—' She left a dramatic pause '—and we have permission for change of use and to take down the internal wall.'

'Brilliant,' said Jason standing up to shake their hands. Tamsyn squealed and dashed to give Daisy a hug.

'I can't believe it. You're going to run your own business,' said Tamsyn followed by a small shriek.

Daisy froze. It suddenly hit home. It had been an idea before, just something that might come about but now it was definitely happening. She would be in charge of her own business. She would be her own boss. She took another long drink of wine.

'Steady on,' said Max, pointing at her almost empty glass.

'I think I need another one.' She downed the last bit.

'You're not driving home, are you?' Jason asked.

'Nope, the motorbike is officially dead and I have no money to replace it,' said Daisy.

'I know someone that might want it for parts,' said Max.

'Sure, it's no good to me,' said Daisy. 'Same again?' She gestured to the table before heading to the bar.

Monty was there waiting. 'You celebrating?' His face was dour.

'Yes. I've just got planning perm—' Daisy noticed Monty's expression and stopped mid-word, making her look like a primary school teacher trying to quieten a class.

'And you thought you'd celebrate in here?' Monty shook his head as he pulled Max's pint.

Daisy pulled back her shoulders. 'Come on, Monty. You're a businessman, you know how it works. There's room for both of us. We can even help each other. If my new gin bar brings people in to the bay they'll be coming in here for meals – well, this is where I'll be recommending,' said Daisy, with a confident nod. Monty appeared to be considering this whilst he made up Tamsyn's martini and lemonade. 'And I'd promote your quiz night. I'm sure people who come in the day to see the restored railway station are less likely to be gin people and more the sort of folk who would enjoy a pint of real ale and a pub quiz.' It was a long shot on her part, but he was tilting his head, which was a good sign. He finally nodded.

'I guess we'll cope,' he said, the reluctance evident in his voice.

'Brilliant. Thanks Monty. You're a star. Keep the change,' said Daisy, handing him a twenty-pound note. Monty took the note and as soon as Daisy had turned her back he checked it under the UV lamp before putting it in the till.

The rest of the evening went well, with Daisy telling the others about her favourite gins she wanted to stock. When Daisy eventually stood up to leave, she swayed slightly, and Max wondered if she may have had one or three too many. Jason waved his car keys, having only had the one shandy he was happy to play taxi and drop the others home.

'You're all right, Jay,' said Max. 'I need to finish this.' He indicated the quarter of a pint still in his glass.

'I can wait for you if you like,' said Jason.

'Nah, you're fine. Get the ladies home. The walk will do me good.'

'Right you are,' said Jason, as he tried to guide the swaying females through the maze of chairs and tables.

Max savoured the last of his drink and wished he'd had more than a slice of toast and an ice-cream all day. He decided to stop off at the kebab place on his way home.

He merrily munched his kebab as he walked along, looking up from time to time to check he wasn't about to bump into someone. It was almost as bad as texting and walking. On his next glance up, he spotted something. Just a shadow, a quick glimpse of someone in the old train station car park.

Max took a couple more bites, rammed the carton into a nearby bin and ran full pelt towards the car park. He had the keys for the padlock but it was quicker to jump up the railings and swing himself over the top. Any noise he made would hopefully alert the intruder and they'd have made off before he got to them. Max sprinted towards the platform where he'd last seen the shadow and saw someone was crouching under the far end of the carriage.

Max stopped and caught his breath. 'Come out. I can see you. The police are on their way.' It was a lie but a quick call to Jason could have him there in a few minutes if it came to that.

He saw the intruder stand up and step out of the shadows.

'Bloody hell, Dad!' Max spun around with his hands on his head. 'If you are breaking in here . . . so help me God . . .'

'No. Of course not. I just need somewhere to kip for the night that's all. I wondered if you might have left it open for your old dad.'

'No, you didn't. You were breaking in.'

'Were you telling the truth about the cops?' Pasco looked shifty as he checked the nearby road.

'No. I was hoping to warn off whatever idiot was thinking about breaking in to an empty building.' Max made a mental note to talk to Daisy about CCTV and an alarm.

'That's good, then. Can you open the place up? Please.'

'No.'

'Can I kip on your sofa instead?

'No.' Max could feel his blood pressure increase at the thought of the two of them crammed into his tiny bedsit.

'Better be here then.' Pasco nodded at the old railway carriage.

'You are bloody unbelievable,' said Max, running his hands through his hair in frustration. 'This is Daisy's place not mine. She'll kill me if she finds you living in it.'

Pasco held his hands up. 'No, not living, only sleeping. I'll be gone as soon as the sun rises. I've noticed you're always here first so she doesn't have to know. I can see you've tidied the carriage out lovely. You're a good worker you are, son. I'm proud of you.'

Max wanted to stick his fingers in his ears. He knew where this was going. Pasco would tell him a sob story and then he'd cave in. It was what always happened, however much Max told himself he wouldn't be persuaded by his father it happened all the same. At the end of the day this was his dad, what else could he do?

'It's been tough coming back to reality after such a stretch inside. I will get on my feet soon enough but—'

'One night only.' Max held up his index finger to emphasise his point and Pasco made a cross over his heart. Max shook his head. 'I mean it. One night and you had better be gone at first light and leave no sign you were ever here. Got it?'

'Loud and clear. You're a good boy, Max,' said Pasco,

pulling him into a reluctant hug and slapping him warmly on the back.

Pasco appeared to wipe a tear from his eye, but Max figured it was all part of the performance. He unlocked the carriage and snatched away the keys when Pasco went to take them. 'Oh no you don't. I need those.'

'You're not going to lock me in?' Pasco looked alarmed. 'I may have developed a bit of a phobia.'

'No, you'll have to wedge this behind the door to stop any intruders,' said Max, handing him a piece of wood from the pile of shelving he and Daisy had smashed up.

'Will do,' said Pasco taking the wood and shuffling something from under one arm to the other.

'Is that a picnic rug?' asked Max, squinting at the thing Pasco had under his arm.

'Yes, it's quite good really. I can wrap myself in the tartan side and—'

'If Jason finds out you've nicked it he'll charge you. You know that, don't you? Jeez.' Max spun around, his frustration propelling him.

'Hang on. I didn't steal this and to be honest—' Max snorted his derision at the comment but Pasco continued '—I am hurt you think I would.'

'Then how come you have a stolen picnic rug?'

'I found it and before you poo-poo my explanation, listen. I saw some youths throwing it to each other in the park and I thought it was an odd thing for a bunch of teenage boys to have. I waited and eventually they got bored kicking it about when it burst open and they couldn't fold it back up again so they left it and I picked it up.'

His explanation was plausible if unlikely. 'Okay, but it's stolen.'

'I didn't know that,' said Pasco, amenably. 'I'm guessing the shop won't want it back now.'

Max had to admit that was unlikely if someone had been sleeping on it. 'Just keep it out of sight because others will jump to the same conclusion I did.'

'You know sometimes it's like you actually want me to fail,' said Pasco.

Max made a series of huffing and tutting sounds. 'Don't be daft. Why would I want that?'

Pasco seemed to consider this before answering. 'So you can put me back in the right pigeonhole. You see, at the moment, I don't fit how you expect me to be and you don't know what to do. Max, you need to accept I've changed.' Pasco put his hands on his son's shoulders and looked him in the eye.

'We'll see,' said Max, and he pulled away.

'Thanks for this.' Pasco stepped inside the carriage.

'Pull all the blinds down, I don't want anybody seeing you're in there,' said Max, ignoring his father's thanks.

Pasco waved before shutting the door. Max watched him pull down all the blinds. How had his father ended up sleeping rough already? There was little more he could do tonight, he shoved the keys into his pocket and walked off as his stomach gave a rumble. To think he'd thrown away the rest of his kebab for that.

Chapter Eighteen

The next morning Daisy stepped inside the old railway building and instinctively knew there was something different. At first she couldn't put her finger on exactly what it was. She stood there as her eyes darted about. Then she saw it. There was no patch of light shining off the clean slate floor. She looked up. 'Max. Something weird is going on,' she called over her shoulder.

Max came hurrying into the room looking like he was about to fight someone. He spun around. 'What?' He was still opening and closing doors as he spoke.

Daisy pointed to the ceiling and when Max stopped for a moment he followed her gaze. They both studied the vaulted ceiling with its exposed beams for a moment.

'What?' said Max sounding exasperated.

'Do you see the inside of the roof?' asked Daisy still pointing upwards.

'Yeah . . .' Max's expression changed. 'Where's the bloody hole in the roof gone?'

'Exactly,' said Daisy, and they both continued to stare.

From the outside, everything looked in order. It had been difficult to spot the missing roof tile before and now it was no longer missing you couldn't see where it had been replaced, but for some reason Max was on a mission to investigate. When he went off in search of a ladder Daisy decided to leave him to it and make some phone calls. She needed to get some workmen in and get some quotes.

The following day the ticket office was a hive of activity with both the man from the Electricity board, an electrician and a builder. Daisy didn't like to stray too far from them; their discussions weren't particularly interesting but she wanted to be there at the point where someone either highlighted a major issue or unexpected cost. Instead there seemed to be lots of mumbled conversations, which were making her uneasy.

At last the group all turned in Daisy's direction, which made her a little self-conscious and she tucked an imaginary piece of hair behind her ear out of habit – there was no need as today her abundant hair was neatly cocooned in a trendy scarf. 'Right, let's have the bad news first,' said Daisy, rubbing her hands together. At least she'd know what level of disaster she was dealing with.

The men all looked at each other and then back at Daisy. At last the man from the Electricity board spoke. 'The wiring needs replacing but I'm happy to reconnect you. Obviously you can't switch on yet.'

Daisy beamed and the electrician spoke. 'I can start work on rewiring as soon as the main building work is finished and like I said before it's a small building, it's not a big job.'

Daisy was surprised. The builder chimed in. 'I can start tomorrow. The job I was working on is having a cash flow crisis so a couple of days without me on site might make them find the money quicker.' A comment that received firm agreement from the electrician.

'Right. All good then?' Daisy wanted to be absolutely

sure and the responding nodding heads gave her the answer she was hoping for.

She handed a key to the builder and decided to have a couple of days off. There was nothing she could do while he was taking the wall out and fitting counter tops. He also knew the electrician and a plumber and was going to call them as soon as they could get to work – he was pretty much managing this phase for her. She was still wondering who her guardian angel was who had fixed her roof; for Daisy it summed up Ottercombe Bay – the sort of community where people helped each other.

She decided her first task would be to have a lie in. She had been getting up super early every day for the past couple of weeks and she was looking forward to some duvet time.

Unfortunately, the next morning she discovered Bug had snuck in during the night – he appeared to have used the stack of library books she'd taken out about gin as a set of steps to get onto the bed and was now snoring loudly at her side, and no amount of nudging seemed to interrupt his flow. When he snored it sounded like someone wheezing into a didgeridoo. Eventually she relented and swung her legs out of bed. She had a whole day ahead of her and no idea what to do with it.

Bug sprang to life, jumped off the bed and started scratching at the door. Daisy decided if she was getting up she may as well take him for a walk. At least then she might be able to get some peace and a chance to start looking at setting up a website for the bar-cum-hot chocolate cabin. She decided she would have a good think about how to market the place because at the moment it felt like it had too many potential guises.

An uneventful walk on a blustery October beach with

Bug was just what she needed to blast the cobwebs away. It also gave her a chance to think about marketing the business, and hopefully the brisk walk would wear Bug out for a few hours and buy her some peace and quiet. She needed to finish reading all the gin books she'd borrowed.

When she got back she did some research on local gin distilleries and found there were a few dotted around not too far away. Her love of gin and desire to make the bar a success motivated her to add to the knowledge she'd picked up on her travels. A couple of emails had her booked in for a distillery tour and meetings with a Head of Sales and Master Distiller as well as samples winging their way to her from a couple of the other craft distilleries. Everyone seemed keen to support her and to share their knowledge of gin which was encouraging.

She had had similar success on the chocolate front with two particularly promising telephone conversations with suppliers prepared to come out to her and go through their hot chocolate offerings. Both were keen to secure an exclusive deal with her, making her feel rather important and slightly scared at the same time – this was a big decision.

By the time Aunt Coral got home Daisy was tired but buzzing. She had made some good connections and the prospect of learning about the products she was keen to specialise in was exciting and new. It felt like a fresh start. The thought of this made her feel guilty. Here she was focusing on the future when she still hadn't solved the puzzles of the past. The locket was still missing and she had made no inroads into finding out what had happened to her mother.

Daisy was miles away as she sucked up a long strand of spaghetti. Her mobile buzzed into life and she looked at the screen. It was the builder and she sat up straight to answer the call. She guessed he was calling to update her on the day's progress and she felt kind of important.

'Daisy, we've got a problem. We need to stop work until further notice.' His voice was stern.

Daisy blinked and put down her fork. 'Why?' Her voice came out as a croak. What on earth had happened?

'Bats.'

Daisy scrunched up her face as she tried to comprehend what he'd said. 'Bats?'

'Yes. There's evidence of bats living in the space above the toilets. We have to down tools until it's sorted.'

'Can you get rid of them or shall I?'

'No. You get prosecuted for that sort of thing. You need to get in touch with the bat helpline.'

Daisy started to laugh and then she sang the *Batman* theme tune. 'Oh, that's a good one. You nearly had me there.' She carried on chuckling with relief.

'Daisy, this isn't a joke. Bats are a protected species. We can't do any more work until it's sorted. I have to go. I'll let the other guys know and I'll wait to hear from you. Okay?'

Daisy stopped laughing. 'Er, okay. Thanks.' She ended the call and saw Aunt Coral looking as worried as she felt.

The next day she learned more than she ever needed to know about bats and spent hours on the phone talking to a variety of people about her bat problem. It turned out the National Bat Helpline was real and incredibly helpful, even if everything they told her made her shoulders sag. Basically, they explained that bats were a protected species and cannot be disturbed and anyone that does risks prosecution. Her builder had done the right thing in stopping work but now she had to wait for an ecologist to pay her a visit to determine what was best for the bats. Until then everything was on hold.

It had all been going brilliantly but now it felt like someone had pressed the emergency stop button. She no longer felt confident to invest any more time or money because the bats could signal the end of everything. If the ecologist said the building work would cause the bats to leave then it was game over and the flying rodents had won themselves a lifetime's tenancy and Daisy's dreams were vaporised. At best it was looking like the opening would be hugely delayed probably even missing the lantern parade so her opportunities for income were quickly slipping away and her chances of failure were increasing.

Daisy needed a break from the bat crisis so she turned her attention to the other thing worrying her. An internet search had pulled up nothing at all about her mother's death. Given she died at a time when the internet was in its infancy this shouldn't have surprised her, but it did. She wasn't entirely sure what she had been hoping to find, but something to give her a starting point would have been helpful. With a heavy heart she gave up searching.

She decided to try and come up with a name for the business but despite making two long lists she still couldn't decide. Her heart wasn't in it now it was all in jeopardy. Half of the names sounded too chocolatey and the other half too alcoholic – perhaps the combination of gin and chocolate wasn't such a good idea after all. She couldn't move forward with anything.

She looked about her for something else to do; she still had a few hours before Aunt Coral came home from work. Bug sat at her feet and looked at her unblinking, with such big eyes he couldn't help but look like he was staring. Daisy was getting used to Bug and his ways. I might as well take the dog for a walk as sit here going slightly insane, she thought. Sitting still had never been a skill she'd been able to master. She put on Bug's collar and for once he looked quite keen to be going out.

A cold wind whipped across the beach and there were very few people about. The wind didn't seem to bother Bug; he was pulling on the lead. She could sense he wanted to have a run and let off some steam. She looked furtively around before crouching down to Bug's level.

'Now, listen up, Bug. If I let you off, you have to come back when I call you. Or alternatively go straight home. Got it?'

Bug groaned and lay down. Daisy sent up a silent prayer and unclipped his lead. There was a momentary delay before Bug leaped to his feet and charged off like a maniac, scuffing up sand in his wake. Daisy laughed as she watched him career about without a care in the world. While he chased about the beach she wandered down to the shore, chose some flat stones on the way and lost herself for a few minutes watching each one skim across the surface of the sea. It was a bit rough today for skimming pebbles but she could still manage to get some to bounce on the surface of the incoming tide. She had spent many a happy hour skimming stones with her father as a child and was pleased to find she hadn't lost the knack. She found it calmed her and helped her see the bat problem as just another hurdle she needed to find a way over.

When she had run out of flat stones she pushed her hands deep into her pockets to warm them up and turned around to watch Bug. She scanned the beach but there was no sign of him. She waited for a moment, expecting him to appear, but there was nothing except the harsh October breeze, which seemed to have more of a chill now. She frantically looked up and down the beach. 'Bug!' she shouted, but it was lost on the wind.

Daisy spent the next thirty minutes marching the length of Ottercombe beach calling for Bug and checking all the nooks and crannies around the fishing boats and beach huts in case he was hiding, but there was no trace of him. The beach café had recently shut up for the winter and there was nobody else about. As she was considering giving up, in the hope he had headed home without her, she heard a faint bark at the far end of the beach and she stormed off in that direction.

At the furthest part of the beach were some steps leading to a series of giant boulders that had once been part of the cliff. She clambered down onto the driest of them while the sea battered the others.

'Bug,' she called again. 'Bugsy Malone.'

This time there was a barked reply. She felt elated that he'd bothered to respond and slightly cross she'd had to come this far to retrieve him. The bark was all echoey and she looked towards an opening at the base of the cliff. A bit of mountaineering later and she was crouching to avoid hitting her head as she looked inside the cavernous hole in the rock. Great Uncle Reg had shared stories of the cave, tales full of smugglers and heroes, but the cave had always been strictly out of bounds when she was a child. It seemed to go back quite a way and she could hear scratching noises echoing around her. Perhaps he'd got himself stuck? She ventured on deeper into the cave calling his name at intervals. She inched her way along, careful where she put her feet because she had no idea how safe it was and it was hard to see. The further she went the darker it became.

The headspace varied greatly as she made her way in deeper, so progress was slow.

'There you are!' exclaimed Daisy, spotting Bug at the back of the dimly lit cave where he was digging frantically. 'There's no buried treasure here, Bug. Come on.' She looked about her, she'd come quite a long way in from the beach and it had been tricky underfoot scrambling over seaweed-covered rocks. It was a relief to have found him at last but Bug didn't look like he was ready to leave. She checked her pockets – she had one doggy treat left.

'Bug!' she called and held out the treat. He paused and turned to look at her, his black face covered in damp sand making it look like he had a beard. 'Come and get the treat, Bug.' Bug went back to digging.

Daisy had to crawl for the next section until she was an arm's length away from him. 'Bug, treat.' She held out her hand. He paused for a moment, trotted over and hoovered up the treat but not before she had grabbed him round his soggy middle and bundled him unceremoniously under her arm.

She started to head back the way she'd come. Crawling backwards was tricky and slow with a dog under one arm. She had to keep stopping to readjust her hold on her wriggling companion. It seemed harder somehow, as though there was less light and the rocks were becoming more slippery than before. The sound of the sea was also louder and echoed as she headed in the opposite direction. It took her an age to make her way back with a struggling Bug to contend with. She was getting tired as she simultaneously tried to hold on to the grumpy dog and clamber over a particularly large rock, one she remembered being not far from the entrance. As they descended the other side her feet didn't meet with damp solid sand as she had expected but splashed into seawater. It was a shock to be unexpectedly up to her thighs in freezing cold water and she gasped. Bug made a bid for freedom and landed with a splash in the ink-coloured ripples and doggy paddled out of reach.

Now don't panic, she told herself as her pulse started to race and fear gripped her. She waded after Bug but when he exited the cave he was quickly engulfed in a wave. 'Bug!' she shouted but she lost sight of him. She was almost out of the cave and the water was getting rapidly deeper. She had to duck down to get out, which meant almost fully immersing herself in the icy water. The tide was coming in and was getting rough as it bashed into the rocks at the cave entrance buffeting her about. It was dusk; almost all the light had been wrung from the day. She squinted to try to catch a glimpse of Bug as another giant wave crashed into the rocks drenching her and immediately chilling her to the core. How had it changed that quickly? More importantly how was she going to get herself to safety?

Daisy made a few attempts to move from rock to rock, the rough barnacles scratching at her soft palms as she tried to grip the surface. Determination and fear pushed her on but every direction was blocked by the encroaching tide and she found herself forced back to the cave entrance for fear of being bashed into the rocks. She pulled out her phone. It slipped and she almost dropped it from her cold wet hands. It was wet, but still working. Gripping it tightly she dialled the coastguard's number that Max had made her add to her directory.

It was a short conversation where an efficient gentleman told her to get to the highest point and to wait as help was already on the way.

She did as she was told and scrambled back up the

nearest large slippery rock, the smell of wet seaweed striking her nostrils. She perched on top and hugged her knees to her sodden chest. With each wave the water splashed higher and the cold seeped into her soul until her whole body was shivering uncontrollably. She called for Bug a few times but she doubted she could be heard over the sea, which was reminding her of its power and dominance with every surge of the tide.

The weak sun became engulfed by dark clouds. A deeper chill descended taking Daisy's hopes with it. A picture of her mother settled in her mind. Was this how she had felt, those last moments before she died? Daisy felt warm tears trickle down her cold cheeks.

She lost track of the minutes as the salt spray whipped her face. The sea was all around her now. Her arms and legs were numb with the cold and she was struggling to think straight as her teeth chattered uncontrollably. She closed her eyes and tried to will herself to warm up. Another angry wave struck the rock drenching her. Panic clawed at her stomach. As the wave receded it tried to pull her into the dark turbulent water with it. She clung to the rock for her life.

Chapter Nineteen

It could have been the wave dousing her already sodden state, but something made Daisy look up from her perilous position. She was clinging to an ice-cold rock now almost submerged in the sea. She had no idea how long she'd been stranded there. Salt water stung her eyes making it difficult to focus. She blinked rapidly. Daisy wasn't sure what she was expecting to see, but the sight of Max manoeuvring the inshore lifeboat close to the mouth of the cave was a surprise, and a huge relief. She was safe.

'Daisy! Stay where you are. Are you hurt?' His voice was soothing and reassuring. Daisy couldn't speak for the chattering of her teeth, so she shook her head and cold wet strands of hair lashed at her chilled face stinging her cheeks.

Max handed control of the boat to Jason whilst another man radioed an update. Max leapt from the boat onto the rock in one confident movement. Before she could think how to clamber from the water Max was already lifting her into his arms. She was quickly deposited into the boat and wrapped in foil like an oven-ready turkey. She'd had better days, and somehow she would have to explain to Aunt Coral that Bug was lost at sea. Max jumped back into the boat making it rock turbulently, which broke her train of thought. He gave her a look that her chilled brain struggled to interpret but she guessed it was somewhere between pity and annoyance. Daisy felt the need to explain.

She discovered that forming words with cold lips was extremely difficult. 'Bug ran off.'

'Bug came home without you. I was speaking to Coral when the coastguard call came through.' Max turned away and increased the might of the boat's engines. Daisy curled up into a tighter ball. Another point to Bug, she thought. The boat skimmed across the water hopping rhythmically over the waves making only a slight spray. The inshore coped effortlessly with the bad weather; if it hadn't been October and she hadn't been frozen to the core, she may almost have enjoyed it. Max squinted over his shoulder at her and she averted her eyes.

'You okay?' asked Jason. Daisy didn't want to talk, she just wanted to be warm again. She nodded and pulled the foil blanket tighter around herself. 'We'll soon have you warm, Daisy. You're doing really well.'

She closed her eyes and tried not to think about how foolish she'd been.

A day in bed with Aunt Coral fussing over her was mostly heartwarming but also partly frustrating. Aunt Coral couldn't seem to get past 'the what might have happened', which meant she was checking on Daisy every few minutes and almost drowning her in cups of tea. Once she was checked over by a medic and her body had returned to a normal temperature Daisy was basically fine. Apart from a few scratches on her palms there was no other evidence of her rescue, assuming you didn't count the front-page news it had generated for the local newspaper who'd made it seem far more dramatic than it had actually been.

The worst part for Daisy was how she felt. She had never felt so stupid in all her life, even including the time she'd sold timeshare in Spain dressed as a pineapple. She'd read stories of people being caught out by the tide and had always thought them idiotic. She had known the tide was coming in but had not registered the speed or that the end of the bay jutted out and would therefore be engulfed by the sea much sooner than the rest of the beach. It was her fault, but it was all because of a tiny canine villain who was getting closer to his goal of doing her in.

Bug was swanning around as if he'd had nothing to do with it and Aunt Coral was crediting him with raising the alarm – in Sea Mist Cottage he was practically a hero. Daisy saw the situation very differently, but she didn't hold a grudge. She had got herself into that mess so she was the one to take the blame. It showed her how easy it was to get caught out and it made her wonder if something similar had happened to her mother, but then that still wouldn't explain what she was doing on the beach in the middle of the night in March.

A few days passed, with Daisy spending most of her time chasing up the ecologist for her bat survey and trying to come up with a name for the bar, although it seemed less and less likely it would ever get off the ground. How could her plans be stopped by such a tiny thing as a bat? Who liked bats anyway? They were basically flying mice that featured heavily in horror movies – unless of course they were getting seriously bad PR, although right now she felt it was all justified. She was reaching the despairing stage as the bats had everything going in their favour and she didn't.

One morning she found herself having a silent weep,

which had caught her off guard. She suspected it was a combination of frustration over the bats and delayed shock. As she sat on the floor hugging her knees and waiting for it to pass, Bug marched in, letting the door bang open to announce himself. They stared at each other and Daisy sniffed back a tear. In an unprecedented move Bug trotted over, pawed at her gently and leaned closer and closer to her until he could get near enough to gently lick away her tears. Daisy still didn't like him being close to her face, but the tender contact softened her heart.

'Maybe you're not too bad after all,' she said, and he answered with a vigorous wag of his tail. Bug tried to lick the rest of her face making her bury her head in her top while he scrambled over her excitedly. Daisy found herself giggling and despite all that was going on, despite everything, she was starting to feel a fraction brighter.

After three weeks the shock of Daisy's rescue had waned and things were getting back to normal. Aunt Coral had stopped asking her how she was every five minutes and she hadn't gone over the 'what could have happened' scenario for at least twenty-four hours. Today was the day of the ecologist's visit and someone from the local bat group had arranged to meet Daisy at the railway building shortly before the ecologist. They were meeting at dusk, which sounded all very cloak and dagger to Daisy.

Daisy was sitting on the platform with her legs dangling down and her backside turning numb from the chill of the concrete when she spotted someone enter the car park. It was a stout woman with a ruddy complexion and a powerful stride.

'I'm Tabitha, Ottercombe Bat Group,' she said, marching up the platform and thrusting a large hand at Daisy.

191

'I'm Daisy,' she replied, her whole body vibrating with the firm handshake.

'And you have bats. How exciting.'

'Not if you have a deadline to meet and a bar to open.' Daisy couldn't keep the despondency from her tone.

'Can I get a look at them?' asked Tabitha, already scanning the building.

Daisy took her inside and showed her the now resident stepladder and the entrance into the loft space above the toilets supposedly where the bats had set up home, although Daisy hadn't actually seen any. Daisy left Tabitha with her head in the loft making ahh sounds. A black car pulled up and a slim man in dark clothes got out, put a black folder under his arm and strode over to Daisy. He looked more like someone from a spy thriller than an ecologist. She'd been expecting long hair and a beard at the very least.

'Miss Wickens? I'm here about the bat emergence survey.'

Before Daisy could get her words out Tabitha was already shaking his hand and introducing herself. 'I'll show you what I've discovered,' she said, leading the ecologist inside.

Daisy pulled her old leather jacket around her. She was cold and fed up. Everyone she'd spoken to had told her bats and their roosts were protected and she couldn't evict them so she already knew what the outcome would be. She had to resign herself to it. She had spent a chunk of Aunt Coral's money on the family white elephant but at least she could pay her back when she got her inheritance at the end of June. Just thinking about it made it seem a long way away especially if she was going to be twiddling her thumbs for the next seven months.

'A-hah,' said Tabitha with gusto, pulling Daisy back from her thoughts. 'This is where they're getting in.' She pointed to the peak of the gable end of the building whilst the ecologist made copious notes. Daisy sighed. She needed to think about shutting up the building permanently – it had been such a waste of time and money.

'Right,' said the ecologist, from behind her. Daisy got to her feet, took in a slow deep breath and prepared herself for the worst.

'You have greater horseshoe bats,' Tabitha butted in, her broad grin one to rival the Cheshire Cat. 'They're quite rare.' At least someone is pleased, thought Daisy. 'Sadly this one didn't make it.' Tabitha opened her cupped hands to reveal a tiny winged creature and Daisy stepped backwards. The ecologist took the bat from Tabitha and placed it in a plastic bag.

'It's a maternity roost,' said the ecologist, sealing the bag. Daisy was resigned. 'They've all departed now for winter hibernation but they'll be back next year. It's important to keep things as unchanged as possible.'

'Right,' said Daisy not really taking in what he was saying. Time to board the place up and forget about it.

'I can't complete a full survey because the bats aren't here so I'll be back in May. But in the meantime you have my permission to continue work.' He waited for a response but Daisy was just frowning. 'This explains everything,' he handed her a leaflet. 'Goodbye.'

'Hang on,' said Daisy blinking. 'Continue work? How can I have bats and meet hygiene regulations?'

'It's fine. They are completely separate. There's no evidence of bats in the main section of the building, only in one section of the loft area.'

'What? I just leave them and carry on?' Daisy was suspicious.

'Yes,' said the ecologist and Tabitha together.

'Brilliant. Thank you,' said Daisy, struggling to believe

this could work but she was willing to give it a go. After all, this man was the expert not her. She waved him off as Tabitha recounted all she knew about the greater horseshoe bat.

'Thanks for coming,' said Daisy, trying to stop Tabitha without appearing too rude.

'It was my absolute pleasure. Please call me as soon as you see the bats return,' said Tabitha.

'Of course.'

'Now I'm off to catch sight of some beaver,' said Tabitha with a nod. Daisy's face froze. 'They're thriving in the River Otter, you know,' she added, pulling her hand from her coat pocket. Daisy hoped she didn't have another dead bat in there. Tabitha handed her another leaflet. 'Good luck with the bar, you can rely on my support and I'm also a member of the OBOS,' she said, tapping the leaflet. 'Goodbye,' she called heartily. Daisy read the leaflet – 'Ottercombe Bay Operatic Society presents their rendition of *Pinocchio*'. She checked Tabitha was out of earshot before she let the laughter escape.

A few phone calls had the workmen all lined up again but they had lost three weeks and the builder wasn't keen to commit to a finish date. With little else she could do she headed off to a local distillery to increase her gin knowledge.

Aunt Coral's little car was weighed down with gin on the way home whilst Daisy was buoyed by her experience. She not only understood the fermentation and distilling process in great detail, she also knew exactly what she was looking for in a quality gin.

Daisy had been able to tour the small establishment, which was located in spare farm buildings on the Somerset border, proving you didn't need a huge factory to set up a craft gin distillery. She was buzzing with all she'd learned, including the origins and history of gin as well as the nitty gritty of understanding subtle differences made by botanicals added during the distilling process and how to describe them to customers. Her big revelation of the day was the discovery that gin was basically juniper-flavoured vodka.

The next day Daisy was in a good mood: the day at the distillery had fired up her enthusiasm and buoyed with new knowledge she was more confident about everything. Her good mood motivated her to take Bug for a walk. She liked the sense of freedom, the smell of the salt air – it calmed her somehow and made thinking easier and clearer. Walking was fast becoming a regular thing. The fact she had Bug with her was a slight downside, but she couldn't stay mad at him forever.

She was smiling as she strode down to the beach enjoying the bright November day and she was sure she could sense Bug's excitement radiating up the lead at the prospect of a run on the sand. Daisy couldn't help replaying the fateful day she'd had to be rescued, thanks to Bug, but when she reached the promenade she could see the tide was in enough to have blocked off access to the rocks and cave. If she let him off he would be confined to the single stretch of beach. They reached the sand and Bug started dancing around her like a lunatic and she knew she'd have to let him off the lead. To bring him here and not let him run around was tantamount to torture and despite Bug's best efforts to bump her off she wasn't the vengeful sort. She untangled her legs from the lead now wrapped around them both several times.

She crouched down. 'Now listen. This is your last chance,' she told him with a wag of her finger, which he strained hard to lick. 'If you run off, I swear, I will not bring you again. Got it?' Bug was snuffling around her feet and let out a giant sneeze as sand got stuck up his nose. 'I'll take that as a firm and binding yes.' She unclipped his lead and he sped off as if his tail was on fire. She chuckled at the sight and realised she was actually becoming quite attached to the small four-legged monster. He charged up and down the beach, darting in random directions whilst Daisy wandered down to the shoreline.

She watched the seagulls; some swooped above her but most of them bobbed up and down on the surface of the water as the waves slowly rolled in. There were definitely fewer gulls this time of year. Daisy wasn't sure where they went or why a few of them stayed. Perhaps, just like humans, some of them preferred to stay by the sea despite the change in weather.

This time she kept a closer eye on where Bug was, listening out for him running past. After a while she was aware she couldn't hear the sound of his paws tearing up the sand. She traced the myriad tracks across the beach, scanning for him but there was no sign and a now familiar feeling crept over her. 'Cock-a-doodle-doo,' she said into the wind.

Daisy strode up the beach. 'Bug!' she called, looking about her for a clue to his whereabouts. There were only the fishing boats, unless he'd already made a bolt for home. She marched over to the nearest row of fishing craft cursing the fact she had thought to trust the manipulative mutt yet again. She rounded the first large fishing boat, her eyes searching for any trace of the dog. Then she heard it, a low growl was coming from up ahead. 'Bug.' Daisy rushed on to the next boat and almost flung herself round its stern to see Bug tugging for all he was worth on a tangled mass of something she couldn't quite identify although the smell made her retch as she stepped closer.

'Drop it, Bug,' she instructed just at the moment Bug pulled with all his might and the boat trapping his prize finally let go. Bug got a better hold on it and began dragging it towards Daisy. She could now see it was a large rotting fish with most of its flesh missing but with the addition of plenty of seaweed. Daisy began reversing away. 'Bug,' she warned. 'Don't you dare.' But Bug was already proudly heaving it in her direction. She stepped backwards and was soon jogging back across the beach with Bug and the rotting fish in hot pursuit.

If she had been watching from a safe distance she probably would have laughed but with Bug, the evil genius, closing in on her with his new favourite thing in the world she was not seeing a funny side. She turned to see Bug on her heels and she could have sworn he was grinning. She was momentarily distracted by the billowing seaweed-wrapped skeleton, which was to be her downfall; her foot caught on a piece of driftwood and in slow motion she tumbled backwards landing with an uncomfortable thud as Bug took a leap with the rotting fish corpse flying behind him like something from a cheap zombie movie. Daisy let out a yelp as Bug plonked the fish remains onto her chest and sat down on her stomach looking almost obedient. The smell was overpowering.

'If you are expecting praise you can think again,' she said, clipping on his lead and scrambling to her feet. She brushed off the fish carcass and seaweed tangle. 'Eurgh. Disgusting.' Bug made a lunge to grab back his prize but Daisy was quicker and she pulled him away brushing at her coat to check there were no remnants although the smell had already clung effectively to her. Bug trotted along beside her looking mightily pleased with himself and she hid a small smile, he was a little sod but despite everything he was growing on her.

Almost as if he sensed her warming to him he decided to squat down and do a steaming poo that, considering the size of the dog it had come out of, defied the laws of physics. But Daisy was somehow still in a good mood and she triumphantly waved a poo bag at him while he haughtily kicked up the grass around his deposit. Daisy steeled herself, put her hand inside the poo bag and swiftly scooped up the excrement. She had taught herself to be prepared for the smell by taking a deep breath beforehand and holding it until the poo was safely bagged, but she was never prepared for the warmth now heating up her fingers through the thin plastic bag. She retched as she tried to tie the knot whilst still not breathing in.

She caught Bug looking at her with his tongue lolling out of his mouth, it looked like he was laughing. Eventually the bag was secure and she could breathe again. She was quite proud of herself, although with her walking behind Bug carrying his crap in a bag she did wonder who was the superior race.

When she reached the Mariner's Arms, Max was coming out. Her first thought was 'that man rescued me', but there was a second thought right behind it. Oh cock, she thought as Max saw her and his eyes travelled to the swinging bag of poo. It wasn't a sophisticated look and she tried to hide the bag behind her back although she knew it was too late. Max was already grinning.

'Someone's been busy,' he said, crouching down to praise Bug who lapped up the attention.

'I'm glad I've seen you,' she said.

'Yeah, why?' Max was still fussing over Bug.

'I wanted to thank you – for the rescue and everything.' She felt embarrassed and it had nothing to do with the poo bag behind her back.

Max raised and dropped his shoulders. 'You're welcome. It's what we do. Good to see you've got him on a lead today.'

She opened her mouth but decided confessing to letting him off wasn't going to do her any favours.

'Here,' said Max, handing her a slip of paper from his pocket, which she took with her free hand. 'I've been meaning to give you this. I spoke to the owner of the Gin Bar in Exeter.' Daisy read the note. 'Ross says you're welcome any time but Tuesday nights are quiet if you want to talk to him. He'll share his contacts and stuff.'

'Are you a regular there too?' she asked.

'No, I taught his kids to swim and he's invited me over a few times.'

'Thanks, this is great. I'll probably go next Tuesday. The sooner the better.'

'Jason seems quite keen to go too. Assuming you want company?'

'Sure, that'd be good. Thanks for this, Max.'

The silence that followed was awkward and Daisy found herself staring at Max's eyelashes before she gave herself a jolt. They were exceptionally long.

'Right, thanks,' she said again inadvertently waving the bag of poo at him. 'I'll let you know about Tuesday.' And with that Daisy, Bug and a full bag of poo hurried off into the evening.

Daisy felt odd and she spent the walk back to the cottage mulling over why that was. She hadn't seen Max since the rescue and whilst she had felt a total idiot at the time those feelings had passed. Something had changed, like sand beneath a wave. There was a lot more to Max than she'd given him credit for; anyone who put themselves in danger voluntarily was worthy of further consideration.

Back at the cottage Aunt Coral was curled up in the living room watching her soaps. Daisy shut the door and stayed in the hall, she didn't want to disturb her. She crouched down to unclip Bug and the smell hit her. 'You stink.' The stench of rotten fish hung over the small dog like a cloud. 'Come on, it's bath time.' She'd seen Aunt Coral do it. She knew which was Bug's shampoo. How hard could it be?

Daisy soon knew the answer. She had put a few capfuls of doggy shampoo in the bath and added a couple of inches of lukewarm water. She had picked Bug up but she wasn't entirely sure what had happened next because now she was covered head to toe in foam along with half the bathroom, although Bug had barely got his feet wet. Every time she put him in the bath he frantically scrabbled about creating masses of foam until he managed to jump out. Catching him was tricky, he could duck and weave better than a New Zealand All Black. Bug pawed at the bathroom door to get out.

'No way. You're not leaving here without a bath.' She put more water in the tub; perhaps her water to bubble ratio was off, she wondered. As the water level increased so did the bubble mountain. It rose above the edge of the bath and both Daisy and Bug watched it grow like an out-of-control experiment. Perhaps she'd put too much shampoo in? She switched off the water, put her arm in to check the temperature and then turned her eyes on Bug – he just gave his usual wide-eyed stare.

'Right,' said Daisy. She meant business and lunged towards him. Anticipating his dash to her left she grabbed the wriggling bundle and deposited him in the bubble-filled bath and he promptly disappeared. Daisy parted the bubbles but there was no Bug. Could he drown in that much water? She started to panic and frantically swept giant lumps of foam out of the way and onto the bathroom floor. 'Bug,' she called. It wasn't that big a bath, where the hell was he? She could hear him scurrying about under the suds but she couldn't see him. As she gave one big sweep of her arm to remove another layer of bubbles the bathroom door burst open. Daisy jumped in fright and Bug leaped up from the foam, out of the bath and escaped downstairs trailing streams of bubbles behind him.

Aunt Coral surveyed the foam-covered bathroom and Daisy who looked like she'd stuck her head in an out-of-control candy floss machine. 'What happened?' asked Aunt Coral looking bewildered.

'Bath time,' explained Daisy, blowing foam off her nose.

'For whom?' asked Aunt Coral, shaking her head and retreating fast.

Chapter Twenty

The evening at the Exeter Gin Bar started off well. She'd had a message from the builder to say the wall was down and the water was connected, so although it was November and they were seriously behind schedule things were starting to happen. Max was wearing the same outfit he'd worn to Reg's funeral, with the exception of the tie, and it reminded Daisy how well he scrubbed up. Unfortunately, despite her best efforts, he was particularly uncommunicative and appeared more interested in looking out of the train window than talking. Although she had impressed Jason with her newly acquired bat knowledge.

The Gin Bar was a short walk from the station. It occupied what had once been a tailor's and still retained a lot of its olde-worlde charm. Ross, the owner, was exuberantly friendly and had loads of useful tips for setting up a bar and some great contacts in the trade. He went through some basics around different standards and types of gin and what, in his opinion, made certain ones stand out from the crowd. This was a conversation Daisy could now contribute to and she was pleased to see both Ross and her friends look impressed with her newly garnered knowledge.

They quickly segued into a full-on tasting session, which Tamsyn had seemed to treat as if it was Tequila shots. None of them seemed keen to spit out the gin and even though they were only having a sip of each it felt to Daisy like it was all adding up. But then this also felt like a bit of a celebration now her own bar was back on track. Ross stocked a lot of gin varieties and in an hour they only scratched the surface, but Daisy jotted down the ones they all liked the best. When they moved around to the public side of the bar and began working their way through the gin-based cocktail menu, Max excused himself and disappeared outside.

'He's not much fun tonight,' said Daisy, who felt her efforts at chatting to Max had been thwarted by his disagreeable attitude.

'Got a lot on his mind,' said Jason, with a knowing nod.

'Under a lot of pressure at work, is he?' Daisy asked. She knew it was uncalled for but, as far as she could see, Max didn't have any major problems in his life.

'Pasco.' Jason put his finger to his lips after he'd said the name, but the finger wasn't in the centre of his lips – he was drunk too. 'And his ex, Jenni with an "i", got engaged.'

'Jenni with one i,' said Daisy, with a giggle.

'Poor woman.' Tamsyn shook her head dramatically. 'I didn't even know Jenni only had one eye.' Nobody was sober enough to explain.

'What happened to Jenni?' asked Daisy.

'Went off travelling and didn't come back,' said Jason.

'Did she die?' asked Tamsyn.

'No.' He shook his head for emphasis. 'She hooked up with a mechanic in Dover and missed her ferry.'

Daisy was still processing this when Ross passed some cocktails and straws across the bar and said something, but it was lost as a pack of wild girls entered the bar with feather boas flowing and t-shirts declaring it was Olivia's Hen Night.

They teemed around the bar forcing Daisy and Tamsyn to grab their glasses and retreat to a table in a dark corner. 'How are the job ideas coming along?' asked Daisy

'I've been thinking about what I was good at in school and seeing if there's a link to a job.'

'Good approach. What's on the list?'

'Spelling and Irish dancing,' said Tamsyn.

Daisy opened her mouth but she couldn't think of anything appropriate to say, so instead she focused on the cocktails. 'They all look different,' noted Daisy, pointing at them. 'Shall we have a try of each other's with the straws?'

'Nope. One, two, three . . .' said Tamsyn and she tipped back her drink in one smooth motion. 'Wow,' she said. 'I could do another of those.' She pointed a finger in the general direction of her glass.

'You didn't even taste it,' said Jason, with a shudder. He and Daisy tried each other's cocktails with their straws while Tamsyn looked on.

They were distracted by a kerfuffle at the bar caused by the hen party making whooping noises. 'It's like the mating call of the baboon,' said Jason, glancing distastefully at the noisy group. A few of the party broke into a slurred rendition of the stripper music.

'Looks like they've got some traditional hen night entertainment,' said Daisy, trying to get a better look at the man among them, who wasn't actually having to strip as the women seemed to be doing that for him. A shirt flew out of the crowd landing on the floor between Jason and Daisy. They were giggling as they looked at the pale blue shirt until realisation finally struck them.

'Max!' they both yelled, jumping to their feet and ploughing into the hen party.

Max was on the floor fighting hard to hang on to his trousers. 'Get off him. He's not a stripper!' shouted Daisy, but the women were making too much noise for her to be heard.

'Enough!' hollered Jason, sounding manlier than Daisy had ever heard him before. 'I'm a police officer—'

Daisy wasn't sure what he said after that because the women clearly thought he was also part of the act and started to excitedly grab at his clothes too. Daisy got pushed out of the chanting circle, her drink-addled brain failing to come up with a better strategy for rescuing her friends. Eventually Ross rang the last orders bell and kept on ringing until everyone took notice. Daisy pushed her way back through the crowd and offered a hand to Jason who was sitting on the floor clutching his ripped shirt to his chest. Max was busy being straddled by the bride-to-be who was oblivious to the bell and was trying hard to kiss him.

'Excuse me,' said Daisy, tapping the woman on the shoulder.

'Yeah, come on, Olivia. Apparently he's *really* not a stripper,' said one of the others.

Olivia burst into hysterics and had to be lifted off an embarrassed-looking Max who was trying to rub the bright pink lipstick off his face, but only managing to smear it further. Daisy offered Max a hand to help him to his feet. He hesitated and Daisy tilted her head. 'Come on. This is my chance to return the favour.'

'What favour?' Max looked puzzled.

'This is me saving you. We're quits now. Okay?' She gave him a cheeky smile.

Max smirked. 'Yeah, right.'

'I can ask the ladies back if you like.' She went up on her toes as if about to try to get their attention.

'No. You're okay.' He took her hand and she pulled him to his feet. She noticed how his stomach muscles clenched as he stood up and how toned his body was. It took her a few moments to drag her eyes back up to his face.

'Are you sure you're not my stripper?' slurred Olivia, staggering back towards them.

'NO!' chorused Daisy and Max together.

Back at the table they found Tamsyn doing a sitting down version of Irish dancing and Jason inspecting his trashed clothing. Max scooped up his shirt from the floor and put it back on quickly discovering it no longer had all its buttons. He let it hang open and sat down opposite Daisy who was forcing herself not to stare at his bare chest – his tanned taut chest with its tantalising smattering of neat chest hair making a path down his lightly sculpted abs to . . .

'Daisy. For Christ sake are you dozing off too?'

'What?' Daisy jolted her head up and tried again to maintain eye contact but all she was doing was opening her eyes super wide and making herself look like she was startled.

'Where's mine?' Max pointed to the row of empty cocktail glasses. Tamsyn still had a straw between her lips, it didn't take a genius to work out what had happened.

Ross appeared at the table. 'I am mortified about them.' He motioned towards the loud women. 'My speciality martinis – on the house. You'll have all this to deal with when you open up.' He laughed and went over to speak to the rowdy group.

'How do you deal with people like that?' said Daisy, realising her voice didn't sound quite right. She gestured towards the hen party who were now boob flashing men through the window. She would be solely responsible in her bar and it bothered her.

'You call the police,' said Jason, swaying towards her and then away again with a silly grin on his face.

'Yeah, you'll be brilliant,' she said, giving his ripped shirt a tug. Perhaps this needed more thought.

'Ohh, I love this shirt,' said Jason, pulling at the shreds.

An hour or so of drinking later she realised it was definitely time to go home when she found herself having a cross purposes conversation with a tall youth.

'It's like everything he does, he does to wind me up. He chews his own toenails. That's not normal is it?' Daisy said, scowling at the recollection.

'Could be a fetish,' suggested the youth.

Daisy pouted as if considering this explanation. 'You see he's black, but I've told him he still has to have a bath but he doesn't get it,' she slurred.

'He doesn't bath? That's disgusting,' said the youth.

'I know,' agreed Daisy. 'Sometimes after he's been on the beach he stinks to high heaven. It's as if he likes smelling like a dead fish.'

There was a long pause before the youth answered. 'Is he a fisherman?'

Daisy swayed away from the youth, narrowing her eyes until they focused. 'Dogs don't fish, you idiot.' She looked about her. Tamsyn was half asleep muttering to herself about joining Riverdance. Jason was blinking repeatedly at his phone as if trying to concentrate. He slowly looked up at her.

'Last train leaves in fifteen minutes.'

'Bye, bye,' Daisy said to the youth, waving him away, and he good-naturedly sloped off towards the hen party. 'You grab a cab and I'll grab . . .' Daisy looked around. They were missing someone. Where was Max? Daisy tried to stand up and achieved success on her third attempt. She felt like an old person. She scanned the bar and located an open-shirted Max who had the full attention of two of the hen party. She was about to wave to get his attention when one of them started to kiss him. She felt something primal course through her. Daisy wanted to march over there but a stagger was the best she could do. Bloody gin, she thought. She unintentionally bumped the chair the kisser was sitting on, which quickly stopped the tongue onslaught.

'Whoops, sorry,' she said, not feeling sorry at all. 'But Prince Charming here needs his beauty sleep. Come on, last train leaving in fifteen minutes.' She had no right to stop him kissing someone but to hell with that, it made her uncomfortable and now was not the time to explore why. She pulled Max to his feet and gave her best cheesy grin to the hen party as Max snaked an arm around her shoulders to steady himself. The four of them thanked Ross too many times and meandered off in search of their last train home.

The next morning someone was drilling inside Daisy's head. She opened one eye to see Bug sound asleep on her pillow snoring so loudly it was making the pillow vibrate. She made a mental note to make sure he was properly shut in the kitchen at night from now on – he escaped more often than Houdini. She gave him a nudge and he grunted to life. He started to lick her face and the stench of his doggy breath made her gag. 'Eurgh.' Dogs and hangovers did not go together.

'I'm never drinking again,' said Daisy, followed by a moan as she headed in search of juice. She knew she was in trouble when she opened the fridge and the small light was like a laser penetrating her brain. She grabbed her aunt's sunglasses from the drawer and put them on. She might have looked like Lady Gaga's granny but at least she was able to look in the fridge without being blinded.

Showered, dressed and on her third black coffee she still felt like someone had forcibly transplanted her organs in the night but at least she'd stopped yawning for the time being. She took two paracetamol and forced down some toast, truly hoping it stayed down. Today she was back onsite at the old railway building; she was keen to see how far the workmen had got and if there was any hope of them being open in time for the lantern parade. She was prepared to get stuck in to claw back some time because the longer the delay the less likely it was she'd still be open by the summer.

She stepped into the fresh November day, took in deep breaths of icy air and lengthened her stride, perhaps a little light exercise might wake her up before she got there?

She wasn't surprised to see Max was already there. He was definitely a morning person, with or without a hangover. He was sitting on the platform nursing a takeaway coffee cup.

'How's your hangover?' She tapped his head as she passed and started to unlock the doors. It was chilly on the platform.

'What hangover?' he asked brightly jumping to his feet and joining her at the door. She gave him a doubtful look, there was no way he was hangover free after the amount they had all put away but he just grinned back at her.

'Go on then, let's see.' He pointed at the door. Daisy turned the handle and they both hurried inside.

The smell of freshly sawn timber hit her first. 'Blimey,' said Daisy her eyes darting around. It looked quite different.

Losing half the wall made it seem much bigger. She ran her fingers along the smooth surface of the newly installed bar top. It was better than she had ever imagined. She turned to face Max. 'What do you think?'

'I think I want a job here.'

'It's yours,' she said, her mouth moving faster than her brain.

'Really?'

'Yep. Any evenings you like.' She didn't want to think too much about her reasons why. She knew he had experience as a cocktail waiter, and she told herself she would need people she could trust and that someone like Max would be good for dealing with any unruly customers, unless of course they were hen parties.

The rest of the morning Max was sickeningly upbeat; she guessed it was an act because he had consumed just as much alcohol as she had. Uncharitably she hoped it was taxing him to keep up the pretence. Daisy felt she had learned a valuable lesson – gin was lethal stuff. And she was pleased she had learned it in someone else's bar and away from the prying eyes of Ottercombe Bay residents. It had also been useful to meet Ross and pick up a number of contacts and tips about starting out in the gin trade and extending the list of gins she wanted to stock.

They spent the morning putting up the big Ottercombe Bay railway sign and were painting the outside of the window frames when Daisy was faintly aware of a beeping and buzzing sound. She turned to see Max leap off the platform then sprint across the car park, dropping his paintbrush behind him.

'What's wrong?' she shouted after him, feeling a shared sense of panic but not knowing why.

'Lifeboat!' Even though he had shouted it he was already a distance away, making it sound faint, and then he disappeared from view.

Daisy was rooted to the platform for a few moments, partly in shock at his sudden dramatic departure and partly at the thought of what he was about to do. He was just an ordinary bloke and yet in an instant he was prepared to drop everything and risk his life for a complete stranger. It was mind blowing. And today he was doing it with a hangover. Incredible.

Daisy went back inside and gave Tamsyn a call. At first when the phone was answered she could only hear heavy breathing.

'Tams? Are you okay?'

When she spoke she was whispering. 'I've been possessed by a demon.'

'Drink plenty of water, it's just a hangover.'

'It can't be. I didn't feel this bad after I had my appendix out.'

'Take a couple of paracetamol, you'll be fine.'

'I suspected someone might have a voodoo doll of me and now I know it's true,' said Tamsyn, with a groan. 'Even my hair hurts.'

Daisy laughed. 'Okay, take care of yourself and I'll check you're still alive tonight.'

'I'd like bouquets of gerberas and pineapples at my funeral,' said Tamsyn, and the line went dead.

Daisy was starting to feel she might have got off lightly.

The lifeboat shout turned out to be an adrift fishing boat despite the person who had called it in being adamant there was someone clinging on to it. A complete waste of time but all of the crew agreed it was far better to bring in an empty boat than a body.

211

'Max,' called Jason, quickening his pace to catch him up. Max stopped and waited. 'How's your head?'

'Like someone started my post-mortem early, but don't tell Daisy. I've said I'm fine.'

Jason looked confused. 'Okay, will do. I have a favour to ask.'

'Sure,' said Max, as they fell in step with each other.

'Can I borrow the keys to the railway ticket office please?'

Max was taken aback; his first thought was Jason must be planning on laying in wait for Pasco who was still sleeping in the carriage more nights than he wasn't despite Max trying to encourage him to leave. He didn't have anywhere else to go, Max knew this for a fact because he'd checked all the options in a twenty-mile radius. He didn't like going behind Daisy's back but he couldn't see his father sleeping rough – he was guilt ridden either way. 'Er, why?'

'I don't want to say.'

It must be something to do with Dad, he thought. Max stopped walking and after a couple of seconds Jason turned around. 'Come on Jason, be straight with me.'

Jason looked at his feet and then slowly looked up. 'I want to do something nice, that's all. I promise.'

Max narrowed his eyes. 'Nothing to do with my dad?'

Jason looked puzzled and amused. 'No. Nothing to do with Pasco. Why? Is he up to mischief again?'

'Mischief? I thought he was public enemy number one.'

They continued walking. 'Not since he came to see me,' said Jason.

'Really? When was this?' Max was unable to hide his amazement.

'Not long after he was released. He called in to the station to let me know he was back. We talked through his plans. He seems to be sorting his life out.'

Max couldn't help an involuntary laugh escaping. 'Seriously, you didn't fall for that old crap, did you? Don't they send you on courses to spot liars like him?'

'I don't think he was lying, Max. Maybe you should try giving him another chance.'

Max stopped dead and Jason held his hands up in surrender. 'It was just a suggestion.'

'Bloody stupid suggestion,' grumbled Max. After a lifetime of being let down it would take a lot for him to trust Pasco again.

'Sorry. Anyway, can I have the keys sometime?'

'We're not working on Sunday; the builders will be there in the morning sorting the guttering but you can have the keys all day if you like.' Max would have to make sure Pasco made himself scarce because that was a whole can of worms he could do without releasing into the wild right now.

Chapter Twenty-One

Daisy was having a well-earned Sunday afternoon nap when her phone rang and dragged her from a lovely dream involving Rufus Sewell. Actually, she hoped it was Rufus Sewell because as she came to the man in her dream looked a bit more like Pasco. 'Eww,' she said with a shiver. Some dreams were really messed up. 'Hi,' she said into her phone, barely registering who had rung.

'Hi Daisy. Could you come down to the railway please?'

'Jason. Hi. What's happened?' All sorts of thoughts rushed through her mind and none of them pleasant.

'Oh, nothing,' he said with a chuckle. 'I just need you to pop down in say half an hour? Okay?'

'Er, why?'

'There's absolutely nothing to worry about.'

'Is this a surprise? Because I hate . . . Hello, Jason?' The call had ended and Daisy stared at the phone. What on earth was going on? She racked her brains as to what bylaw she might have violated and her mind leapt to Max and the carpet. What had he done with it?

She was feeling slightly more awake when she opened the door to someone bouncing around a lot like Tigger, but less stripey. Tamsyn was jumping about as if she was on something quite strong, her loose bunches springing around her shoulders.

'What's going on?' asked Daisy with a yawn.

'I can't say,' said Tamsyn, balling her fists up near her face like a child on Christmas morning.

'But you do know?'

'No,' said Tamsyn.

Daisy grinned. 'Then why are you excited?'

'I don't know. But Jason told me it's something special and it has to be good then, doesn't it?'

'I guess,' said Daisy, not convinced. She hated the anticipation and the not knowing, it churned her stomach up. The doorbell sounded again and she went to see who it was. This many visitors on a Sunday was unheard of.

'Hi,' she said to a bored-looking Max.

'I've been summoned to the railway building. I thought we might as well all go down together.'

'You too?' The mystery was growing making Daisy uneasy.

'Apparently,' said Max, with his usual nonchalant air.

'What's going on then?' asked Aunt Coral emerging from the living room.

'Jason has planned something special and we're all to go to the railway building now,' said Tamsyn, checking her watch and starting to gesticulate wildly at the door.

'Oh, let me grab my coat,' said Aunt Coral and the others exchanged looks.

'Why not?' said Daisy. 'The more the merrier. Let's get this over with.'

'I'll drive,' said Aunt Coral grabbing her keys.

The makeshift gate was already open and Aunt Coral drove straight in. Jason was standing outside the door looking very smiley indeed. Daisy was in the back with Max and her stomach did another flip as she scanned the area, but she couldn't see any obvious changes. She could see Max doing the same and he looked apprehensive too. They exchanged grimaces and the car pulled to a halt.

'This stop is Ottercombe Bay, everyone leaving us here please take all your belongings,' said Tamsyn in a nasally train announcer voice. Aunt Coral giggled and got out of the car. Daisy and Max climbed out of the back seats and followed an over-excited Tamsyn up onto the platform where they all exchanged welcomes with Jason.

Daisy tried to peek inside the window but it was too dark to see anything. Jason jangled the keys to get everyone's attention and Daisy clocked they were Max's set. She gave him a questioning look but he just pouted in reply.

'Thanks for coming at short notice—' started Jason.

'Get on with it, Jay,' said Max fidgeting from one foot to the other.

'Right, yes. I wanted to do something to the building, which I hope you will all think is an improvement.' Daisy's eyebrows shot up, she had a bad feeling about this. 'I hope you like it,' he said, flinging open the door and standing back. Daisy thought she might be sick. What had he done? She wasn't sure if she wanted to look because when she had left it yesterday it was all looking pretty perfect as the carpenter had been in and it was actually starting to look like a bar.

She stepped gingerly inside, her eyes darting about in a frantic search to spot the surprise. If he'd wallpapered her beautiful bare brick wall she'd kill him. Daisy was still scanning the room when a small whirring noise started above her head and made everyone look up. At picture-rail height there was now a narrow shelf going all the way around the room and on it were two model trains zipping

216

along. Daisy's frown changed to a smile – it was difficult to do anything else while watching the trains whizz around the track.

Jason popped an anxious face around the doorframe. 'Do you like it?'

It was the last thing she was expecting to see, but it fitted in perfectly. 'I love it, thank you,' she said, giving him a brief kiss on the cheek. 'But what did all this cost, Jason?' She followed the trains around the room and back again noting the little touches of model shops, people, stations and trees dotted along the model trains' route.

'Nothing. The track and those trains are Reg's from the shed.'

'You're kidding me?'

'Nope, straight up. And I have another three engines in perfect working order so you can swap them over to add a little interest.'

'I can't believe they still work after being in our damp old shed for ages,' said Aunt Coral.

'They just needed a little TLC and some lubricant and they were good to go,' said Jason. When Max sniggered behind him Jason gave him a stern look.

'Roll me in glitter and call me a unicorn,' shrieked Tamsyn, making Aunt Coral put her hands over her ears. 'You are bloody brilliant,' she added, launching herself at Jason and proceeding to kiss him firmly on the lips. She released him and they gazed at each other – both looking stunned. Jason licked his lips. Tamsyn pulled him back to her and they staggered out onto the platform. Once outside the chill of the day didn't seem to dampen their embrace and the kissing continued.

'I like it too, but I'm not snogging you,' called Max to Jason. 'Thank God those two have finally got it together.'

'Well, it's a lovely surprise,' said Aunt Coral, apparently oblivious to what was in full swing outside. 'It will be an excellent draw for children, and it's too high for them to reach,' she continued but Daisy and Max weren't listening – they were watching Jason and Tamsyn through the window.

'Get a room,' called Max and Daisy elbowed him in the ribs.

'I'm so proud of you, Daisy,' said Aunt Coral. 'You have done such a brilliant thing in restoring this old building. Reg would have been thrilled.' She wiped away a tear and Daisy gave her a hug. She wasn't sure why but she was feeling emotional too. Perhaps it was having everyone there and seeing it nearly finished.

'Can we go now?' asked Max, looking tired and bored. 'I'm missing the football for this,' he protested, when he was met with hard stares.

'Okay,' said Daisy linking arms with her aunt and walking outside. Jason and Tamsyn were in a particularly passionate embrace as they passed them, with Jason now pinned to the Ottercombe Bay sign.

'Mind my sign,' said Daisy.

'All aboard,' said Max, followed by an imitation of a train whistle.

Tamsyn suddenly pushed Jason away and started to gasp for breath.

'What's the matter? Tamsyn?' Jason was trying to comfort her but she was firmly pushing him away.

'Please go,' she said, holding a hand to her chest as she took a gulp of air.

'Jason, please,' said Daisy, putting an arm around Tamsyn. Jason nodded and backed away. She had no idea why Tamsyn was reacting like this but if she had asked him to leave then Daisy felt she should support her and find out her reasons later – however Tamsyn-style bonkers they may be.

'What's wrong?' Daisy asked, distressed by Tamsyn's obvious discomfort.

'Can't breathe?' gasped Tamsyn, and she started to shake.

'Are you asthmatic?' asked Daisy.

'Are you allergic to coppers?' asked Max, who received a death stare from both Daisy and Aunt Coral.

Tamsyn shook her head and took a big rasping breath.

'Max, my prescription's in the boot, get it would you?' instructed Aunt Coral stepping forward. 'Tamsyn, now calm down. You're getting yourself flustered.'

Max came back with the prescription bag and handed it over.

Aunt Coral tipped out the box of painkillers and gave the empty paper bag to Tamsyn. 'Breath into this. Deep and slow,' said Aunt Coral who had a comforting arm around Tamsyn's shoulder whilst Jason paced about, a safe distance away, at the other end of the car park.

Max tapped Daisy on the shoulder and beckoned her to one side. 'Should I call the quack? Or an ambulance?' he asked, keeping his voice to a fraction above a whisper. He shot another look at Tamsyn who was doing as she'd been told and looked most odd as the crackling bag rhythmically inflated and deflated.

'No, I think it's a panic attack,' said Daisy, concern etched on her face.

'What's she panicking about? Kissing Jason?' He stepped back and failed to hide a splutter of laughter with a fake cough.

'I don't know, but stop being mean.' Although Daisy could feel a snigger tickling the corners of her own lips.

219

'See, you think it's funny,' said Max, poking Daisy in the ribs making her snort out a laugh. Aunt Coral shot Daisy a look and she punched Max on the arm.

'Stop it,' Daisy said, going all serious.

She went to join Tamsyn – if she stayed with Max he'd get her into more mischief. 'I think we should get you home,' she said to Tamsyn and the paper bag bobbed up and down in agreement.

Back at Aunt Coral's there was lots more fussing around Tamsyn and sweet tea for everyone, although Daisy had no idea why. She figured it was Aunt Coral's default answer to anything traumatic, however minor. When Tamsyn's breathing had returned to normal and her face looked the right colour, Daisy decided it was time for some answers.

'What happened back there, Tams?'

Tamsyn puffed out a breath and put down her cup. She pouted and appeared to be thinking through her answer. 'At first, it was "Hurray. I'm kissing Jason" and then I realised it wouldn't work out and I felt like I'd won and lost him all in the space of one kiss and then my heart went all thumpy and I couldn't breathe.'

Daisy was frowning as she tried to make sense of it. 'You realised from one kiss your relationship with Jason wouldn't work?'

'Yes,' nodded Tamsyn emphatically.

'Boy, he is one ba-ad kisser.'

'No. It wasn't the kiss. Don't you see?' Tamsyn looked forlorn and she shook her head.

'Not at all. Sorry.'

Tamsyn leaned forward. 'He's a policeman. Policemen are generally quite blokey. I know some of the others at

220

the station and they already tease Jason for being . . . a bit . . .'

'Nerdy?' offered Daisy.

'If you like. He's not like them. He doesn't go out drinking and falling into bed with someone else's wife or—'

'Does that happen a lot?' Daisy was interested in the gossip at the local nick.

'All the time,' said Tamsyn. 'And when they do have girlfriends they're well . . . more like you than me.'

'What do you mean?' asked Daisy, unsure if she should prepare herself to be offended.

'Pretty and confident.'

'But, Tams, you're pretty and confident too.'

'Not really,' she said, her face the picture of sadness as she looked down at her colourful clothes. 'I'm a bit different.'

'No, you're not—' protested Daisy but Tamsyn cut her off.

'Don't Daisy. I know people think I'm a bit odd. I can't help it and I don't want to change and be someone I'm not, so I deal with it. But it would be wrong to make Jason deal with it too.'

'That's a rubbish reason. You *are* different but in a good way. Like a limited edition.' Tamsyn looked surprised. 'Jason's an adult, you can't go making those sorts of decisions for him. Plus the fact you're probably missing out on a lovely relationship and lots of great sex.'

'Daisy!' Tamsyn blushed. 'I know I'm right, it's doomed.'

'You don't know that. Didn't the cards say something about you and your soul mate? What if it's Jason?'

Daisy must have struck a chord because Tamsyn looked like someone had zapped her with a freeze ray gun. Eventually she moved and spoke. 'I wouldn't want to go against the cards.'

As they continued to chat Daisy was aware Aunt Coral was opening the front door and within moments a worried-looking Min was engulfing Tamsyn and checking her over as if she'd been in a major motorway smash. Tamsyn's mum was an older version of Tamsyn, although her style of clothes was more vintage, her hair and features were strikingly similar.

'Mum, I'm fine.'

'Let's get you home,' said Min, helping Tamsyn to her feet. She seemed to spot Daisy for the first time. 'Oh, hello Daisy. Are you all right?' she said, and there was a flash of concern in Min's eyes. She reached out a hand towards Daisy and then let it drop to her side.

'Yes, thanks. I'm good,' said Daisy, standing up and seeing them to the door.

Min stopped abruptly, turned and leaned in close to Daisy.

'You know, I gave all my evidence about Sandy to the police,' said Min, her dark eyes conveying concern.

Daisy was taken aback. 'What evidence? When?' Daisy looked from Min to Tamsyn and back again. Min's mouth lifted at one side. Daisy could feel the sympathy emanating from her. The familiar sensation of the pity of others.

Min stroked Daisy's arm gently. 'The vision I had of your mum the night she died.'

'What vision?'

Min's gaze drifted off. 'It was dark and the sea was rough. I saw her face emerge from the water. She looked serene.'

Daisy swallowed hard. 'Go on.'

'That was it. Someone was saving her.'

'But she wasn't saved.' Daisy wanted to shake the woman. There was a long pause.

'No. Not exactly,' said Min, at last.

'Not at all,' said Daisy, her expression frosty although she felt as if she was overheating. What was Min going on about?

'But there was someone with her when she died. I hope that's a small comfort,' said Min. She turned to leave. 'We'll see ourselves out,' she added, guiding Tamsyn through the hall and Aunt Coral stepped aside.

Daisy watched them go, she had no idea what to think.

Once the front door was closed and they had disappeared from view, Aunt Coral shook her head. 'Don't take any of her mumbo jumbo on board, Daisy. She's a raisin away from being a total fruitcake.' But Daisy couldn't dismiss what she'd said quite so easily.

Chapter Twenty-Two

It was December and outside it felt like winter had a firm grip on the bay. Thanks to the bats the building works had been greatly delayed but items on the To Do list were being ticked off at a rate of knots now. Apart from some painting, signage, printing of drinks lists and flyers and a thorough clean the bar was on track to open in time for the lantern parade. Daisy had also managed to drum up some interest from the local paper, which was probably because everyone was fed up of seeing burned-out sheds on the front page.

Tamsyn had popped round for no apparent reason and was warming herself by the fire. 'Watchya doing?'

'Tweaking my job advert for the newspaper.' Daisy handed it to Tamsyn and sucked the end of her pencil.

'You're holding interviews for the bar?' said Tamsyn when she'd finished reading.

Daisy nodded.

'Really?' asked Aunt Coral, putting down her newspaper. 'I thought it was just you and Max to start with?'

'I'm hoping we'll get busy quickly in which case I'll need a bit more than just the two of us.'

Aunt Coral looked dubious. 'But it's winter. Half the businesses are closed.' Daisy was frowning. 'I love your optimism but I think perhaps you need to see how things go before you take someone else on.'

Daisy was thoughtful. 'Maybe I just need some agency staff for opening night and around Christmas.' Daisy was thinking out loud.

'Ooh, ooh, ooh!' shouted Tamsyn.

'The funky gibbon,' said Aunt Coral, followed by peals of laughter. Daisy and Tamsyn both stared at her.

'What?' asked Daisy, her left cheek twitching.

'Oh, never mind. You're both too young,' muttered Aunt Coral and she went back to her newspaper.

Tamsyn grabbed Daisy's arm. 'I'll be your agency staff for opening night. And I'll be your extra staff whenever you need someone. I'm bored witless most evenings. Pleeeeeease.'

This had the potential to be a total disaster. Daisy loved Tamsyn but that didn't make her the ideal employee and she wasn't sure working together would do much for their friendship. Daisy was hoping for someone with lots of cocktail bar experience but how likely was that this time of year? Tamsyn was looking at her the same way Bug did when she ate a bacon sandwich.

'Have you ever worked behind a bar?' asked Daisy tentatively.

'No, but more than anything I want to work with you.'

'I need someone experienced and—'

'I'm used to taking orders and dealing with customers from the beach café,' said Tamsyn in a rush. 'And I'm keen to learn. I've watched Tom Cruise in *Cocktail* twenty-eight times.' She grinned at Daisy and she knew she wasn't lying.

'Okay, but I can't promise regular hours.'

'I love you. You're the best boss ever.' Tamsyn pulled her into a hug and squeezed hard.

'Okay, okay. Come to the railway building at ten Wednesday morning and Max and I will go through the basics.' Daisy truly hoped she hadn't made the worst decision ever.

Ten o'clock Wednesday morning, Daisy opened the doors and looked outside. Old Man Burgess was leaning against the building and Tamsyn was chatting to him.

'Hello, Mr Burgess, I'm afraid we don't open for a couple of days.'

'Hello, Daisy. I know. I've come for an interview. Tamsyn said you were recruiting.' Tamsyn was nodding as she helped him to stand fully upright.

'Er . . .' Daisy was lost for words. 'You'd better come in.'

Max settled Old Man Burgess down on the long bench while Daisy used this as an opportunity to show Tamsyn how to use the coffee machine. 'It's okay,' said Tamsyn waving her away. 'I know how to use this. You interview Mr Burgess.'

Daisy gritted her teeth. She'd speak to Tamsyn about this later. She went and sat next to the old man who was unravelling the longest scarf she'd ever seen. 'I'm so sorry Mr Burgess but I think there's been some confusion,' started Daisy, but it appeared that either Mr Burgess didn't hear or chose to ignore her.

'I get awfully lonely, Daisy. Since my wife died I just sit at home all day and it's not good for me. Even Nesbit has left me.'

'Has he flown off again?' asked Daisy, feeling something tug at her heartstrings.

'No, he's being acclimatised before his release.'

'That's good though,' said Daisy, giving his gnarled hand a pat.

226

'But I have no purpose any more. So when Tamsyn said you were recruiting I thought how marvellous it would be if I got myself a little job. Just a few hours a week.' He was smiling broadly and Daisy swallowed hard. This was going to be like drowning a kitten.

'I'm after someone with experience,' she said.

'Here's my CV,' said Mr Burgess, handing over a printed sheet of A4. 'I used to run the restaurant at the Smuggler's Rest years ago and—'

'I loved that pub,' said Max butting in. 'They did the best scampi,' he added turning to Daisy who was skim reading the CV.

'And before the pub you ran a tea shop in Salcombe?' she asked.

'Yes.' Mr Burgess nodded with enthusiasm unbefitting of his age. 'I know I'm not your perfect candidate but I'm reliable and honest.'

Daisy was warming to him. 'Thanks Mr Burgess. I appreciate you coming in but until we get off the ground I don't know if there'll be enough work for any of us.'

'It's all right, Daisy. I understand.' He looked awfully sad making Daisy feel like a monster.

'Here you go, Mr B,' said Tamsyn plonking down a perfect cappuccino in front of him. 'Why don't you have Mr B as emergency cover? He lives really close so you can call him in when you need him.'

'I don't think—' started Daisy but she was cut off.

'That would be lovely,' said Mr Burgess. 'Thank you. Both of you. This means the world to me.' He wiped away a tear.

'You're welcome, Mr B,' said Tamsyn with a beaming smile, leaving Daisy bewildered as to exactly how she now had a third employee.

Once Mr Burgess had finished his drink and left, Daisy turned to Tamsyn who was trying to memorise the cocktail ingredients. 'Why did you tell Old Man Burgess I was recruiting?'

'You said you wanted experienced people. I don't know anyone with more experience.'

Daisy could see where she'd gone wrong and let out a sigh. 'He's lovely but . . .'

'He'd make Mrs Overall look like Usain Bolt,' said Max, appearing at her shoulder.

'Exactly.' She felt awful at the thought that she'd probably never call him.

'You know you could employ him just for an hour a day. It would get him out of the house and he's got tons of experience,' said Max, with a shrug. He had a point and a few good part-time workers were better than nobody at all. But it all depended on whether or not they had any customers.

'I think we'd make a great team,' said Max, giving her the briefest of glances.

Daisy stopped what she was doing and chewed her lip. 'I guess Old Man Burgess brings experience, Tamsyn has enthusiasm, I've got the business acumen and you're the muscle,' she said with a wink. 'I suppose we'll be okay.'

'I meant you and me,' said Max under his breath as Daisy walked away.

After months of preparation, hard work and the distribution of a rainforest's worth of flyers the opening day had finally arrived. Daisy was pleased she'd managed to keep the bar's name a surprise and was thrilled the sign writer had covered the new logo in a white film so the name boards were all in place but nobody could read them yet. It had been a struggle coming up with something appropriate what with it being part gin bar, part hot chocolate cabin housed in an old railway – it was definitely an unusual mix. She had a new outfit for the grand opening too: a simple black dress, which fitted her well, and if Max spilled something down it, it wouldn't stain.

She had organised her stock, updated her book keeping, checked her payments system was working, got in extra change for the till, put posh hand wash and hand lotion in the toilets as well as giving the whole place another thorough clean. Daisy looked around her. The bar looked perfect. Specially made staggered shelving displayed her selection of gins next to a neat row of optics for those that featured frequently in cocktails. The wooden bench had come up lovely with a comfy seat cushion in what Jason called GWR green. Under the back window were four high tables with bar stools and another six stools around the bar. The rest of the area had small square tables and simple wooden chairs. The end wall was all bare brickwork and made an interesting feature with the scattered framed photographs showing off the building's heritage. And overhead the model trains whizzed by excitedly. Looking at it now she was massively grateful to Aunt Coral for all she'd invested. Daisy had to make a success of this for both of them. She felt a tiny bubble of excitement about the evening ahead. There was no more she could do but twiddle her thumbs for the next eight hours until it was time to open.

Daisy wandered along the coastal path, found a bench and sat down. She looked out across the sea and breathed in the cool fresh December air. It did smell different. She remembered her mother saying you could taste the salt in the air. Daisy had spent many an afternoon with her tongue lolling out, not unlike Bug, but she had never managed to actually taste the salt.

She could see a couple of dog walkers on the beach and a fisherman tending to his boat. She watched them for a while. She wondered what her mother would think about today. Here was Daisy about to open her own business. Daisy couldn't stop her hand going to her neck. She missed her locket and she missed her mother. Being here she thought about her all the time. Everywhere there were memories – the beach itself was where they found her cold, lifeless body – and whilst Daisy hadn't witnessed it she had a clear picture in her mind. It sent a shiver down her spine. She wanted to find out more about what had happened but right now she needed to focus on the bar.

Daisy's earlier calm had evaporated by the time evening descended. 'What if nobody comes?' said Daisy, wiping down the counter for the umpteenth time.

'Chill out, they'll be here. It was splashed across the local paper and it's been the talk of the bay for weeks. People will want to come for a nosey at the very least. Relax,' said Max, briefly putting an arm around her shoulder. Daisy paused for a moment. It was nice to have Max's arm around her, she liked it and she liked him. She looked at him with his hair under control for once and in his new smart trousers, crisp white shirt and waistcoat – he looked gorgeous. A smile crept across her face.

'What?' he asked, noticing her looking at him.

She was recalling the body he was hiding under his shirt. She gave herself a mental shake. Max was still waiting for a reply. 'A waistcoat suits you.'

Max went to speak but Tamsyn appeared like a whirling dervish. For once her more flamboyant side was slightly reined in. Daisy had chosen a long flowing Tamsyn-style skirt for her to wear but in dark grey with a lace-edged white shirt. She looked smart, but she still looked like Tamsyn. She threw off her coat, washed her hands and almost jumped to attention at Daisy's side. 'Right, Boss. What shall I do?'

'Max has got the cocktails covered so you can join me in panicking about no one showing up and then you can chop another lime or grapefruit if you like,' she said, offering her a knife.

'Seriously?' said Max, pointing to the two large platters of sliced fruit.

Tamsyn tilted her head. 'What do you mean no one? There's loads outside already,' she said.

Daisy and Max rushed to the window to look. Jason was standing at the bottom of the platform slope chatting to people at the front of the queue and there were lots more milling about the car park area.

Daisy swallowed hard and checked the old railway clock on the wall. 'Shall we start pouring out the freebies and let them in?'

'Yes, Boss,' said Tamsyn with a salute.

'You're not going to call me that all night, are you?' asked Daisy, with a twitch of her cheek.

'Is it annoying?' asked Tamsyn.

'A bit,' said Daisy.

'Very,' added Max, and Tamsyn gave him a thump.

'Are you and Jason going to be okay?' asked Daisy. Not much had been said since Tamsyn's panic attack and she knew the two of them were avoiding each other.

'We'll be fine. It's for the best,' said Tamsyn, but the look in her eyes upset Daisy. She knew she had to do more to help her friend but tonight wasn't the right time.

They soon had trays of small sampler gin and tonics on the counter and bowls of olives on the tables.

'Ready?' Daisy asked and received two firm nods in response. She took a deep breath and opened the door to a spontaneous round of applause and a couple of whistles. Jason shushed the crowd and Max confidently climbed a ladder up to the main sign on the old building.

'Wow,' said Daisy, pushing back her hair. 'I am thrilled so many of you came tonight. Thank you. I just want to say that today wouldn't be possible if it wasn't for my Great Uncle Reg and we'll be raising a toast to him inside.'

'Hear, hear!' shouted someone from the back. She wasn't sure if it was in reference to Reg or the drinks.

'Without further ado. I am very proud to welcome you all to opening night at . . .' she left a little pause and she indicated to Max that now was the moment to pull off the sign's plastic covering, which he did in a smooth motion at the same time as Daisy announced the name, '. . . Locos,' she said proudly. Max grinned at her from atop the ladder and she beamed back as everyone clapped.

The rest of the evening was a blur of people and chatter. Daisy surprised herself with how knowledgeable she was about the different gins; she'd been swotting up for weeks now and interspersed with her tales of gin from her travels it had customers enthralled. There were lots of locals, in fact most of the town appeared at some point during the evening, and many stayed for the freebie and an additional drink, apart from Monty who only popped in for a few minutes. Daisy was pleased to see him and although he sniffed at her balloon glasses and shiny bar tops, he was rather taken with the train set and wished her every success, which was good of him and more than she had expected.

Aunt Coral had sobbed off and on throughout the evening due in part to how proud she was of Daisy but mainly due to her large gin consumption. Before Daisy knew it it was almost eleven o'clock. As she was keen to keep hold of her licence, she politely but firmly thanked her guests then herded them on their way. When the last stragglers had left and they finally closed the doors, Daisy, Jason and Tamsyn all slumped onto the bench seat.

'I'm sooooo knackered,' said Tamsyn.

'Come on, tidying up to do first,' said Max, as he came back from locking the new car park bollard in place. There was a series of groans and everyone got reluctantly to their feet apart from Aunt Coral who tried but wobbled a lot and sat back down.

'I think I'll wait here,' she said, in a slurred half whisper.

The four of them set about collecting glasses, stacking the glasswasher and wiping down surfaces.

'I can't believe someone left their glass in the loo,' said Jason, shaking his head as he put it on the counter. 'Some people, really.'

'Maybe they were multitasking?' suggested Tamsyn.

'That's what worries me,' said Jason, and a weak smile passed between them.

With the four of them working, and the glasswasher already having been on a couple of times during the evening, things started to look orderly quite quickly. Jason rounded up Aunt Coral and Tamsyn. 'Come on you two,' he said to Daisy and Max who were arguing over what to do with a remaining half of a grapefruit.

'I think I'll walk back. I need to clear my head,' said Max, giving Daisy an unreadable look.

Daisy faltered. Everyone was watching her. 'Erm . . . yeah. Me too.' She felt all giddy and then slightly panicked about what she was doing. Seizing an opportunity to be alone with Max – this was not part of the plan.

'Okay, if you're sure,' said Jason, and he and Tamsyn steadied a meandering Aunt Coral, steered her through the door and closed it behind them.

'You did well tonight,' said Max, his eyes closely studying Daisy's face making her feel a warm glow rise from her core.

'So did you.' She realised her voice had gone a little husky. She looked up slowly and their eyes met and she knew what was going to happen next. Her heart was speeding up while her head was full of question marks. Max bent forward and their lips touched. Was this a good idea? No. Would it change things between them? Probably. Did she want to do it anyway? Yes.

The kiss took over and they were lost in the moment until Max started to pull at her shirt and she broke free. 'Hang on, let's think about this,' she said, quite breathless.

'Let's not,' said Max and he kissed her again.

Then something distracted him and he glanced at the window. Daisy turned too and saw the shadows change in the darkness – there was someone outside, most likely a local looking for one last freebie.

It was enough to kill the moment. Max pulled away from Daisy who had been rapidly warming to the idea of carrying on. 'You're right,' said Max, looking awkward. 'Sorry.'

'No, no, it's fine. More than fine.'

Max looked distractedly out of the window. 'I'll just check everything's okay outside then we'll make a move.'

'Great,' said Daisy, trying to cover her tinge of embarrassment at getting carried away. It was definitely for the best; she needed to have a think about this before they went any further. She would be looking to sell up and leave next summer, but that was quite a while away and some fun with Max between now and then might be, well, fun.

234

Daisy locked up whilst Max patrolled the perimeter. She put her hands in her pockets and walked over to him. 'You okay?'

'Hmm,' he said distractedly. 'Er, yeah. Sorry. We all locked up?'

'Yes, we are.' She appraised him. He was gorgeous when he was smartened up.

Max put an arm protectively around Daisy. 'Okay?'

'Yeah,' she replied, enjoying the closeness of the gesture and they set off for home as unbeknown to them a figure watched from the shadows.

Daisy didn't sleep well; she was thinking through every tiny detail of the evening, particularly her kiss with Max. She had hoped she would get a repeat performance when he dropped her home but he seemed preoccupied and had only given her a hug and then walked off.

Her alarm woke her and she dragged herself out of bed, made some toast and said a brief 'Good morning' to Aunt Coral who was nursing what looked like a monster hangover. Daisy left her with her an Alka-Seltzer and went to work. She didn't need to get there this early, she wasn't opening up until the evening but she had some work to do on getting the hot chocolate cabin side of the business up and running.

She stood outside for a few minutes grinning inanely at the sign. She was glad there was nobody about to witness it but just looking at the name on the little railway building made her happy. She loved the fact it was hers, all her own work with the help of some good friends, and it felt terrific. This was a master class in setting up a business for resale. All the time she was investing here was about making Locos the best it could be and for it to be turning a profit before she had to put it up for sale and get top dollar. She'd be able to repay Aunt Coral and have the money she needed to travel.

Daisy's first big test was the lantern parade. With only a day between opening and the parade it was all a bit too close for comfort but Daisy had already shown she was up for a challenge and this was no different. She had sourced and tested a number of hot chocolates and had settled on a good quality real chocolate flake variety – it was more expensive but gave a rich and smooth flavour she was sure children and adults would adore. As soon as she'd tasted it she'd been transported back in time to when she was a little girl and Great Uncle Reg would melt his special chocolate chips into hot milk – it tasted exactly the same. She had also found a creamy white hot chocolate and a sumptuous dark version too. A variety of syrups including some sugar free also made for a multitude of variations but all were available with whipped cream, chocolate shavings and marshmallows – obviously.

The lantern parade was akin to a launch party for the hot chocolate side of the business and because it was a great opportunity to promote Locos Daisy was prepared to put the cost down to marketing.

Daisy was testing her favourite combinations in small measures to decide on her finalists for the big event when there was a knock on the door.

'Hiya.' Tamsyn popped a head around the door as Daisy crossed one off the list. Dark chocolate with peppermint was probably better suited to a smaller audience.

'Perfect timing, Tamsyn. Tell me what you think of these three flavours for after the lantern parade.' She produced three filled shot glasses and gestured for Tamsyn to try them.

She lifted the first one tentatively to her lips and Daisy leaned in, keen to judge her reaction. Tamsyn closed her eyes and took a sip. 'Blimey, it's gorgeous. Mega thick and creamy.'

'Great, that's our standard offering, try this one next.' She offered the next glass and Tamsyn wrinkled her nose.

'White chocolate?'

'Yep, try it.' Daisy was smiling, she knew how amazing it tasted with the most delicate hint of vanilla.

'Scrumptious,' said Tamsyn, draining the glass and licking her lips. 'It's like drinking a bar of white chocolate.'

'That's the general idea.'

Tamsyn picked up the last one without being asked and took a sip. 'Ooh is there a hint of cherry?'

Daisy nodded. 'I'll serve it with cream and a drizzle of sauce, it's like a black forest gateau in a glass.'

'They're all amazing. I'm going to be the size of a house working here,' said Tamsyn, sticking her finger into the glass and mopping up the dregs.

Daisy was pleased with Tamsyn's reaction; she hoped everyone else felt the same tomorrow night.

'Are we having food too? Because I was thinking we could make something nativity themed like cow pies and donkey sausage.'

Daisy wasn't sure how these were related to the Christmas story but neither sounded appropriate. 'It's okay. Old Man Burgess is making some shortbread stars.'

'Oh goody,' said Tamsyn, jiggling on the high stool. Something fell from her pocket. Daisy bent to pick it up and placed *The Beginners' Guide to Tarot Reading* on the bar.

'Are you dabbling in the occult again?' asked Daisy, with a grin.

'I'm thinking about doing Tarot readings on the side,' said Tamsyn, pulling a pack of Tarot cards from her bra.

'Okay,' said Daisy, getting an ominous feeling.

'Can I practise on you?'

Daisy was already shaking her head. 'I'm not sure, Tams. Tarot's not my kind of thing. Have you done it on yourself yet?'

It turned out to be a good distraction technique. 'Not really. I guess I should do me first,' said Tamsyn and Daisy vehemently agreed.

Tamsyn shuffled the cards and slowly separated the deck into three piles in front of her. Daisy watched her intently. Tamsyn turned over four cards and Daisy scanned them quickly.

'What do they mean?' asked Daisy.

'They all mean something slightly different in relation to the main card.' Tamsyn touched the card above the three in a row. 'Most readers use their psychic intuition to read them as well as their knowledge of the cards.' She sounded well informed.

'Right. What does your psychic intuition tell you about these?'

Tamsyn touched the top card. 'This is the two of swords. I've had that before and I think it means a decision is needed.' Tamsyn touched the first card in the row of three with her fingertip. 'This is my Past. Hmm, Page of Wands, now what does that mean?' She rifled through the Tarot book. 'Ah, a bringer of news. It could be someone who's always been in my life.'

'Jason,' said Daisy getting excited.

'Or you.'

'Oh,' said Daisy. 'Carry on.' She was getting quite into it.

'This is my Present,' said Tamsyn moving her finger to the next card and scrabbling through to the right page in the guide. 'The nine of wands denotes completion of projects and the number nine is associated with the Moon. It warns of delusions and dreams not being as they seem.' She looked up from the page.

'Are the cards telling you you're wrong about keeping Jason at a distance?'

Tamsyn ignored her and moved her finger to the last card. 'My Future.' She took a deep breath and Daisy waited while Tamsyn checked the book. 'This card is Judgement, Karma or The Angeli; it means a second chance.'

Daisy clapped her hands together making Tamsyn jump. 'They're telling you to take another chance with Jason.'

Tamsyn gathered the cards up. 'I'm not sure. I wasn't getting that as a psychic message.'

Daisy stopped Tamsyn by placing a hand on top of hers. 'What does your heart tell you?'

Tamsyn hurriedly got off the high stool tipping the cards onto the floor. Daisy rushed to help pick them up.

Tamsyn looked panicked as she pointed at the strewn cards and a single one lying face up – the death card. 'Oh no, I don't need to look that one up.'

'It doesn't mean anything, Tamsyn.' Daisy saw the word death and quickly collected it up with the others.

Tamsyn gasped. 'But Old Man Burgess is making the biscuits for the lantern parade tomorrow.'

Daisy laughed. 'I'm sure we'll all be fine.'

Chapter Twenty-Three

Daisy and Tamsyn were on their way back from grabbing sandwiches for lunch when Tamsyn spotted Jason coming out of the fudge shop. She ran to catch him before he got into his police car. 'Jason,' she called from the other side of the road.

He looked across at the sound of his name but his expression wasn't the usual happy smile she'd come to expect or even take for granted.

'Hiya,' said Jason, his hand on the car door.

'Actually, Jason, I'd like to explain the other day and the kiss and everything.'

'It's fine.' He didn't look fine.

'Okay, but I don't want either of us to get hurt.'

'I'm not sure avoiding things is the best approach to not getting hurt.'

'I think it is in our case. I'd worry we'd both feel we had to change and try to be the person the other one wants us to be.'

Jason looked as if he understood. 'Just promise me one thing?'

'Anything,' said Tamsyn, brightly throwing open her arms in an elaborate Tamsyn-style gesture.

'Don't rule us out forever. You know in the future there might be a time when it would be right for us to be together and I'd hate to think we let it pass us by.'

Tamsyn hesitated. 'Okay. I promise.'

'Good,' said Jason, appearing to relax a little. 'Did you fancy coming round tonight for a *Doctor Who* marathon? It's just me, Max and a couple of large pizzas.'

'I'd love to,' she said. Daisy hovered nearby not wanting to interrupt.

'You're welcome too, Daisy, if *Doctor Who* and pizza float your boat,' said Jason.

'Sorry, *Doctor Who* kind of sinks mine, but thanks for asking.'

Whilst everything seemed fine between Tamsyn and Jason, Daisy couldn't help feeling something fundamental had changed.

Lantern parade day dawned and Daisy knew it was going to be one of those days that dragged on forever, a bit like Christmas Eve when you were a child. The parade wasn't until the evening and she couldn't make the hot chocolate until just before the parade started because she needed to serve it hot. She had managed to get hold of a ten-litre hot water urn, which the manufacturer assured her would heat milk just as efficiently as it did water although the urn would need a thorough clean afterwards. Daisy decided the cost was a worthwhile investment to enable her to serve real hot chocolate on the promenade thanks to an extension cable they were going to rig up from the beach café.

Daisy and Tamsyn decided to put up some lanterns of their own. Daisy wanted it to look traditional and as close to what the Victorians would have had as possible whereas Tamsyn favoured anything brightly coloured and preferably sparkly.

'How about this?' asked Tamsyn, holding up some bright pink glittery paper.

'No way,' said Daisy.

Tamsyn didn't reply, she thumbed the paper with a glum look on her face.

'What's up?' asked Daisy, pausing at the top of a stepladder with a cylinder-shaped lantern in her hand.

'I saw Jason last night.'

'Oh, yeah. How was *Doctor Who*?' Daisy tried hard not to pull a face like she was eating a sour sweet.

'Max was there, it wasn't totally awkward but I could tell Jason wasn't relaxed. I've ruined things between us.' Her shoulders slumped forward and Daisy came down the stepladder and put an arm around her. 'Things will settle down again.'

Tamsyn pouted. 'What if the cards were right? What if I should give me and Jason a second chance?'

Daisy exhaled. 'I don't think one kiss was even a first chance to be honest.'

'Hmm, maybe not. I just want some sort of sign it's the right thing to do.' Tamsyn scanned the bar as if waiting for something to happen. It made Daisy glance about too but everything was silent.

A sudden banging on the door made them both jump. 'Cock-a-doodle-doo,' said Daisy, her heart leaping in panic. She rushed to unlock the door.

'Hello Daisy, I've come to give you a hand ahead of tonight,' said Old Man Burgess, shuffling inside. How a frail old gent could knock on a door that hard was beyond Daisy. She looked across at Tamsyn and she gave a weak smile, Daisy guessed Old Man Burgess was not the sign Tamsyn had been hoping for.

*

Night descended on the bay and Daisy went into full-on efficient-boss mode. She had Tamsyn checking the list of everything they needed to serve the drinks remotely and Max was tasked with loading it into the back of Tamsyn's car. Once on the prom they did everything in reverse and set themselves up on the beach café's picnic tables, which had been pulled out of winter storage. Daisy filled up the urn with milk, switched it on, checked the temperature gauge and set to work on measuring out the chocolate flakes into the plain white mugs Tamsyn was putting out in neat rows.

Daisy received a text from Jason to say the children were setting off from the church and her stomach did a flip. This was like the gin bar unveiling all over again but this time she felt she probably had harder critics because if kids didn't like something they were brutally honest.

Before long they could see the lights appear in the distance. There was a mass of glowing objects bobbing along – it was lovely to watch the lights snake their way down the hill. As the group grew closer so did the accompanying jolly chatter. Daisy checked the temperature gauge on the urn and all was well. Max was standing by with the whipped cream. A wicked thought danced through her mind but the sight of lanterns turning onto the promenade brought her back to the present.

Daisy marvelled at the variety of lanterns as the children and accompanying adults proudly neared them. It was a sight to behold with the different coloured lanterns all glowing in the dark, but what touched her most was the look of sheer delight on the children's faces. They lined up their lanterns by the sea wall to be judged and then all at once the children seemed to rush towards the picnic tables for their hot chocolates. Old Man Burgess did his best at queue management but it was rather like trying to herd hyperactive cats.

They got in a rhythm with Daisy reeling off the choices and calling out the order and Tamsyn filling the appropriate mug with milk and syrup if required and then passing it to Max for toppings and delivery to the child. It was nice to catch a glimpse of the children's faces as they sipped their drinks – not one had pulled an 'I don't like it' face, which was miraculous.

Before long they were serving the last few stragglers and Daisy at last started to relax. People hugged their mugs as the judges delivered news of the winning lanterns and prizes were handed out. Empty mugs started to come back thick and fast accompanied by heartfelt thanks and praise for the drinks with the general view being it was a million times better than last year. In exchange for each returned mug Old Man Burgess handed out a Locos leaflet, which had taken Daisy ages to design but looked worth it now they'd been professionally printed. Tamsyn and Daisy carefully stacked the dirty mugs into boxes, the glasswasher would be busy this evening.

'I think we can call tonight a resounding success,' said Max, giving Daisy an impromptu hug that made her go all awkward and a bit giddy. She was starting to wish their kiss hadn't been interrupted the other night.

'Er, yeah. Well done team. Top effort.' She tucked her hair behind her ear and tried to ignore the knowing look Tamsyn was giving her.

It was still early when she opened up, a couple of days later; now Max was on the paid staff he wasn't there every morning. She liked being there on her own. She loved being able to hear the key turn in the lock with a thunk and step inside her own little empire. Perhaps empire was stretching it a bit but it was the most she had ever owned and it was somewhere she felt at home, which struck her as odd because that was a phrase she never used.

She set about giving the counters and table tops a proper clean and when they were done she decided to bring in some more tonics from the old railway carriage, which was acting as their storeroom. Up until now Max had been bringing in any stock from the carriage but Daisy was no wimp, she was sure she could manage.

She checked her keys and tried what she thought was the right one in the lock. It didn't feel right. She tried another but it didn't fit like the first one. She tried the first key again and then realised the problem was there was no resistance, no lock to turn. It was already open. Somehow they must have forgotten to lock it up last night. Cautiously she turned the old door handle and peered into the gloom. With all the blinds down there was no light at all. Then she heard something. She listened carefully. Was it an animal? Or a motor of some sort? It was someone snoring!

Daisy crept back into the main building, picked up a bottle of gin from the display, taking care it wasn't her most expensive, and headed back to the carriage. She pulled the door fully open and jumped inside making her presence known with her bottle of gin held aloft.

'Bloody hell!' came a voice from the previously snoring tartan bundle.

'Pasco?'

'Oh, Daisy, good morning. How are you?' Pasco blinked and tried to sit up.

'What the hell are you doing in my railway carriage?' As she spoke she noticed the tartan picnic blanket he was wrapped in. 'You're the thief.' She pointed at the blanket. 'Where's my locket?' She stepped forward with the gin bottle still in her hand.

Pasco shuffled backwards. 'Now hang on. Don't jump to conclusions like Max did. I found this blanket.'

'I don't believe you. I'm calling the police.'

'Now we all know you mean young Jason Fenton and he's a lovely lad who won't take kindly to you wielding a bottle near my head, now will he?'

Daisy was still thinking through what to do when someone came up behind her making her scream and she swung the gin bottle in their general direction.

'Daisy!'

'Max, I nearly hit you!' Daisy slowly lowered the bottle. She was shocked how close she'd come to bashing him with it. He seemed momentarily cross but his attention was quickly diverted elsewhere.

'Dad!' Max looked exasperated and ran his fingers through his hair. 'What's going on?'

Pasco got to his feet and started to bundle up his make-shift bed. 'I'm sorry, son, I know you said to be out early but look.' Pasco lifted up an alarm clock. 'I still have five minutes before this goes off.'

Daisy stared at Max and gripped the gin bottle. 'You knew?'

'What?' said Max, looking wrongfooted. He ran his teeth uneasily along his bottom lip.

'You bloody well knew your dad was sleeping in here. That's why you've been all "I'll fetch the stuff from the carriage" and "I'll get there early". You complete and utter shit,' she said, giving him a forceful shove with the gin bottle, which he deftly caught as she let go and stormed out of the carriage.

Max watched her disappear into the bar and then turned back to Pasco.

'Thanks for dropping me in it, Dad.'

'Sorry, but she'll come round when she sees there's no damage done.'

'No damage?' Max shook his head, his expression incredulous.

'I don't suppose there's a cuppa going, is there?' Max went to reply but instead emitted a growling noise. 'No. Okay. I'll be off then,' said Pasco.

Max rubbed his hand across his stubble and went after Daisy who was now pacing up and down the platform.

'Were you in on the thefts too? Have *you* got my locket?'

'Bloody hell, Daisy, calm down. This is all my dad's doing, it's got nothing to do with me.'

'But it has,' she said, more calmly. 'You knew he was sleeping in there. You've been using me all along.' She threw up her hands. 'I am such an idiot.'

'No, look it's not like—'

'Piss off, Max. I don't want to hear it.' Daisy strode back into the bar and slammed the door behind her.

Pasco gave a small cough behind Max. 'I don't suppose you've got a couple of quid for a coffee have you, son?'

'No, and what's more I will never give you another penny. You have done it again. You always mess things up. You are the most selfish person on the planet. Mum was right about you.'

'Steady on there, Max. I know you're upset but . . .' said Pasco looking hurt.

Max stepped closer to his father and lowered his voice. 'Will you do one thing for me?'

Pasco gave him an endearing lopsided look. 'I'd do anything for you. You know that.'

The attempt at endearing didn't seem to work on Max. 'Leave Ottercombe Bay. Never come back and never get in touch with me again.'

Pasco gave a small laugh. 'Well, there's three things on your list, son . . .'

'I mean it, Dad. I've had enough.' Max turned and walked away.

Chapter Twenty-Four

Tamsyn and Jason were at an uneasy point trying hard to be relaxed in each other's company. What was meant to be another pizza and *Doctor Who* evening with friends had ended up as just Jason and Tamsyn because Max had cried off for some reason. They were sitting on Jason's firm and durable sofa watching the television and she couldn't think of a time she'd been happier with the possible exception of when her parents had bought her bunk beds so her imaginary friend had somewhere to sleep.

Tamsyn drank the last of the supermarket cola and hoped the aftertaste would soon disappear. She leaned back to study Jason and he viewed her a few times before eventually giving her his full attention. 'What?' he asked gently.

'There was another thing stopping us being . . . you know.' Jason didn't look like he did know. 'In a relationship,' she added.

'What exactly?' He paused the DVD.

'You want to go out with Daisy, don't you?' said Tamsyn. Jason looked as if he'd been hit in the face with a chair. 'It's all right, don't worry. I don't mind. I mean, I'd choose Daisy instead of me. She's prettier, funnier, braver, more adventurous—' She was counting the attributes off on her fingers when Jason interrupted her.

'Wow, let me stop you there,' he said, flicking off the television and turning to face her properly.

'Don't deny it, please.' Tamsyn looked a little sad as she flattened down a tuft of his hair that was having a rebellious moment. 'I can see how you look at her and I don't just mean since she got back. I remember how you watched her all the time when we were children. Have you always loved her?'

Jason's eyes were wide. He let out a long slow breath. 'No,' he said emphatically. 'I haven't always . . . there was a time when I had a huge crush on her, that's true. I was about six and to be honest there was nothing I wouldn't have done for her. Do you think she knows?'

Tamsyn rolled her lips together. 'Probably, but I think a girl like Daisy gets used to men feeling like that about her. She won't hold it against you.'

'I hope not, it's all in the past. It's not how I feel now.'

'How do you feel now?'

Jason broke eye contact and sighed. 'To be honest when she turned up in the bay again I did kind of revert to my schoolboy self and six-year-old me was mightily pleased she was even talking to me. But I quickly realised we've all grown up.'

'But you must have wanted to go out with her, she's lovely.'

Jason looked serious. 'I agree, Daisy is lovely but we both know she's not right for me.'

Tamsyn tilted her head to one side. 'And do you think I could be?'

'I'd like to find out.' Jason angled himself slowly forward as if moving in for a tentative kiss.

'Great. I'll think about it,' said Tamsyn, shuffling to the other end of the sofa away from Jason and she turned her face back to the television's blank screen. Jason slowly filled his lungs with air and turned the television back on.

When the credits rolled at the end of the episode, Tamsyn rearranged herself to sit crossed legged on the sofa. 'Mum says it's destiny.'

'Uh-huh,' said Jason ejecting the DVD.

'She said it was meant to be, the cards told her.'

'Just like they told her an unexploded bomb was going to be washed up in the bay?' asked Jason.

'Technically we still don't know if she was correct about that one because the tide might have taken it out again.'

'Okay.' Jason returned the DVD case to its place in his ordered collection.

'She sees more darkness before the sun for Daisy. I hope she can cope with more darkness.' Tamsyn bit her lip.

'I'm sure she'll be fine,' said Jason. 'Do you want another cola?'

Tamsyn wasn't sure on either front.

Daisy had bottled, corked and shelved her anger at Max letting Pasco use the carriage as a squat but being in close proximity to him now was making it bubble up again. They had been working the evening shift together and Max had a permanent frown etched on his face, which annoyed her immensely. It was *his* fault they were barely talking, *he* was the one who had gone and spoilt everything, so why was *he* frowning? She could barely look at him because every time she did it reminded her of how he'd taken her for a fool – all trust was gone.

As the last customer finally left and Daisy locked the door behind them the forced smile she'd been wearing slid from her face. Max was leaning back against the counter undoing the top buttons on his shirt. He'd stopped frowning.

'I don't know about you, but I'm knackered,' he said, as the corners of his mouth tweaked.

'Me?' said Daisy, the bubbles of anger started to fizz inside her. 'I'm still furious.'

The furrow returned to Max's forehead. 'Pasco sleeping in the carriage was meant to be for one night—' he started and that was enough for Daisy's cork to blow.

'Even one night was too much. You had no right to let him sleep here. You went behind my back.'

'Daisy, he's my dad.'

'I don't care. You could have at least bothered to ask me.'

'And what would you have said?' Max's tone was inching into the challenging territory.

'That's not the point. The point is you used me. You only helped out around here so your thief of a father had somewhere to squat!'

'That's not true. I helped out because I wanted to.'

'Or were you just wheedling your way in to get a job?'

'You're crazy.' He looked exasperated.

Daisy's expression changed. 'Were you in on the burglaries?'

Max was visibly rattled. 'Shit, no. That had nothing to do with me and how dare you say—'

But Daisy wasn't listening. 'Has my necklace been sold?' She was further annoyed by the tears springing to her eyes at the thought of her mother's locket.

'I don't know!' shouted Max. 'I'm not a thief.'

'Your father is.'

'Just because he's been in prison doesn't mean he's guilty of every crime that happens around here. You're as bad as everyone else.' His voice tailed off and he gave Daisy a look of disgust.

'Maybe everyone else is right.'

'Fine. Believe what you like,' said Max struggling to unlock the door.

'Fine,' agreed Daisy, wanting to push him through it but instead she shoved him out of the way, wrestled with the key and opened the door. The few awkward moments seemed to stretch on interminably until Daisy stepped out of the way and Max stormed outside. Daisy slammed the door behind him but it didn't give her the satisfaction she had hoped it would. She was mad at Max for having got mixed up with his father and ruining everything. But worse still, she was nowhere nearer to finding out where her locket was.

Christmas seemed to have crept up on Daisy. Only two weeks to go, but she didn't need to do much. She'd topped up her stock at Locos in case they had a rush of people out for Christmas drinks. Tamsyn had strung up some fairy lights and Max had brought in some real holly – she hadn't asked where he'd got it from. It was all the railway bar needed to make it feel traditionally festive but not over the top.

She wasn't a big fan of the festive season. It had always seemed to be focused on bringing families together and since hers never could be it had felt a little pointless. Her father had frequently worked over Christmas so apart from the day itself she had often found herself home alone watching old movies. Since her dad had moved to Goa she had continued the tradition and let everyone else's excitement wash over her. But it looked like this year was going to be different.

'Tamsyn is coming round later to help decorate the tree and I'd like a hand with wrapping some presents if you don't mind,' said Aunt Coral. 'Isn't it exciting? They're predicting a white Christmas for the Midlands but I bet we miss out. Such a shame the coast can't hold the snow. I guess it's the salty air.'

Daisy didn't answer – she was staring open-mouthed at the giant Christmas tree that was filling a whole corner of the small living room and blocking out the television completely.

'Daisy?'

'Yes, sorry. Fine,' she replied trying hard not to comment on the ridiculous size of the tree.

Aunt Coral put an arm around her. 'It's magnificent isn't it?'

Daisy managed a twitch. There were no words. Thankfully Bug walked over to the tree and promptly cocked his leg against it, which summed up Daisy's thinking on the matter perfectly. Before he had time to relieve himself Aunt Coral had scooped him up and transferred him to the back garden where he vehemently barked his protest.

That evening the small house was filled with the scent of mulled wine and the sound of a decidedly dodgy Christmas album. Despite Daisy's misgivings, after a couple of glasses of Aunt Coral's special mulled wine she was enjoying the evening even though she could see no point in covering the giant tree with the multitude of homemade decorations Tamsyn had brought only to have to take them all off again in a few weeks' time – utterly pointless.

Daisy picked up a brown lump attached to sparkly ribbon and gave it a once over. It clearly was something Tamsyn must have made as a small child. It was either a Christmas pudding or a lump of poo. Tamsyn caught Daisy inspecting the bauble.

'I made it myself,' said Tamsyn proudly.

'That's what worries me,' said Daisy, twirling it in front of her eyes.

'I watched this programme all about crafting your perfect Christmas. I've been making these for weeks. I've already filled our tree at home. Aren't they fab?'

Daisy helped herself to another glass of mulled wine; she'd need it to get through the rest of the evening.

Tamsyn paused with a wonky-eyed robin halfway to a branch. 'You never see Turkey eggs for sale. Always chickens and sometimes ducks but never turkey. Why is that?'

'Is this a cracker joke?'

Tamsyn looked puzzled. 'No, it's a real question.'

Daisy pondered it for a moment. 'I have no idea.' Tamsyn was funny, she seemed to worry about things nobody else gave a passing thought to.

When the last string of homemade pom-pom tassels had been hung and the lights switched on they all stood back to admire their handiwork. Aunt Coral put an arm around both of them. 'Well done, girls. It looks terrific,' she said, giving them both an affectionate squeeze. Daisy felt something stir deep within her, which could have been festive cheer, or the feeling of accomplishment at filling the enormous green spruce, or more likely too much spice in Aunt Coral's mulled wine.

Things were still strained between Daisy and Max but having to work together five nights out of seven meant they had had to call a truce. Daisy wasn't happy with the situation but Max was still protesting his innocence and as business was steady she needed him – they were stuck with each other for the time being. They had to get along as boss and employee.

255

'I hear your Christmas tree is pretty spectacular,' said Max, rubbing the glasswasher smears off a glass at the start of another shift.

Daisy couldn't help herself. 'It looks like 1974 vomited on it.'

Max looked taken aback but he laughed all the same. 'Now I definitely want to see it. I'm sensing you're not a fan of Christmas. Am I right?'

'I've never got what all the fuss was about to be honest. I understand if you're religious but I'm not, it's just another day.'

'And I thought I was a Bah Humbug, but you're the full Ebenezer.'

Daisy looked shocked. 'I'm not that bad. I don't mind other people enjoying it. All I'm saying is I don't get it. Are you going to tell me you dress up as chief elf and carry Santa's sack?'

Max raised his eyebrows at the double entendre but gallantly let it go as Daisy was already colouring up. 'No, I'm not a dressing-up kinda guy. But I like my full turkey dinner, preferably home cooked.'

'You cook?' Daisy didn't mean to splutter the words out but she'd been caught off guard.

'I wish I could cook a full roast but spaghetti bolognaise is the peak of my abilities. I usually go to the Mariner's; Monty's wife does a cracking Christmas lunch.'

'People make such a fuss about it. It's just a roast dinner, it's no biggy. But then they go and spoil it by insisting on Brussels sprouts and I don't believe they're anyone's favourite vegetable.'

'Reg liked them.' Max started to stack more glasses, making sure they were all neatly in line.

Daisy scanned her memories; she couldn't find much

about Christmas in Ottercombe Bay – she'd been seven the last time she'd spent the festive season here. It was still odd that Max sometimes knew more about her family than she did. 'What do you do after lunch on Christmas Day?'

'I like to crash out with a few beers and a crap movie.'

'Now the crap movie I totally get. That is something we can agree on.' Which is rare these days, thought Daisy.

'I think there's too much pressure on people to spend loads of cash.'

'Totally agree,' nodded Daisy. 'All the adverts tell you you should be buying diamonds and—'

'New sofas and tellies.'

'Exactly. When the poinsettias they're selling at the supermarket for ninety-nine pence would be fine.'

Max laughed. 'You cheapskate.'

'Hey. They're great, no one has to know how much they are. It's the thought that counts.' She'd already decided to get one for Tamsyn's mum and dad, Old Man Burgess and Aunt Coral although she needed to buy her something else too, she was staying in her home rent free and she had stumped up a sizeable sum to get Locos off the ground. Daisy was having a think when she noticed Max was staring at her. 'What?' There was only a faint hint of irritation in her voice.

He gave a short smile. 'Nothing,' he said, turning back to focus on restocking the mixers. Daisy turned away, at least this was better than fighting all the time but it didn't mean he was forgiven.

Chapter Twenty-Five

Daisy was tired when she got in on Christmas Eve and presented Aunt Coral with her poinsettia. She figured it was safest to hand it over now, she didn't have a good track record with plants. Aunt Coral gave an odd grimace of a smile. 'It's lovely, thank you,' she said, taking it to the kitchen. Daisy followed and watched her remove it from the decorative wrapping, give it some water and place it on the windowsill next to two other identical plants.

'Oh,' said Daisy.

Aunt Coral was quick to reassure her. 'It's fine, I really like them. They must be the trendy gift this year: I had one from Mrs Brightling for taking her shopping and one from work. Once they've soaked up some water I'll spread them about the house. Now, would you like a glass of sherry?'

Daisy tore her eyes away from the trio of red plants and wished she hadn't been such a cheapskate. 'Yeah, go on then.'

Aunt Coral handed her a glass. 'Come and look at this,' Coral said, excitedly. Daisy followed her into the living room, trying to take a sip as she went, which didn't work. It became obvious what Daisy had been brought to look at. Where there had once been a small dark sofa and a chair there was now a huge pale cream sofa and two matching chairs and with the giant Christmas tree there wasn't a lot of room for much else. The sofas reminded Daisy of giant mutant marshmallows.

'What do you think?' prompted Aunt Coral tilting her head at the mountainous furniture.

Daisy bent forward and Aunt Coral whisked her sherry glass away, the proximity of it to the masses of pale fabric was likely putting her on edge. Daisy sat down and felt as if she was being swallowed by the sofa. At first it was alarming but she quickly relaxed into it. 'Wow, this is seriously comfy.'

'I know,' said Aunt Coral grinning. 'I've wanted them for ages and now I can afford it. We just need to keep them this colour.'

Daisy gave a doubtful nod. With Bug in the house they didn't stand a chance.

Christmas morning dawned and Daisy was woken by someone opening presents on her bed. She rubbed sleep from her eyes and sat up to see Bug's bottom wriggling about enthusiastically with the rest of him inside a large Christmas stocking. When he reversed out he had a mouthful of ripped wrapping paper. It was early and Daisy was confused by what was going on. She was pretty sure she hadn't gone back in time to her childhood so it was very odd to find a stocking perched on the end of her bed.

She shooed Bug away and with a disgruntled snort he jumped to the floor and swaggered out. 'And a merry Christmas to you too,' she called after him. Daisy reached forward and dragged the stocking towards her. There was a pretty tag attached to it and in swirly gold writing it read 'Love From Father Christmas'. Daisy laughed out loud at the peculiarity of it but she tipped out the presents all the same.

After a frenzied few minutes ripping open the paper like a small child she sat and surveyed her haul. There was an accounting book, which was a very useful gift. There was a small make-up bag containing a lip balm and something claiming to be lip scrub, which Daisy wasn't too sure about but she'd give it a go anyway. There was the dinkiest set of mini nail varnishes in pretty colours, lots of white chocolate, which was her absolute favourite, and a new case for her mobile phone. But this wasn't just any old case – when she turned it over she saw the back was emblazoned with a photograph of Locos. Aunt Coral must have taken it on the sly, thought Daisy, examining the impressive result.

A tentative tap on her open door made her look up. Aunt Coral was hovering with two mugs of tea.

'Happy Christmas, love,' she said, coming in and placing the mugs on the bedside cabinet. 'I see Father Christmas has been,' she added, with a wink.

'You are officially bonkers,' said Daisy, reaching up and giving her aunt a tight embrace.

'Oh, it's just a bit of fun. I bought a pre-filled stocking for Bugsy, then Min said she always does one for Tamsyn and I wouldn't want you missing out.'

'It's really kind of you and these are fab presents. Thank you.'

'You're welcome.'

'I didn't get you much,' said Daisy, feeling embarrassed at the dull jumper waiting under the tree for her aunt. If she'd realised about the stocking perhaps she could have done something similar but what she would have put in it she had no idea. Support tights and Nivea face cream sprang to mind and she blinked to try to banish the thought.

'Don't be silly.' Aunt Coral patted her hand affectionately. 'It's just lovely to have you here. Christmas is a time for families.' Daisy brightened – perhaps today was going to be okay after all. 'Right, we'd better get a wiggle on, we need to be on the beach in forty minutes,' Aunt Coral added rising quickly to her feet.

'Why?' Daisy pulled up the covers, she hadn't planned on getting up yet.

'Christmas Day charity swim,' said Aunt Coral, as Daisy's eyebrows jumped. 'It's traditional. Come on, snap to it.' Daisy's eyebrows remained where they were.

Daisy was relieved to discover she wasn't actually required to go swimming. She and Aunt Coral were on the beach to cheer the swimmers on, along with a surprisingly large crowd of people. Aunt Coral was filling paper cups with mulled wine from a large flask and as ten thirty approached people Daisy had assumed were also watchers started to strip off their layers to reveal swimming costumes. There were also quite a few people dressed up – three Father Christmases, a nun, a man in a large pink tutu and plenty of people in Santa hats. But the most worrying was the man who whipped off his large coat to reveal a lime green mankini. Daisy turned away only to come face to face with a gorilla. She stepped back in alarm. The person in the gorilla suit started making monkey noises and banging its chest. 'Very good,' said Daisy, with as much enthusiasm as she could muster on a cold December morning and hoped that would be enough to make the idiot go away.

'Isn't it exciting?' asked Aunt Coral, hugging her cup of mulled wine as the steam swirled off the surface.

'Oh yeah,' said Daisy. In her mind it was total and utter madness. She was sure she'd read about someone dying doing this the other year and was trying to recall the details when someone pinched her bum. She shot around to see the gorilla lolloping away. Great, she thought, an idiot and a pervert.

A man walked down to the water shouting something about the swimmers gathering around and a large portion of the crowd followed him to the shore. Daisy had a better view now of the swimmers. She searched the crowd for faces she knew but there were only a few, alarmingly Old Man Burgess was one of them. While she was pondering the health risks once again someone pinched her bum. A flash of temper swept through her and this time the gorilla was going to get a piece of her mind. Daisy swung around quickly grabbing the gorilla by the arm and pulling him back sharply, making him land with a thump on the sand.

'Hey!' came the plaintive cry in a voice she recognised. The gorilla pulled off its mask. 'That was a bit rough,' said Tamsyn, looking disgruntled. 'It was only a bit of fun.'

'Sorry, I thought it was some pervert.' Daisy offered Tamsyn a hand and pulled her to her feet. 'Great costume by the way. I take it you're not swimming in it though?'

'Er, yeah of course I am. It's cold in there you know.' Tamsyn jogged ape style down the beach to join the others, putting her mask back on as she went.

Daisy looked about for lifeguards and spotted a bored-looking Max hugging a bright orange torpedo buoy and chatting to an equally bored-looking St John Ambulance cadet. Despite the cold, Max was wearing a jacket and shorts and she didn't rush to drag her eyes away from his muscular legs. Without warning, someone in full wetsuit, mask, snorkel and flippers loomed in front of her making her take a step back, narrowly missing Aunt Coral's toes.

'Sorry,' came the muffled reply through the snorkel.

'Jason?' Daisy peered closer.

'Can't stop, took me ages to squeeze into this. I think I may have put on a little weight since last year.' He shuffled awkwardly to the shore where everyone was forming an orderly line.

'Remember once around the *outside* of the red buoy and first one over the line wins,' shouted the loud man.

'What line?' Daisy asked Aunt Coral.

'They hold up a bit of ribbon once they are nearly at the shore.'

'Right,' said Daisy, catching another glimpse of Max who had wandered down to the water's edge as if to show willing.

'Three, two, one. Go!' This was accompanied by a loud hooter, which made Daisy jump, and all the swimmers raced into the sea. The serious ones were recognisable in their immediate desire to get swimming whereas a lady in a giraffe onesie and Tamsyn were still only ankle deep. Jason tried to wade in but the tightness of his wetsuit was restricting movement and he fell into the water with a huge splash and automatically started doing the breaststroke despite only being in about two feet of water.

Daisy started to laugh; this was actually quite good fun. The crowd of watchers were cheering everyone on and they got particularly excited when the leader reached the red buoy. Tamsyn on the other hand was still at the wading stage albeit up to her shoulders. As she started to swim a flaw in her plan quickly became apparent. The gorilla suit was quite heavy and the addition of water meant Tamsyn was barely able to keep her head out of the water and lifting her arms out appeared to be an impossibility. Daisy watched the gorilla slowly start to sink. Instinctively Daisy started to run forward but Max was already diving into the water and swimming efficiently to Tamsyn's rescue. Daisy stopped at the water's edge, it was going to be freezing in there and Max looked like he had it covered. No point getting cold and wet for no good reason.

The crowd cheered as Max grasped Tamsyn but she didn't sound as pleased. 'Get off, Max. I'm fine,' she shouted from behind the mask.

'You're struggling,' said Max, towing her back to shore.

'No, I'm not,' insisted Tamsyn, but her protests were drowned out as the other swimmers raced for the finish with a lanky teen just pipping the early leader to the soggy ribbon finish line. The crowd clapped and then immediately dispersed; some went to congratulate the winner, others produced towels to wrap around loved ones as they emerged and the rest headed off home.

Daisy watched Max unceremoniously drag Tamsyn into the shallows. She clambered to her feet, tugged off her mask and trudged over. She was a bedraggled and forlorn sight like a giant wet dog.

'Poor you,' said Daisy. 'At least you tried. You need to get out of this soggy costume. Have you got a towel?' Daisy scanned the beach and saw a pile of towels nearby.

'Minnie Mouse one,' said Tamsyn, miserably and Daisy dutifully fetched it. When she returned the last of the back markers were wading to shore. It was good to see Old Man Burgess emerge unscathed. Jason, however, was lying in the shallows with waves breaking over him like a beached whale albeit an undernourished one. Daisy helped Tamsyn out of the costume while a few people helped Jason onto his flippers.

'What did this cost you?' asked Daisy, wringing out a sleeve of the gorilla costume.

'Only twenty-five pounds plus a deposit but they explained I get that back.'

Daisy held up the sopping costume. 'I'm not sure you will.'

After damp hugs and lots of Happy Christmases, Daisy and Aunt Coral walked back up the beach. Daisy was feeling chilly, she couldn't imagine how cold the swimmers were. She clapped her hands together to warm them up. 'That was fun but I'm ready for turkey now.'

Aunt Coral linked arms with Daisy. 'With that in mind I've invited a couple of people for dinner,' she said, giving her arm a squeeze. 'I won't see anyone on their own at Christmas.'

'Who?'

'You'll see,' said Aunt Coral, tapping her nose and Daisy smiled at the gesture. She remembered her aunt doing this when she was a child. She suspected it would be a couple of the local elderly.

After they'd returned to the warmth of the cottage, opened their other presents and Aunt Coral had made suitably appreciative noises over the gift voucher as well as the jumper they were soon in the kitchen concentrating on the final run down to Christmas dinner. Appropriately cheesy Christmas songs blared out of the radio. Daisy felt quite cheerful. The table was set and looked festive with a poinsettia theme, bright red crackers, two bottles of Châteauneuf-du-Pape and four balloon glasses hastily borrowed from Locos.

There was a knock at the door and Aunt Coral sprang away from the Brussels sprouts, whipped off her apron and started to fuss with her hair, which made Daisy notice for the first time that she had done her hair especially nice today and was wearing a dress Daisy hadn't seen before that flattered her fuller figure. Daisy paused and checked over her own outfit of jeans and panda sweatshirt. She shrugged to herself: she'd do. She could hear jovial voices carrying through from the hallway as festive pleasantries were no doubt exchanged. She got ready to greet whoever was joining them.

'Merry Christmas, Daisy,' said an over-enthusiastic Pasco as he barrelled into the kitchen and pulled her into a warm hug making her slop the gravy over the side of the saucepan.

Daisy opened her mouth to answer but most likely the expression on her face was communicating her murderous thoughts accurately. She looked past Pasco to Aunt Coral who was pulling a 'be nice' face. This was stretching Daisy's charitable side to the limit. Despite the anger bubbling inside her she pulled herself together – after all it was Christmas Day.

'Merry Christmas, Pasco, this is a surprise.' At least she was being honest. Why on earth would Aunt Coral invite the local felon to share Christmas dinner with them?

'Look Daisy, about me sleeping—'

'No, no, it's forgotten,' she said, emphasising her point with an overly cheesy grin. Obviously it wasn't forgotten at all but what could she do?

A knock at the door had Aunt Coral scuttling off leaving Pasco and Daisy to exchange awkward looks.

They both waited to see who the last guest was. Aunt Coral appeared first. 'We're all here, let me sort the drinks.' She stepped aside to reveal a reluctant-looking Max hovering in the hallway hugging a poinsettia plant. He looked more shocked than Daisy had to see Pasco and that gave her an odd sense of satisfaction.

'Oh, a poinsettia, how lovely,' said Daisy, taking it from him and doing what she'd seen Aunt Coral do the night before. Cheapskate, she thought.

Chapter Twenty-Six

Dinner was an odd affair with Daisy and Max avoiding eye contact and Aunt Coral and Pasco appearing to do the opposite. There was a familiarity between Pasco and her aunt, which Daisy wasn't expecting. When they retired to the living room with refilled wine glasses Aunt Coral and Pasco took to the new armchairs leaving Max and Daisy to share the sofa. Daisy decided to do a little probing.

'How long have you two known each other?' she asked, taking a sip of her red wine but keeping her focus on their responses. They seemed to instinctively look at each other before either ventured an answer.

'Since secondary school?' offered Pasco.

'Junior school,' scolded Aunt Coral. 'You joined at the end of the last summer term.'

'Yes. We'd moved up from Paignton. I can remember you like it was yesterday.' He was looking at Aunt Coral fondly and then seemed to snap out of it. 'Did you know she used to have bunches with great big bows on?'

'No,' said Daisy, with a snigger. It conjured up an odd sight. 'I bet you were quite something.' It was difficult to find the right words when you had a weird picture of your fifty-something aunt in bunches.

'Gorgeous, she was,' said Pasco and Aunt Coral giggled coyly. What was going on with those two?

Christmas afternoon was thankfully more relaxed than lunch, due to the wine consumption, and they all settled down for the obligatory crap film. Pasco slept through most of it, Max had a little doze when he thought nobody was watching and Aunt Coral shed a tear at the sad bit whilst Daisy munched her way through half a box of Matchmakers.

Aunt Coral went to busy herself in the kitchen and with Pasco still snoozing in the armchair Daisy and Max eyed each other warily from opposite ends of the sofa. Daisy didn't like the edgy atmosphere between them – it was Christmas Day after all. But even Christmas was not going to make her feel any less used by Max. She had stupidly trusted him and that gnawed away at her. She'd had her suspicions but had ignored them. It hurt her more than she wanted to admit.

She picked up her glass of red wine as a distraction. As she turned towards him he was reaching out to her and the unexpected contact of Max's hand on hers made her jump, sending the wine swirling around the balloon glass like a trapped tsunami that spilled in a dramatic fashion onto the middle of the brand-new pale-cream sofa. Daisy gasped in horror and this was echoed by Aunt Coral walking into the room. In an instant Pasco was awake. He picked up his glass of white wine and threw it over the deepening red stain making everyone gasp again.

'Will people *please* stop throwing wine on my new sofa!' said Aunt Coral, marching over to inspect the damage, her bottom lip looking decidedly wobbly. Max was glaring at Pasco.

'It's a known fact white wine counters the effects of red,'

said Pasco. 'I was helping,' he added in case it hadn't been clear.

'I'm so sorry,' said Daisy, rushing out of the room to fetch a cloth.

After they'd all had a go at cleaning the sofa it was decided a professional cleaner was needed. A tea towel was laid over the offending stain and Daisy and Max were relegated to sitting on cushions on the floor.

After a tea of turkey sandwiches and cake, that nobody had room for, Pasco and Max thanked Aunt Coral all the way to the front door.

'Look, I'm sorry I didn't get you a present or anything,' said Daisy, as Max put his coat on and Aunt Coral eagerly helped Pasco with his.

Max shrugged. 'No need, I'm not keen on poinsettias anyhow.'

'Noted,' said Daisy. 'See you at work tomorrow then.' Daisy was planning on opening each night on the build-up to New Year's Eve in the hope of grabbing whatever trade there was.

'Looking forward to it,' said Max, and he turned and followed his father out of the house.

Aunt Coral held on to the door and she and Daisy watched them go huddled up into the glistening evening. She was about to turn away when Max slowly looked back over his shoulder and he gave a warm smile when he saw Daisy was still watching.

'Right, let's shut the door, it's freezing,' said Daisy, taking control of the situation. She must have looked like a love-lorn teenager gazing after him as he went down the lane and Aunt Coral wasn't much better. But it was what Max thought of her that bothered her most.

*

January went by in a blur even though the winter months were quiet. She settled into a routine with her staff on lean hours and longed for Easter and the start of the holiday season. She was barely covering her costs. Daisy found herself in February back on shift wearing a damp shirt with a moody Max for company. The washing machine had died mid cycle and the shirts inside were the only ones she had because, as usual, Daisy was behind with her washing. This one she had attempted to dry with a hair dryer. Thankfully Aunt Coral was getting the washing machine fixed, so Daisy only had to cope for a few more hours with the overpowering smell of fabric softener, which hadn't been properly rinsed out. Max passed her and wrinkled his nose. 'What air freshener are you wearing?'

'Ha, ha. It's a long story. You okay?'

Max pulled a face that indicated he wasn't. 'It's nothing.' It wasn't her causing his annoyance, since Christmas they seemed to have called an uneasy truce.

Daisy was concentrating on a large cocktail order but out of the corner of her eye she was watching an agitated Pasco in discussions with Max. Max was leaning over Pasco whose smile betrayed his body language. Daisy wished she could lip read, it would be such a useful skill to have. The suited man she was serving interrupted her with a last-minute change of one of the cocktails just as Daisy saw Max pass something to his father, but the distraction meant she didn't see what it was.

When she looked over again, Pasco had gone and Max was heading back to the bar with his teeth clenched. Max banged about putting glasses in the glasswasher until the inevitable happened and one of the balloon glasses smashed. An array of muffled swear words drifted through.

'That's another £3.50 you've cost me,' called Daisy.

'Take it out of my wages,' came the humourless reply.

Daisy finished serving her customer and stuck her head round the doorway to the small kitchen area. 'I was joking. What's got your thong in a tangle?' She smiled to emphasise she came in peace but Max wasn't looking at her, he was still picking bits of broken glass out of the glasswasher.

'It's nothing.' He didn't appear in the mood to discuss it.

'Okay, will you give me a hand cashing up later? I've not banked the cash for ages and it's built up. There's quite a bit of money in the safe and not much in the account. I need to pay it in first thing tomorrow.'

Daisy had assumed Max would help her and was already returning to the bar when he replied. 'Can't it wait and I'll do it myself in the morning?'

Daisy pulled a face. 'I'd rather do it tonight.'

'Why?' Max was still looking disgruntled. 'We're both tired. Let's do it tomorrow. Okay?' But he didn't wait for her to reply, he had already returned to the glasswasher. Daisy felt her hackles rise. She hated being told what to do. A customer waved a note indicating they were waiting and she went to serve them; she'd deal with Max later.

The end of the shift couldn't come quick enough. Daisy was rehearsing in her head a little speech about how she liked working with Max but at the end of the day it was she who made the decisions.

'Right I'm off,' called Max, pulling on his jacket.

'Hang on,' called Daisy who literally had her head in the safe.

Max turned around with the look of a teenager being summoned to the Headteacher's office. 'What?'

Daisy was crouched down in front of the safe. 'There's money missing from the safe,' she said, flicking through the bundles in front of her. Max didn't answer. Daisy swivelled around to face him. 'I was making up the bank book for paying in tomorrow and we're short.'

'It's late – you've probably added it up wrong. You said yourself we haven't paid in for ages. Leave it until tomorrow.' He zipped up his jacket and turned to leave.

Daisy didn't like his dismissive attitude. 'Aren't you going to ask how much is missing?'

Max stopped in the doorway. 'What's it matter? It'll be an accounting error. The safe was locked.'

'A hundred and fifty pounds is missing,' said Daisy. Without taking a breath she continued. 'What did you give Pasco earlier?' Her mind was awash with questions and the biggest one of all was: had Max taken her for a fool yet again?

Max's expression changed rapidly from bored to annoyed. 'Are you accusing me of stealing?'

'No, I'm asking you a question. I saw you give Pasco something earlier and now I'm wondering what it was.' Her pulse started to race, she'd not seen Max look this cross. Maybe it wasn't wise to tackle him but she couldn't let this go.

Max shook his head. 'I gave him forty quid.'

'Only forty?' Daisy was feeling brave.

'Yeah, because that's all I had.' Max put his hands in his trouser pockets and pulled out a set of keys and some loose change, which he slammed down on the counter top. 'Search me if you don't believe me.' Daisy stood up but didn't move forward. 'You don't believe me do you? You think I've stolen it.'

He was right. She should have sacked him after the fiasco of Pasco sleeping in the carriage then maybe cash wouldn't be missing now. 'One hundred and fifty pounds has gone from the safe,' she said, pointing at it with one of the bundles of notes in her hand.

'I am not a thief.' His voice was cold, the look on his face was making her think maybe she had jumped to the wrong conclusion.

Daisy's mind was whirling. 'Who else could have taken it?'

'Anyone who has a key for the safe.'

'That's you, me and Old Man Burgess. Are you saying it was him?' Her shoulders tensed. They both knew Mr Burgess was so trustworthy he made Mother Teresa look like Al Capone.

Max strode towards her and snatched the bundles of cash from her. He started counting out the money and ticking it off in the cashbook. She felt an odd sense of satisfaction when she saw him come to the same conclusion as her, even though it confirmed she was one hundred and fifty pounds short. 'Did I make a mistake?' she asked.

'No,' said Max, looking puzzled.

'Then someone has taken a key and stolen it. Where do you keep your keys? Could Pasco have taken them?'

'There you go again!' Max was back to angry. 'If it's not me it must be someone in my family.'

'And is it?'

'You are bloody unbelievable. First you accuse me and now you're accusing my dad.'

'Someone has stolen it and right now I'm £150 down. What do you suggest I do?'

'Stop blaming everyone else.'

'What? Are you accusing me of fiddling my own books?' Daisy's temper was spiralling out of control.

'If the cap fits.'

'Piss off, Max. I've never stolen anything in my life. It's

not me with a police record.' Daisy felt a pang of regret as soon as she'd said it and she knew she'd hit a nerve.

Max shook his head. 'That's a low blow, Daisy.' He marched towards the door and she followed him. He turned back to face her. 'And by the way. I resign,' he snapped.

'No need, you're fired.' As she was about to slam the door she heard someone outside.

'Hello,' came the heavily accented male voice.

'We're closed,' said Max gruffly.

Daisy popped her head outside. Her eyes widened when she saw who was standing further down the platform and she suddenly didn't want Max to leave.

Chapter Twenty-Seven

'I am not 'ere to drink. I am 'ere to see Day-zee.' The man's thick French accent cut through the crisp night air.

Max looked from Daisy to the stranger and back again. 'She's all yours, mate,' he said, striding off along the platform before being quickly swallowed by the darkness.

'Er, thank you,' said the Frenchman politely. He turned around and beamed a warm smile at Daisy.

'And what the hell do you want, Guillaume?' she asked, folding her arms protectively across her chest.

Guillaume opened his arms wide in an elaborate show of affection and tried to pull her into an embrace. Daisy instinctively stepped away from him. Had he forgotten how they had parted? The screaming and shouting, the accusations and the loss of everything they'd worked for? Seeing him was not helping her mood at all. She hated surprises and this was one of the worst.

'Ahh, now come on, Day-zee. We are friends, *non*?' Guillaume went to step forward again. Daisy stepped back and held up the palm of her hand as if stopping traffic.

'Guillaume, what do you want?'

'I want you, Day-zee. It's always been you.' He looked at her with his dark, sad puppy dog eyes.

Daisy was beyond sceptical.

'How did you find me?'

He seemed to think for a moment before answering. 'Your name. It was in the paper and it came up when I search on the internet.' He looked quite pleased with himself. Daisy groaned. It was too simple to trace people these days and she was sure for many people this was a blessing but right now it was unbelievably annoying.

'I don't want you here. You should leave.' It was exactly what she was feeling and the words tumbled out without any vetting by her brain. Guillaume looked wounded, but then he was good at that. She gave a shiver as the chill of the night cut through the thin cloth of her shirt.

'But I have come to congratulate you on achieving your dream. You always wanted your own business and now . . .' He splayed out his arms and turned on the spot, making Daisy look around herself. He was right, this was all hers but she hadn't got here on her own. It was thanks to many other people and right now she wished one of them in particular was here. Even if he was a giant pain in the arse.

Daisy sighed heavily, she was tired from both the shift and fighting with Max. 'What do you want, Guillaume?' As he puffed up again looking like he was about to reel off a rehearsed speech she stepped in. 'Apart from me, that is.'

His shoulders slumped. 'I would like to talk things over with you. Make peace.'

'Look, I've just finished a shift and I'm tired . . .' She was hoping he could fill in the blanks for himself but as Guillaume was still looking at her hopefully it appeared unlikely. 'Are you about tomorrow?'

'Yes, I am staying at the public house.'

'We open at ten, if you get here at about nine you can

talk while I work. Okay?' Daisy figured he would be easier to say no to after a good night's sleep.

'Wonderful, I will look forward to it. Good night Day-zee,' said Guillaume, leaning in for a kiss but Daisy scooted through the door and shut it quickly calling 'Bye' over her shoulder. She knew too well where Guillaume's kisses could lead and she had far too many problems complicating her life right now, another was definitely to be avoided.

She didn't sleep well. Her night was disturbed by her brain going over and over the argument with Max, worrying about what had happened to the money and trying to ignore Bug alternating between snoring and farting on the pillow next to her.

When she finally hauled herself out of the house the next morning she wasn't in the best frame of mind to face Guillaume or to scrutinise their failed relationship. It perplexed her why he was here. Theirs had been a passionate affair interspersed with lots of rowing. There was a strong attraction between them but what excited her about Guillaume also infuriated her. Him turning up unexpectedly had stirred up old feelings she didn't want to examine.

Guillaume was looking nonchalant and very French, leaning casually against the railway building. Daisy was able to watch him and take in the details she had forgotten as she walked across the car park. He exuded confidence and charisma as he drew lugubriously on a cigarette – a habit she'd forgotten how much she hated. His dark hair was shorter now and it suited him. He was dressed in his usual smart and stylish look making him look like he had just stepped off a catwalk. Any woman would have killed for his cheekbones and despite his moody appearance he was attractive.

He turned when Daisy neared and his expression

softened – reluctantly she felt something react inside her. She had to keep a rein on her treacherous body. She needed to listen to what he had to say and then send him on his way: he was a distraction she could do without and yet another man she knew she couldn't trust.

'You are looking beautiful this morning.' He eyed her appreciatively.

Cut the crap, Guillaume, she thought. 'Come in and I'll get you a coffee.'

He settled at the bar with a double espresso whilst Daisy set about stacking the glasswasher, which she'd failed to do the night before. Scenes of the previous evening flashed through her mind. She didn't want to think about what she'd said to Max. She had gone over and over it most of the night, the fact she'd essentially called him a thief was pricking her conscience just as the remaining glass shards pierced her fingers as she removed them from the bottom of the glasswasher.

'Day-zee, I am sorry for everything that happened in Rouen.' Something about the way he pronounced it brought an image of the town to mind and she felt a longing to be back there enjoying the culture and the French way of life. It was a beautiful part of the country and at the time she had harboured hopes of settling there. She shook her head as if to try to bring her mind back to the present. Guillaume gave her an odd look and continued. 'It was all my fault. I thought to make things happen with the business we had to think bigger.'

Daisy listened whilst she pulled out the next rack and stacked more glasses. 'You gambled with our future.'

'Only on something I thought was certain to make us money but I was wrong. Let me try to put things right between us.'

She looked up and could see the genuine regret in his eyes. Oh, those deep dark eyes that attentively held her gaze. He was saying all the right words but she had to keep things in perspective. 'Thank you for apologising.'

'What else can I do?' He bent forward across the bar. 'I want to make it up to you.'

'There's no need. But thanks for coming.' Daisy shoved a stray piece of hair back into her bandana and returned her attention to the glasses.

'You have lost your barman, *oui*?'

'*Oui*. I mean, yes.' Daisy hadn't really thought of Max as a barman before, he was just her friend who had helped her get Locos off the ground and now worked alongside her. Although he was getting paid for it and his father had been receiving free lodging, unbeknown to her. She hated the fact she just couldn't let it go.

'Can I step in and help you? Work his shifts for a couple of weeks until you find a replacement. My way of saying sorry and a chance for us to be able to part as friends.'

She paused and looked at him. It was a kind offer but there were doubts at the back of her mind. 'Why would you do that, Guillaume?'

'Because I am a nice guy,' he said, finishing with a broad smile that had it been a toothpaste commercial there would have been a zing and a sparkle bouncing off his teeth. 'And I want to show you I am sorry.'

'But it will cost you money to stay here and the job doesn't pay much.' Given what it had cost him to travel to Devon she was quickly working out Guillaume was going to be heavily out of pocket. She had her hands on her hips as she watched him closely.

He scrunched up his shoulders and laughed childishly.

'There is no fooling you,' he said, wagging his finger playfully. 'I 'ad a little win on zee horses.'

Daisy raised a questioning eyebrow. 'A little win?'

He chortled. 'Okay, it was a good win. I thought I should use it to put things right between us.' Daisy looked sceptical. 'Come on Day-zee, I am trying to do the right thing 'ere. I could give you the money or I could be more use to you by working the bar for free.' He raised his shoulders theatrically. Could he be any more French?

Daisy sucked in a breath. She couldn't actually see a downside with the exception of her being in close proximity to a handsome and charming Frenchman for a couple of weeks. All she had to do was keep her hands off him. Surely she could manage that?

A couple of days of working with Guillaume and she was already having lascivious thoughts about him. Daisy was taking an afternoon break back at Sea Mist Cottage and preparing herself for another evening shift in close proximity to her ex by dunking a digestive and mulling over the memories of his body when the digestive broke and disappeared to the bottom of her tea. 'Cock-a doodle-doo!' she hollered.

At the same time Aunt Coral arrived home. 'Hello,' she said looking as if she was trying hard not to laugh at Daisy's choice of expletive. She really needed to stop saying that. 'Here's the money I owe you.' Aunt Coral handed her an envelope.

Daisy's brow furrowed as she picked up the package, her eyes widening at the wodge of twenties inside. 'What do you mean the money you owe me?' Was this how Alzheimer's started?

'The money I borrowed from the bar,' added Aunt Coral,

but Daisy was still looking blank. 'For the washing machine. The cashpoint was out so I called in to Locos but you were at the Cash and Carry and Mr Burgess opened the safe. It took him four goes you know, his arthritis is shocking poor man. Anyway we're all square.' Aunt Coral started to get out the chopping board appearing oblivious to the fact that all colour had drained from Daisy's face.

Daisy licked her lips and wished her throat didn't feel as dry as Ottercombe beach in July. 'How much did you borrow?'

Aunt Coral looked surprised the conversation was still continuing. 'One hundred and fifty. It's all there.'

'I'm sure it is. It's just . . .'

Aunt Coral was watching her with a small knife poised. 'Are you okay?'

Daisy blinked. Okay was the last thing she was. 'I need to go out.'

'What about your cuppa?' asked Aunt Coral, picking up the mug.

'You have it,' called Daisy, grabbing her jacket and heading out the front door.

Aunt Coral took a swig of the tea and then recoiled at the grittiness of the floating biscuit. 'That's disgusting!'

What a nightmare, thought Daisy as she strode purposefully towards Max's flat. She felt awful, everything he'd said about her jumping to conclusions was true. She had automatically believed it was Max and his vehement denial had only solidified her belief. She was deeply in the wrong and now she had to eat humble pie.

Daisy knocked on the door, folded her arms and then unfolded them and then shoved her hands in her pockets, this was mortifyingly uncomfortable. A shadow appeared

282

at the door. When Max opened it his annoyance at his visitor was evident in his eye roll.

'I'm here to apologise.' She could see into the small bedsit and was surprised by how neat and tidy it was and how unlike the bachelor pad she had imagined. It just went to show how wrong you could be about people, which was something she was learning in spades today.

'Go on,' said Max, looking vaguely interested.

'Aunt Coral has just given me this back.' She pulled the envelope of money from her pocket and showed him as if presenting evidence.

'Coral's the thief? Now there's a turn up,' said Max, but there was no humour in his voice.

'Apparently the cashpoint was out and Old Man Burgess gave her the money from the safe but nobody passed on the message to me . . .' She shuffled her feet awkwardly and regarded Max, hopeful of forgiveness.

'That's it?'

'I'm sorry,' she said, with an uneasy smile. 'I just . . .' Her shoulders dropped. 'I'm really sorry, Max.'

'It's all back to normal. Just like that is it?' The sarcasm was plain.

'The job's yours if you want to come back.'

'I thought your boyfriend had taken over?'

'He's not my boyfriend and it's only temporary. Do you want your job back or not?' She wasn't going to beg.

'No, thanks. I don't want to work somewhere I'm not trusted. You can stick your job,' he said, and firmly shut the door in her face. Daisy gave a slow blink, she deserved it but it didn't make it any easier to take.

That evening Guillaume turned up on time wearing a crisp white shirt, fitted black trousers and oozing mystique.

Tamsyn was quickly charmed despite Daisy giving her a multitude of warnings.

'OMG! He's scrummilicious,' declared Tamsyn, excitedly clapping her hands together. 'And it's so romantic that he's tracked you down.'

'Shh,' said Daisy, steering her out of earshot. 'That's as may be but he's off limits.'

'Why?' asked Tamsyn, her childlike face tilting to one side.

'Because . . . he's . . . you know . . .' Daisy pursed her lips and looked at Tamsyn.

Tamsyn nodded and then it changed to a headshake. 'No, not really,' she said, looking perplexed. 'You and Max can't seem to get it together even though you row like a married couple.'

'Er, no we don't.' Daisy was indignant.

'Er, yes you do,' said Tamsyn in a mimicking tone. 'Anyway Ghee-Home looks super sexy, I'd fill my boots if I were you.'

Daisy had given up trying to help Tamsyn pronounce his name correctly as it had ended up with Tamsyn looking like she was doing some particularly strenuous facial exercises whilst making what had sounded like whale noises so 'ghee-home' was the best they had been able to achieve.

'Thanks for the advice but I've been there before, remember? It ended badly and I have no desire to repeat the exercise.' But the truth was she did have desire. It was there zinging away every time she looked at him; her disloyal body was filled with longing for Guillaume and there was nothing she could do to switch it off.

Chapter Twenty-Eight

It was surprising how easily Daisy fitted back into a routine with Guillaume. It was true they had been together for a while and familiarity imprints itself on your psyche. Despite all the things he had done wrong in the past she still liked him as a person and he was working hard now. If only he had worked hard in Rouen things could have been different, she thought. She still cared for Guillaume and still fancied him rotten but she didn't love him – she was sure of that. But he was fun to be around, easy on the eye and helped take her mind off the mess she'd made with Max.

Daisy hadn't seen much of Max since her apology and she'd tried to convince herself he was not worth bothering with but the truth was she missed not seeing him around. She had heard on the grapevine Pasco had got a job at the caravan park and was staying on site; at least the railway carriage was safe from that particular squatter for the time being. Daisy knew she was better off without any of the Davey men in her life muddying the waters but sometimes it was easier said than done.

As they finished late on Saturday night Guillaume poured Daisy a Clotted Cream gin, her favourite to drink neat, and slid it along the bar Wild West style. Daisy caught it just in time. 'Would you like to do something relaxing with me before I leave at the end of next week?' he asked, his voice sounding sexier than ever. Daisy's mind jumped to the bedroom and she blinked away the X-rated images rampaging through her brain.

'What did you have in mind?' She took a long taste from her drink enjoying the buttery richness whilst watching his every move.

'A boat ride?' He inclined his head. 'There is something mesmerising about the sea. Its rhythm. Its powerful thrust.'

She felt a shiver run down her spine and it wasn't the gin making her jiggle uncomfortably in her seat. 'Er, I don't know. I think it's best we keep work and . . . other things separate.' She was proud of herself. This was the right thing to say. She looked up and Guillaume was right in front of her and getting slowly closer until his lips were almost touching hers.

When he spoke his voice was husky. 'I disagree.'

'You kissed him?' screeched Tamsyn, looking appalled.

Daisy hesitated. 'You said he was sexy and, I quote, "I'd fill my boots."'

Tamsyn shook her head. 'Well, I've thought about it now and this is a man who wrecked all your hard work and broke your heart. Do you have no self-respect?'

Daisy was taken aback by how vehement Tamsyn was. 'That's all in the past. He's being helpful now. Shouldn't I make the most of him?'

'No, you shouldn't. Men like him will always come out on top, which leaves only one place for everyone else.'

Daisy opened her mouth, but Tamsyn was already leaving. 'There are worse places to be than underneath Guillaume!' shouted Daisy, but Tamsyn didn't look back.

Only four months left to go then she could take the money, sell Locos and get the hell away, she thought. She stomped into the kitchen making Bug take a little interest. He stretched and a small trump escaped.

'You have it easy,' she told him. 'If you like someone you sniff their bum and if you don't you growl at them. See, it's easy.'

Bug sat down in front of her and tilted his head on one side as if he was listening.

'It's confusing being a human. Maybe I should apply doggy logic. Who do I like or, in doggy terms, whose bum do I want to sniff?' Daisy recoiled at her own words. 'Actually, let's not apply doggy logic at all or I'll be on my own forever.'

She needed to make some decisions. Guillaume wasn't planning on staying long, which was good and it also left a small opportunity for a brief fling. She had to concede that the thought greatly appealed to her. However, if she did have a brief fling it could make everything complicated. Bug was still looking at her. 'Right, first decision is I'm NOT going to have sex with Guillaume,' she said, emphatically.

'Oh, well that's lovely,' said Aunt Coral from the doorway, making Daisy jump. 'I thought you were talking to someone.' She scanned the room.

'I thought you were at work?' Daisy stared at Aunt Coral feeling the familiar sensation of her cheeks flooding with colour.

'Sorry. I didn't go in today, I had a migraine. I was snoozing upstairs when I heard the door slam.'

'Right. Cup of tea then?' Daisy sprang to her feet and started to busy herself. Despite her embarrassment at least she had sorted one thing out, now all she had to do was tell Guillaume the kiss was a one off and nothing else could come of it. Easy.

'What do you mean you still want me to hire a boat?' Daisy was tired, it had been a long shift at Locos and she still had to finish up. Guillaume seemed irritated with Daisy for not wanting to restart the relationship and now he was going on about boats.

'I want to see more of the coastline.' He gave a firm nod.

'Then walk the coastal path. It goes all the way around to . . .' Daisy paused to think. 'It goes a really long way.'

'No, I need a boat.' He shook his head firmly. 'You must know someone.'

Daisy knew a couple of the fishermen but she didn't think it was likely they would let her borrow their boat. 'Just ask in the pub. Monty will know who to speak to.'

'Will you ask for me, please? My English is not good.' Guillaume gave her a wide-eyed look.

She chuckled. 'Your English is better than some of the locals.'

'*Putain!*'

Daisy knew this was a swear word and she held up her hands.

'I am sorry,' said Guillaume, trying to grasp her hand across the bar but she managed to whisk it away just in time. The less physical contact they had, the less likely she was to reverse the no-sex decision. 'I am trying to do something nice for someone special.' His eyes were pleading. 'I just need a boat.'

'Do you need someone to skipper it?'

He shook his head. 'No, I can drive it. I just need it for a few hours to see—'

'The coast. Yeah, I get it,' she said, thinking the opposite. 'Leave it with me and I'll ask around.'

'Thank you Day-zee.' He gave her a kiss on each cheek and she felt her resolve crumble a little.

'What sort of boat?' asked Monty, looking like one of the fishermen had hooked his top lip and was about to reel him in.

Daisy shrugged. 'Something small and motorised.'

'I know a guy who'll know.' Monty waved someone over. Daisy turned around to see Max standing with his hand still on the door. She huffed. Really?

'Actually, Monty, I don't think that's such a . . .' she started, but Max had now joined her at the bar. 'Hi,' she said turning away and beginning to fiddle with a beermat.

Monty was pouring Max a pint. 'Daisy here is after finding a boat. I figured you'd know of one she could borrow.'

Max finally looked at Daisy. His features appeared hardened and it saddened her. 'What for and for how long?' mumbled Max, appearing reluctant to join the conversation.

'Just sightseeing. Guillaume wants it for a couple of hours to see the sunset.'

'You going with him then?'

Daisy hadn't decided yet. This was clearly what Guillaume wanted – a chance to rekindle their affair. If she went it was definitely going to test her no-sex rule to the limit. 'Yeah,' she said, wondering if Max cared about her going off with Guillaume. 'It's the kind of spontaneous crazy romantic thing he comes up with.' She found herself tilting her head in an overly girly gesture.

Max frowned harder. 'When?'

'Um, sometime within the next week, but otherwise I don't think it matters.'

'Leave it with me,' said Max.

Daisy hovered. 'Is that a leave it with me and I'll be in touch shortly or . . .' She didn't want to finish the sentence with 'or a leave it with me but I'm not planning on doing anything for you ever again.'

Max turned slightly, he was still frowning. 'It's a leave it with me because I need to speak to a couple of people and I'll let you know as and when.'

'Okay, thanks.' She managed a small smile. Monty passed Max his pint and held his hand out to be paid. Max looked from Monty to Daisy and back again.

There was a slight pause before she sprang into action pulling a note from her pocket. 'Oh, let me get that.'

'Thanks,' muttered Max begrudgingly and he moved away from the bar.

Daisy shoved her hands in her pockets along with her change and, feeling awkward, she disappeared up the stairs to the guest rooms above. She knocked on Guillaume's door. She could hear him inside having a muffled conversation in French. The talking stopped. 'Who is it?' he asked.

'Daisy.'

There was more muffled French and then the door opened. 'Come in Day-zee. It is wonderful to see you.'

'No, you're okay thanks.' She leaned against the doorframe. 'I've got someone looking for a boat for you. Have you checked the weather forecast?'

'*Pardon*?' He looked confused.

'If we're taking a boat out at dusk we need to make sure the weather is going to behave itself. We want a calm sea and good visibility. You don't want to have to call out the lifeboat to rescue you.' She chuckled and quickly tried to dismiss the image of Max on the inshore that had popped into her mind.

Guillaume raised his chin a little as if trying to see her from a slightly different angle. 'I need the boat on Thursday.' He swallowed and then smiled broadly. 'I think Thursday is good weather.'

'That's not a lot of notice but I'll see what I can do.' She turned to leave and he grabbed her hand, making her jump.

'Thank you,' he said staring deep into her eyes, which for once didn't have her thinking passionate thoughts, this time she just felt uncomfortable and she couldn't think why.

'You're welcome.' She carefully pulled her hand free and hurried downstairs, through the door and into the hubbub of the bar. She headed for Max's usual spot to find he now had company.

'Hi,' said Daisy, feeling as out of place as a lamb chop in a fruit bowl.

Jason stood up and banged his leg on the table in the process. 'Ow. Hello Daisy. Lovely to see you. And you do look well.' Jason however looked like he was possibly going to have some sort of seizure as a result of the levels of embarrassment currently flooding his system.

'Stop wittering, Jason,' said Tamsyn. 'Join us,' she added, gesturing for Daisy to pull up a chair. Max was giving Tamsyn a sideways look but she was ignoring him.

'No, you're all right,' said Daisy. 'Any chance of getting a boat for Thursday?'

Max sipped his pint. 'What's the rush?'

'Weather should be okay on Thursday and he's planning on leaving here soon.'

Max failed to hide his delight at this statement. 'He's not stuck around long, has he?'

291

'Can you get a boat for Thursday or not?' Daisy's tone was cool. She knew exactly what Max was implying and she wasn't going to rise to it. She wouldn't give him the satisfaction.

'Like I said I'll make some calls and—'

'Fine. I'll wait to hear from you then.' Daisy turned back to Jason and Tamsyn. 'Sorry to interrupt your evening. I guess I'll see you sometime.'

Daisy spun around and left. She couldn't help feeling upset that she hadn't been invited out for a drink. Sure they had asked her to join them, but it was an afterthought forced by toe-curling levels of embarrassment. They had made their choice and they had chosen Max. If she'd thought about it rationally of course they were always going to choose Max. They all grew up together, they were friends long before she came back to the bay. She was the interloper, and however close she and Tamsyn had become she would always be the outsider. Daisy sniffed and blinked. She wasn't going to cry. Shedding tears served no good purpose other than to let others see your weakness. No, she wasn't a crier, she thought, as she roughly wiped away a tear.

She wasn't entirely sure how she found herself on the jetty on a windy February evening that Thursday. The sea was choppy and the tide was on the turn but they still had a few hours before they would have to have the borrowed boat moored up again. Guillaume was in the boat familiarising himself with the outboard controls. His initial excitement at learning Daisy had sourced a boat had quickly disappeared and he now seemed decidedly edgy. But Daisy had to admit she had similar feelings. Should she go with him or not? Could she handle being in a very confined space, for a romantic boat ride along the coast with a sexy Frenchman? She was pretty sure Guillaume was still trying to rekindle their affair. She didn't want a full-blown relationship but it had been a long time since she'd had sex and what harm could one night of passion do? In a split second she made her decision.

'Give me a hand,' said Daisy, lifting a leg onto the edge of the small craft.

'Uh? *Non*.' Guillaume held his hand up to stop her and she stiffened.

'What's up?' She was standing with her leg still cocked looking like Bug at a lamppost.

'I am sorry Day-zee. I want to do this alone.' His voice was melodic but the words were sharp. 'You can wait for me at the pub if you like?'

'What the hell is going on?' asked Daisy, returning her foot to the jetty.

'I am going for a boat ride. Like I explained I want to explore this beautiful place. I am an adventurer and I want to see—'

'Quit the bollocks.'

Guillaume looked like he'd been slapped in the face. He laughed awkwardly. 'Day-zee, what are you talking about?'

'It is almost dark, the sea is getting choppy, you don't know your starboard from your arse and you want to go out on your own to look at the coastline. Do you think I'm a total idiot?'

'Not at all.' His expression changed. 'I need to do something for both of us.'

'Like what?' He gave the classic Gallic shrug. 'Then tell me what it is?'

'Trust me. It is a surprise.' He fired up the outboard motor and the small boat purred into life. 'Bye Day-zee. I will be back in a couple of hours. Go home, please.'

293

She thought about shouting some expletives at him but it was unlikely they would be heard over the engine. Where was he going? Perhaps he had arranged something as a way of saying goodbye to her. Just goodbye would have been enough and the sooner he said it and left the bay the happier she'd be. So much for her one last night of passion, she thought. She imagined she'd be cuddled up in Guillaume's arms right about now, not marooned on the jetty with her hair billowing in the wind.

She watched the boat disappear out of the bay and continue to follow the coastline. Daisy made a snap decision and instead of going back to Aunt Coral's she jogged up onto the headland to see if she could still see the boat. Perhaps he wasn't going far – maybe Lyme Regis or Weymouth? She scanned the water until she spotted the small boat now far in the distance. She watched and unless she was very much mistaken Guillaume was no longer following the coastline – he was now heading directly out to sea.

Chapter Twenty-Nine

Daisy was standing on the cliff top watching the small boat carry Guillaume further out to sea. The wind cut through her coat making her shudder. She had a bad feeling about this. What should she do?

She took a deep breath. Guillaume had been a slippery character in the past but he'd never been in any serious trouble. There were a few cash and carry fiddles, but she had no reason whatsoever to suspect he was up to no good now. Daisy felt a little better for this thought process. Perhaps she just needed to go and have a large glass of wine and forget about it. Yes, that was exactly what she would do. Another gust of night air gave her the nudge she needed to go home. It was times like this she missed her old motorbike.

She had a long chat to the man in the fish and chip shop whilst he explained the secret to his excellent fish and chips, and she did a good impression of someone rapt by the deep-frying process whilst her brain continued to mull over the situation with Guillaume. If it was some big romantic gesture then what on earth could it be that required a small motorised boat to be out on a choppy sea?

Walking home her phone beeped. For a moment she hoped it was a text from Guillaume saying he was back, but it was just a silly game demanding attention. But next to the game app was the Find My Phone app and it was calling to her. She had Guillaume's phone set-up; well, assuming he still had the same phone and it still worked. She slowed her pace, clicked the app and hoped it would show he was in Weymouth. A small dot started to flash. The small dot was way offshore and it wasn't moving.

The wind was getting up now and she knew the impact that would have on the sea. Whatever her guess as to why Guillaume had taken the boat out, the fact remained he was now way offshore in a tiny boat in the dark with little sailing skills and a possible storm brewing. Daisy fumbled with her phone as her brain fumbled with her dilemma. Eventually she called Jason and proceeded to offload all her concerns in one long diatribe.

'Daisy, stop. One thing at a time. Is Guillaume in danger?'

'He might be.' She bit her lip when she thought about it. The non-moving dot in the English Channel might simply mean he had broken down. She didn't want any harm to come to him, especially if he was off doing something romantic for her when she had no intention of reigniting their relationship.

'Is this a lifeboat call out?'

'I don't know, I don't think so,' said Daisy, feeling overwhelmed by confusion.

'Right, I'll meet you at Locos in five minutes. Okay?'

'Okay, thanks.' Feeling somewhat relieved she ended the call and flicked up the Find My Phone app. The dot was still stuck in the middle of the blue mass of ocean but it was no longer in range. Perhaps the boat's engine had failed and he'd drifted out there. Maybe Jason was right, perhaps it was a lifeboat call out.

She stopped for a moment and looked around her. She wasn't sure why but she had an odd sensation someone was watching her, but there was nobody there. At least she couldn't see anyone. It was dark now and the wind was starting to whistle around the town, which meant the sea would be starting to cut up rough. She put her head down and strode off towards Locos.

Jason and Daisy could see each other approaching from different directions. Jason swung the small patrol car into the kerb and jumped out.

'Are you okay?' he asked.

'Yeah, I'm just confused and I don't want to get anyone into any trouble.'

'Daisy, if someone has done something against the law that is their issue not yours. Has someone done something illegal?' Jason's expression was cheerily expectant.

'I don't know,' said Daisy shaking her head. 'The thing is, Guillaume wanted me to hire him a boat, which he said was for him to see the coastline, but I thought it was for us to go out and watch the sunset and . . .' She paused. She didn't need to reveal anything else about what her expectations may have been about the evening. 'But anyway, he went on his own, which just seems an odd thing to do and the weather isn't great and he doesn't know much about boats.' She ran out of steam.

'He doesn't have a criminal record. I checked,' said Jason. Daisy raised her eyebrows. 'Always best to be proactive.'

'I don't know if he's up to anything but I do know he appears to be stranded in the English Channel.'

'Let's put the lifeboat call out. It's getting rough out there; he is in potential danger, which is enough to get a crew in the water. I'll make sure I'm in the boat so if there's anything untoward going on I can step in. We'll get him back safe. Okay?'

'Thanks, Jason.' Daisy was swamped with relief. She may not want to rekindle her romance with Guillaume but she certainly didn't want anything to happen to him.

'Let me get the last known coordinates of his phone from your app then you can stay here. I'll be able to keep you posted. I promise.'

Jason quickly got what he needed from her mobile, handed it back and jumped back into the small patrol car like he was in a low-budget cop show. Daisy watched him go but already she knew she couldn't sit in the bar and wait to hear from him, she needed to be on the beach. She wanted to make sure Guillaume was all right and felt over-whelmingly responsible for both letting him take the boat and for sending the lifeboat crew out after him. By the time she got to the beach the lifeboat was already in the water. She thought the beach was deserted until behind her she heard the crunch of pebbles as someone strode purposefully towards her.

'Shit, I missed the shout,' said Max, out of the darkness. 'Tell me it's not your idiot boyfriend in that bloody boat?'

Daisy bit her lip as she tried to form a sentence to rebuke his comment but it simply wasn't possible. She winced.

'I knew I shouldn't have agreed to it. Bloody hell. I thought you said he was familiar with boats.'

'He said he was. But from the way he studied the motor I don't think he knows much about them.'

'So now he's risking three more lives, and for what? Some sightseeing trip?' Max looked around and then back at Daisy. 'I thought you were going with him?'

'So did I,' said Daisy, staring out at the ink-black water

spitting out a white froth as it angrily pummelled the shoreline.

'What's going on?' said Max, spinning around like a clumsy toddler doing a pirouette.

'He's stuck in the middle of the sea and . . . where are you going?' Daisy started to follow Max even though he was ignoring her and was marching back the way he'd come. 'Max!'

'You stay there, I'm just checking something out,' called back Max. Daisy jogged to keep up with him and as she drew level he shook his head. 'I see your listening skills haven't improved.'

'Nor have your manners.'

They both put their heads down against the wind and with the faintest of smiles battled on up to the headland. The wind on the top was fierce now and Daisy could feel panic rising as they neared the edge. Max stopped dead and Daisy almost bumped into him.

'Why is there a car parked there at this time of night?' Max was pointing to an ancient Astra estate car in the small car park. They both looked around but there was nobody else about.

'Is your boyfriend a crook?' asked Max, setting off again.

'He's not my boyfriend and, no, he's not a crook.' They marched on in silence away from the bay following the coastal path towards the cove. Max slowed his pace.

'What are we doing exactly?' asked Daisy, raising her voice to be heard over the now howling wind.

'Stop shouting. I'm following a hunch.'

Daisy grabbed his arm and spun him around. 'Will you tell me what's going on or at least what you think is going on.'

Max was looking annoyed, most likely at her volume.

She lowered her voice and leaned closer. 'Please,' she added and let go of his arm.

Max strode further along the path and then beckoned her to join him. They were standing on the edge, above the cove, and Daisy looked uneasily down to the rocks below her.

'The cove was where Pasco used to do his dodgy deals and his petty smuggling.' Max indicated the cliffs in front of them with a thumb.

'But Tamsyn said the cove isn't safe because of all the rock falls and that's why they closed the path off to stop you getting down there.'

'Which makes it an ideal spot—'

'—if you were up to something.' Daisy finished the sentence.

She realised the implications. 'Hang on a minute. You think Guillaume has been duped into something dishonest?'

Max pulled a face conveying his thoughts quite well. 'Not duped, no.'

'Who is jumping to conclusions now? You've met him a couple of times and now you think he's the brains behind something illegal.'

'I wouldn't go that far. He didn't strike me as a genius, bit of a jerk if you ask me. Actually a great big—'

'Really? Is now the time to have this argument?' Daisy had her hands on her slim hips.

'Guess not,' said Max lowering his voice.

Daisy walked forward and peered over the edge. Max grabbed her by the arm making her start.

'Shit, Max, you nearly pushed me over.' He still had a firm hold on her and her heart was racing and it wasn't entirely because of the proximity of the cliff edge.

'Look,' said Max, pointing to the small patch of beach waiting to be swallowed by the approaching tide. 'There's someone down there.'

Daisy squinted. 'I think there's two people.'

Max guided her back from the edge and let go of her arm. 'I'm going to sit it out and see who they are. You go home and I'll call you.'

Daisy laughed. 'Why does everyone keep sending me home like I'm some sort of silly little girl? I'm staying put.' She folded her arms defiantly.

Max shook his head. She hoped he wasn't going to argue with her. He stepped away and for a moment she thought he was going to leave her there but instead he crouched down behind a nearby bush. Daisy joined him. 'They don't do this in James Bond,' she said, with a smile.

Time stretched on and there was no sign of anyone coming up from the cove. Perhaps they'd been mistaken; it could have been shadows playing tricks. Eventually her thighs started to burn so she sat down on the cold ground. She could no longer feel her fingers despite them being in her coat pockets. There had been no update from Jason but then she wasn't sure he would get a signal in the middle of the sea. The earlier excitement had waned and she was considering going home for a coffee; there wasn't anything she could do here and Jason would let her know if Guillaume was okay soon enough.

Then Max tapped her arm making her look up. He pointed rapidly past the bush. Daisy peered around the spikey plant to see if she could see anything. The tide had come in further and the beach was no longer visible in the cove.

Daisy repositioned herself and had another look down to where the sea was swirling ominously in the tight confines of the cliffs. 'There's nobody down there. Those people must have been washed out to sea or there was nobody there in the first place.' Daisy went to stand up but Max forcefully pulled her back down, making her land on her bum. She stifled the urge to yell because she could sense from Max all was not well.

Max put his hands up and mouthed 'sorry' and then pointed forwards and down. Daisy squinted in the darkness but could see nothing and could only hear the wind whipping around her chilled ears. But then she saw something move. Two silhouettes were moving along where the slope had once led down to the small secluded cove. Her heart started to race. She tried to get a good look at them but it was too dark. She wondered who they could be and what they were doing on an unsafe cliff on a night like this, but most of all she wondered if they had any connection to Guillaume. She was very glad she wasn't on her own.

Chapter Thirty

Daisy and Max watched silently in the darkness as the two figures clambered over the barricade that was in place to stop people following the path down to the cove. They heard a yelp as one of them tripped.

'It's a woman,' whispered Daisy, instantly feeling foolish for hiding behind a bush. 'They aren't criminals – they've been for a shag on the beach. And now we look like we're dogging. Cocking hell, Max.' She was immediately cross with Max for having stirred up her doubts about Guillaume and even angrier with herself for going along with it. This couple were clearly unconnected to whatever Guillaume was doing out at sea, which was most likely completely innocent.

Max put his finger to his lips and Daisy reluctantly fell silent. They watched the couple climb up the last few steps and stop to look out to sea. The man started speaking into a mobile phone and although they weren't close enough to hear the conversation they could tell he was irate. It was oddly addictive spying on someone like this; she was fascinated by who this couple were and if nothing else it was taking her mind off the worry that she'd called the lifeboat out on a wild goose chase.

'Now what?' said Daisy, digging Max in the ribs.

'Shh, I'm thinking.'

'Then we could be here all night. I say we—' But her sentence was cut off by the sound of music. The blast of a Crazy Frog ringtone bellowed from Daisy's pocket as her mobile sprang into life.

'Hello?' she said, her voice hushed.

'Daisy, it's Jason. Guillaume is safe. Stay where you are. I can't give you any details but this is now part of a criminal investigation.'

Daisy was listening but she was also looking at the two faces looming over the bushes watching her and Max carefully. This close their features were clearer. Neither of them was smiling. Her heart started to pick up its pace, her mind swirled and her muscles tensed as panic took hold.

'Okay, thanks for your *help*. Bye.' She very much hoped Jason would pick up on the emphasis on help: her pitiful attempt to tell him she felt in danger. Max slowly stood up. It was some comfort he was at least level with the stern man looming over them. Max reached for Daisy's hand and pulled her upright, keeping tight hold of her, which caused something to zing in the pit of her stomach.

'Hi Buddy,' said Max sounding friendly. 'Sorry if we startled you.' He turned to Daisy. 'Come on, babe, let's go home.' He guided Daisy from behind the bush, gave a cursory nod at the other couple and walked towards the town.

Max put his arm around her and pulled her in closer to him and whispered. 'Just keep walking. Do what I do. Okay?'

His reaction was frightening her but the warmth of his body close to hers was reassuring. 'Okay,' she said swallowing hard and trying to keep her breathing steady. She wanted to ask him what the hell was going on. She wanted to run. She wasn't entirely sure why but something in her psyche was saying 'RUN' and it was hard to ignore.

Her heart was racing and the blood was thrumming loudly in her ears. She noticed Max, who was nearer the edge, had guided her to walk on the grass and off the pathway. It was more uneven underfoot but definitely safer should anyone have plans to push you over the edge. A furtive glance over her shoulder and Daisy saw the couple were following them. A knot of anxiety clenched in the pit of her stomach and despite all logic her instincts kicked in and she bolted.

Max lurched forward but it was too late, Daisy was already sprinting away. He heard the footsteps behind him and turned as the man was throwing a punch. Max dodged and the punch caught him in the shoulder knocking him off balance. Max stumbled backwards as more punches came his way. As he landed with a thump he expected to get a kicking but could see his assailant was now under attack from someone else. He blinked through the darkness. He couldn't believe his eyes.

'Dad?' asked Max from his prone position as Pasco landed a second right hook on his assailant. Max's mouth dropped open.

'Get to Daisy, Max. She needs you,' said Pasco, as he dodged the retaliating blows. The man was far younger than Pasco but for the moment they seemed evenly matched.

Max rolled over. Daisy was still running but the woman was in pursuit and was gaining on her fast. Max scrambled to his feet and set off at speed, taking to the path in a bid to catch up. Daisy wasn't looking back, she may not have known she was being chased. Why were they being chased at all? Who were these people and what the hell was that stupid French goon caught up in? Max pushed himself to run flat out in a bid to reach the woman before she reached Daisy.

Max was soon gaining on them. Daisy was nearly at the small car park and thankfully there were some streetlights but there was nobody else about. Ottercombe Bay at night was dead and there were no properties nearby. Max pulled his phone out of his pocket whilst still running but it was a difficult manoeuvre. He hit Jason's number and put it to his ear – it was really awkward to run like this.

'Answer the bloody phone, Jason.' His breathing was heavy as he watched Daisy disappear off the path and onto the main pavement into town. He expected the woman chasing her to follow but instead she stopped at a parked Astra and got inside. Max slowed for a second; Daisy was out of immediate danger. He filled his lungs with air but continued to jog along. The woman was obviously doing a runner, it had just looked like she was chasing Daisy because she was running in the same direction. The relief he felt was overwhelming.

He slowed to a walk and was considering running back to help Pasco or continuing after Daisy when Jason answered his call. 'Jason, I'm up on the headland with Daisy, we've been attacked by two people and . . . shit!' Max shoved his phone back in his pocket and sprinted after the Astra now heading after Daisy and not out of town as he had expected it to. This running lark was tiring; he was fit but cars, even old Astras, went much faster.

The wind was gusting straight at him, which hindered his speed as he tried in vain to keep the car in his sights as it sped off, skidding slightly when it took a bend too fast, and disappeared from sight. He pushed himself to keep going but he simply couldn't maintain this pace for much longer.

Max was considering stopping because he had no idea which way Daisy or the car had gone when he heard the sound of screeching tyres and scraping metal up ahead and it spurred him on. He turned the corner near the Mariner's Arms and saw the car rammed up against the railings. He carried on running and the scene became clearer. The car had been stopped by a stinger, a belt of studs purposely thrown under the tyres to puncture them. Two police cars were in the pub car park. He turned his attention back to the road suddenly realising there were two armed officers shouting at him to get down. Max stopped, lay down and did exactly as he was told. His heart was thundering in his chest, and drawing in air was difficult when you were lying face down on tarmac.

'Hang on, that's Max,' shouted Jason from nearby. 'What are you doing?' he added, approaching him. Max slowly rolled onto his side and looked up to see an automatic weapon pointing at him and Jason next to the armed officer with his hands on his hips.

'Hiya, mate,' said Max, breathlessly. 'The bloke you're looking for is up on the headland fighting with Pasco.'

Jason got on his radio but someone more senior was already directing officers into a car and they screeched away. Jason helped Max to his feet and he watched as the woman was removed from the Astra, handcuffed and escorted to the other police car.

'Where's Daisy?' asked Jason.

Max closed his eyes. That was going to be his question. 'I don't know.'

'I need to sort things out here. Can you find her?'

Max nodded and set off towards Locos taking in big gulps of air as he walked. His mind was awash with questions. He had no idea what he'd witnessed, who those people were or where the hell all the armed police had sprung from. His only comforting thought was that Daisy had avoided a confrontation, but where was she now?

He took out his phone and dialled her number. It went to voicemail. He took a deep breath and started jogging. When he reached Locos he could see there were no lights on, which wasn't a good sign, but he would go and check inside anyway. He slowed to a walking pace and checked all around the building. 'Daisy!' He knocked on the door but there was no reply. He was standing on the platform thinking through his next move.

A click behind him got his attention and for a second he expected to see the stern-looking man from the headland with a cocked gun. As he turned around the door of the carriage opened and a frightened-looking Daisy emerged, glancing around her like a startled animal.

Max had a million things running through his head that he wanted to say to her but instead he opted for pulling her into a hug and holding her tightly. He could feel her trembling. After a bit Daisy gently pushed him away.

'What the cocking hell is going on?' she asked.

'I wish I knew. Come on, I'll walk you home and we'll get Jason to fill in the blanks in the morning.' He needed to track Pasco down too and check he was all right but getting Daisy home was his priority and she didn't need anything else to worry about right now.

Daisy locked up the carriage and they walked slowly across the car park giving Max a chance to fill her in on what had happened to the woman who had chased her whilst Daisy explained how she'd cut down a side street to get away. As they reached the sea wall they could see more police cars had appeared and there was a flurry of activity around the pub, which was lit up like Christmas.

'Poor Monty, he won't be happy about all this,' said Daisy, turning to walk home.

'I dunno, he'll be charging them top dollar for fancy coffees. He'll be raking it in.'

They neared Daisy's road and heard a car approaching behind them. As it went past they could see it was yet another police car. The car screeched to a halt, slammed into reverse and sped back towards them. Daisy and Max stopped walking and watched two officers leap from the vehicle.

'Max Davey?' said one of them.

'Yeah,' said Max, looking bewildered.

'Max Davey, I am arresting you on suspicion of being concerned in the supply of drugs under section 4 of the Misuse of Drugs Act 1971. You do not have to say anything, but it may harm your defence if you do not mention when questioned something you later rely on in court. Anything you do say may be given in evidence. Get in the car please, sir.'

'What?' said Max. The policeman opened the car door and gestured for Max to get in. 'Actually, nothing makes sense tonight. Let's go, boys.' Max shook his head and willingly got in the police car. One officer got in next to him, the other got in the driver's seat and they drove off leaving Daisy shivering on the pavement.

Chapter Thirty-One

When Daisy woke the next morning she lay there for a few minutes hoping it had all been a dream but if she was honest even her craziest dreams made more sense than the events of last night. As she was trying to order her thoughts the bedroom door opened and Aunt Coral came in with a cup of tea.

'Morning, love. I'm not working today. I wondered if you'd give me a hand cutting the Buddleia back. Are you all right?' she said, taking in Daisy's glazed expression.

Daisy took the proffered tea. 'Thanks and no, I'm not all right at all.'

Aunt Coral sat on the bed and Bug came and joined her (after three failed attempts to jump up Coral took pity on him and picked him up). She listened intently and nodded in the right places until Daisy had finished her story.

'So Guillaume is safe because Jason saved him and Max saved you but he's been arrested for supplying drugs. Is that right?'

She had hoped it would make a little more sense once she'd gone through it out loud but it still made no sense at all. Daisy snatched up her mobile and rang Jason's home number, when there was no reply she tried his mobile but it went straight to voicemail. Daisy threw back the covers. 'I need to see Jason. Perhaps he can explain everything.' She wished somebody would. She headed for the front door hoping Tamsyn would know where to find him, and then thought even popping next door in her pyjamas probably wasn't socially acceptable so she scurried back to put something else on.

Tamsyn also had no idea where Jason was so they decided to go to the police station together in Tamsyn's car. Daisy went through the events of the previous evening again, as much for herself as for Tamsyn. If she was voluntarily going into a police station she may be asked to make a statement and it would be nice if she had some understanding of what she had witnessed.

'Jason sent a text last night to say no *Doctor Who* because he was on an emergency. I just assumed it was an RTC. That's road traffic collision,' added Tamsyn proudly.

Daisy eyed her friend. 'This was no RTC.'

'I think you should turn yourself in,' said Tamsyn, her face deadpan.

Daisy blinked. 'What did I do?'

'You got Max to hire the boat that Guillaume had to be rescued from.'

Tamsyn had a point.

The police station where they were holding Max was a few miles away, gone were the days of one in every village. The car journey gave Daisy time to studiously inspect her fingernails.

When they got there Tamsyn made a big deal of making sure her car was parked properly in the space despite Daisy pointing out that being crap at parking wasn't actually an offence. Inside there were quite a few people but a distinct lack of anyone who looked like a policeman.

'Shall we ask for Jason?' said Daisy, feeling unsure. 'Or Max?'

'I'm guessing they'd be more likely to send Jason out to the front desk to explain things to us.'

'Oh, okay then,' said Tamsyn, seemingly oblivious to the sarcasm.

Daisy joined what she hoped was the right queue and waited. Behind her she heard raised voices. It was one of those moments where you knew making eye contact could be a disaster but still something tells you that you have to look. She turned to see Pasco reversing through some double doors with Max poking him in the shoulder. 'You think it makes everything else all right? What about the locket? Did you think I wouldn't recognise it? Was it you who—' Max stopped dead as he realised who his audience was.

Daisy was shaking as she looked from Max to Pasco. Her mouth had gone dry and she was struggling to make sense of what she'd just heard. She stepped out of the queue and walked right up to Pasco. 'Did you steal my mother's locket?'

Pasco turned to Max who was looking uncomfortable and raking his hands through his hair, which was even more messy than usual. He looked a state – tired, unshaven and still in yesterday's clothes.

'Daisy, let's go somewhere and have a talk.' Pasco rested his hand on her shoulder and she shrugged him off.

'No, I think a police station is the perfect place to discuss a theft.' She stood firm and stared him down.

Pasco's eyebrows shot up. As if on cue Jason strode purposefully through the double doors.

'Max, you are free to go but don't go disappearing in case we want to check any facts.' Max gave him a derogatory glare, which Jason didn't seem to notice. 'You too, Pasco.'

312

'Hey, I'm innocent,' said Pasco, hastily trying to usher everyone out of the police station.

'See you later,' said Jason, giving Tamsyn a little wave.

'Stop,' said Daisy, forcefully. 'Jason, where is Guillaume?'

'I'm off,' said Max, putting a hand on the door. Nobody responded so he slunk out closely followed by Pasco.

'Guillaume has been charged with possession of drugs with the intent to supply.'

'Where is he?' Daisy's voice was gruff and implied she wanted to do him harm.

'He's not here. The criminal gang he was doing business with were being watched by a bigger police operation. The local force didn't get much of a look in.' Jason appeared thoroughly disappointed by this.

'Right. Who were the people who chased me and Max?'

'Guillaume was a middleman. He was meant to collect the drugs from another boat at sea and then pass them to those two at the cove. It was all a bit last minute; apparently the deal was meant to be next week but when they had a tip-off someone was onto them they brought everything forward. Hence they picked the cove not realising it wasn't accessible.'

'You know Max had nothing to do with it.'

'Yeah, they still interviewed him for half the night because he hired the boat and the others weren't talking but Guillaume eventually came clean. He exonerated you of any wrongdoing too.'

'I should bloody well think so.'

'He admitted he only came here to set up the drugs handover.'

'Duped again,' said Daisy.

'Yes, well. I still have a bit to finish up here then I'm heading home. It's been quite a night.'

'If I wanted to bring charges for theft, do I speak to you?'

Jason's tired face registered some interest. 'You can. What and who are we talking about?'

'My locket and Pasco.'

Jason looked surprised. 'Do you have proof?'

'Not exactly but—'

'You know if it wasn't for Pasco keeping watch on you— Well, all I'm saying is if it hadn't been for Pasco stepping in to save you . . .' His speech was speeding up and he looked agitated.

'Save me?' Daisy was sceptical.

'These people Guillaume is mixed up with are career criminals and the woman who chased you was carrying a knife.' Jason's usually jovial expression was beyond serious.

Daisy tried to take in what he'd said. 'A knife?'

Jason blinked slowly. 'If Pasco hadn't been keeping an eye on you . . .'

'Pasco was watching me? What, like a stalker?'

'No. He was suspicious of Guillaume and he's been worried about you . . . and Max too. He had quite a bit of useful information to impart, some of which we've been able to back up with CCTV footage. Anyway, I have already said far too much. But go easy on Pasco. I honestly think he's turned over a new leaf. And your lift is waiting.' He indicated Tamsyn's head peeping through the door.

'Thanks, Jason.' Daisy reached up and gave him a peck on the cheek.

Jason blushed slightly. 'Out or I'll have you arrested for assaulting a police officer.'

Armed with this new information Daisy scanned the street outside for Pasco but there was no sign of him or Max.

'Where've the others gone?'

'Pub, I think,' said Tamsyn.

'At this time in the morning? Come on, I need to talk to both of them.'

Unsurprisingly they found Max and Pasco in the first pub they came to. Neither looked pleased to see them walk in.

'Would you mind getting me a Diet Coke please, Tamsyn?' said Daisy, who was eager to speak to Max and Pasco alone. Tamsyn dutifully went to the bar and Daisy pulled up a chair.

'Daisy, I have had a shit night. Please can you have a go at me later after I've had some sleep and bought some ear plugs?' asked Max.

Daisy ignored him. 'Pasco, where is my mother's locket?'

Pasco frowned and signalled to Max who put his hand in his pocket. Daisy could hardly believe her eyes when Max unfurled his fingers in front of her to reveal her locket. Daisy sobbed as she took it from him and clasped it tightly in both hands. The relief of being reunited with it was immense. She uncurled her fingers and stared at it. Every detail etched in her memory exactly how she remembered it and now it was safe again. Daisy sniffed and roughly wiped the tears from her eyes. Now wasn't the time for sentimentality, now was the time for angry accusations.

'Which one of you stole it?'

Pasco leaned forward to rest his elbows on his thighs and brought his hands together to create a steeple shape. 'I'm not certain it is stealing if you are taking back your own property.'

Daisy gave a hollow laugh but seeing the stony looks on both Pasco and Max's faces she stopped. 'What do you mean your property? This was my mother's.'

Pasco shook his head slowly and pursed his lips. 'That locket is a Davey family heirloom. It's been passed down through my family for generations. It's French.'

'I know,' said Daisy, feeling bewildered. She clutched the locket tighter between her fingers.

'I think one of my ancestors probably stole it during the French Revolution.' Pasco took a deep breath. 'I'm sorry I took it without explaining. It looked like old Reg had left the window open and I thought I'd shut it to put off any passing thieves.' Daisy's eyebrows danced at the irony. 'I just saw the locket there on the cabinet and I knew it was the same one.'

None of this made sense. She was sure it was her mother's. She looked down at the locket in her hands and blinked slowly. 'But it was with my mother's things.' Daisy's voice was small and unsure.

Pasco looked uncomfortable. 'I was a bit of a rogue back then, always in and out of the cop shop, and I wore the locket all the time. I guess they just mixed it up . . .' His eyes darted about and he let out a long slow breath.

There was silence for a few moments before Daisy spoke. 'It can't have just been a mix-up. Can it?' She looked from Pasco to Max and back again but neither was making eye contact with her. 'My dad always said that was what happened but it didn't feel right somehow.' She thought of all the times her father had dismissed her thoughts on the necklace as fantasy. Had she really been wearing a stranger's locket all this time? She turned the locket over carefully in her hands. Perhaps she had projected onto the locket the significance she wanted it to have? She was no longer sure of anything.

'I'm sorry, Daisy. The police weren't as meticulous back then. Mistakes happened,' said Pasco.

Max was watching Pasco carefully and his eyes narrowed slightly as Pasco cleared his throat.

Daisy looked up, her expression melancholy. 'I guess this is yours.' She held out the locket to Pasco. 'You said you wore it all the time?' she said, as the locket slipped from her fingers and into Pasco's outstretched palm. She felt the pain of its loss return. She turned quickly to look at Max. His expression revealed everything. 'You recognised my . . . the locket. Didn't you? You knew all along it wasn't my mother's! Oh my God. I've been so stupid. Pouring my heart out to you and all along . . .'

Max's expression changed with a jolt. 'No, that's not how it was.' He paused as Daisy stood up. 'Daisy, don't jump to conclusions, listen to—'

But Daisy had had enough of listening and she cut him off. 'Did you know it was Pasco's locket? Yes or no?' Daisy was resolute.

Max looked down and nodded. Daisy waited for him to offer an explanation but he said nothing. She watched him for a moment. He couldn't even lift his head to speak to her. A lump rose in her throat and she swallowed hard before turning and walking out without another word.

Chapter Thirty-Two

Daisy lay on her bed with Bug snoring happily beside her. She hated to admit it but feeling him there was a comfort. How could so much change in twenty-four hours, Daisy wondered. She had managed to let two men treat her like an idiot. Perhaps that was the bottom line: she was an idiot. One minute she was having fun with Guillaume and supposedly going off on a romantic boat ride and the next he was in a police cell and she was here alone. Guillaume was only using her as cover for his smuggling operation.

Max must have been laughing at her behind her back; he had known all along the locket was nothing to do with her mother. All the times she talked to him about it being the crucial link to what happened and all the while he had known it was a red herring. How could he have kept that from her? How could he have let her waffle on like a deranged fool? It was cruel and unnecessary.

Daisy rolled over and studied the calendar. It was early March. She had less than four months until her sentence in Ottercombe Bay was over. With the locket returned to Pasco it seemed there was no mystery to solve. If she kept repeating that to herself over the next few months then

318

she could walk away from Ottercombe Bay having laid her mother properly to rest forever.

A couple of weeks later Max was strolling towards the pub after a thankfully uneventful day. 'Pasco,' he shouted, as he recognised the figure up ahead in the street. When his dad didn't turn around he tried again. 'Dad.' This time Pasco stopped, turned and waited for Max to jog up to him.

'Hiya Max, you all right after—'

'What's going on?'

Pasco held his hands up. 'What have I done now?'

'Not now. I've been going over everything and it's what you did the night Sandy died that's bothering me.'

Pasco's cocky expression was gone. He stared at Max, a frown making his usually warm features appear harsh. 'Nothing to do with me.'

'Then how do you explain your locket winding up with Sandy's stuff?'

Pasco clicked his neck as if trying to release some tension. He cleared his throat. Something he did when he was uncomfortable. 'Like I said, son, it was a simple police cock-up. They make them all the time. And to be fair it's not the most manly piece of jewellery; you can see how it could have happened can't you?' He placed an arm around Max's shoulder in a conspiratorial gesture.

'No. I don't buy it. It's too much of a coincidence that *your* locket ended up with *her* things. Come on, let's have the truth.'

Pasco ran his fingers over his stubbled chin as if considering his answer. 'Truth is police cocked it up.' He gave a blasé shrug of his shoulders.

Max shook his head, he was losing his patience. 'How about this for nearer the truth. You were off on a smuggling

319

trip and Sandy is on the beach and she spots you but before she can tell anyone you knock her unconscious and she drowns?'

Pasco tried to laugh it off but Max could see the concern on his face and it made him uneasy. 'You should write murder mysteries; you have a wild imagination.' Pasco threw up his arms with dramatic effect. 'This is the sort of stupid rumour that can damage a man's reputation. Don't you go saying this to anyone else.'

Max locked eyes with him. 'Did you kill her?'

Pasco's expression was one of dismay. He shook his head. 'I won't dignify that with an answer.' He started to turn away from Max but Max held him firmly by his shoulder.

'Daisy deserves to know the truth. And I bet my version of events is a damn sight closer to the truth than yours.' He let go and didn't wait for Pasco to respond, he was already striding away. The fact his father hadn't profusely denied murder was laying heavy on him and he feared it was a sensation that wouldn't go until he knew the truth.

The warm spring weather had brought the trees to life, the seagulls were back in full chorus and as the holidaymakers returned the sleepy town was waking up. Daisy needed it to be a good season. Locos was busy because Easter was fast approaching, the celebrations for which appeared to start early thanks to Daisy's Singapore Sling cocktail promotion, and she was rushed off her feet. If she never had to make a Singapore Sling again it would be too soon. She swore she'd be making them in her sleep. With no Max or Guillaume, Daisy and Tamsyn were working flat out. On the plus side, it meant she didn't have time to dwell on recent events. However, a little more time for sleep and general relaxation would have been welcome. In between customers Tamsyn passed Daisy a piece of paper and when she had a moment to catch her breath she studied it.

Daisy read the handwritten note.

22nd March is Tamsyn Turvey Day. Starting at your house at 8.30am. No need to be dressed. No money required.

  Jason x

Daisy reread the note before handing it back to Tamsyn. 'What's it all about?' she asked.

'I'm not sure. What should I do?'

'Definitely go,' said Daisy, the curiosity was already making her itch.

'Really? It sounds like a plot to get me to go out with him.'

'And is that so bad?'

Tamsyn pressed her lips together. 'The cards are still looking favourable for us. But . . .'

'What is stopping you?'

'You,' she said bluntly.

'Oh, I'll be fine. Old Man Burgess will be in, I think we'll manage.'

'No, that wasn't what I meant. We're in a love triangle. You, me and Jason.'

'First I've heard of it,' said Daisy, her eyebrows drawn together. 'And I think I would remember.'

Tamsyn pulled a face. 'I figured you knew Jason has a thing for you.'

Daisy shook her head. 'I think you've got it wrong. Have you seen the way he looks at you?'

'I'm more interested in the looks he gives you.' Tamsyn was forlorn.

'That's just testosterone at work, Tamsyn; he's not serious.'

'But if he likes you then he can never be a match for me. I believe people need to fit together like puzzle pieces.' She was linking her thumbs and forefingers together as she spoke. 'I'm looking for someone like me. No point wasting time trying to ram in a puzzle piece that's never going to fit.'

'Sometimes you talk such sense. You should listen to yourself sometimes. Not *all* the time, just sometimes.' Daisy was surprised by her own words but it was true, occasionally Tamsyn provided insight and clarity often when you least expected it. It was also true that most of the time she spoke as if she was reporting from another planet.

'I'm worried he'll be comparing me to you. I do it a lot. And you win every time.' Tamsyn hung her head and Daisy felt awful but had no idea why.

'You shouldn't do that. You're a unique and beautiful person – inside and out.'

'Thanks but I don't know what to do about this.' Tamsyn waved the note.

'What would Bilbo do?' asked Daisy. 'Apart from rub his ring.' She giggled at her own joke.

'He wears the ring,' said Tamsyn, rolling her eyes. 'I think Bilbo would go.'

'Then you should too and with an open mind. See how you feel at the end of it.'

'Mmm, okay,' said Tamsyn and she carefully folded the note and put it in her bra.

Max approached the caravan park and the sight of smoke had him quickening his pace but when he got nearer he could see it was the remnants of a controlled fire. It looked like someone had been burning an old carpet.

Max peered closer; it bore a striking resemblance to the cat pee one from the old railway carriage, which he'd paid a bloke a tenner to dispose of a few months back. Max turned his back on it and knocked on a dilapidated caravan nearby.

Pasco's face lit up at the sight of his son on the doorstep. 'Come in. I'll put the kettle on,' he said, walking away and picking up a dirty plate as he passed the arm of the sofa it was resting on.

'What are you burning?' asked Max, staying where he was.

'Just some old carpet. People dump all sorts up here,' said Pasco, with a conspiratorial wink.

'You'd better have a permit for setting fire to it or Jason will be after you. I'm surprised he's not here. A wisp of smoke and he appears like the genie from the lamp just in case it's another shed going up.'

'It's covered by the site permits and all health and safety regulations were followed, don't you worry. And it's likely we won't see any more shed fires.'

'Why's that?' Max had an ominous feeling creeping over him.

'I caught the little sod who's doing it. I told him he'd end up like me and I think it scared him off.' Pasco looked pleased with himself.

'You sure?' Max was doubtful.

'Coupled with the fact I was sleeping in the shed at the time. I think that freaked him out.'

'Have you told Jason?'

'No, and I'm not going to. Anyway, come in.'

Max was reluctant but with his father retreating inside he could do little else but follow him. Shutting the door behind him, Max looked around the caravan. It was small and untidy but it wasn't the total tip he'd been expecting it to be. 'Coffee?' asked Pasco.

'Please.'

'Sugar?' Max shook his head; his father didn't know him well at all.

It was becoming more awkward by the second. He felt guilty for wanting to escape the situation. There was only one reason he was here: Daisy. He knew Pasco was hiding something and until the truth was fully revealed Max would always be public enemy number one in Daisy's eyes and he couldn't bear it. He knew he had let her down and finding out exactly what Pasco's involvement was in her mother's death was the least he could do, even if it meant Pasco would be returning for a longer stint at her majesty's pleasure. If he had to make a choice then it was Daisy and the truth over Pasco and his lies.

Pasco hurried through with the drinks and slopped them slightly in his eagerness to sit down. 'It's great to see you,' he said, with a smile, which quickly faded as he studied Max's face. 'What's wrong?'

Max picked up his mug and looked about for a coaster; when he couldn't see one, he wiped away the wet ring it had left with his hand. 'It's Daisy . . .'

Pasco seemed to relax. 'Girl trouble hey? You've come to the right place.'

'No, it's not that. She needs to know what happened to her mother.'

'Only Ray would know about that,' said Pasco nodding sagely.

'I'm asking you what *you* know.'

'Why?' Pasco became defensive, leaning back and folding his arms.

Max tried to soften his tone. 'Because if there is any

324

possibility you know even the smallest piece of information about what happened to her, it may help Daisy to lay it all to rest.' He was pleased with himself for staying calm. He sipped his coffee to stop him launching into a full-blown interrogation. He tried in vain to relax a little. When Max put down his mug and looked up his father was scratching his chin.

Pasco cleared his throat. 'I wish I could help, son. I really do.'

Max felt his shoulders tense. He decided to try another tack. 'What do you remember about that night?'

Pasco blinked. Gotcha, thought Max, trying hard not to let it show. Pasco pulled the sort of face you pull after a tequila shot. 'Ooh, you're talking about something that happened a very long time ago. And my memory's not what it used to be.' He tapped the side of his head and gave a tinkle of a laugh.

'But in a small place like this, someone dying must have been a big tragedy. Something that would stick in your mind. Sort of like the local version of when JFK or Princess Diana died; they say you always remember what you were doing when you heard about those sad events.'

Max watched Pasco shift in his seat and clear his throat again. He rested his forearms on his thighs. 'I remember there was a party.' Pasco spoke slowly and deliberately. This was what Max was after. 'I didn't go. I was working. That's all I know,' said Pasco, maintaining eye contact with Max. If it hadn't been for the tell-tale throat clearing Max may even have believed him.

'Where were you working?'

'I don't remember now. I think I was helping out a mate.' He picked up his mug as if to signal the conversation was over.

'Where?' Max wasn't going to let it go easily.

'Er . . .' Pasco seemed to be trying to recall or was he simply conjuring up a believable lie? 'Here at the caravan park.'

'In March? What's there to do in a caravan park that time of year?' He had to force himself to keep the tone enquiring rather than accusatorial.

'There's a lot to do ahead of the Easter holidays and it was cash in hand.'

'You remember that clear enough.' Max couldn't hide his sarcasm. 'You and Mum were still together. If you walked home from here you would have taken the coastal path and must have walked past the beach where she was . . .'

'I walked through town. I went straight home. I saw nothing. I had nothing to do with Sandy's death.'

Pasco's voice was firm. Max wasn't going to get any further but he knew his father well enough to know he was hiding something and it worried him greatly.

'Can I ask you something, Max?'

'Sure,' said Max, finishing his coffee.

Pasco studied his son. 'Why don't you believe me?'

Max narrowed his eyes as he pondered the question. 'Because you've let me down in the past and it feels like too much of a coincidence that your locket just happened to get mixed up with Sandy's belongings at the police station.'

Pasco's lips made a flat line. 'I know I've not exactly been reliable over the years but coincidences do sometimes happen. And you have to leave the past behind and move on.' Pasco held Max's stare for a moment and then relaxed back into the sofa. He'd given Max something to think about. Maybe there was a chance Pasco was telling the truth and perhaps there was no more to be gained by raking over the past.

Chapter Thirty-Three

Tamsyn was woken by the sound of Jason's voice and by the time she'd opened her eyes he was placing a tray on her bed. It was the 22nd of March.

'Good morning,' he said ridiculously cheerily.

Tamsyn rubbed her eyes like a small child, yawned and blinked. 'What's all this?'

'Your mum let me in. This is the start of Tamsyn Turvey Day,' said Jason proudly. 'Toast and tea and a yellow rose because I know you like those,' he added pointing to the things on the tray. Tamsyn couldn't help the beam of a smile spreading across her face. She had a feeling she was going to enjoy today very much.

Their first stop was her absolutely favourite place, the donkey sanctuary, and thanks to Jason knowing the vet's cousin she was allowed to spend the morning being a keeper. 'You all right?' called Jason, from a safe distance as Tamsyn flung manure and straw into a wheelbarrow.

'Yeah, this is great.'

'I've never seen someone enjoy mucking out before.'

'It's ace. I definitely want my own donkey,' said Tamsyn, her face serious.

Next there was feeding and grooming and before she

knew it she was out of her green overalls and borrowed steel cap boots, and sitting with a cup of coffee in the sanctuary café.

'This has been the best day ever,' she said. 'Thank you, Jason.'

'Drink up,' he said with a grin. 'You're only halfway through.'

He was so kind and thoughtful, she thought. If today was about showing her what things would be like to be his girlfriend he was selling himself well.

'You know you don't have to do any of this,' she said.

'It's not a bribe. I'm not expecting you to declare your undying love for me or anything.' He gave a strangled laugh. 'You're my friend and I want you to know how special you are. That's all.'

The next stop was another favourite of hers. The freshest local fare from the fish and chip van eaten on the sea front with a wooden fork with seagulls swooping above them in the hope of snatching a stray chip. It was a beautifully sunny day and the sea was rolling tamely onto the beach – it didn't come much better in Tamsyn's book. When she thought she was too full to eat anything else Jason produced a cake box from his rucksack.

Her eyes were like a bush baby's. 'Is it?' She was too excited to finish the sentence.

'Scones and clotted cream,' he announced, flipping open the box lid. Tamsyn was in heaven.

After a delicious fresh scone, which crumbled in her mouth, she licked her fingers and was interested by the mix of chip vinegar and clotted cream. 'Jason, that was amazing. Thank you.'

'Uh-uh,' said Jason with a shake of his head. 'Not done yet.' He checked his watch. 'Come on.' He held out his hand

and Tamsyn took it. His fingers were warm and curled gently around hers. They both looked at their entwined hands and grinned. Something was starting to feel right.

A short drive brought them to the old picture house: a newly restored cinema that had stood empty and neglected for years until someone had had the inspiration to get a lottery grant and transform it. Now it showed old films as well as new ones at weekends, staffed by a fleet of volunteers.

Tamsyn read the sign on the glass while Jason checked the car was locked.

'Sorry, Jason. We've got the wrong day. It's not open.' She pointed to the sign.

'It's not open to the public but when the Super is a keen movie fan . . .' He rapped his knuckles on the glass and a tall man appeared and opened the door.

'Welcome to the Ottercombe Bay picture house,' he said, standing back.

'Wow,' said Tamsyn, tiptoeing inside.

She could feel the excitement building as they chose seats in the middle of the empty cinema and waited for the film to start. She had no idea what it would be but she already knew she would love it and when the titles to *Tangled* appeared on the screen she knew beyond any doubt she also loved Jason.

Max rested his body on the outside of the caravan while he waited for his father to appear. Eventually Pasco hurried out and locked the door behind him. Max could see he'd made a special effort. He was freshly showered and shaved. Whatever their genetic background there was something about the Davey bloodline that had them growing a five o'clock shadow at about three in the afternoon and a dark one too. Pasco's hair was as neat as Max had seen it in a while and he was even wearing an ironed shirt. Max brushed at the front of his own t-shirt – it was clean and ironed but he hadn't exactly made an effort. Pasco slapped him on the back, his face was lit up at the prospect of an evening out with Max. Max felt a pang of guilt but he had a strong suspicion Pasco was still hiding something about Sandy's death and he was determined to get to the truth, however uncomfortable, whatever the consequences.

'How was your day?' asked Pasco and Max spluttered a laugh at Pasco's enthusiasm.

'It was fine. How about yours?'

'It was good but it's a whole lot better now I'm going for a drink with my son.' He gave him another slap on the shoulder and this time he left his hand there. His dad was incorrigible.

On the way into town they talked about football, but Max wanted to steer the conversation towards Daisy so he asked his father how well he had known Reg.

'I think you knew him better than I did and most likely you knew a different man to the one I did years ago.'

'What makes you say that?'

'You only have good things to say about him and, let's say, me and Reg didn't see eye to eye on a few things.'

'Like what?' Max was intrigued. Reg was the most reasonable person he had ever known. He had given Max good advice and just before he died he had been helping him investigate possible courses to enable a change of career. He felt a pang of guilt that, apart from the brief stint at Locos, he'd done nothing to progress this. Reg was a good man through and through, and instantly Max could see where there could be an issue with Pasco.

'Coral,' said Pasco, with a brief look in Max's direction.

'Coral?' Max's eyebrows shot up. 'What – you were going out with her?' Max could feel himself gearing up to tease him and he stopped himself.

'Don't be cheeky, she's worn well and she's still the caring person she always was. I'll have you know she was a beauty in her day.'

'She's a lovely person, I agree with you there,' said Max, considering his next question. 'What was the problem with her Uncle Reg?'

'It wasn't just Reg it was Arthur too, Coral's dad. They both thought I wasn't good enough for her, and to be fair they were right.'

For the first time in a long while Max felt defensive of his father. 'That's a bit narrow minded of them.'

'Nah, I would have been the same if I'd been them. I was a hoodlum with no steady job and a growing police record. Not exactly textbook husband material, which was what they wanted for Coral. Someone she could settle down and have a family with.'

Max looked puzzled. 'But she's never married. Has she?'

'Nope. She looked after her brother and Daisy after Sandy died and then she cared for Arthur and Reg. I guess she never found the right man.'

'And you fell in love with Mum,' Max prompted.

'Er, yeah. It's no secret she was pregnant when we got wed. She could have done better than me too.' Pasco looked remorseful.

Max's mind was whirling. He'd never done the maths; he didn't even know when their wedding anniversary was, for Christ's sake. They'd split up when he was in his teens. He observed Pasco. There was no need to ask if he was his biological father – that was blindingly obvious – but the fact he'd been conceived out of wedlock was a bit of a surprise. While they walked along in companionable silence, Max ran through a store of memories as the puzzle pieces started to fit. All the things his mother had shouted in the heat of a row, all the times his father had talked of being trapped, it all started to make sense.

'You all right?' asked Pasco, after a few minutes.

Max swallowed. He was now thinking back to Christmas Day – the way Pasco and Coral had been with each other. He'd exchanged looks with Daisy at the time and laughed at the clumsy flirting between the two of them but now he felt he understood the situation better. They'd been the couple who were meant to be, but with Coral's protective family and his father's wayward nature their lives had gone in different directions.

'Dad?'

'Yes, son,' said Pasco looking thrilled at being called Dad for a change.

'You and Coral.' Max felt painfully awkward and he ran his finger round the neck of his t-shirt even though it wasn't tight. 'You shouldn't waste any more time.' Pasco was looking puzzled and Max was getting more embarrassed by the second. There was a reason men didn't talk about stuff like this. 'She obviously likes you and you like her. Why not ask her out or something?' He wasn't sure what older people did in this sort of situation.

Pasco gave a hearty chuckle. 'I think we're past anything like that but we're still friends, which means a lot to me.'

'Yeah, but sometimes friends isn't enough.' He wasn't sure where it came from or who exactly he was talking about. 'If you care for her, then you should tell her. I'm sure she feels the same way about you . . . but goodness knows why.' He affectionately slapped his father on the shoulder and Pasco revelled in the contact. Max was grateful for the breeze as he was swiftly starting to overheat – they were striding uphill, it was probably the exertion.

'After all this time, do you think I should?' asked Pasco.

'Definitely,' said Max. They walked across the Locos car park. 'The past has to be laid to rest and the sooner you do it the sooner everyone can move on.'

Pasco glanced at him wearily like he knew he was no longer talking about Coral.

Daisy and Tamsyn were having a quiet night, when the door opened and Max walked in Daisy had to hide her surprise. She'd seen him about but they'd not spoken since she'd walked out of the pub the morning after the drugs bust. She busied herself with polishing a glass and watched him closely. He looked his usual scruffy and unshaven self but she kind of liked it. She figured whatever he did to his hair it would always look unkempt. It struck her how alike he and Pasco were in looks as he followed Max to the bar, if Pasco was an indication of what Max would look like in a few years' time then his future looked bright.

She raised her chin as they approached. She needed to stay professional. 'What can I get you both?' she asked.

Max seemed to notice her for the first time and he blinked slowly showing off his long eyelashes. A quiver of something she didn't want to think too hard about went through her body.

'These are on me,' said Pasco, standing very straight. 'Have whatever you like,' he said, handing Max the cocktail list. 'I've got my wages.'

'I kinda know this inside out,' said Max. 'I'll have a dirty Martini,' he said, looking straight at Daisy. She almost giggled. What the hell was going on? She reminded herself

333

that Max was still the enemy, the man who had made her feel a fool.

'No problem. And for you, Pasco?'

'What do you recommend?'

She pretended to appraise him and then suggested what she did to most of the men who asked. 'How about the Opihr oriental spiced gin with ginger ale and a slice of orange?'

Pasco licked his lips. 'Sounds perfect.'

'Actually, I think he'd love the rhubarb and custard cocktail,' said Max.

Daisy straightened her shoulders. 'Okay.' She wasn't going to argue.

As Daisy made the drinks, Pasco and Max chatted convivially. She handed over the glasses and gave Pasco his change. They stayed sitting at the bar and took their first sips.

'Wow, it's amazing,' said Pasco bobbing his head appreciatively. 'It's rhubarb and custard in a glass. I love it.' He took a long sip and closed his eyes.

'Good. I like a happy customer.'

'How's Coral?' Pasco asked and Daisy noticed Max was suddenly very involved in stirring his drink.

'She's good, thanks.'

'I hope you don't mind me asking but does she have any special friends at all or anyone she sees regularly or . . .'

'Bloody hell, Dad,' said Max, barging into the conversation. 'Is Coral seeing anyone?'

Daisy was slightly taken aback by Max's forcefulness and the unexpected questioning.

'I don't think so. No.' She looked at Pasco whose expression resembled a Bond villain working out his next dastardly plan. 'Why?' she asked tentatively.

'They liked each other years ago but never did anything about it and—' started Max.

Pasco cleared his throat and Max stopped talking. Daisy and Max stared at Pasco. When he spoke it was soft and full of emotion. 'We did go out but in secret. Nobody knew. Your granddad and great uncle were not keen on her dating a lowlife like me and I don't blame them. When it got harder for her to get away the relationship went a bit off the boil.' He turned to Max. 'I got together with your mum, which was the end of me and Coral.'

Max was frowning. 'You slept with Mum when you were meant to be in a relationship with Coral?'

'I told you I wasn't good enough for either of them.' Pasco looked contrite.

'I guess that didn't work out well for any of you,' said Max.

Daisy was impressed with Max's composure assuming, like her, this was the first time he was hearing this.

Daisy busied herself with loading the glasswasher and served the few more customers who came in, but the whole time she was distracted by Pasco and Max, who were deep in conversation close by. Max bought another round and continued his evening. It was nice to see him even if it was odd with him on the other side of the bar. She missed him. She felt pathetic for even thinking it, but it was the truth. They had been a good team and despite all the arguments they worked well together. If only he had been honest about the locket things could have been so different, she thought.

As closing time approached and the other customers drifted off, Tamsyn went home and Daisy found she was wiping the tables down with only Pasco and Max left at the bar. When she approached, Max was talking to his father.

'Do you want another drink? Because it'll have to be a lock in or I'll lose my licence.'

'No, we'll finish these and be off,' said Pasco, but the look that passed between him and Max said otherwise. Pasco checked there was nobody else in the bar and let out a long slow breath. 'Look, Daisy.' Pasco leaned over and placed a hand on top of Daisy's making her halt what she was doing. 'I fixed your roof tile.'

They all looked up at the same time. 'Thanks, I wondered who'd done that,' said Daisy, starting to retrieve her hand.

Pasco kept a hold on it. 'And there's something else. Your mother's death was a tragic accident.'

She looked at him with tears pooling in her eyes. 'You don't know that.'

'Yes, I do,' said Pasco, his voice calm. Daisy was shocked. 'I was there the night she died.'

Chapter Thirty-Four

Daisy looked from Pasco to Max and back again. 'Is this for real?' A hollow laugh escaped. This had to be some sort of sick joke.

Max motioned for Pasco to continue. Pasco thumbed Daisy's hand gently as he spoke. 'It was the early hours of the morning and I was in a boat not far from shore. I saw a figure on the headland. It was a woman in a long flowing dress. I watched her for a while.'

'My mother?' Daisy's voice was barely a whisper. Her eyes fixed on Pasco, her attention gripped by his every word.

'Yes, it was your mother. She was dancing, spinning around like she didn't have a care in the world. I remember thinking how happy she looked.' He paused and Daisy's stomach filled with knots. 'What happened next, happened in the briefest moment. Sandy stumbled and fell over the edge. Her dress billowed for a second before she disappeared into the sea.'

Daisy couldn't help the gasp that escaped and Pasco instinctively gripped her hand. 'Are you okay?'

'Yes, please carry on,' said Daisy, swallowing back the tears threatening to erupt.

'It was a rough night and I struggled to turn the old

337

boat around. But I kept on battling and I got to her as quickly as I could. I dived off the boat and swam to where she'd entered the water.' Max gave an eye roll at the picture of heroics he was describing, but Pasco ignored him and continued. 'It took me a while to find her but when I did I fought with the waves to pull her out of the water and onto the beach but . . .' He swallowed hard. 'I'm truly sorry, Daisy. She was already dead.'

Daisy didn't speak for a moment, the information overwhelming her. 'She wasn't pushed?'

Pasco shook his head. 'There was nobody else there; she just tripped and fell.'

'She didn't jump?' Daisy was frowning hard. She had to be completely clear and rule out all the possibilities that had tortured her over the years.

Pasco gave her a warm smile. 'No, she definitely didn't jump. It was an accident. There was nothing anyone could have done to save her.'

Daisy blinked hard and willed the tears not to erupt as she tried to take it all in.

Max noisily placed his empty glass onto the bar. 'Exactly why were you in a boat at night?' he asked, his voice stern.

Pasco shot him a look. 'Max, you know one day you will have to let go of all this anger,' said Pasco, looking genuinely concerned.

'You've given her the hero version, now tell her what you were doing there,' said Max firmly.

Pasco let out a long slow breath and turned back to Daisy. 'I was smuggling. It's what I used to do. Not any more, mind.'

Max learned forward. 'Don't you see? He panicked because he was up to no good as usual. He didn't call an ambulance—'

'Because there are no phones on the beach and I didn't have a mobile back then and at any rate it was too late to save her.'

'We only have your word and how reliable is that?' Max sat back.

'But he tried to save her,' said Daisy, her forehead furrowed into a deep frown.

'He left your mother on a beach in the middle of the night, wet through, freezing and alone and he did what he always does. He ran away.'

Daisy bit her lip. Running away was something she could relate to. A shudder went through her as if someone had walked over her grave. She could picture her mother just how Max had described, her lips blue, her hair and clothes soaked. Daisy blinked rapidly but her gaze was on Max. She could see the animosity in his eyes; he was proving a point about his father as much as he was revealing the truth to Daisy.

'There was nothing anyone could have done for her, Daisy.' Pasco's voice was soft and soothing, his face full of regret. 'Believe me, I tried.'

Pasco let go of Daisy's hand, sat up straight on the bar stool. He had pulled the locket from under his t-shirt and was repeatedly turning it over and over in his fingers, something Daisy had done many times herself when she was troubled.

Daisy stared at the necklace. 'And the locket?'

'I wore it all the time back then. When I realised Sandy had gone and I had a boat full of tobacco drifting out to sea, I panicked, and as I got up it must have got caught on her clothing. I always thought I'd lost it in the sea that night. I used to go beachcombing to see if it would wash up with the tide. And yet all these years you were keeping it safe.'

Daisy looked from the locket to Max and back again. It hurt her that he had known who the real owner was, and it struck her perhaps this wasn't the first time he'd heard Pasco's version of events. She blinked back the tears, pulled herself up straight and looked directly at Max.

'Did you know?' Daisy's voice was heavy with emotion. Max looked puzzled. 'Did you know it was an accident?'

'God, no! This is the first time I've heard this, I swear. I figured he was keeping something back, which is why I cornered him tonight.' He turned to Pasco for support. 'Tell her.'

'He didn't know anything, Daisy. I've never told a soul about what happened that night.'

Daisy wanted to scream and lash out. A forceful emotional cocktail swept over her and she knew she had to get away. Her head was swimming with a jumble of facts, her emotions unexpectedly unleashed like a warring dragon in one of Tamsyn's fantasy books. She hastily handed the keys to Max and without a word she walked out.

Daisy walked and walked until her legs ached. She found herself on the far east promenade striding back towards the headland. It was like a beacon calling to her. From the promenade she could see the distance from the cliff top to the sea – it was a huge drop with rocks at the bottom. A chill went through her and she wasn't sure if it was the evening's temperature drop or the thoughts of her mother's last moments causing it. She ploughed on, keeping her head down, until she'd rounded the east side of the bay, past the cave where Max had rescued her and along to the main beach. This was the beach Pasco had talked of. This was where they had found her mother the next morning.

Not washed up as people had suspected but dragged there by Pasco. This was where her mother had died. It was an odd comfort to know nobody had hurt her and she hadn't committed suicide, but knowing the facts hadn't changed the end result and it felt slightly more pointless that a simple stumble had been the cause.

Daisy flopped down onto the sand. Her lips trembled and she pressed her fist to her chest. She pulled up her knees and at last she let go. She released the tears that had been burning her eyes and with them she tried to let go of the burden she'd carried all these years. A sob turned into a wail and she yelled out her pain, the sound fading into the night. Daisy ran her fingers through the sand, digging them in hard and feeling the grains catch under her fingernails. She raked at it as the sorrow clutched at her heart. She rested her throbbing forehead on her knees and sobbed until there were no more tears to come.

Daisy took a couple of days off work leaving Tamsyn and Old Man Burgess manning Locos and spent them either curled up in bed or pacing the beach. It was where she felt closest to her mother. Aunt Coral had provided a bottomless supply of tea and listened to her retell Pasco's version of events countless times as Daisy tried to seal the facts in her mind. It was as if she was grieving for Sandy all over again. The pain cut through her, a physical relentless ache. The only small consolation was that her mother had not been totally alone.

All the time Bug had not left her side, even if she went to the toilet he nudged the door open to join her, which she could have done without but the fact the little dog sensed her distress was comforting. Now she knew the missing pieces of the story perhaps she could make peace with the past but right now that felt like it was a long way off.

A few shifts at Locos had Daisy back in the swing of some form of normality, but the revelation about her mother's death still dominated her thoughts. The initial local excitement at the drug smuggling bust had long since dwindled and she had hired some more help before the season got into full swing. She still had Old Man Burgess working the odd mornings on the hot chocolate shift and alongside her and Tamsyn she had a bouncy Australian named Maddison at weekends who was a fast learner and already a popular attraction with the local men.

A few times she had seen Max at a distance jogging on the beach but they hadn't acknowledged each other. She was confused by her feelings for Max. She still wasn't sure she could trust him. It wasn't long until her forced stay was up, but for the first time it felt odd to think of leaving the bay and saying goodbye to everyone, including Max. Stick to the plan, she thought. She was managing enough heartache at the moment so self-preservation told her to keep a safe distance from him.

She had seen Pasco in town a couple of times but she had put her head down and walked on. Whilst knowing what happened had helped her start to lay her mother's ghost to rest, it had also highlighted how Pasco had selfishly kept this information secret for all these years solely to protect himself.

Then one balmy evening in early May Pasco walked in to Locos and made himself comfortable in the corner of the bar. Maddison was already working through a big order so Daisy took a deep breath and decided to be the bigger person. For the time being they were all still living in the bay. She put on her best professional smile and went to serve him.

'Evening, Pasco. What can I get you?'

'Hello, Daisy.' His voice was warm and similar to his son's. She dispelled the thought of Max that burst into her brain. 'I'd like to try this cocoa gin,' said Pasco, studying the specials board. 'What mixer does it come with?'

'If you like gin and orange it works well in a cocoa martini?' suggested Daisy.

Pasco licked his lips. 'Sounds perfect.' Daisy set to work on the cocktail and tried to ignore Pasco watching her intensely. It wasn't unusual; people liked to watch when she mixed cocktails, there was a natural fascination, but right now she could have done without his scrutiny.

She handed him his finished cocktail and he thanked her and paid. She waited while he sipped it, closing his eyes and savouring the flavours. 'Delicious.' She was expecting something else, but he turned slightly to look across the room signalling the end of the conversation. She should have felt relieved but oddly she didn't. She took a couple of the orders from Maddison to occupy her mind and stop her overthinking her feelings.

Despite everything, tonight she was drawn to Pasco. She wanted to talk to him and she also didn't. He was the link to the past, he was the one person who witnessed her mother's final moments and now he had shared them.

'Pasco?'

He swivelled around to face her. His face was weathered but still handsome in a roguish way. 'Yes, Daisy?'

'Thanks for telling me the truth about my mother. I know it all happened a long time ago but I think it's helped me to know.'

'I should have told you before. Not just for your sake but for my own. I've been carrying it with me for too many years. Time just puts distance between you and the event, it doesn't heal anything.'

They exchanged smiles and Daisy got back to work.

As the days lengthened and the weather warmed up, May became increasingly busy and business increased at both ends of the working day. The sun had brought in young families and the recent arrival of the bats had brought out the bat watchers in force, which was excellent for evening trade. With the greater horseshoe bat being quite rare, there were only a handful of nursing roosts located in Devon, making Locos something of a mini wildlife attraction.

When Daisy got back to the cottage late one night she kicked off her shoes and flopped onto the sofa. 'Boy I'm tired.'

'Was it busy?' asked Aunt Coral, switching off the television and giving Daisy her full attention.

'Yeah, we had a leaving do in and they were pretty much working their way through the cocktail menu, which is excellent for the takings. We also had the usual faces out in force.'

'Pasco?' asked Aunt Coral. 'Was he in tonight?' Daisy had noticed Aunt Coral asked after him a lot lately.

'Yeah, Pasco was in. He's doing all right for himself now he's got a steady job. Maybe you should ask him for a coffee or something.'

Coral eyed her suspiciously. 'Now why would I want to be spending time with Pasco Davey?'

'Who are you kidding? You two are like a couple of teenagers when you get together. What is stopping the two of you?'

Aunt Coral took a deep breath. 'That was all a long time ago. We're different people now.'

Daisy felt sad for her. 'I had a little chat to him recently actually.'

'Ooh what about?' Aunt Coral bent forward.

'We talked a little about my mother, he had some funny memories of her. I think it's helped him telling me about what happened the night she died.'

Aunt Coral reached out and clasped Daisy's hand. 'It was never going to be easy.'

'No. But I like the idea of her dancing, even at the end. It feels kind of fitting she was acting a bit whacky. Just how I remember her.'

'They were whacky times,' said Aunt Coral.

'I don't mean drugs,' said Daisy, quick to clarify what she'd meant.

'Oh, everyone did a little weed back then.' Aunt Coral gave a cheeky shrug of her shoulders.

Daisy's expression changed. She stared at Aunt Coral her frown tightening. 'Did they? I thought that was the sixties not the nineties.'

'Oh they were rife in the nineties. Not all the time. We weren't addicts or anything. Just a bit of weed on the beach and at parties. Harmless stuff.'

Daisy's eyebrows hitched up a notch. 'I bet my dad didn't see it like that – he's dead against drugs.' She watched her aunt's expression.

Aunt Coral broke eye contact as her gaze darted around the room looking at anything apart from Daisy. 'Perhaps I should go to bed,' she said, picking up her empty sherry glass.

'I can't believe my dad would sit back and let you do drugs?' Daisy felt she was questioning a fundamental fact about her father.

'I wish you'd stop saying drugs. There's a huge difference between weed and something like heroin.' Aunt Coral looked agitated.

'But still, Dad is against all of it. He'd never condone it.' But as she finished the sentence she saw her aunt sneer. '*He* didn't smoke the stuff. Did he?' Daisy waited for her aunt's response.

Aunt Coral stared at the carpet and said nothing. Eventually she looked up slowly and sighed as she made eye contact with Daisy. She nodded. 'We all did, love.'

Daisy was still frowning. 'I don't believe it.' This didn't make any sense. Her father had always had a strong anti-drugs message especially when she was at university. He was always reminding Daisy of the dangers. She thought he was just being over protective but now everything looked very different.

'I'm sorry, Daisy. We're none of us perfect, you know. And like I said it was never anything heavy and everyone was doing it.'

'What changed his mind?' Daisy's suspicion was growing. 'How did he go from casual dope smoker to anti-drugs vigilante?'

Aunt Coral looked cornered. 'I've said too much. This shouldn't be me having this conversation with you, it should be Ray. Only he can tell you how things changed.'

There was a long pause where the two women sat uncomfortably in the small living room with Bug snoring on the rug, oblivious to the confrontation swirling above him.

Daisy looked shocked as realisation dawned. 'I'm so stupid. It's only after Mum's death that he's been anti-drugs isn't it?' She didn't wait for a response. 'My mother smoked marijuana as well. She was high on the stuff wasn't she?'

Daisy stood up, her breathing was fast and she was

overheating. Aunt Coral gave a brief nod. Daisy raked her hands through her hair. 'Shit. That's what killed her. She was off her head.' Daisy started to laugh. It wasn't driven by humour but by a sick grasp of the situation. 'That's why she was dancing on the bloody headland. Not because she was free and happy but because she was stoned.'

Aunt Coral wiped away a tear and Daisy felt a brief pang of guilt. She knew she shouldn't be calling Aunt Coral to account but nobody else was here. Her questions were coming thick and fast now and she couldn't stop herself from firing them all at her aunt. 'Did you tell the police about the marijuana?'

'No,' said Aunt Coral, taking a hanky out of her cardigan sleeve and blowing her nose. 'We agreed it would only make things worse. And we didn't want the papers getting the wrong idea, making out she was a drug addict or something. It was just a—'

'A bit of weed. Yeah, you said. But the thing is it killed my mother.' Daisy was aware she was failing to control the anger spiralling up inside her.

'I am sorry, Daisy. But it was just bad luck that Sandy went up onto the headland without anyone noticing.'

Daisy was boiling with anger and she knew she was only going to start shouting if she didn't leave and calm down.

'And was it bad luck you were all too stoned to look for her?'

'We thought she'd gone home and then when we got back we all crashed out. Nobody meant for it to happen. You have to believe me. It wasn't anyone's fault.'

Daisy couldn't look at her aunt any more. She grabbed Bug's lead, clipped it on and picked him up from his comfortable spot. 'I'm going out. I don't know when I'll be back.'

A walk on the cliffs was out of the question. Somewhere that had so often been her go to place was now the last place she wanted to be. Bug was confused by the change in routine but seemed to perk up as a fresh wave of smells hit his squashed nostrils and he trotted along merrily at the lively pace Daisy was setting. Daisy's head was full of questions she wanted to ask and answers she didn't want to accept. After all this time, the key piece of information had never been revealed. No wonder her father had been adamant it was an accident and it explained why he always appeared to blame himself – of course he blamed himself, it was *his* fault.

If just one of them had gone after her before that fateful moment my mother would probably still be here now, she thought. Daisy hadn't noticed she was crying until the tears dripped off her chin. She angrily wiped them away. This felt so unfair and somehow worse. It could have been prevented. She walked on taking deep breaths as she tried to calm herself down. Blinking away the tears she crossed the road and tried to ignore the drizzling rain.

A thought struck her and she stopped dead, making Bug jerk on the lead as it pulled taut. He gave her an unhappy look. She pulled out her phone and rang her dad. She didn't care what time it was in Goa. She had a question she needed to ask.

Chapter Thirty-Five

After a lot of holding on, whilst various people searched for her father, a bright and familiar voice finally came on the phone. 'Baby, how are you?'

Daisy was gripping the phone tightly. 'Who was looking after me the night Mum died?'

'Er . . . what's wrong, Daisy? Has something happened?'

'Dad. I just want a straight answer for once. Who was looking after me the night Mum died?'

There was a long pause on the other end of the line before he eventually spoke. 'It was Reg.'

A long silence followed while Daisy processed the answer. She had almost forgotten about Great Uncle Reg and instantly felt bad for her lapse. He had been the one person who had always been there for her so this news shouldn't have been a surprise.

'Right. Thanks.' She was about to end the call.

'Daisy, I can tell there's something wrong. What's brought all this up again?'

Daisy rolled her eyes. He made it sound trivial. 'Aunt Coral has explained that Mum died because she was off her face on marijuana and everyone else was too and that's the reason nobody went to find her and why she died—'

Her voiced cracked and she had to take a steadying breath '—because you were all too stoned to look for her. How could you?' She was shaking her head as she spoke. She felt she would never be able to understand.

After a pause he spoke. 'I'm sorry, Daisy. I've spent all these years . . .'

'Lying to me about it?'

'Trying to protect you.'

'From what? Doing dope like you and Mum used to do?'

'From knowing your mother wasn't perfect.'

The sentence hit her hard. She listened to her father's breathing on the line and she knew instinctively he was crying. They cried silently together for a moment, the distance between them lost.

She heard her father take a deep breath. 'Daisy, nobody knows if that's why she died. It may have had nothing to do with it.'

'Someone saw her the night she died. She was dancing and twirling on the tip of the headland. She lost her footing and she fell.'

She heard her father sob and despite how cross she was with him it broke her heart to hear it. She listened to him cry openly and felt her heart ache for him. Despite everything she knew, Sandy was the love of his life and his world had been shattered beyond repair when she died. This was reopening an old wound and laying it bare.

'Who saw her?' he asked at last.

'Pasco Davey.'

Pasco oddly now seemed like the hero of the story. The man who had risked his own life to pull Sandy from the sea and try to save her while her own husband was in a drug-fuelled slumber.

'Pasco?' There was a hint of irony in his voice.

350

'It's a long story.' Daisy was feeling overwhelmed with the fatigue of her emotions and didn't have the energy to explain further.

'Please know that I love you, Daisy. I have to go.' Her father's voice was choked with emotion and before she could protest the line went dead. In a flash of frustration she wanted to hurl the phone at the footpath, but what good would it do? She was weighed down with sadness. The rain was spitting on her and adding to her despair. Bug shook off some of the rain, sat back down and patiently waited for Daisy to continue their walk. Daisy noticed she was shivering, the water had penetrated her thin jacket and was dripping off her hair and mingling with the tears. She heard a distant voice and slowly turned towards it.

'Daisy?' An equally sodden Tamsyn was coming into view. 'You all right?'

Daisy and Bug were a bedraggled-looking pair when they finally made it to Tamsyn's front door.

'Come in. Give me Bug, I'll take him home and explain to Coral. Although I'm not entirely sure why you can't go back there.'

Daisy looked forlorn. 'She knows why,' she said, in a tired voice. Any anger had abated and she was left with only a hollow sadness. Tamsyn ushered Daisy into the living room where she was greeted warmly by the rest of the Turvey family while Tamsyn wrapped Bug in an old towel and marched off.

It was a bit like being in someone else's house at Christmas. Everyone was overly friendly when all Daisy wanted to do was curl up into a ball and cry. All the times she had wished for the truth, to know all the details, and yet here she was overwhelmed by everything she'd found

351

out. Maybe there was something in the saying 'be careful what you wish for'. Perhaps she would have been better off not knowing.

'You poor mite, you're frozen. Let me put the fire on for you. Sit yourself down,' said Tamsyn's mother Min. 'Alan,' she then hollered in contrast. 'Fetch a blanket.'

A well-weathered Alan appeared with something swirly draped over his arm. 'What's the fire on for, Min? It's bloody May.'

'Can't you see the girl's cold?' Their good-natured bickering had amused Daisy as a child. 'What else can I get you?' asked Min.

'I'm fine,' said Daisy, looking the opposite of fine. Her usually bouncy caramel curls lay dull and lank from the rain and her fine features were red and puffy from crying.

'Good thing they caught that boyfriend of yours,' said Alan, plonking himself down in the well-worn armchair.

'Alan,' admonished Min, her face contorting with the effort of trying to convey her message.

'He wasn't my boyfriend,' said Daisy, staring at the perfectly uniform flames of the gas fire. 'But yeah. Good thing they got him.'

'Beautiful girl like you can have her pick of men,' said Alan. 'The right one will come along when you least expect it. You'll see.'

'Oh, do shut up, Alan,' said Min, shooing him up from his chair and out of the room. 'Go and do something useful,' she said, kissing him as he went past. 'He's neither use nor ornament,' she said to Daisy with an apologetic smile.

'Do you think there is a right one for all of us?' asked Daisy.

Min sat on the arm of the sofa next to Daisy and took

her hand in hers. 'No, I don't actually. But there is a right one for you.'

Daisy twisted in her seat to look up at Min. 'What makes you so sure?'

Min gave a weak smile. 'I get messages.'

'From Mum?' Her heart clenched at the thought of her mother.

'Sometimes,' said Min. 'I say messages but it's more vague than that. I have these thoughts that aren't my own.'

'And what did Mum say or think about me?' Daisy was looking up at Min, her eyes eager like a child.

'An overwhelming sense of love,' said Min, giving her hand a squeeze. They heard Tamsyn returning. 'I should stop now,' said Min, getting up.

'No, please don't.' Daisy reached out and gripped her hand.

Min eyed her fondly. 'She likes what you've done with Locos but fighting with your father upsets her.'

Daisy felt a chill go through her and she let go of Min's hand as if she'd received an electric shock. Tonight was the first time she'd spoken to her dad in months. How could Min have possibly known? The door clunked shut as Tamsyn came inside.

'That dog thinks he has staff. I dried his feet but he kept lifting up his paws. It's still raining out there. How are you feeling?' she asked, finally appearing in the living room.

Weird was how she felt, if she was being honest, but all she said was, 'Better, thanks.'

Daisy wasn't sure where she was for a moment when she was wrestled from her dreams. She looked about the Turveys' spare bedroom and it all came flooding back to her – it was morning and she'd stayed the night at

Tamsyn's as the thought of facing Aunt Coral had been too much.

'Daisy, you need to come downstairs.' Tamsyn was standing by the door, her voice was low and urgent. By the time Daisy had fully come round Tamsyn had gone. Daisy padded downstairs yawning as she went.

Aunt Coral was at the foot of the stairs with Tamsyn. She looked tired but appeared dressed for a trip to the theatre, wearing smart trousers and a blazer-style jacket with matching scarf. 'I just wanted to say goodbye,' she said.

Daisy blinked fast and tried to summon her thoughts. 'What do you mean?' It was all too confusing for this time in the morning.

'I'm truly sorry about everything, Daisy, and the last thing I want is for you to leave this close to having completed your year in the bay. It wouldn't be right for you to miss out on your inheritance. I thought if I went away for a few weeks then you wouldn't leave?' The last bit came out like a question.

Daisy shrugged. She realised for the first time in forever, running away hadn't actually been her first thought and it interested her but she was too tired to analyse it. 'You don't have to.' Daisy tried to stifle a yawn and failed. Whatever she felt about that fateful night and her aunt's involvement she didn't want her to feel she had to leave – this was her home.

'I've been thinking about having a bit of a holiday for quite a while now, this gives me the excuse I needed. My boss isn't impressed but he's agreed the time off and I got a great last-minute deal,' she said, turning to Tamsyn who nodded happily.

'Holiday?' asked Daisy, feeling quite slow on the uptake. 'Are you taking Bug?'

'No, dear. He can't come on a twenty-two-day cruise,' said Aunt Coral, with a chuckle. Daisy's eyes widened. 'Bug will be fine here with you.'

'I've always wanted to go on a cruise. The exotic destinations, the glamorous dresses . . .' Tamsyn seemed to get stuck with her list. 'The big boats.'

'We fly to Barbados and then we're going all around the Caribbean. I'll send you lots of postcards.' Coral stepped forward. 'I'll really miss you, Daisy.' She pulled Daisy into a hug and held her for a moment. Aunt Coral sniffed back a tear as she let her go. 'I hope you can forgive me,' she said, and she hurried out to a waiting taxi.

Tamsyn was wittering on about how amazing the Caribbean would be as they both waved off a teary Aunt Coral and Daisy's sleep-fogged brain belatedly asked whether it was just a turn of phrase when she said 'we'? And if it wasn't who was she going on a twenty-two-day Caribbean cruise with?

Chapter Thirty-Six

Daisy was looking forward to her night off; it had been a busy weekend so a Monday in the pub with Tamsyn was exactly what she needed. Actually, she would have preferred a bottle of wine at home but Tamsyn had been insistent. With only four weeks to go Daisy was getting demob-happy. The accounts were looking healthy and the solicitor had confirmed everything was on track to release the final instalment of her inheritance as planned. She was then going to put Locos up for sale, repay Aunt Coral and jet off to South America. Everything was coming together. She still had some niggles in the back of her mind, but that's all they were. She wanted to do more travelling – it had always been her dream and nothing had changed, nothing at all. So why did she feel uneasy about moving on?

'Slippers,' said Tamsyn, as they walked in the warm evening air.

'Yes,' said Daisy, bracing herself for Tamsyn's next question.

'I mean, how dangerous do they sound?' Daisy was frowning. 'Imagine the inventor saying, "I've invented slippers, they go on your feet. Do you want to try them?" You'd think you were going to slide to your doom, wouldn't you?'

Daisy started to laugh and Tamsyn continued. 'And who was the cruel person that put an "s" in lisp?'

They were giggling as they entered the pub but Daisy's laughter quickly faded when she saw who was sitting at their usual table.

'Oh, no, Tams. I'm not spending an evening of awkwardness with Max,' said Daisy, bolting for the door, but Tamsyn artfully blocked her.

'Wait, please listen. It's not about you and him it's about me and Captain Cuddles.' Daisy raised her eyebrows. 'Because you two aren't talking we have to see you separately and we feel we can't mention the other one and it's making us sad.' Tamsyn's face was brimming over with unhappiness making Daisy relent slightly.

'All the trust has gone, Tams.' Daisy looked across at Max; she wished that wasn't the case but how could she even be friends with someone she no longer trusted and who had made her feel such a fool?

'Please just have a drink with me and Jason. You can pretend Max isn't there.' Tamsyn's face was pleading.

'Look at his melancholy face,' said Daisy, glancing at Max who, from his expression, she surmised had just learnt of the devious plan himself.

'That's an odd phrase – melon-cauli. Is it because vegetables look sad?'

Max now looked like the lesser of two awkward conversations. Against her better judgement, Daisy took a deep breath and headed over to the table, with Tamsyn squeaking her delight behind her. Max stood up like he was about to walk out and Daisy felt hopeful because that way she would have done as her friend asked and they'd avoid the uncomfortable silence or unholy row that was likely to engulf the evening – she couldn't be sure which way it would go.

Max rubbed his stubbly chin during a hushed conversation with Jason who was sporting a similarly pleading face to the one Tamsyn had displayed. Jason stood up and gave Daisy a brief kiss on the cheek.

'You okay, Captain Cuddles?' she asked Jason, with a grin, sitting down in the chair next to Max's and angling her body away from him.

'Yeah, good thanks, I was just saying to Max—'

'I can't sit through her ignoring me all night in a pathetic attempt to make a point. I'm going to save you the trouble and leave,' said Max, picking up his almost full pint and starting to drink it at speed.

'Excuse me. I think I made my point when you finally revealed yourself to be a lying scumbag,' said Daisy, getting to her feet and squaring up to Max.

'Oh, this was a bad idea,' said Jason, quickly standing up and putting a shoulder between the two of them.

Max stepped around Jason. 'When did I lie?' he asked, looking irritated.

Daisy's jaw tensed. 'In my book, not revealing key information is the same thing. You knew the necklace was Pasco's.'

'It only dawned on me when I saw an old photo of him.'

'But you knew what it meant to me and yet you let me continue to believe it was my mother's.'

The fight seemed to go out of Max and he lowered his voice. 'I never meant to deceive you. Surely you can understand I was torn. Pasco's my dad.'

'You could have talked to me about it. That was all you had to do.' Daisy was more sad than cross as she studied his face. 'I thought we had something you and me.' Daisy held her breath; she hadn't intended to reveal quite so much but it was said now. Tamsyn was watching them closely and Daisy saw her reach out and grip Jason's hand, not in a loving way, more akin to how she imagined couples held hands as the *Titanic* sank.

'Not enough to make you want to stay in the bay.' Max's voice was heavy.

'I never had a good reason to stay.' Daisy felt her pulse start to quicken.

'People are a good reason.'

Was he saying he should be her reason? 'People let you down.'

'Like your French boyfriend?' Max was back to being snappy.

Daisy's lips formed a thin line. 'You'd buggered off!' she said, her voice rising again.

'You sacked me from the bar.'

'I thought you resigned?'

'You gave me no choice. You accused me of stealing!'

'You let me down and worse still you hurt me.' As the emotions took over she knew she couldn't say any more, the mixture of anger and wounded pride was a fatal combination and had ruined many a great woman's speech. She stepped away but Max grabbed her arm, the contact made the tiny hairs on her arms stand to attention.

'I never meant to hurt you, Daisy.' His eyes conveyed his regret.

'But you did,' she said, pulling away.

Max watched her leave the pub. Jason and Tamsyn were staring too as if watching the climax of a soap opera.

'That went well,' said Max, finishing the rest of his pint swiftly. 'I think I'll make a move too.'

'How do we sort this out?' asked Tamsyn, after Max had gone.

'Maybe it's not ours to sort out,' said Jason looking thoughtful. 'Sometimes there's too much getting in the way.'

Tamsyn pouted and shook her head. 'I'm not giving up on those two yet.'

A few days later, after a long walk, Bug flopped down on the mat by the back door. 'Basket,' said Daisy, pointing at his bed. He let out a groan and stayed where he was. She knew by now Bug was far from stupid but he was lazy. A thought shot through her mind. Perhaps she could teach him something while Aunt Coral was away? She never shied away from a challenge.

Two hours and the best part of a bag of dog biscuits later Bug was still looking at her as if she was demented. It didn't matter how many times she put him in the basket, repeated the command or rewarded him there was nothing that would make him do it on command. She poured herself a large glass of wine and put it down to experience; another point clocked up on Bug's side of the scoreboard.

'Cock-a-doodle-doo,' she muttered. He was definitely sleeping in the kitchen tonight.

That night Daisy fell asleep quite quickly, but she was soon woken by the sound of Bug's whimpering interspersed with the rumble of distant thunder. The weather had been hot and stormy all week. Daisy huffed, hauling herself out of bed, and shuffled to the kitchen where Bug was hiding under the table. She sat on the floor with him for a bit until he had settled and when she could no longer hear the rumbling she returned to her bed.

It felt like only a few moments before the scenario was repeated. This time it wasn't cute or funny and she had zero patience left. She trudged to the kitchen and flung open the door; all she needed was a well-timed flash of lightning to make it look like a scene from a horror movie.

Bug was sitting in the middle of the floor looking at her expectantly. She was tired and she was grumpy and she definitely couldn't hear thunder this time. 'Bug, ignore the storm. It's just being a bastard,' she said firmly.

Bug paused for a moment and then trotted off and got obediently into his basket and wagged his tail like he was mightily proud of himself.

'Bastard. Not basket you . . . oh never mind. Well done, Bug,' she said, going over and giving him a scratch on the head before returning to bed for what she hoped was the final time.

A week later the West Country was experiencing some unusually harsh weather. The wind had been building all day and now the rain was coming down in bucket loads, making it seem even more vicious as it lashed at the cottage windows, and the accompanying wind howled down the passageway. There was something different about storms on the coast. They had an increased ferocity thanks to tidal surges. It wasn't something that frightened Daisy – she had seen enough of them growing up, even on occasion marvelling at the ferociousness of it when standing on the headland with her father and watching the sea churning below. It was mesmerising: beautiful and slightly terrifying at the same time.

It was Monday night; Locos was closed and she was making her way through a bottle of wine on her own. Tamsyn was meeting Jason and Max at the pub and she was fed up with arguing with Max. A bottle of wine wasn't the best solution, she knew that, but sometimes it did make you feel better and at least she would sleep tonight. She poured herself another large glass, flicked on the television and curled up with Bug, who reversed his plump backside into her ribs until he was perfectly comfortable and settled down for a nap.

She must have drifted off because the sound of knocking on the front door jolted her awake. For a moment she thought she was in bed with a hot water bottle, then realised she was slumped on the sofa at an odd angle with Bug tucked up against her. She unfolded herself as the knocking turned to banging.

'All right. All right. I'm coming.' When she heard the slur in her voice she remembered the wine and eyed the empty bottle whilst struggling to unfold her foot from underneath her. Her right leg was asleep and tingled into life as pins and needles made her wince. She hobbled to the front door, hoping all the effort would be worth it. She must have looked like a dead ringer for the Hunchback of Notre Dame, limping into view dragging her dead leg and trying to straighten her neck with a series of shoulder gyrations. She looked at the figure at the door; they were engulfed in swirling rain, which explained their incessant knocking. The figure turned when she opened the door.

'Max?' He was wearing a huge raincoat and stepped inside without waiting to be asked. 'Er, you're wet.'

'No shit, Sherlock?' said Max, shaking his head and spraying her with water not unlike Bug did after a bath. She rubbed at her lips remembering to check her mouth for any signs of stray dribble.

'Still stormy then?' She gazed behind him at the torrential rain outside.

'We need to talk.' Max looked resolute, his hair darker than usual and his face shiny from the rain.

'Now?' Daisy felt the recalcitrant teenager in her huff. She wasn't mentally equipped for this right now.

'Yes, now. Tamsyn says – Have you been drinking?'

Daisy closed her eyes. She didn't want to lie but she also wasn't keen to admit she'd been drinking alone either. 'Just a glass . . . or two. Why? Is it against the law? Because you'd know all about breaking the law, wouldn't you?' She wobbled slightly, maybe it had been a tad more than two glasses.

'Daisy, we have to stop this. We're just going over old ground and it's getting everyone down. The way I see it we have two options. We either put the past behind us and give it a go, you and me. Or we keep in this continuous loop. Which will it be?'

It sounded simple when he put it like that. Not exactly the words of a die-hard romantic. But even through her wine-fogged thoughts, Daisy knew he was right. It didn't help at all him being right. If they were to ever get together then she had to let go of the past. Stop raking over all the old arguments and move on and she wasn't entirely sure she could because that meant trusting someone again. If she did then she had to be able to have total confidence in Max and trusting him meant laying herself open to being hurt yet again.

'You think we can move on just like that?' asked Daisy, trying to click her fingers and puzzling over why she couldn't.

'I don't see why not. I mean, I've forgotten about you accusing me of stealing and getting me to hire a boat for a drug dealer.' He gave a cheeky smile. 'Come on Daisy, take the plunge.'

Daisy felt pressured and more than a little panicked by being put on the spot. She wondered if she could ask him if he would wait for an answer. It would give her time to sober up and more importantly to think things through, weigh up the pros and cons and get her head around what she was doing. Before she got to voice her thoughts there was a faint buzzing and Max seemed to make the decision for her. He sprinted out the door. Not too keen on waiting for a response then, she thought.

'Lifeboat!' hollered Max, belatedly as the front door was whipped shut by the force of the wind outside and it slammed behind him.

'Cock-a-doodle-doo,' said Daisy and Bug barked his agreement. At least this gave her time to think. Perhaps some more wine would help her too.

Chapter Thirty-Seven

She was settling herself down with *Plus One* on the television and another bottle of wine when her phone sprang into life; before she could speak Tamsyn commenced a monologue.

'I'm worried. Are you worried? I know you say you don't care about Max, but I know you do. Maybe not like I care about Jason but you still care. Should we wait or go to the lifeboat station? I don't know what's best. We won't know much sooner either way. What do you think?'

'Hello,' said Daisy wearily. 'Sorry, what are you talking about?' She let out a giant yawn making her jaw click. Her head was foggy.

'The storm. Jason and Max are on a lifeboat callout in the worst storm we've had in years.'

Daisy perked up. She peered out of the window and watched the virtually horizontal rain being chucked forcefully at the windows. It did look pretty bad out there and Daisy was already imagining the lifeboat being manhandled by the sea and it almost sobered her up. 'Right. What should we do?' asked Daisy, waving a finger at the window as if she were remonstrating with the weather.

'I can't sit here any more, I think I'm going down to the lifeboat station. At least I can make tea for the wives and girlfriends and feel like I'm being useful.'

Daisy nodded heartily and then realised that wasn't a lot of use on the phone. 'Good idea. Let me know what happens,' she said, pulling her hoody tighter around her even though she wasn't cold.

There was a delay from Tamsyn. 'You're not coming with me?'

'Do I need to?'

Tamsyn made a noise that sounded like she was blowing out air. 'No, not if you don't want to.'

Daisy watched the rain lash against the windows. 'Okay then take care.' She hung up and snuggled back down on the sofa much to Bug's annoyance as he had taken over her seat while she'd been looking out of the window. Daisy switched off the television. She wasn't really watching it. It was dark outside now but she could still hear the insistent wind.

She wondered if she should have gone. But like Tamsyn said, at the lifeboat station there would be wives and girl-friends of the crew, and Daisy was neither. What was she to Max? Ex-sort-of-friend-and-employer? It wasn't the same. It didn't mean she didn't care about Max. Of course she cared. She was in the worst place she could be – a no-win situation. She needed to clear her head and figure this out, some very strong coffee was called for.

Two mugs later, she was wired with a slight headache and a plan. The more she thought about Max being on the lifeboat in the storm the more she realised, despite all his faults, of which there were many, she did care for him quite a lot. Having him back in her life had been one of the best things about being back in the bay. They annoyed the hell out of each other but somehow that came from a deep-rooted place of caring about each other.

'Bye Bug, I'm going to tell Max that I care about him,' she said. Bug blinked and then closed his eyes. He didn't seem impressed with this revelation. Daisy stroked his head. 'I quite like him, you see.' Telling Bug somehow made it more real. 'I need to go now.'

She grabbed her coat and tugged on her wellies with great difficulty; standing upright was still somewhat of a challenge. She opened the front door to what felt like someone hosing her down. She dragged on her hood and marched off towards the beach.

The sky was dark but she could still see the deep clouds moving at speed as the rain drove its way under her hood. As she walked she thought about Max. He was infuriating, but just the image of him in her mind brought a smile to her face. Could two people who annoyed the crap out of each other embark on a worthwhile relationship? For a moment she imagined translating the anger into passion and a shudder ran through her. He was attractive, that went without saying: his dishevelled roguish look had grown on her. More than once she had fantasised about ripping off his top. Bloody hell, why had she wasted so much time being cross with him? She put her head down and determination with a hint of lust and a lot of wine and coffee drove her on.

When she reached the turning to the beach she could see the abandoned cars of the lifeboat crew strewn along the road down to the lifeboat station meaning they were still out on the shout.

Daisy found Tamsyn huddled near the station entrance hugging a mug of tea.

'You came!' Tamsyn sloshed tea everywhere as she threw herself at Daisy.

'I couldn't sit at home while our friends are out in this.'

'Friends? Is Max *just* a friend?'

Daisy paused. 'No,' she said and Tamsyn's face lit up. 'He's also an almighty pain in the arse.' Tamsyn's face dropped. 'But he came by earlier with some notion of us giving things a go and . . .' Tamsyn gave her another hug and spilled the rest of her tea.

'I knew you'd see sense eventually.'

'No promises,' said Daisy, turning to watch the sea with a hint of a smile on her lips. She couldn't take her eyes off the waves. Giant thunderous ones battering the shoreline. The thought of Max being out there rubbed away her smile.

'I need more tea,' said Tamsyn waving her empty mug. 'You want one?'

'No, thanks.' Daisy shook her head. She couldn't pull her eyes away from the giant rollers. She scanned the sea meticulously for any sign of the lifeboat, her feet and hands growing colder by the second as the wind whipped off the sea and up the beach chilling her. She stepped outside and battled to stay upright but continued her careful search for any sign of the orange vessel. Her stomach was doing backflips and this time it wasn't the wine and coffee mixture. It was seriously dangerous out there and Max and Jason were at the mercy of the sea.

Daisy swallowed hard. She knew now how much she cared. All she wanted in the world was to see the lifeboat appear and to see Max safe. But there was no sign of it.

Tamsyn returned with a fresh mug. 'It's a yacht about three miles out,' she said, dipping her chin towards the small office inside the station where a mumbled exchange with the lifeboat could be heard.

'Right. Are they all okay?' asked Daisy, stepping back inside.

'Yeah, they do this all the time. Doesn't stop everyone worrying though,' Tamsyn said.

Daisy dragged her eyes away from the beach for a moment and caught sight of the radio operator looking worried and it drew her attention. She started to walk towards the office and the words hit her as she approached.

'. . . Man overboard? Confirm? Who is it?'

The radio crackled a response before Jason's voice could be heard. 'Yes, confirmed it's Max. He's roped but he's—'

Daisy was frozen to the spot. She knew Tamsyn had joined her and another woman but her hearing was fuzzy and the room started to spin around her. She gripped the doorway of the office and took deep breaths until she was back in control. All she could think was if he's in the sea, then he's dead. Just like Mum. On a night like this nobody comes out alive.

'Daisy?' Tamsyn was standing in front of her, trying to force her mug at her. 'Here, sit down and drink this. He's roped. He'll be okay.' But Tamsyn's furtive glances at the radio operator and pale complexion told her otherwise.

Daisy listened to the one-sided conversation of the operator speaking to the emergency services. 'Ambulance . . . Ottercombe lifeboat station . . . Member of crew unconscious . . . Max Davey . . . Still at sea but due to shore shortly . . . He's receiving first aid on board.'

The minutes passed desperately slowly until a wave swelled and receded and they at last caught a glimpse of the lifeboat. Daisy felt a sob escape and she quickly tried to take hold of her emotions. A commotion broke out on the beach as an ambulance drove onto the sand and two paramedics jumped out. The radio operator joined them

369

but he was shaking his head too much for Daisy's liking and his expression was grim. They got a stretcher out of the ambulance and she thought she was going to be sick.

After all this time, it took something like this to make her realise what Max meant to her and in a flash she'd lost him.

The lifeboat neared the shore and the others ran down to join the tractor and trailer waiting for them. Daisy couldn't move. She didn't want to witness this. She didn't want to see a lifeless Max. Tamsyn was gripping her hand tightly and she realised she was crying. Daisy started to panic. How could this be happening?

Tamsyn tugged on her arm and pointed to the lifeboat. The sea was still raging up the beach like an uncaged wild animal. Daisy closed her eyes. She needed to be strong.

'Daisy!' She heard her name being carried on the wind but she didn't want to believe whose voice it was.

She opened her tear-stained eyes to see Max, who was conscious and being forced onto a stretcher by the two paramedics. Daisy let out the breath she hadn't realised she was holding and a sob escaped.

'Cock-a-doodle-doo,' said Daisy, breaking into a mess of laughter and tears as the tension released its grip on her shoulders. Max was alive.

She launched herself into the stinging wind and hurtled across the stones. Max shoved the stretcher to one side and pulled Daisy into a tight hug.

'I thought . . . I thought . . .' She couldn't finish the sentence. 'You're bleeding, Max.' She reached for the blood trickling down his face and he winced.

'Just a bump. I mistimed my jump and the yacht lurched at the wrong moment. It's fine.' He said this more to the paramedic who was trying to get a look at the wound.

'Come on,' said Daisy, steering him back towards the lifeboat station. 'They can patch you up inside. Let's get you in the warm.'

'I thought you'd never ask,' said Max, his eyebrows dancing cheekily.

Down on the beach Tamsyn was smothering Jason in kisses. 'I love you sooooo much.' She hugged him again for emphasis. 'You are as brave as Aragorn and I'm seriously proud of you. Of all of you!' She shouted the last bit at the other crew members and some of them looked up from securing the boat to the trailer.

In the warmth of the lifeboat station Daisy hugged a hot cup of tea and shivered uncontrollably while Max argued with the paramedics who wanted to take him to hospital. She closed her eyes and tried hard to steady her juddering limbs as she lifted the mug to her lips and took a sip.

'Daisy.' Max's voice was soft and tentative. She opened her eyes and smiled at him crouching in front of her, sticky strips now holding his cut together. 'You okay?'

'I'm fine. It's you who got knocked unconscious.'

'Only for a minute or two.'

'You could have drowned.' The conversation was too raw for Daisy and she went back to sipping her tea.

'I'm sorry.' Max's eyes were cast downward.

Daisy felt she needed to clarify things. 'Which of the many things you've done to piss me off are you apologising for exactly?' Maybe her brain wasn't quite back to normal yet because her words came out a bit harsher than she'd intended, especially after what had just happened.

Max surveyed his feet like a naughty schoolboy. 'For nearly drowning. For letting Pasco sleep in the carriage. For not telling you the moment I recognised the locket.

For not realising how much I'd hurt you. And for being a general bum hole.'

A smile finally pulled at the edges of Daisy's lips. 'Is General Bum Hole higher ranking than Captain Cuddles?'

'All day long,' he said, looking a little surer of himself. He pulled a small black velvet box from his pocket. 'This is a family heirloom that's been passed on to me, but I'd like you to have it.'

Daisy put down the mug, rubbed her hands together and took the box from Max, her eyebrows knotted in puzzlement. She opened it and a smile lit up her face. 'The locket. I can't take this. I've already kept it for far too long.'

Max shook his head. 'No, you should have it. Pasco gave it to me and whilst he may have been able to pull off wearing a fancy locket, I'd just look ridiculous.'

'I don't know.' Daisy paused, her eyes studying the locket. Despite knowing the truth, she still felt a connection to it.

'It suits you.' Max took it from the box and fastened it around her neck.

Daisy's hand immediately closed around it as the cool metal touched her skin. It felt right.

'I have missed this so much, thank you.' She looked up and the slightly vulnerable look about him made her smile.

'It was only going to sit in a drawer.'

Daisy stood up quickly, a little too quickly as it turned out making her feel dizzy, she reached out for support and Max was there. 'Steady on, what's the hurry?'

'I was going to kiss you,' she said, the wine still having a loosening effect on her tongue.

'Then I understand the rush and the fainting. Happens all the time.'

Daisy gave him a playful thump. 'Do you want this kiss or not?'

Max appeared to consider it. 'What sort of kiss is it going to be?'

'Do you want a diagram?'

'I meant is it a thank you kiss or a let's start a relationship kiss or a you're a hero and I can't control myself kiss. All of which are completely acceptable by the way.' Max loosened his hold on Daisy and she stood firmly on her own without swaying.

'It's definitely not the third one,' she said, taking a step closer to him. 'It could be the first one or . . .' Daisy tucked a stray piece of hair behind her ear and looked into Max's eyes. He was trying hard to appear cool and unconcerned but she could see the trepidation nestled there.

'We could just give the kiss a try and see if it gives us any clues,' suggested Max, bobbing his head as if mulling over the prospect. 'I mean, I don't mind if you don't?'

Daisy's grin spread across her face. 'Okay.'

Max put his arms around her, bowed his head a fraction and Daisy pulled him slowly to her until their lips met. Daisy found it was a little hard to kiss when you were smiling this much. The kiss felt easy with just a hint of passion – very unlike their liaisons to date. She had no doubt a relationship with Max was going to be tumultuous but she owed it to herself to give it a chance. Daisy pulled away at a point where she hoped she'd left Max wanting more.

Max put his finger to his lips. 'That felt like a number three to me.'

Daisy gave him a thump. 'It's a two, you idiot.'

'Can we handle a two?' asked Max, his eyes searching hers.

Daisy didn't want to bring the mood down. If she thought about this too much it would spoil everything. 'I don't know, all we can do is give it a go.' He gave a tentative smile and she pulled him into an even deeper kiss.

Chapter Thirty-Eight

When Daisy woke the next morning the world seemed quite different somehow. Although when Bug snored loudly and woke himself up she realised some things hadn't changed at all. She scratched him behind his ears and he gave a stretch and let out a squeaky trump from the effort of jumping off the bed. Daisy yawned and reached for her locket. She had slept well, only now she recognised her sleep had been disturbed since she'd lost the locket. She switched her phone on and saw a message from Max, she smiled before she'd even read it.

Hi Please can I borrow your old helmet for fancy dress at work. They said I can't come as Lifeboat crew again this year lol M

It wasn't exactly what she'd been hoping for but one kiss did not a relationship make she reminded herself. Right now she didn't know if this was going to be a very short-term one that ended when she went travelling or one of those awkward long-distance affairs. She shoved her thoughts to the back of her mind, strolled through to the kitchen, let Bug out in the garden and popped some bread in the toaster.

Daisy wondered where her old helmet was, she'd left it in the hall and it had stayed there for ages and then disappeared. Daisy had no use for it since her bike had died and Jason had taken it to the motorbike graveyard. Aunt Coral had either chucked it out or put it away somewhere. She set about tidying up her room – she didn't know where her kiss with Max was heading but just in case it led back here she didn't want her messy ways putting him off and it was high time she got in the habit of making her bed anyway.

The helmet was still puzzling her and she went through various cupboards and the shed but there was no sign of it. She remembered the cupboard above the stairs and went to have a look in there.

'Gotcha,' she said, spotting the helmet peeking from behind a box at the back of the cupboard. She reached in and pulled the cardboard box out of the way. Curiosity got the better of her and she had a rummage in the box. There were bundles and bundles of postcards and letters. Daisy sat on the floor with a bump. Everything she had ever sent to Great Uncle Reg he had kept and there was a lot, way more than she'd realised. She lost an hour rereading her messages and remembering how much she'd loved exploring new places but how hard it had been to be constantly working. It felt good to think she could just sightsee when she went to South America. At the bottom of the box an old photograph album caught her eye. She lifted it out and instantly felt a familiarity with it. She couldn't be certain but she thought she remembered it from her childhood. She carefully brushed off the dust and along with the helmet took it downstairs.

She sat at the kitchen table, took a deep breath and opened the album. There on the first page were pictures of her as a baby with both her parents. The sight of them hit her like a punch to the stomach. The happy family beamed back at her. Her mother was beautiful. Daisy wasn't sure she looked like her, it was difficult to see yourself in others although the mop of bouncing golden curls was definitely the same. Daisy studied each photograph in turn. Under some were comments in neat blue biro. It wasn't her father's hand-writing, she assumed it must be her mother's. Daisy ran her finger along the sentences as she read them, trying to imagine her mother jotting down the notes.

She turned the page to see a picture of her younger self in blue dungarees sat in a high chair with a sunny smile on her face, waving two spoons in the air. Underneath was written 'My little two spoons having dinner'. Daisy moved on to the next photo of them sat on a picnic rug on the beach but something pulled her back to the high chair photograph; she wasn't exactly sure why.

An hour later she was serving chocolate milkshakes and iced frappés, which were proving to be popular now Ottercombe Bay was experiencing the calm after the storm. The sun was out and Old Man Burgess had to keep sipping iced water to stop overheating.

'Hiya,' said Max, striding in, wrapping his arms around Daisy's waist and placing a kiss firmly on her cheek making her insides tingle. 'You smell gorgeous,' he added letting her go. That was the reassurance she had needed, an open show of affection told her last night wasn't a one off created by the drama of the situation.

'Thanks, it's just body spray but anyway . . .' She was jabbering like a smitten teenager; she needed to pull herself together. 'Here,' she reached behind the bar and handed Max her old crash helmet. 'I've given it a clean but you might want to have a go too.'

'Brilliant, thanks,' said Max, kissing her again.

'Who are you dressing up as?'

'Ahh, you'll see,' he said tapping his nose.

'My aunt's back next Thursday, and I'm thinking of doing her a welcome home tea if you wanted to come.' She watched him hopefully.

A smile spread across his face. 'That would be great, but I'm hoping to see a lot more of you before then.' He pulled her into his arms and gave her a tantalisingly brief kiss.

That was more like it, she thought.

Over the next week or so they did see a lot more of each other, with Max turning up after his shift at the swimming pool to help finish off at Locos and walk Daisy home.

'I can't believe Aunt Coral's back tomorrow. Twenty-two days has gone quickly, loads has happened,' said Daisy, squeezing Max's hand. She wasn't quite sure how she'd get Aunt Coral up to speed without making her hyperventilate. She'd definitely have to brush over the lifeboat drama.

'I can give you a hand getting things ready if you like.'

Daisy sniggered at the thought of them being all domesticated and making cucumber sandwiches together. 'You don't have to.'

'No, I want to,' said Max. 'If it's a chance to be with you then I'd even make fairy cakes.'

Daisy grinned, her heart was running away with itself and she had no way of stopping it, and perhaps she didn't want to. They were enjoying each other's company and with only days left in the bay she wanted to make the most of it. Her imminent departure was the elephant in the room between her and Max – neither of them wanted to spoil their time together by bringing it up.

It was Thursday afternoon and a production line of sandwiches was in full force in the kitchen when there was a flurry of car horns outside. Daisy wiped her hands on a tea towel and went to investigate with Tamsyn hot on her heels. As she gave the porch door a shove she realised she had been mistaken about the car horns. Outside the cottage was a smug-looking Max sat on her old motorbike. Only it no longer looked old and knackered it looked old and shiny.

Max revved the engine. 'You want to take her for a spin?' he asked, handing her the crash helmet.

'You fixed it?'

Max went all modest. 'With some help from Jason and the internet. Sorry it took forever, we struggled to get some of the parts.'

'This is amazing. You're amazing.' She reached up and gave him a long lingering kiss. 'Thanks, Max. This is brilliant.'

'I thought you might be needing it soon.' He lowered his eyes.

'I had better see how she goes,' said Daisy, avoiding the insinuation in his voice by taking the helmet and getting on the bike.

Being back on the bike was such a joyous feeling. Daisy had always preferred bikes to cars; the freedom, the connection with the vehicle and the speed had had her hooked from an early age. She turned back into Trow Lane and stopped the bike; the sun shone on Sea Mist Cottage making even it look happier somehow. She was buzzing, but that was more to do with how pleased she was about Max doing this for her. All the times she'd fallen out with him he must have been returning to this secret project and it made her feel humble and extremely grateful.

After more kisses of thanks she got back to work on the buffet food whilst Jason and Max puzzled over how to put up the gazebo Daisy had borrowed. Daisy had only invited a few people to start off with but now it seemed over twenty people would be descending on the tiny cottage.

'Ham and chicken for the carnivores, cheese and egg mayo for the veggies,' said Daisy, checking her list. 'How are the veggie fillings coming along?' she asked Tamsyn.

'Cheese are all done and the eggs are in my pocket warming up.'

Daisy's eyebrow twitched. She should have known better than to ask by now but sometimes she couldn't help herself. 'You know we need to boil the eggs not just warm them up, right?'

Tamsyn giggled. 'Of course I do. But if you put an egg straight from the fridge into boiling water it'll crack, if I warm them in my pocket first they don't.'

Daisy had to admit for once Tamsyn was talking sense. 'Okay great. Thanks for all your help today, Tamsyn, you're a star.'

'I love working with you,' said Tamsyn. 'And it's nice to see you and Max together.'

'It's early days,' said Daisy, instinctively glancing out of the window at Max wrestling with a green canopy. 'I'm not sure what happens after South America.'

'I think you two will be fine,' said Tamsyn, with a knowing look.

Daisy went out to give Max a hand as a confident-looking Jason came inside. He tapped Tamsyn on the shoulder and she spun around. He wiped a smear of butter off her rose-tinted cheek and she froze at his touch as a million butterflies took flight in her stomach.

'Are you happy, Tamsyn?'

'Yes,' she said, without hesitation.

'Sure?' His voice was back to his usual hesitant tone.

Instead of answering she reached up and kissed him hard on the lips. Their teeth bumped uncomfortably and at the same time she felt something pop near her tummy and for a second she thought the millions of butterflies were escaping, but when the wetness seeped through her pants she remembered the eggs. This never happens in films, she thought.

When the taxi pulled up outside there was a flurry of activity in the small cottage as everyone hid and there was an abundance of shushing from Jason. Daisy hung on to Bug who was squirming uncontrollably as the taxi receded and the footsteps approached. They could hear lots of girly giggling when the key went in the lock and the door swung open. Daisy waited a moment and gave the signal. Everyone leaped from their hiding places in a chorus of 'Surprise!' to find Aunt Coral in Pasco's arms and them both looking red faced and shocked. Thankfully Pasco didn't drop her in alarm.

'Cock-a-doodle-doo,' said Daisy before turning to Max and whispering, 'Does this mean what I think it means?'

'Depends on what you're thinking and right now I have some shocking images in my head that I'm never going to be able to erase,' said Max.

'Welcome home,' said Daisy, a little belatedly. Aunt Coral wrapped her in a hug and Bug wrapped himself round her ankles.

'Hiya Dad,' said Max, and Pasco pulled him into a manly embrace. 'You look . . . tanned.'

'Can't beat the Caribbean for sunshine, son,' said Pasco, slinking a protective arm around Aunt Coral's shoulders.

Daisy knew her eyebrows were unnaturally high on her forehead but it was difficult to act nonchalant when you were confronted with something like this. 'I take it you both had a good time?' Daisy felt awkward; it was like she was asking them directly if they'd slept together. As if sensing her discomfort Max put an arm around her.

'The best,' said Aunt Coral, giving Pasco a lovelorn look. 'But it's nice to be home. More than anything I'm thrilled to see you're still here.'

'For a bit longer,' said Daisy. She felt Max's arm squeeze her just a fraction tighter.

Aunt Coral disappeared into the throng for a while and Daisy busied herself with making sure everyone had a drink and snatching kisses from Max at every opportunity.

'You know I'm going to miss you so much while you're away,' said Max, too many beers had likely loosened his tongue.

'I'll miss you too,' said Daisy. 'But I can't not go.' The guilt weighed heavy on her that she was about to abandon him and their fledgling affair.

Max was already nodding. 'I know and I agree. You have to go. I'll still be here. Assuming Emma Watson doesn't visit in which case I can't guarantee it.' He gave a cheeky shrug.

'I understand,' said Daisy, and they held each other's gaze.

The plan had always been to put Locos up for sale, which would give her the cash to go wherever she wanted for as long as she pleased, but was that still the right thing to do?

'Daisy, love, come here,' said Aunt Coral, pulling Daisy into a bear hug breaking the intensity of the moment with Max. 'I have missed you so much.' Aunt Coral wiped away a tear. 'I'm truly sorry about everything that happened before—'

Daisy stopped her. 'It's all forgotten. Let's just look

forward,' said Daisy, returning the hug. She looked over her aunt's shoulder at Pasco and Max chatting companionably. 'You and Pasco?'

'It's a long story,' said Aunt Coral, flushing wildly. 'Where's my Bugsy?' she said, as Bug danced around her ankles desperate for attention.

'I'll let it go for now but when everyone's gone I want to know more,' said Daisy, although she didn't want too many details, what she'd seen when they walked in the door had been quite graphic enough. 'Oh and look at this album I found,' said Daisy, handing her aunt the old photograph album.

'Oh, I say,' said Aunt Coral, putting down her wine glass and taking the album from her.

'They're mainly of me as a baby.' Daisy turned to the page with the picture of her in a high chair. 'Is this my mother's handwriting?' She pointed to the jotted note underneath.

'Yes, that's Sandy's writing,' said Aunt Coral, peering closer to read the words. She chuckled. 'I'd forgotten she used to call you two spoons.' She tapped the photo. 'You couldn't feed yourself but you insisted on having a spoon in each hand.'

Daisy's brow furrowed. Something had popped into her head and it was all starting to fit together.

'Was two spoons like a nickname?' asked Daisy.

'Yes, exactly, she used to say—' But Daisy didn't hear the rest, she was already pushing her way through the hall to find Tamsyn who was locked in an embrace with Jason. Daisy couldn't wait for her to come up for air. She tapped her insistently on the shoulder until she broke free.

'Tamsyn, do you remember at the Donkey Sanctuary when you tried to connect with me spiritually and find out something I didn't know?' The words tumbled out in a rush.

Tamsyn ran her fingers over her swollen lips. 'Yeah, I was rubbish.'

'No, you weren't. Could the message you got that day have been *two spoons* rather than *teaspoons*?' asked Daisy, holding her breath. This was the connection she'd been trying to make. The message had been two spoons, her mother's nickname for her. Tamsyn was psychic after all.

Tamsyn pondered this for a moment. 'No, absolutely not. It was definitely teaspoons.' She turned away before Daisy could protest and resumed snogging Jason.

Daisy was about to have another try when she felt Max's arms snake around her middle and pull her away. 'You all right?' he asked, his face full of concern. She was about to explain but in that moment she realised it didn't matter. Her mother would always be with her in her heart, and it turned out there was space for more than just her. Everything was slotting into place and at last she felt at peace and happy as she sank into Max's kiss.

Chapter Thirty-Nine

Carnival day in Ottercombe Bay was always a big event and Devon had warmed up in celebration. Everything looked brighter. All the holidaymakers that were staying anywhere nearby came to see the spectacle and most of the people from town were either in the procession itself, organising it, or running a business that would make money because of it. As Locos wasn't on the procession route, Daisy decided her best bet was to be part of the carnival.

Daisy was sitting on the wall at the recreation ground watching the floats trundle in whilst Old Man Burgess directed them to be judged ahead of the procession. A vampire float was almost grounded on the speed hump and the onboard black-cloaked individuals looked momentarily pale. She heard someone call her name and turned to see a large green bottle shuffling clumsily towards her.

'Tams?' Daisy squinted at her friend. She could see quite clearly and didn't need to squint but she couldn't believe her eyes. Tamsyn was dressed as a bottle of gin. Her attention was drawn by the noise of shouty men announcing the arrival of the inshore lifeboat pulled by a large tractor and followed by a mass of lifeboat crew all looking rather like they may have been to the pub first.

Daisy wasn't good at making long-term decisions but for now she'd decided she wasn't going to put Locos up for sale. She had invested so much in the business and it was one of the few things in her life she was proud of. She had a great team she could trust to keep it afloat while she was away and she had enough money for now.

Tamsyn had been thrilled when Daisy had told her she wanted her to step in as Locos' manager and she'd been quick to get sashes printed with the bar's logo on the front and back for publicity at the carnival. Daisy didn't argue even though she didn't want to wear the bright green sash because it made her feel like a beauty pageant contestant.

After a lot of hanging about the procession finally got underway. It was a long time since Daisy had been in the carnival and hearing the music and the crowd made her realise how much she enjoyed it. Excited children lined the streets waving flags and balloons as bystanders merrily threw their hard-earned pennies into the collecting buckets.

At the end of the procession spirits were running high, especially amongst the firemen who appeared to be giving free lifts to anyone who fancied one and a few people who definitely didn't. Daisy spotted Max sauntering over and her heart leapt at the sight of him. In her mind she could easily reduce him to a slow-motion image and apply advert-style music over the top. Yes, he was rough around the edges but that was part of his charm, along with his wayward hair and ridiculously long eyelashes. He approached and she remembered she was wearing the bright green sash and started to wrestle to get it off. As Max neared her she gave the sash one last tug pulling it sharply over her head.

Despite the noise levels of the jolly folk surrounding her she heard the tiny snapping sound. In that split-second she watched her locket sail through the air on a direct trajectory towards the nearest drain. Daisy fumbled forward in an attempt to stop it but it was dropping towards the grille and the murky depths beneath at a rate of knots.

Her stomach lurched at the thought of losing her beloved locket again but a large hand intercepted the falling jewellery and saved it just inches from impending doom. She looked up to see a grinning Max clutching the locket and its broken chain.

'If you didn't want it any more, you only had to say.' He had a twinkle of mischief in his eyes or it could have been beer.

Daisy's hand was already on her chest covering the space where her locket always sat. 'I couldn't bear to lose it again. It means everything to me.'

Max guided her away from the road and the masses of people. 'It means a lot to both of us. In a funny way it brought us together. I mean, not a classic love story, but it's our story.' Max handed the locket back to Daisy and she carefully put it in her pocket.

'It is,' she said, linking hands with Max and relishing the familiar zing at the contact. He was in his lifeboat crew uniform, and despite the bright yellow waders there was something sexy about it – most likely the toned body hidden underneath.

Daisy looked about taking in the bedlam around her; Tamsyn was lying on the grass as Jason tried manfully to pull her free from the gin bottle costume whilst Old Man Burgess gave instructions. Over the noise she heard a bark she recognised and started to panic. She had left Bug with food and water locked up safely at the cottage – or so she hoped. She scanned the crowd frantically at ankle level for the small black dog. Through the throng she saw her aunt and Pasco approaching with Bug at their heels.

'How did it go with the solicitor?' asked Aunt Coral looking tense.

'Good. Everything has now been signed over to me. I've transferred the money I owe to your bank account plus a little interest. My year in Ottercombe Bay is at an end.' This was something else Daisy was mightily proud of. It had been an eventful year and she had learned so much. Now it was time to reap the rewards.

Aunt Coral's face drained of colour. 'What happens now?'

'Ah, about that,' said Daisy, with a wary glance at Max. 'I'm leaving on Tuesday.'

Aunt Coral's face fell and she looked to Pasco who pulled her closer to him.

'And me,' added Max, beaming.

'What do you mean?' asked Aunt Coral, looking anxious.

'We're both leaving on Tuesday because we're off on a tour of South America,' said Daisy. 'We'll be away for six whole weeks and then we'll both be coming home to Ottercombe Bay.'

'Oh that's marvellous.' Aunt Coral squeezed Daisy and Max tight. She eventually let go and dabbed at her eyes. 'You don't know how pleased I am. Having you back here means the world to me. Oh look at me getting all senti-mental.' She wiped away more tears.

'It's okay. Ottercombe Bay feels different somehow. More settled. More like home,' said Daisy, with a nod to Pasco. She credited him with helping her lay to rest the ghosts of the past.

'And it'll be safer too, once I get my fire-resistant shed

business off the ground,' said Pasco. Aunt Coral eyed him proudly as he and Max started to discuss the details.

Aunt Coral pulled Daisy to one side. 'Reg would have been pleased,' she said, looking wistfully off towards the sea. 'And your mother too.'

'I agree but I'm not doing it for them. I'm doing it for me.'

Aunt Coral gave a deep happy sigh. 'However much you fight it, you have to listen to your heart eventually.'

'Thanks for everything,' said Daisy. Her heart was full to bursting having the people she loved back in her life, which was on a much more stable footing than it had ever been before. Bug yapped his annoyance at being left out.

Without warning a huge wasp flew into Daisy's face and became tangled in her hair. She pulled away from her aunt and started to scream. She frantically swiped at her hair trying to get the wasp out without being stung. Her heart was racing as panic gripped her. The angry buzzing hitched up a notch and so did Bug's barking.

'Bastard!' shouted Daisy, as the wasp broke free and flew off, in the exact same moment Bug pulled his lead from Aunt Coral's grip and raced off towards home.

'Oh no,' said Aunt Coral with a gasp, her fingers shooting to her lips. 'He's chasing the wasp.'

Daisy reddened. 'It's okay. I think you'll find he's heading home to his basket. Maybe we should do the same.' Daisy linked one arm through her aunt's and the other with Max and wondered how you went about untraining a dog.

**Loved your time at Ottercombe Bay?
Then escape to the Cotswolds with Beth and Leo . . .**

The perfect book for any season – includes
an exclusive short story!

Available in all good bookshops now.

As the sun begins to set on Sunset Cottage, an unlikely friendship begins to blossom . . .

A hilarious and sweet love story that will warm your heart.

Available in all good bookshops now.